HAMELN

NJ KNIGHT

ALSO BY NJ KNIGHT

<u>Short Stories</u>

"The Rules of Sabertooth Sanctuary" in *Mixed Bag of Tricks*

"A Merry Little Séance"

First published in the United States in 2025 by Murasaki Press LLC
Copyright © 2025 by Nancy Knight
Cover illustration and design by Sarah J. Coleman

First Edition—2025/layout by Britta Jensen, Interior Art by Douglas E. Draper Jr., editors: Britta Jensen and Heidi Asundi

Murasaki Press LLC
PO Box 152313
Austin, TX 78715
U.S.A.

School and bulk sales of this book can be purchased for business or promotional purposes. For more information, e-mail info@murasakipress.com

Join the author's mailing list at https://www.nancyknight.net/

Library of Congress Control Number: 2025917804
This book has been catalogued for libraries as follows:
Names: Knight, N. J., author. | Draper, Douglas, 1982- illustrator.
Title: Hameln / N.J. Knight.
Description: Austin, TX : Murasaki Press, 2025. | Series: Hameln, bk. 1. | Summary: Five teens team up to solve the scourge of rats and magical secrets in the medieval city of Hameln. | Audience: Grade 7 to 12.
Identifiers: ISBN 978-1-966241-02-7 (hardcover) | ISBN 978-1-966241-01-0 (paperback) | ISBN 978-1-966241-00-3 (ebook) | ISBN 978-1-966241-03-4 (audiobook)
Subjects: LCSH: Young adult fiction. | CYAC: Teenagers--Fiction. | Coming of age--Fiction. | Fairy tales. | Fantasy. | BISAC: YOUNG ADULT FICTION / Fairy Tales & Folklore / Adaptations. | YOUNG ADULT FICTION / Fantasy / Historical. | YOUNG ADULT FICTION / Family / Siblings.
Classification: LCC PZ7.1.K65 H36 2025 (print) | LCC PZ7.1.K65 (ebook) | DDC [Fic]--dc23.

*To my Chaos Crew.
You're my forever favorites.*

In Hameln fair,
choose words with care,
else Fate will stop your tongue.

No babe aware;
no crazed mind share;
the past remains far-flung,
the truth is yet unsung.

—Hameln Setting Stone Inscription,
Author Unknown, Date Unknown

SEVENTEEN YEARS BEFORE

The heat in the cottage was like an anvil pressing on Rachel's chest, burning her air-starved lungs as she stubbornly continued to fight for breath, both for herself and the child she was struggling to bring into the world.

The coarse bedsheets and wet cloth on her forehead grounded her, kept her present even as the pain threatened to pull her under. There was a soft rustling at the night-dark window beside her, but she screwed her eyes tight against the gleaming eyes and teeth she knew her mind would conjure—had conjured—ever since Rachel learned she was pregnant.

"You're nearly there, dearest," Elisabeth murmured directly into her ear. Rachel felt Elisabeth wrapping one hand more firmly in her desperate, slippery grip while bracing Rachel's lower back with a strong arm. Only Elisabeth, her oldest and dearest friend, understood what Rachel's near silent labor really meant—that her bone-deep pain was too much for words or tears. Hopefully Elisabeth sensed nothing of her fear.

Elisabeth's sister, Agathe, looked Rachel over critically, timing the contractions, measuring the progress, and seeming to find her wanting, like poorly spun yarn. Agathe, whose clever eyes and sharp mind never missed an opportunity—or a weakness. "When I tell you to push— "

"Yes, yes, I know," Rachel gasped, crouched up, knees bent and preparing to bear down. Were those whispers, or just the trees outside? Was there even a difference anymore? "This isn't my first birthing."

"Well, it's your first from that side of the bed," Agathe grumbled. "And it is nearly time to meet your babe. When I tell you, push."

The icy chill Rachel felt down her spine as the older woman's eyes surveyed her feverish body had less to do with labor pains and everything to do with the truth that would soon be discovered. Would her friends, the Council, the entire town know immediately? Or could Rachel hide the truth just a little longer...

"Push now, Rachel. Now!"

With strength she didn't know she still possessed, Rachel nearly fell forward on her face, only Elisabeth's practiced arms keeping her upright long enough for Agathe to catch the squirming, blood-slick infant. Another push, and Rachel's vision went white, softening to gray as she slumped down on the bed, losing the fight to stay awake.

Instead of the soft cries or indignant shrieks one would expect in the first moments of a newborn's life, there was silence. Elisabeth tended to Rachel anxiously, stanching the blood and waiting for her to rouse. She thought of bringing out the eye-watering salammoniac from one of the many medicinal bags hanging from the silver chatelaine around her waist but ultimately decided to let Rachel rest. After all, Elisabeth knew exactly what a silent birthing room meant.

"Is the child...?"

Agathe didn't let her finish. "*He* is fine. Or, as fine as can be expected, given the circumstances." The disgust in her voice was clear, but it was tinged with thinly veiled fear. So, this was why Rachel insisted her friends come alone.

"Is he malformed in some way?" Elisabeth hurried over to the cleaned and swaddled babe, then stopped short at the strange sight. Piercing green eyes stared out from his dark face with a steady intelligence that no newborn should possess, paired with a full head of dark curls. The child was handsome. But it was the curious, calm, *inhuman* gaze that made her tremble for her friend.

The preternatural gaze that was currently caught at something beyond Elisabeth's shoulder.

She turned quickly, already feeling absurd. As if the child could see out the window, as if there would be something there to see … The world seemed to blur in that instant. Was that a fur-covered snout, bleached bone fingers, and glittering teeth? Or just weak moonlight reflected in the glass? No, there *was* something there. A green package, soft and small, dangling from the now-open sash. Baby's first ghastly mobile.

Shaken, Elisabeth turned back to her friend's sleep-still form. "Oh, Rachel. What have you done?"

1

HAMELN, DECEMBER 1258

"No! Please stop—" Clare woke at her own hoarse cry. She found herself curled up in a corner of her bed, sweaty and shivering in her twisted woolen blanket, heart still racing from the nightmare that had plagued her for the last decade, as her family disappeared around her.

First when her older brother, Nic left. Followed by her parents. Then her grandfather.

Now Cas.

Clare focused on slowing her breathing, swiping the damp curling hair from her neck and sitting up to look around her familiar room. Early morning light limned the stout dresser and her brown cloak hanging on a hook by the door. She listened intently past the blood pounding in her ears for the familiar sounds of Cas in the kitchen preparing his breakfast of tea and bread, both with ample amounts of honey.

She shrugged her tunic on over her chemise and loudly pulled her door open with an exaggerated yawn to hide her lingering distress. "Morning," she mumbled, ruffling her younger brother's dark curls in exactly the way she knew he hated.

But Cas' keen gaze didn't seem to miss her bloodshot eyes or worse-than-usual bedhead. "Good morning. Did you have the dream again? The invisible bloodsucking—"

"Yes," she answered shortly, moving around the room rather than meeting his questions head-on. Her baby brother had enough to worry about this week, without adding her recurring nightmares to his burdens.

"Hmmmm." He nodded while biting into his honeyed bread and perusing what looked suspiciously like an order for the forge. "You know, I'm probably going to be staying right here, annoying as ever. If Father Stephen gets his way—"

"And he usually *does*," Clare interrupted with an impatient snort, swiping his cup while he chewed, gulping down the rest of his tea. Cas well knew her disdain for the holy man who'd set his sights on taking her brother from her years earlier.

He frowned, picking at crumbs on the table absently. "Right. Then I'll still be here. Just not right here, where you can pilfer my breakfast. Best of both worlds."

Clare snorted companionably, unwilling to have this conversation again. No need to remind him that there was no guarantee he wouldn't be sent much further afield: to the Everstein Castle or King Rudolf's court or somewhere else neither of them had ever even imagined. *I just want to enjoy the day with my brother.* She walked to the window, opening it to check the day's weather as she braided back her long brown hair.

Even from a storey above, the festival commotion was nearly overwhelming—raucous bells, sharp whip cracks, vendor calls and giddy laughter throughout. "Food's better at the Nixe, anyway," she responded absently. *Far away from me, just like the rest of our vanishing family.* Her gut twisted, and she was suddenly a lot less interested in food.

"Aunt Aggie wanted to see you," Casper offered, while he looked over his papers. "Why are you bothering with Aunt Aggie's orders right now, anyway? She's busy enough that she'll probably forget she even asked for you."

She ignored his questions, instead nodding toward the paper in his hand. "Don't *you* have more important things to worry about right now? Like preparing for your test?"

"I just wanted to make sure you had the supplies you need," he answered. "You know, before…" He trailed off, suddenly very busy wiping crumbs from their overlarge dining table, a rare useful wood-working piece their grandfather left them.

"Before you leave. Right." her tone was bright and brittle, failing to mask her sorrow that after the Obolen ceremony, Cas was setting off for a life that she would never know. "Well, I think it's time to get this doomed day started."

On a typical day, Hameln carried the aroma of the surrounding deep evergreen forests, the Weser River winding past, and the dusty golden wheat ground down at the mills. The hours at her father's smithy added the sharp tang of hot metal in water as Clare molded it with force and fire, her hands and her will. The air was usually quiet, monotony punctuated only by Clare's hammer and the hourly bells of St. Boniface, reminding the village that time marched on regardless of man or God.

Obolen was not a typical day in Hameln.

Stepping outside, she felt it immediately: there was magic in the air today. It hummed, shimmered, and twisted, like a held note in the air, waiting impatiently for the song to follow. Clare closed her eyes to listen more closely, sitting in the moment before facing the day and all its changes. Despite herself, she smiled at the excitement that curled in her stomach. *Anything could happen.*

She took a deep breath and held it in her lungs until they burned. Her slowing heartbeat counted the moments like a muffled

drum in her chest while her skin tingled, numb and sensitized at turns.

The trouble with magic was that you never knew if the change it brought was fortuitous or dangerous—even those who traded a lock of hair. And though she was only sixteen, Clare had learned long ago that most change wasn't for the better.

Even now, she smelled the fried sausages and dough that Hans prepared every day of the weeklong festival; the hoppy beer that would drown out most everyone's anxieties or failures; the fresh-hewn timbers used to build the trials stage months earlier.

Clare heard the low, familiar buzz that would soon crescendo into a dull roar as both neighbors and strangers filled the streets, shoulder to shoulder, straining to see more of the festivities, when the children of Hameln—five to fifteen years of age, anyway—presented their wares, their talents, their very selves to be judged for the Obolen by the Council. The Obolen festival was the week that many had waited for their entire young lives, when the region's nobles and Hameln's elders gathered to decide where each child's talents could best be used—and who would reap the rewards.

Of course, not every child strove for a place among the generals, monks, guild masters, or courtiers. There were many who wished nothing more than to stay with their loved ones and make their home where generations had before them. The sweet, careworn face of her best friend, Lucie, came unbidden to Clare's mind at the thought. Not everyone wanted to run away from Hameln.

Maybe just the best of them.

And for Clare, "the best" meant her brothers. Nicolaus, with his eyes flashing gold, his burnished head thrown back in quick laughter, broad shoulders taking any burden as if it weighed nothing at all. And her younger brother, quiet young Casper, body brought low by an injury to his leg that never affected his mind. As a silversmith, Casper's clever fingers were always testing, creating, changing the world with his inventions to be what he knew it could—and should—be.

Lately she had tried to ignore Casper's narrowed eyes and wrinkled brow. It was more proof that his mounting anxiety had finally outmatched his thirst for success. If all went well, his adventure would finally begin after Obolen. Just like their brother Nic's had, nearly ten long years now.

Even before disease had taken her parents and Count Berchtold had taken Nic, Clare had never hoped to be chosen in the Obolen. She always intended to make her own fate, joining one of the caravans that passed through town or exploring the wilds, charting her life by the stars her mother had loved so dearly. There was no room for "Clare the Adventurer" in Hameln.

Instead, her life was the forge behind their house, exactly where Clare would be this morning, after breakfast at the Nixe and, with any luck, news from Nicolaus.

Clare knew how most of the town saw her: an odd, temporary ornament. Even Clare's status as a guild member was in name only —the guild masters had spent the better of two years trying to convince her to try for the Obolen herself, if only to give her father's forge to another. Someday, they assumed, she'd find her proper place behind the Nixe's bar or in some man's marriage bed. She was expected to be a responsible, respectable daughter of Hameln who would do her duty: provide the next link in the chain of her family's line. *A chain I sometimes feel tightening around my throat.*

Clare shook the dim thoughts from her head, and quickened her stride down the cobblestone street made unfamiliar with festival bustle. Today was the day they'd hear from Nic, and the news would be good. *I'm sure of it.*

No matter what, it was better that Nic find fortune and glory out in the world than returning to Hameln for a pale half-life of ruined hopes and sidelong glances. Clare could live with the town's unceasing ambition, but not with a broken brother.

Casper's presence at the monastery would be nothing new, of course. He'd been roaming the halls of the great Gothic cathedral since he could talk. The problem was, once he entered the gates at

Midsummer, he wasn't coming back home to Clare. And she hadn't been able to follow him beyond the church for six long years now.

"Why doesn't Father Stephen want me to come back? Did I do something wrong? Are my sins too big for God to forgive?" Ten-year-old Clare looked up at her father, rubbing angrily at the tears that fell without permission.

"No!" Her father's voice never registered much lower than a bellow, but his volume was like a snarling bear woken before Beltane. "Damned fool Christian ideas. You know, your grandfather wouldn't have any but his wife and daughters handle the books. He knew the power of a woman's intellect."

"And he won't take it out on Cas, will he? Cas loves school so much." Clare knew something vital in Casper would break if he were banished from the school, too.

"Clarebear, listen to me." At his young daughter's confusion, Thomas' face regained some of its softness, and he reached down to pull her close, smelling of leather, smoke, and honey. "This isn't about you, your goodness or your mind. There was no sin that you committed. The church doesn't allow women in their school, so we will simply school you here. Does anyone know more about medicine than your mother? Can any hold as many figures in her head as your Aunt Agathe? You will not want for books or knowledge, not in my house."

"And what if I want to learn to be an adventurer, like grandfather?"

Thomas' smile was warmer than the blast furnace. "You still have his North star, right?"

She wrapped her hand tightly around the pendant hanging from her neck. "Mama said it'll always guide me true."

Clare clutched at her necklace, the way she couldn't hold onto Casper. The cool, smooth lodestone set in old Viking gold, a coin more than 200 years old, if her Afi could be believed. Etched in the metal surrounding the black rock was a crude eight-point star. Her fingers traced it lightly, as familiar to her as her own skin.

It had since been joined by a second charm Casper crafted for her, a tiny iron sword no longer than a nail. By rubbing the sword against the lodestone, it would point northward, no matter where she stood. "Polaris only shines at night, after all," Casper had told her, looping the necklace over her head, bowing low so he could reach without losing his careful balance. "Now you'll find your way no matter where, or when, you are."

"Guide me true," she murmured the closest thing to a prayer she knew, tightening her grip on the charms before entering the Nixe to face her aunt. Aggie would have no time for her whirling emotions.

Clare walked through the inn doors and let the nostalgia—for a different time, a different dream, a different version of herself—roll over her, golden and bittersweet. She used to practically live at the bar, keeping her Uncle Matthias company or running small errands for the patrons between tall tales of distant lands. She used to dream of the day she would join them on one of the many roads out of the village. *Anywhere but this quiet, secretive town.*

As expected at this hour, the dining room hummed with low voices and affable laughter, but in addition to the usual mingling scents of fresh bread, stale ale, and careworn travelers, music filled the air.

Clare stopped short, scanning the room before venturing further into it. Her narrowed eyes passed over the candlelit tables, dark-haired Jakob already filling tankards at the bar and the circle of locals seated around the cavernous fireplace, before spotting the source.

Instead of seeing the grizzled royal huntsman, Wolfhart, in his usual corner, Clare found herself staring at the most beautiful boy she'd ever seen. His thick black curls lay in an artful mess over his dark brow, while his startlingly green eyes stared into the middle distance while he performed. For a single instant, Clare felt his gaze sharpen and hold her own as the door closed behind her. He grinned at her, quick and easy. She frowned back instinctively at the unlooked-for recognition. It wasn't the music that caused the hair on her neck to stand on end. *Am I about to be charmed or scammed?*

His right hand kept an almost martial rhythm on the tabor that hung from his left side, while his fingers flew over the three holes of his pipe, creating a dizzying combination of notes that climbed jauntily up and up. He tipped his curly head in time as the staccato tune crescendoed, achingly sweet, before slowing into a single, otherworldly note that flushed her cheeks and broke her heart.

He's a stranger; it's best to keep a close watch. She silently justified her careful attention, though of course there were often many strangers at the Nixe. It was Obolen, and there would be countless more before week's end.

He lowered his instruments with a flourish to hearty applause as Clare walked the perimeter of the dining room, trying to make herself as small as possible. She didn't have time for more drama in her life and she sensed that this newcomer brought it with him effortlessly, riling his audience up and then taking as much gold and adoration as he could. Clare made her way to Aunt Agathe's office, surreptitiously keeping the young man in her line of sight as he accepted kind words, food and drink.

She noted the sharp, wild look in his eyes and the quiet amusement on his face as he winked at a particularly appreciative female patron. The blonde tourist, dressed as a white-robed goddess, giggled back at her friends while waving her distaff in time to the music. Stiffening her spine, Clare felt the magic recede and forced herself to look anywhere else but the beautiful boy. *Stay wary*, she reminded herself.

Using a lifetime of dealings with drunks and deceivers, Clare ignored the fizz in her bloodstream and the heat in her cheeks—in her experience, the excitement of new faces arriving only led to the heartbreak at their leaving while she stayed behind.

As a child perched on the roof of the forge, Clare dreamt of discovering the Grey Cottage deep in the woods to defeat the evil witch who lived there. More than once, amused neighbors caught her just outside of town with a too-large sword and a determined chin, both stolen from her father.

Her father Thomas blamed her Aunt Agathe for Clare's excursions, forbidding his daughter from the tavern she operated. Agathe scoffed at her brother-in-law's accusations, instead blaming Clare's idle hands. There was always plenty of work at the Nixe, the inn her beloved grandfather had founded once he decided to sell his ship and settle in Hameln. Round and round the fight between them went, only ending when Clare inherited her father's forge.

Clare had slipped past the bar into the narrow hallway that ended at her destination. Agathe's office, no more than a broom closet, lined in shelves at the back of the building, was empty. Clare wasn't concerned. Aunt Aggie always came back to her books, like a blackbird to her nest. "The inn is my life, and it's all in these books," Aggie once told a much younger Clare, who would later sneak a peek at one of the ledgers.

Clare never outgrew her disappointment over the dated rows of inventory and untitled lists of names. She wouldn't find her adventure there. Just hard facts, an ancient oversized desk and a particularly uncomfortable chair.

Aunt Aggie appeared after just a few moments, a whirlwind of brown curls and quick steps, mumbling under her breath and snatching up a pencil and paper to jot something down before looking at Clare with her warm, shrewd smile.

"My darling girl, it's so good to see you here. I take it Casper told you I wanted to see you? Or was there something else you needed?"

This was her Aunt Aggie, Clare thought ruefully. She had a hundred thoughts flying through her head, but she was always ready to add another. She prided herself in knowing all that happened within the town walls. "No, no, I'm here at your request. And dying of curiosity since yesterday's late-night message," Clare replied, her smile bright, if a bit empty, sensing that another responsibility was about to be given to her.

"Good, good!" Aunt Aggie sat behind the desk, looking over the piles of papers that were always just on the verge of toppling over.

"I've got it here somewhere, a letter from Wolfhart … He knew I'd be looking for help, you see, with the Obolen …" Her nimble fingers seemed to touch each sheaf of paper, careless of the precarious balance maintained. "And don't think I've forgotten your birthday coming up in a few months. We must celebrate …"

Clare rolled her eyes good-naturedly while Aggie continued her hunt. Seventeen wouldn't mean much for her, who'd already settled into her comfortable Hameln routine.

"—yes! Here it is." Aggie plucked a piece of paper that seemed completely random to Clare's eyes. Clare held her breath, but while the pile the letter had slipped from trembled, it didn't fall.

"You might have noticed Lukas, the musician here this morning," Aggie opened the letter, rereading its contents as she spoke. "He's got some talent, but more importantly he's not afraid of hard work. Lukas comes highly recommended by Wolfhart, and with your brother leaving us soon …"

Clare's anger was instant and white-hot. "You've replaced Casper already?" *Was it so easy for Aunt Aggie to usher her own nephew out and a new laborer in?* "And with some newcomer, a-an *auslander*, at that? We've still got six months, even if he is chosen!" Clare heard the nasty, snarling tone of her voice, but couldn't stop the words from crawling up her throat.

Aggie's slight, still form and cold eye stopped the rant. "Yes, he has six months. To prepare for his life to change completely. Whether here or elsewhere, he's going to use the Obolen as the stepping stone to all his future accomplishments." She sat behind her desk. "And *we*, my dear, have six months to do the same. Lukas is bright enough and wants to make his way in the world. Casper can teach him the ropes, and maybe Lukas can even help around the smithy, if you'll have him."

"I won't," Clare bit out, stung by the charity Aggie seemed to provide to everyone but her own blood. "But *you* enjoy your new help. Any word from Nic?"

Aggie peered at her, calculating and close, before allowing the subject change. "No," she answered calmly. "Not today. But perhaps Berchtold will have news. I'll ask him at the Council meeting."

"Please do." Clare suddenly felt stiff and sore, as if she'd fallen from a tall height. "I'll see you at the square, Aunt Aggie."

"Of course, Clarebear." Clare noted Aggie's blank face, the surest sign that she was concerned about her niece, and a trait she shared with Cas that never failed to annoy Clare. Especially when it felt like it changed *nothing*. "I'll see you and Casper at the ceremony."

2

er Royal Highness Princess Sophia of Everstein was destined to rule over … something at some point or another. She was trained in all the appropriate arts of a proper German noblewoman, including how to appreciate music, compose detailed correspondence, and compliment arrogant men in multiple languages. She'd been taught the politics of all the neighboring lands since birth and knew every boring detail in how a royal household was to be run.

Even her wild brown curls were habitually subdued into the complicated twists and braids that her grandmother had taught her from birth, and her fashionably embroidered skirts were kept spotlessly clean. She was a glittering ornament and the perfect complement to her brother, Freddie the Everstein heir.

But when her mother, the Imperial Countess, left the castle—and she often did, there was so much to do in a busy principality—Sophia vanished as well.

Instead, she became Castle Everstein's cunning little Sophie, who was currently sitting quietly in the corner of the kitchens, absently petting the cook's ancient and fearsome rat terrier.

"Do you think we'll have a few handsome soldiers to join the guards?" a young pink-cheeked laundress asked the room, starry-eyed over the thought of a new beau.

If information was power, Sophie was determined to be the best-informed person in the castle.

One of the stable boys snorted into his stew. "I imagine the Countess is more concerned with bringing on advisors she can mold to her liking. Last week I overheard her telling one of them she needed him to try to be as intelligent as the horse he rode."

"As long as it isn't a battalion of soldiers that I'll have to keep fed daily," the perpetually scowling cook complained, wrist-deep in dough.

With news as exciting as the renowned Obolen in Hameln, Sophie was eager to hear all the details and what they could mean for her home.

"The real question is, will she bring back a decent brewster? We haven't had a good stein of ale with our meals in an age!" This from Sophie's favorite scullery maid who was generally more likely to smile at the princess than shoo her away.

Listening may not be enough this time, though, she thought, still combing her fingers through the dog's wiry fur and sharing her pastries in exchange for its quiet companionship, while everyone around her continued to gossip about the festival and the changes it brought every ten years.

According to her intelligence, the Obolen, a sort of ceremony, occurred over six months. First, there was the weeklong festival, when mathematicians and engineers, musicians and poets, artisans and craftsmen presented themselves to the Hameln Council. Afterward, the chosen participants were named and further sorted into the specific guilds, the militia, Castle Everstein, or Saint Boniface's famed university.

Most importantly, the Obolen ceremony occurred only once every ten years. The next time it came around, she would be old, married off to some lord or another, possibly even pregnant and bedridden.

"No, I can't sit this one out," she determined, standing up, much to the comfortable pup's dismay. She had to experience *something* for herself, and she had decided that this festival was it. "I'm going, whether mother allows it or not." That meant she needed an ally.

Sophie didn't bother announcing her arrival to her father's dark laboratory, calling out only when it became clear he wouldn't notice her presence himself. "If only your subjects could see you now …"

Johann of House Everstein, Imperial Count and Knight of the First Order of the Dragon, blinked owlishly at his daughter from behind soot-covered goggles. He was surrounded by piles of books and papers, vials of powders and liquids, and more than a few half-eaten meals.

"Did I miss dinner again? Is your mother threatening to bring the bishop in to remind me of my duties as an Everstein?" He flipped his goggles up over his high forehead with one hand as he ran his fingers and eyes over the pages of his journal again.

"No, she's moved on to ordering the staff to clean your laboratory while you sleep," Sophie replied with an arched brow and a gleam in her dark eyes.

That got his full attention. Johann's dark head snapped up, shoulders suddenly high and tense. "She wouldn't!" He gripped his papers protectively to his chest while Sophie laughed.

"Of course not," she answered, walking over to a crowded workbench to pluck a particularly large, pockmarked rock off it. "But God's bones, your face …"

"Hilarious," her father's look was withering. "And be careful with that! I sent for it from Aquitaine. They believe it's a piece of the firmament itself. It might be the missing element I need to finish the process."

"Lead to gold?" Sophie may not have fully understood her father's experiments, but she was a good daughter. And no good daughter could resist her father's childlike delight in his scientific endeavors.

"Gold! This is beyond gold!" Johann waved his hands wildly, as if clearing the air of her ridiculous suggestion. "I'm talking about a perpetual-motion machine, a never-ending energy source! We would no longer live at the whim of the seasons, or even the sun. A mill that grinds flour no matter how low the river runs or a plowshare with no need of oxen to pull it through the earth! We could revolutionize, well, the world!"

"A carriage that never stops to rest the horses?" Sophie quickly caught her father's excitement and ran with it. "Or … kitchens that bake all our favorite desserts while the bakers are fast asleep?"

"Precisely!" Johann's smile was wide and bright, and his hazel eyes gleamed with pride at his daughter's quick mind. "This could be the breakthrough I've been waiting for my whole life."

"Well, I'm sorry to interrupt you. But I do need your help." Sophie put the rock back with considerably more care than she had picked it up. "There are a few mysteries in the world that I want to uncover for myself. Starting in Hameln."

"Hameln?" Johann cocked his dark head, as if weighing her words. "The Obolen festival then? Is this mere curiosity, or …"

Sophie held his gaze, clear but calm. "I need to know how it works," she said, appealing to his own quest of knowledge. "How it affects our people. And the chance won't come again for another decade, after all."

His gaze remained leveled on her face before his own transformed into a boyish grin.

"I know the temptation to strike out on your own can be unbearable. You're an Everstein, after all." Johann moved to press a kiss to the top of her head. "And I am sure you will find adventure enough to fill that book of yours. But it is a delicate process, with many interests converging and colliding. If you do this, etiquette will demand that you honor Father Stephen and the mayor's household. And your mother will demand that you behave in a manner befitting the House of Everstein."

Sophie quashed the urge to pout at his admonishments. This was the type of caution and propriety she expected from the Countess, not her dear father. She wanted—needed—a grand adventure, and time was running out.

"And what do *you* demand, Papa?" In that moment, Sophie sought to look every inch the submissive noble daughter. *If Maman could see me now*, she thought. Though her mother would never even entertain this conversation, she knew.

"Go discover something grand," he replied sternly, before succumbing to a wide smile. "Though I insist that Heinrich drives you straight to Saint Boniface, and safely through the door. And don't you lead him astray."

"The ample rains this season have saved the crops, but there are worries that the rivers are overflooded. As you know the trade routes depend on ..."

Freddie's mother sat beside him in the Council chamber, wearing the same small, enigmatic smile on her fair face that she showed every guest she received, eyes narrowed just past friendly attention and inching into intense concentration. Countess Katherine was always in control of both her emotions and whatever room she was in.

Meanwhile, Freddie, Sophie's brother, stared at the iridescent sapphire and crimson peacocks climbing the golden walls. They seemed to dip and twirl before him, and his vision swam.

Freddie despised those peacocks, his only companions in the monotony.

Instead of providing valuable counsel to his mother as he'd hoped, he sat quietly during every interminable banquet and reception, attempting to count each one, before his eyes lost their focus, one swirling tail of feathers mingling with another.

He'd never made it past 137.

Freddie caught himself shifting uneasily in his seat, and forced himself to be still, straighten his back, and pay attention to the droning advisers who were actually allowed to speak. To make his mother proud.

If only he could handle his official duties like his sister. Sophie, who slipped in and out of her noble persona like it was a fine mink robe. Comfortable, of course, but much too fine for everyday wear. Meanwhile, his own role as heir felt more like a hair shirt, itchy and ill-fitting.

Freddie normally enjoyed the day-to-day realities of his life: touring the estates, managing the lands and meeting with honest representatives of the towns and hamlets under Everstein protection. *I could learn more speaking to our farmers, hearing what actually plagues our people.* He wondered if the others in the room could read his thoughts on his face.

Abruptly, his mother dismissed her advisors. Freddie found himself saying and doing all the proper, perfunctory things as they shuffled out the door until he was alone with her.

"It is 536," Katherine said, smiling at her son. Freddie quickly went over the last few moments of the meeting, searching for the number she was referring to.

"Peacocks. On the wall?" she added.

He ducked his head, relieved that his dark skin wouldn't easily betray the blush sweeping over his cheeks. "I was simply admiring the splendid furnishings of our reception hall, *Maman.*"

"Yes, I admire them whenever Brandenburg speaks, as well," she answered conspiratorially, turning from the table with a bright gleam in her blue eyes. She looked out the grand window overlooking the River Emmer, a sedate tributary of the powerful Weser that cut through the rolling green hills of the Everstein lands.

She looked so lovely in that moment, golden hair shining in the morning sunlight and graceful neck craning to see the peaceful vistas surrounding them. "Are you ready for our journey? It will be a short visit, but you will have a much more active role in this year's Obolen."

He perked up. "Active role?"

"Accompanying me. Aiding me in choosing this year's initiates, and our own apprentices," she answered.

Am I prepared for the politics of the Hameln Council? Something in his chest fluttered, then bloomed. It was time for Prince Friedrich of Everstein to do his duty, to smile and flatter and maneuver his way to greatness for his noble house. To make a difference, instead of merely playing a prince. *Finally.*

Freddie knew it was his mother's first Obolen as the Everstein representative, but he would never know it from her calm expression and steady hand.

In fact, most of this Council was new to the ceremony. Four years ago, a plague had ripped through Hameln, and if reports that Freddie had seen from the city were accurate, no home came through unscathed. The illness was made even more terrible by how rare it was for such an event to affect this seemingly charmed town —this was the first such plague to visit Hameln that Everstein advisors had ever seen. Now Count Berchtold was the only familiar face on the Hameln Council that had led the Obolen just 10 years ago.

"Yes, *Maman,*" he said, finally answering her earlier question. Freddie glanced up at the Everstein coat of arms, the silver lion rampant on a field of blue, helmed by even more peacock feathers spilling out of a golden crown. The symbol of his family's strength. *My strength, for my people.* "I am ready."

3

Lukas' name seemed to be everywhere this morning, much to Clare's annoyance.

"I heard he's Johann's illegitimate son by one of the castle servants. He's got the Count Johann's dark skin and green eyes, after all. He's traveling with his father's protection, but that's just about all the Countess will let the boy have. He wanders the kingdom, but no other noble will take him on, fearing her anger," Clare overheard an old man gossiping about the bard with his compatriots at the Glückshaus board.

"That's absurd—old Johann only loves his gold!" Another man answered with a sidelong glance after rolling a seven and placing a coin. "No, he's a child of the Grey Cottage. His mother was a witch, and they were chased from their village years ago. He uses his cover as a traveling musician to avenge his dead mother's honor after all these years. I'd watch your back with that *auslander*; never know when he's going to use his dark skills against you."

Clare, who had just decided to stop listening, paused at a mention of the mysterious Grey Cottage. Anticipation coursed through her veins that she would *finally* get a good story.

"Have you seen the way he's dressed?" Vogt snorted, turning his attention from the game and gesturing to his own tame brown outfit to emphasize his point. Locals rarely participated in the masquerade aspects of the festival. "He's not exactly sneaking around, looking like that. The colors are absurd, but the cloth is as fine as you'd see on the king himself. And the boy is a natural talent."

Clare wrinkled her nose, before nodding grudgingly at that truth.

"Bastard or witch's welp, he'll find his place in the world, especially with a man like Wolfhart speaking for his good character," his friend agreed as he reached for the dice.

"Wolfhart!" Another grey-bearded regular slapped his knee after rolling his die and earning a jackpot to a chorus of his competitors' groans. "Where is that old cuss, anyway? Seems like an age since I saw his grim face around these parts …"

"Last I heard he was in Goslar searching for a missing girl. Word is she was foolish enough to wander into a bear cave …"

Clare shook her head, and flicked her brown braid over her shoulder, disappointed that there was nothing new to be learned about Lukas's connection with the mysterious Grey Cottage. And such a wide array of opinions gave her leave to feel any way she wished about the musician.

She wished Lukas would go away. All he did was remind her that Cas would be gone soon.

Clare's mind flitted morosely to her birthday Aunt Aggie had mentioned. *Seventeen soon, and facing down a lonely life in Hameln,* she thought. She shoved the last of her porridge in her mouth to mask a self-pitying grimace. She'd have to be careful, hide her anxieties.

"Let Casper enjoy the celebration," Clare murmured to herself. "Enjoy Obolen."

"Remember last Obolen?" her old friend Jakob asked with a wide smile and friendly brown eyes, breaking into her thoughts. He ambled over to her end of the bar, picking up her now-empty bowl. "We couldn't find any live entertainment, so we just invited anyone who wanted to perform up on stage? That's how we learned Josef had such a beautiful singing voice. And there was that old woman who made an entire fistful of coins—*someone else's* coins—disappear …"

Clare smiled into her coffee cup, before finishing that up, as well. "That's right. Some of those coins showed up in Casper's and my shoes later that night." Jakob's answering chuckle was warm. "The show was great until Josef opted for twirling two still-on-fire torches like batons," she reminisced.

This time, Jakob laughed with his whole body, throwing his head back and clutching his chest with one hand. "One of them flew into the crowd, and Nic's hair nearly caught on fire! He poured the whole table's beer to try to douse the flames …" He paused, narrowing his bright blue eyes at her cautiously before continuing. "He would have loved this year's festivities, though. Live music and enough *reibekuchen* to feed an army."

Clare's good feelings soured in an instant at the mention of Nic missing so much for so long. "Too bad he's too busy being in the army to join us," Clare responded bitterly, ducking her head down and rising from the wooden barstool, silken soft after years of use. Perhaps Jakob wanted to reminisce, but the thought of her last days with Nic a decade ago still made her chest ache.

"It's not too late, he may still show up …" Jakob trailed off, tilting his head and eyeing her carefully.

She forced herself to smile, tossing her braid over her shoulder and looking him directly in the eye. "Thanks for breakfast, friend."

"Any time, Clare."

With a short wave, she turned to leave, but not before giving the lingering Lukas a wide berth. She hoped to avoid his clever eyes for as long as possible, avoiding the change he brought with him. Besides, it was past time to stoke the fires at the forge and organize the day's wares for Cas to sell at the Christmas Market. *Assuming Casper had his wits about him and even remembers his daily festival duties.* The usually conscientious youth had a lot to prepare for this year.

Like the rest of his life, without me.

As she reentered the streets, an indignant yowl startled her from her gloomy thoughts, followed by the loud crack of heavy wood meeting flesh. She froze and scanned the crowd already gathering. After a few seconds, her eyes settled on a familiar group of leather-studded patrolmen leading a struggling tourist to one of the makeshift cells built for unruly revelers. This particular fool was well-dressed, though his clothes were a bit old-fashioned. And no one could miss the shiny golden crown sitting atop his gray head.

There were a few troublemakers every year, and the Hameln patrol knew what to do with them. She moved to escape the gawking crowd and get to work, when she heard a collective gasp and a sharp yank at her sleeve.

"What, young one? So eager to leave my company?" The drunken buffoon had somehow slipped from his captors' grasp, snapping his jaw as he leered down his long, pointed nose at her, eyes dark and tongue lolling as his crown slipped further down his brow. "Let us leave here together. I can show you sights you'd never dream to see in Hameln."

Clare huffed in annoyance. He clearly thought she was easy pretty. *His mistake.*

"It seems you are engaged elsewhere, *sire*," Clare sneered at the strange reveler, stomping on his foot and pushing him away as the patrol surrounded them, twisting his arms behind his back. "Enjoy ruling over your cell."

"We've got him, Clare. Sorry about that," one of the patrolmen grimaced in apology as he hauled the king of idiots back into the waiting arms of the patrol. "He's a slippery one. Like holding a net of eels."

"Let me go, you *miststück*!" The fool cried out.

"No harm done." She knew the patrolmen probably didn't hear her over the colorful curses the man shouted at the entire town.

The crowd cheered in appreciation as the patrolmen dragged the drunken king away, before quickly finding entertainment elsewhere. *There was always something else to astonish in Hameln's Obolen,* she mused.

Clare moved toward her forge, passing by pastries and trinkets for sale, and a beer garden packed with revelers. The world came to Hameln to catch a glimpse of the master artisans, tacticians, and politicians who would one day lead them all, but she could only drum up interest in one thing.

The gold they'd leave behind.

Clare walked briskly through her front door, reaching for her heavy leather apron before heading to the back of the house, outside to her forge. It was time to get back to work, and she hoped the hard labor would help quiet her fears over Casper's future, and her own. After all, she couldn't force him to forgo the Obolen. And she didn't really want to, if it meant his unhappiness.

She skipped down the stairs quickly, headed to the back toward the smithy that led out into the sun-soaked courtyard where she met with her potential customers. Inside, Clare's tools lined the far wall, ready and able to fulfill any task that she put her mind and muscle to doing. This morning, it would be making nails.

As she felt each familiar, well-worn tool, something settled deep in her chest like a cat curling into a contented ball. At least within these four walls, Clare knew that if she could imagine it, she could shape it with iron and fire.

Opening her eyes, she knew she wasn't ready to let go of her fears for a future without Casper after the Obolen Ceremony, or even her anger at the outsider coming to usurp his place at the Nixe. But she couldn't let her little brother jeopardize everything he'd worked for just to make her less alone. Which meant accepting reality, and possibly the help of that insufferable bard her aunt had brought into their lives.

Let's get to work.

"Didn't start without me, did you?" her brother called as he loped toward her.

She opened her mouth to ask him where he'd been—before

remembering: he was fine-tuning his presentation. *Enjoy the time you have left,* she reminded herself. "No, you're just in time."

Clare and Casper quickly fell into an easy rhythm. He pumped the bellows, practiced and steady, as she worked between two iron bars in the fire, turning and shaping the yellow sockets while they cooled to black, then returning them to the heat.

After breaking off the heads, she began drawing the points with practiced motions, holding them firm with her long, tapered tongs. She tapped the red-hot heads with the heel of her hammer, turning all the time. She moved through quickly, methodically—turn and taptaptap; turn and taptaptap—pausing periodically only to wipe the beads of sweat from her brow and work-rough hands. They should have a sheaf of nails to sell at the market by noon.

She was comforted, if not fulfilled by this work. Moving her body in familiar ways in a well-known place, and having real proof that the work was *useful,* eased her soul. Most days lately, she shared this space with Jakob instead of Cas. Sweet, careful, reliable Jakob, who read her moods and needs and offered unconditional support. He was Nic's best friend from before; the level-headed counterbalance to Nic's more volatile, quick-fire style. Jakob sensed her loneliness, recognized it in his own life, and seemed to make it his responsibility to keep her spirits afloat just with his steady presence.

She hoped for, rather than expected, the same wordless solace from her little brother. Cas was better at actively fixing problems, after all.

She soon lost herself in the soothing, familiar ritual of her craft in the otherwise chaotic week. Even the soot on her face and arms were a comfort; she was hard at work, as if it were any other day.

"Are you angry at Aunt Aggie, or me, or the world right now?" Cas asked, his eyes sparkling and avoided the steam deftly as he stacked more firewood.

"Why choose just one? You know me, I work best with many irons in the fire." She paused in her work to waggle her eyebrows and gesture toward the hearth with her hammer.

Casper groaned. "Dad's terrible jokes aside, Jakob and I honestly think the *auslander* will be a great help around here, for you and—"

Clare doused a near-finished head in the water, letting the steam interrupt Cas for her. "So now I have you and Jakob deciding what's best," she sniped at him. "Lucky me, not having to face my own problems in life."

"I don't think he's the type of problem that you can just bang away at, Clarebear." The little snot didn't even have the decency to sound chastened.

"But you're certainly welcome to try." An unfamiliar, amused voice sounded from the open doorway, rankling her further. She turned to find Lukas, the dark-haired *auslander* musician, had silently entered the smithy, with no apparent compunction over eaves-dropping.

"That's—that's not what I meant!" A pink blush bloomed over Casper's face as he let go of the bellows to face Lukas. "She's a blacksmith and—"

"Leave it, Cas," Clare rolled her eyes as she banked the coals in the furnace, poking more viciously than strictly necessary. "There's no reasoning with a fool."

"I'm Lukas, actually, and it is a pleasure to meet you." Lukas moved forward as if to catch her hand. When she failed to put her tools down, he instead raked his hand through his unruly curls and flashed her a wide, bright smile. She was a bit dazzled despite herself. "I was told there may be work for me at your forge."

"You're delusional if you think you can just march in here unan-nounced and be welcomed into my smithy," Clare shot back, her feelings slipping out of her control. "This is a business, and I depend on hard work, not a catchy tune."

"So put me to work." Lukas spread his arms, his expression open and mild.

"Well, you've asked for it now." Casper grinned good-naturedly at the older boy, as if they were sharing a joke. It felt like it was at her expense.

"Shut up, both of you." She closed her eyes and breathed in deeply through her nose. There was too much work to do for them to just stand here arguing, and she needed to remember her duties.

"You." Clare pointed to Casper. "Keep pressing."

"And you." She locked eyes with Lukas and immediately felt electricity surge through her limbs. If either of them noticed, she would blame the heat from the furnace for her suddenly flushed skin. "Aunt Aggie says you're trustworthy enough. And I assume she told you the consequences of crossing Hameln's blacksmith," Clare spoke slowly, as if he hadn't said a word. There was too much to do. *And not enough hands to get it done*, she admitted to herself.

The bard, wide-eyed, simply nodded. It placated Clare's simmering anger. Just.

"You can take those finished pieces to Pieter's stall at the Christmas Market, then," she continued, smoothing her expression, determined to be professional. "There are tourists out there looking to take a piece of Hameln home, and last I checked, we *are* still in the business of making money."

4

Sophie had never set foot in Hameln. The growing city was leagues west of her ancestral home, after all. Beyond the busy harbor, Hameln itself was shielded by walls ten feet tall and multiple guard towers interspersed at the dozens of roads and bridges leading in and out of the center of town, like spokes on a wheel. *A rather intimidating welcome,* Sophie thought, admiring the general busyness of the people thronging about. It calmed her nerves to see so many people who didn't seem to care about her comings and goings at all. *I should be able to slip in and out with ease,* she thought gleefully. As long as she didn't run into her Maman, at least.

The circular town center had white stone and half-timber buildings that lined the roads leading to the *hochzeitshaus* in the town square. It was the tallest of the buildings by far—besides Saint Boniface monastery, towering to the south, of course—an open, friendly Romanesque building with tall arched windows that beckoned all to celebrate the Yuletide inside.

As her carriage wove through the crowds in the wide streets, Sophie felt a rush of excitement, and a touch of anxiety. The first potential snag in her plan was quickly approaching: how to blend in once she left the carriage. For once, Sophie was grateful for one of her mother's ridiculous court events to help her clear it.

Her mother, Countess Katherine, had insisted that she participate in this year's Samhain masquerade, and she had felt more than a little ridiculous in the shimmering bejeweled blue satin gown and iridescent butterfly mask that made her look more like a living doll than a real girl. She shivered at the thought—to be another toy on the shelf, malleable and silent, filled with her mother's motivations and desires, instead of her own hopes and dreams. Determination filled her again. *Not this time.*

But that same absurd costume was her greatest asset now, she reminded herself, rubbing the smooth, cool fabric under her warm palms. Because for the next week, and to Sophie's delight, everyone else in Hameln was hiding who they were, as well. The town's Obolen festivities were filled with kings and queens, fairies and fauns, sorcerers and enchantresses. The god of thunder taking a long pull from your tankard may just be the town drunk. The wicked witch with her blood-curdling cackle could be your own sweet grandmother. That goblin street beggar drawing you near with his piteous pleas may instead press a gold coin into your hand. It instantly added to the magic and mystique of the boisterous festival for Sophie—she would never know exactly who she was celebrating with.

But as the carriage rumbled down increasingly narrowed streets, she saw that not everyone was participating in the masquerade: there were also many exasperated locals dodging drunken embraces as they made their way through the streets to carry on with their lives. Sophie decided her written account wouldn't be complete without their experiences, and made a note to seek out a particularly talkative native before she left town. She needed the full Obolen experience, after all.

Sophie caught a passing blonde girl's eye and they shared a smile before the girl bowed her head over what looked like a blade and was lost in the crushing festival crowd. A frisson of fear rose in her stomach at the sight. *Perhaps it was just part of her costume?*

Sophie shook off her disquiet as the carriage rolled on, deciding to bask in the delicious smells of fresh-baked pastries, fried sausages and sweet white wines instead. The Obolen competitions began today, and Sophie glowed with the knowledge that for the next week, the world had converged on Hameln. *I am free of Maman's grip!*

After all, Hameln's most famous export wasn't flour. It was the young boys and girls who dreamed of becoming world-builders through the town's Obolen. The competition was used to select Lower Saxony's best and brightest. Sophie was determined to chronicle every moment of the pageantry and passion, starting with this week's Obolen festival.

Her carriage finally stopped in front of the imposing monastery. Her father had given her strict instructions to look for her mother, Countess Katherine, there. She was to deliver his missive and then follow her mother's instructions. But he never said she had to do so *immediately.*

Time to talk to all the right and wrong people. How else was she to discover everything about the town that her Maman had tried to stop her from seeing?

She looked up at the grand facade of Saint Boniface, its older basilica overcome by Gothic gables, pinnacles, and arched stained glass. Sophie accepted Heinrich's waiting hand gratefully as she stepped down. *I will act the perfect young noble lady. Right up to the church doors, anyway.*

"Thank you, Heinrich," Sophie said, looking around her distractedly. "If you'll leave my traveling pack here, I wish to walk the grounds. It was a tiring journey, and a stroll will refresh my spirits before meeting with Father Stephen."

Sophie knew Heinrich wasn't a fool. But she knew he was also keenly aware of the first rule in dealing with Sophie: Let someone else deal with her.

"Of course," he responded stiffly, before hopping onto the

carriage. "Have a pleasant Obolen, my lady." And with those parting words, she was finally alone to set on her grand adventure. Which definitely wouldn't happen at the church, with Maman's allies watching.

Picking up her pack, Sophie tightened the hood of her traveling cloak around her now-masked face and headed for the center of town.

Now to find a quiet spot to watch and listen …

"A lock of hair to tell your fortune, dearest?" Sophie's thoughts were interrupted by a willowy woman with spiky silver hair that puffed out of her head like a dandelion. Sophie, who had paused by the wooden stall to find her bearings, now glanced over the tall woman's shoulder at the scores of clear glass lockets adorning its walls filled with … something. Lots of somethings. She moved closer, peering at the strange trinkets, and realized it looked like blood.

Intrigued, Sophie met the woman's too-large eyes directly. "Are you selling those? What are they? What do they do?" she asked eagerly.

The strange woman moved to grab her hand. Her fingers seemed abnormally long, and Sophie almost couldn't dodge quickly enough to escape her reach. "I sell information, of course. These are just mementos from my customers. Perhaps you are more interested in the past? Those readings are more expensive, of course—a boon or a thimbleful of blood, if you're interested? No need to worry, it doesn't hurt a bit."

Sophie stepped back, fighting to hide the alarm and disgust coursing through her, curiosity now tempered with the threat of small, casual violences. Though the nobles she spied upon at Maman's gatherings usually sold information with fewer trinkets and far nastier smiles. "Not today, thank you," Sophie answered, papering over her own disgust with a polite smile. "But if you could point me in the direction of the largest inn in town?"

"You're looking for the Nixe. Just turn left at the intersection ahead and follow it north. You can't miss it." The woman turned her long neck away, and called out to another reveler passing by on the crowded street, as if she had never even noticed Sophie.

Sophie hurried on her way. The louder the crowd, the easier it was to slip through it with as little fuss as possible. And it made staying at the nearby Nixe an absolute no-brainer, even for a young traveler who knew almost nothing about this city.

As soon as she passed through the inn's heavy wooden doors, Sophie felt the comforting mantle of anonymity settle over her shoulders. No one noticed her, and none would care even if they did.

She moved smoothly to the bar, then waited for the harried dark-haired gentleman tending it to notice her. Sophie reckoned he was not yet twenty, with a steady gaze and hand despite the never-ending flow of drink orders and idle conversation lobbed at him. She found his smile was warm, if impersonal. Watching as he even threw in a few goodhearted chuckles at a particularly garrulous customer, Sophie decided she liked this potential source immediately —if only to overhear what his gregarious customers related to him.

A few minutes later, the bartender—Jakob, she'd heard someone call him—finally made it to her corner of the bar. "How can I help you, miss?"

"Good morning," she responded, still hooded but careful to meet his bright blue eyes and smile winningly. She found smiling at him was much more fun than when she had to smile for Maman's courtiers. "I'm interested in a room."

"We've no more individual rooms; they're always the first to go during a festival week. But if you're willing to share a space, there's a bed to be had," Jakob said, keeping a careful eye on the demanding crowd that still vied for his attention. "That'll be two pfennig a night, ten for the week, young lady."

Sophie passed him ten pfennigs without a word, nervously readjusting her mask. She was careful not to seem pleased or disgruntled at the price point. He didn't need to know how little experience she had paying for anything.

Not that it mattered. Jakob seemed too intent on keeping order in the boisterous dining room to pay attention to anything but the coin going into the Nixe's coffers. His fingers combed through his thick dark hair absentmindedly, and he was already moving away from her. "You'll be in Room 12 upstairs, then. Whichever bed looks empty is yours."

"Thank you," she said. Sophie slipped off the barstool. Instead of heading for the stairs, she made her way toward a quiet corner where she could observe the dining room and all the people in it—as well as pull her paper and quill from her pack. The day's first Obolen initiates would begin presentations within the hour at the main stage outside. She could soak in the Carnival-like atmosphere with no one looking over her shoulder. After the show began, that's when people would really start talking.

It's time to see what this Obolen is all about.

A few blocks away, Freddie found himself comfortably settled in the mayor's spacious guest rooms, thanks to Wilhelm's ever-accommodating daughter, Lucie. He remembered her fondly, if vaguely, from past visits to Hameln. But he was too anxious to give her more than a distracted smile before heading to his mother's neighboring chamber. It had been ten years since he had seen the Hameln Council. He wanted to ensure they saw him as the Everstein heir, not a meddlesome child.

"I am glad we have come to a mutually beneficial understanding, Countess," Freddie heard Count Berchtold of Ebernberg's low voice reverberate through the receiving hall as he entered the room. Freddie frowned, disappointed. *Even when I'm in the same building, Maman keeps me away from the important conversations.*

"A pleasure, as always, Berchtold." Katherine extended her hand to their ancestral ally for him to kiss in a move that was somehow both friendly and dismissive. The brunet was half a head taller than her, and yet Maman never seemed to look up to him. Freddie only hoped to one day emulate his mother's consummate grace and efficiency.

The count, pale and lithe, briefly touched his lips to her hand and swiftly retreated, nodding and clasping Freddie's shoulder as he passed. Freddie had known the man his whole life and still felt he knew nothing about him. He'd been hoping a round of negotiation would become a gateway to his own relationship with the mysterious noble. As peers, even.

"Did I miss anything crucial?" Freddie made his voice light, uncaring. He couldn't let her know it rankled that she still didn't trust him with the more delicate parts of regional diplomacy.

Katherine's careful smile turned genuine at Freddie's arrival, and his tense shoulders loosened a bit. She bounded back to her desk, skirts flouncing, her joy was contagious.

"Berchtold? He's a kitten. And a *terrible* liar," she replied, moving toward the mirror at the wall to make those minuscule adjustments to her fair hair and spotless, glittering blue skirt that Freddie found as endearing as they were unnecessary. "Father Stephen's the one you have to look out for. He's as ferocious toward Obolen rivals as that kitten's angry mama."

For a moment, watching his mother's reflection, an image came to mind—his grandmother's dark, withered visage melting into his mother's pale face in front of that same mirror. He shook his head briefly, reaching for the chair in front of him for balance, as his vision snapped back to reality.

"Are you ill?" Katherine was at his side in a moment, all loving concern.

"No, no." Freddie looked down at her anxious face, every feature her own. "Just all the festival excitement. Nothing a good, hard ride and some fresh air won't cure."

"Soon enough." Katherine squeezed his shoulder before moving toward the door, clearly eager to play the part of Council leader. "Let's go enjoy today's performances. I hear there's a young engineer with quite a few clever machines to show. He might even turn your father's head. Maybe you can help me figure out how to pry the boy away from that jealous old monk."

5

The entire Council was seated on the Obolen stage, just right of the lectern where each child would display their wares, as it were, for the next seven days. Clare shook her head in disgust, then quickly schooled her expression into one of bland interest before Casper, who was beside her, could notice.

This wasn't about her, she reminded herself. *This was about his dreams to build a better world with his own hands. Whereever that leads him.*

She allowed her dark eyes to skim over the Council's now-familiar faces, going through a silent, snarky roll call. Yes, there was Countess Katherine, icy blonde and regal. She was joined by her son, Frederich, said to favor his father with his dark skin and wide-set eyes. But the expression in that blue gaze was all his mother's—determinedly not bored or entertained at all. Typical nobles, she scoffed.

In six months' time they'd be taking their apprentices back to Castle Everstein, training them to be footmen and tutors and ladies-in-waiting—whatever skills the household needed, ensuring they'd never have a reason to return to Hameln again. *For better or worse.*

Next to them was the more mysterious Berchtold, whose stronghold in the Weserbergland Mountains housed the lion's share of Lower Saxony's armies. Clare's heart swooped low in her chest as his eyes fixed closely to hers. Did he recognize Nic's features in her face? *Would he have news of her dear brother, if I only had the nerve to ask him?* But his eyes had already focused on Lukas, who had silently appeared beside her.

Well, of course. He looks like a lunatic in that chaotic red, gold, and green jacket of his.

Lukas didn't seem to notice the attention he'd earned from the stage as he soaked in the atmosphere.

No doubt composing an epic poem to thrill us all at this very moment, she thought, rolling her eyes.

Turning back to the stage, Hameln's mayor sat next to Ebernberg. Clare wasn't surprised to notice his discomfort. This was Wilhelm's first Obolen as mayor. In another thirty years, he'll be as bored as the nobles. She wondered briefly where her old friend Lucie and her mother, Margarethe, were viewing the ceremony. To her dismay, her best friend usually left Hameln with her mother during the weeklong Yuletide festival, begging off to protect Margarethe's nerves from the chaos. But on an Obolen year, the mayor's wife and daughter were expected to be in attendance, if not on the main stage itself. *Where were they?*

Clare watched the far corner of the stage, where Father Stephen was meditating—or merely dozing. *If he doesn't lift his face and pay attention when Cas presents himself, I'll tear that cowl right off of his bald, blind head.* This was the man who held Casper's hopes and dreams in his hands. Already, she was searching for a small pebble to throw at his head just in case, weighing the pros and cons of eternal damnation for her brother's sake.

"Whatever you're plotting, I request fair warning beforehand." Lukas' low voice, smooth as silk, lilted with undisguised humor. He grinned down at her. "I don't want to miss the action."

"I don't know what you're talking about. Did you get those pieces to Pieter?" she asked coolly. A glance toward Casper showed her that he hadn't missed the exchange, or the tension telegraphed by her stiff posture.

"Just as you commanded," he said. "Look, we had a rough start. Let me introduce myself properly. I'm Lukas. You're Clare, right?" He held his hand out in easy friendship, and Casper quickly grasped it when it became clear that Clare wouldn't.

"I'm Casper, her brother. You're here to help out at the inn, right? What brings you to Hameln?" Good old Casper, with his bright brown eyes and kind smile.

"I'm here for the spectacle, you could say. There's no better place for that than Hameln, I'm told. Especially during an Obolen." Lukas looked around the restive crowd, seemingly invigorated by the activity around them. "You're an initiate? What's your skill?"

Lukas eyed Casper and his box of intricate devices before moving to take the cumbersome load from the younger boy. "Did you need help with that? It looks heavy," he said, hands out in friendly offering.

Casper awkwardly juggled the box, just out of Lukas' reach, Clare noticed. "Thank you, no," he said with the same carefully cheerful smile. "Some of these are very fragile—and I am not."

"Oh, I didn't mean to—" Lukas began, before Clare waved her hand at the two of them, a silent order to be quiet. Countess Katherine had just moved to the front of the stage.

But before Katherine had even opened her mouth, a scream, sharp and piercing, cut through the air. Clare winced at the note, thinking it came from a jubilant and off-key Yuletide reveler from earlier.

The crowd parted, and she spotted the drunken festivalgoer who had grabbed her earlier, his disheveled crown falling to the ground and his body collapsing behind it, jerked forward like a puppet whose strings were suddenly cut. His movements were unnatural and grotesque enough to convince Clare that this wasn't just another drunken outburst.

The crowd continued to move away from him swiftly, the fear of another deadly plague never far from anyone's mind.

Clare pushed Cas back from the danger. "Stay away!"

Only then did she move forward against the surge of bodies. With a start, she realized that Lukas had inexplicably moved with her. *Just like a minstrel, too caught up in the drama of the moment to understand that his life might be in danger.*

Aunt Agathe's commanding voice cut through the low, panicked rumblings coming from the spooked crowd. "Stand back! We must get him to a doctor!"

Clare knelt beside Aunt Agathe, attempting to grasp at the fallen king's shoulders to lift him, his crown rolling to the ground forgotten.

"Easy, now. Let's get him to the Nixe," Aunt Aggie directed.

Together, they and Mayor Wilhelm picked up the surprisingly light man and hauled him to the Nixe. She tried to ignore her jumping pulse, determined to seem responsible in the face of danger, instead of excited at the prospect of adventure.

Once they arrived, Lukas cleared a table for them to lay him down, and Clare slammed into his back in her haste to search for a pulse at the reveler's throat.

"Sorry," she mumbled hastily, still focused on the fallen tourist.

As soon as she touched the man's skin, Clare felt *wrong*. Her vision blurred and vertigo had her clutching both the table and the charm at her neck, as if that could help her find her footing as easily as it helped her find true North.

What is happening?

It was Lukas' strong, gentle fingers at the small of her back that brought her back to herself. She looked up at his concerned face. Her vision slowly sharpened as her unfocused brown eyes met his green eyes.

"You're fine. Just take a deep breath through your nose, and out through your mouth." His voice was strangely reassuring, which annoyed her enough to snap her back to the emergency at hand.

"Yes, of course I'm fine!" Shrugging off his hands, she returned to the man passed out in front of her. If she noticed the flash of hurt in Lukas' eyes before his expression returned to faint amusement—*again*—she wouldn't acknowledge it. Seeing a real emotion meant making space to feel something about his handsome face.

"He's been stabbed through! I can feel the wound just here," Agathe's voice was low and distinct as she examined the man's gut from the other side of the long dining table he was laid out on. Dark red blood was seeping out and staining his clothes at an alarming rate. "I don't know how much the monks can do for him. If Rachel were here——"

"Rachel made her decision years ago." Wilhelm cut Aunt Aggie off with a sharp nod in Clare's direction. She felt Lukas stiffen next to her, but she didn't understand the name, or the mayor's gesture, or what either had to do with her.

Hesitantly this time, she reached for the stricken man's pulse point and focused on his wheezing, unsteady breathing. Something under his skin seemed to roil, like a burlap sack full of cats. For an instant, she thought she felt her fingers sink through soft fur instead of skin, and she jerked her hand away from the dizzying sensation.

At that moment, Father Stephen's men burst through the doors. His face was enough to remind her of everything she was— and wasn't—in Hameln. This wasn't her problem, and it was time to leave this to the Council members, who all seemed merely alarmed rather than scared. No matter how frightening it was to her.

The festivalgoer roused suddenly. He sat up straight, staring blindly ahead and speaking low and distinct.

"… dare attack me … risk the Obolen … my wrath …"

She instinctually moved closer, but couldn't make out any meaning. His speech slipped through the air, oily and dark, and her mind recoiled at the sounds even as she tried to grasp them.

What was *wrong* with her? Her vision doubled again, sometimes seeing an ashen-faced man who blubbered in fear—sometimes a weaselly face covered in whiskers and short grey hairs, a sharp-toothed muzzle sprouting out where a nose should be.

Is it the plague? she wondered. *Is this how my short, pointless life ends?*

Father Stephen held the patient up, feeling carefully around the wound, his unseeing eyes squinting in concentration as he pondered what his hands felt. Clare knew he could make out shadows and shapes, and then only in bright light. Then the abbot set him back down on the table with a firm hand, and called for Berchtold's help moving him into a private bedroom. Clare hadn't seen the Count enter, but suddenly his overwhelming presence filled the room. He placed his hand on her shoulder briefly. The calm she felt was instantaneous, and she clung to the feeling that spread through her chest as if she were rescued from drowning.

The Council will help him, of course they will. Though it wasn't every day there was an attempted murder in Hameln, all will be well. Reluctantly, she moved back and let them get to work.

She only hoped Cas was far away from whatever was happening in the Nixe.

6

Immediately after the wrecked Obolen ceremony, Sophie had breathlessly slipped through the Nixe's doors and found a dark, quiet corner in the dining room, making herself as small as possible, practically vibrating with excitement. *This is what I came here for: an unexpected spectacle, a rush of excitement, and just a touch of danger.*

When was the last time one of her mother's carefully orchestrated events was ruined? And not by Sophie?

This was an attack in the bright sunshine, in front of hundreds—no, thousands—of witnesses. Who would dare cut a festivalgoer down mid-ceremony, with all the law of the region there to see you do it?

Sophie watched the two younger villagers from across the large dining hall—a strong, pretty, brown-haired girl and the wild-looking boy who clearly wished to hold her up, if only she wouldn't cut his hands off for touching her—stepping back to let the adults get to work. If she remained out of sight, she could always slip into the victim's room, try to talk to him, get a better look at his wound—or at least see if anyone suspicious returned to finish the attempted murder.

Hours later, Sophie's quiet perseverance paid off. The monks were gone, taking their pungent ointments and quiet prayers with them, and the wounded man was left in a private room with a single guard: her old friend Jakob. As soon as he ducked out to use the privy, Sophie ducked in.

Sophie blanched at the sight that awaited her. The pallor of the man's grey skin was alarming, and she watched his body jerk periodically, as if his arms and legs decided it was time to make a go of it out in the world, independent from the rest of his body. *And this after they worked so hard to heal him?*

There was so much blood. Already a dark, ominous red was blooming through the thick white bandage around his torso. Sophie held her breath, trying to still her heart.

"Excuse me, sir," she whispered, willing her voice to somehow sound both gentle and firm. "Can you tell me what you saw? Who attacked you? Did they take something from you, or tell you what they wanted?" Sophie sensed she was speaking too rapidly, barraging the man with questions, and forced herself to pause and wait for a response. But she feared if she paused a moment, she would lose her nerve entirely.

The impotent anger she saw in his eyes strummed up both pity and disgust in her heart that she hoped he couldn't see on her face. *Stay calm and show no emotion. You're here for the facts.* She remembered her father's words, taking a deep breath and maintaining her silence.

He didn't seem to notice her internal struggle. He grabbed her hand with what felt like a cold, clammy claw. Making what was clearly a mighty effort, he pushed words out of a mouth contorted with pain. "Hameln … will pay … for this treachery."

"Hameln? Are you saying your attacker was from the town, or that the attack was *for*—"

Before she could finish her question, the man's entire body seemed to erupt up and outward into a squeaking, seething flood of fur and claws and pink, wiry tails.

Paralyzed with shock, Sophie was pushed aside and to her knees, with tiny claws pricking her skin and fur tickling her face. Bringing her hands up defensively, she was pitched onto her back by the frightening mass of … *Christ's teeth, they're rats.*

A swarm of rats had exploded from the man's death bed.

"Get away from me!" Sophie's screams were barely heard over the squealing rodents that she was desperately trying to keep away from her face. She couldn't breathe, she couldn't think, there was nowhere to *go*.

"What is happening here?" Jakob's voice thundered, his panicked entrance upsetting the chair Sophie had placed in front of the door. He got no farther than the doorway before stumbling backward in confusion and fear as hundreds of rats raced for the now open door.

Jakob ran away and Sophie fought to regain her footing to join him, unsure if he even noticed her in the room. She had to get out, before she was discovered or captured. She would escape while the dead man's disappearance—or was it transformation?—distracted the building.

I will figure out what the hell just happened.

"Things are going to get messy here, Freddie." His mother was moving about Freddie's bedroom, pointing out his belongings to her maid, who then shoveled them not-so-delicately into his travel sack. "After we speak to the crowd that is being assembled, I want you back at the castle. You can report back and keep our advisors calm."

"But I think I can be of more use to you here, Maman." Freddie hated the pleading note in his voice, but he hated the thought of being sent away even more. "Your diplomacy has served us well; let me see it in action."

Katherine had stilled at his words. Freddie could practically see her contemplating all the angles as she stared into the distance, brow furrowed and fingers tapping against his bedpost, but she eventually shook her head. "I'm sorry, Freddie. There's a murderer in Hameln, and I have to get you to safety. You are the heir."

As her maid finished packing, Katherine sent her to Mayor Wilhelm's personal stables.

"Prepare Freddie's horse. He's leaving now," she ordered the flustered young woman.

As usual, the Countess had planned for every contingency.

"When I am gone, it will be your job to keep this family going." All of Katherine's formidable attention was now on him. "And we need a representative at Castle Everstein that I can trust when our allies start asking questions."

"But I can help." Freddie winced at the wheedling tone of his own voice. "What I mean is, I have begun a relationship with these people. I can be your eyes and hands where you need them. Even the smaller details that you need taken care of …"

She took his hand sympathetically as he slumped back down into an overstuffed armchair, unable to hide his annoyance. "Your loyalty and sense of duty are a credit to this family, my love. But I need you back home because I have to have someone I can trust at my back. No matter what." Her words were warm, but her tone was frigid.

He pushed his disappointment down. "Yes, of course. Nothing is more important than the safety of all of our subjects. I'll await your instructions from the castle."

"Good," she nodded before straightening her back and heading for the door. "Now it's time to salvage what we can of this festival."

❄

Within the hour, most of the town had reassembled at the Obolen stage. Nothing traveled faster than gossip, and the frightened festivalgoers were eager for news. Sophie was eager to see how they were going to explain the catastrophe that still had her legs weak and her hands trembling. The restive crowd's anxiety was often punctuated by squeals, both human and rat, as the two populations uneasily navigated around each other. Sophie kept raising her own skirts higher than was strictly proper, ensuring the rats swarmed past instead of being caught in her skirts.

While all of the usual representatives from the town were on stage—the guild masters, the mayor, Father Stephen—Count Ebernberg was notably absent. Sophie hoped that meant he was tracking the murderer down at that very moment—and not looking for her.

She fastened her butterfly mask more securely to her face and sidestepped a tail that she saw just in time to avoid. *Disgusting*.

Her mother stepped up to the edge of the stage with sorrowful eyes and a slight smile. "Thank you all for your patience at this trying time. We have worked swiftly to uncover the truth about today's shocking events, including the identity of the man who was struck down in front of us all today." Sophie recognized Katherine's calming voice, low and measured. She often used it whenever Sophie had just ruined a perfectly good courtly introduction. "Even now, Count Ebernberg has called his most trusted men to Hameln to ensure the safety of the town and all the people in it."

The tension in the crowd went slack at the mention of the celebrated war chief. Sophie heard approving murmurs all around.

"And so, I bring you the sad tidings: it would appear that we had a disgruntled would-be initiate," the Countess continued. "In his grief over disappointed hopes, he cut himself down before others could take their chances at the Obolen ceremony."

"That is *not* what happened," Sophie spoke out emphatically, forgetting in her frustration that she was still trying to steer clear of her mother and the notice of the investigators. "Who commits suicide by turning into a *swarm of rats*? God's bones!"

While those around her in the crowd began inching away from her explosive anger with shuffling feet and sidelong glances, she cringed in instant regret over drawing attention to herself. Soon others cried out in similar frustration.

"What about the ceremony?"

"My family has waited years for this!"

"What are we doing about these rats?"

The last question was emphasized by another squeal and muffled thud, as a well-aimed kick sent another rat flying toward the stage.

"To those who have already exhibited their talents, you will be placed," Katherine responded, and Sophie sighed in relief. Either her mother had not heard her, or she simply wouldn't bother to hear what a young girl had to say. It was the usual dynamic at home, as well. "And to those who had not yet participated, rest assured: the Council will be in contact with each of you to ensure that the sanctity of the ceremony is not defied."

With that pressing question answered, many of the festivalgoers moved rapidly down side streets and into the many buildings lining the town square, perhaps not satisfied but more interested in escaping the vermin than demanding information. But many of the townsfolk remained, waiting to hear more about the confusing rumors concerning strange happenings at the Nixe directly after the ceremony's interruption.

"What's going on at the Nixe?" Josef's aged father demanded. "Is it safe? Are we safe?"

"As for the matter of the sudden influx of rodents at the Nixe," Katherine's lip curled. "We are not only aware of the issue; we are working to contain it. Your city and all who inhabit it are safe."

With a parting wave, Sophie watched as her mother descended the stage, and the rest of the Council quietly followed after her. The murmuring crowd followed the noble's cue and dispersed.

Sophie, still shaken by her close call, moved easily within the crowd, attempting to get lost in it while she determined what her next move was. The Council—including *her mother*—wasn't going to tell Hameln the truth about the Rat King's murder, she realized with chilling clarity. *It is up to me to figure it out.*

But before she could even exit the square, she felt a heavy weight on her shoulder, and hoped to God it was a hand rather than another kicked rat. "What exactly do you think you are doing here, spitfire?"

Sophie twisted around, panicked at being caught. "Freddie! I-I can explain!"

Her brother narrowed his blazing blue eyes at her, looking just like their father after a particularly disappointing experiment. "Start talking."

7

After the Countess' announcement, an agitated Clare and anxious Lukas were quick to track Casper down in the thinning crowds and take him home.

"I don't want to alarm you, but I may be ill," Clare whispered to Cas as they walked, before turning to include Lukas in their conversation. Though her dizziness had faded, she still felt a bit weak, and very confused. "You both may want to head straight back to the Nixe without me."

"Look, I don't know what kind of guys you usually bring home," Lukas replied with a sidelong look in her direction. "But I'm not the type to leave a sick girl to her own devices. Especially when my other option is a rat-infested inn."

"I'm not dying or anything," she scoffed. "I don't think. But something happened back there, the things I saw, or *think* I saw ... I might have been hallucinating."

"Lucky for you, I know my way around a sickroom." Lukas' voice was breezy, as if they were discussing which tavern to frequent.

Clare stopped in her tracks as a rat scurried ahead of her with a half-eaten sausage in its teeth. "There's been a murder in Hameln."

"And you're in shock," Lukas replied. His tone all flippant indifference while he was carefully not touching the small of her back.

"I don't know if you noticed, but I'm not exactly a delicate girl," she said, glancing disdainfully at his hand before walking forward again with more pride than vigor.

"No, you're a strong, terminally stubborn girl. Even more reason to ignore anything you might say to deter someone looking after you," Lukas said, oh-so-reasonably.

Was he actually steering her toward her own home, as if she wouldn't know the way backward and blindfolded?

"How terrible could it possibly be to depend on someone else?" Lukas asked.

"I'll let you know when I try it," Clare shot back, quickening her pace. She would not be handled like a skittish horse.

"It's been a long, stressful day." Lukas continued walking, looking ahead as if she hadn't responded. "And if you are ill, this would be an amazingly terrible time for us to leave you alone. Right, Cas?"

Cas had regained a bit of the color in his own shell-shocked face. Clare frowned at his quiet misery. Her little brother never reacted quickly under stress. He readjusted his viselike grip on his box and glanced at a small group of rats snipping and snarling at each other a few feet away before responding. "I can call for one of the monks, Clare. Of course, we won't leave you."

There was a strange pressure lingering in her head that was making it difficult to continue arguing, or to even remember why she should bother. Rubbing her temples, she begrudgingly acknowledged their wisdom. "Yes, you're right. Home first. Then we can figure out what the hell is going on."

The trio reached the house soon after, and Cas directed Lukas to fetch some firewood as he eased Clare into a chair at the kitchen table.

"Good riddance," she mumbled into her hands as she waited for the medicinal brew that Casper was preparing for her.

"You know, I'm actually surprised at you, Clare," Cas said as he moved awkwardly through the room, filling the teapot and reaching for the loose-leaf white willow bark tea they kept on a particularly high shelf. "After watching you sit at the knee of every traveler who sets foot in the Nixe, I thought you'd get on with Lukas like wildfire."

"He just rubs me the wrong way." Clare propped her head on her arms now, idly watching her brother work. "He's so ... practiced."

That earned her a short laugh that quickly died in Casper's throat at her dark look. "Yes, I suppose he does practice quite a bit. He is, after all, a traveling musician. Being good at his job is how he's kept from starving." He readied her cup as the water heated.

"No! It's not that, it's ..." she huffed in annoyance, frowning down at the worn tabletop as she searched for the words. "He's not *real*. He acts like it's all a game or ... or one of his performances, including the Obolen and even this murder. I don't know how to trust someone who doesn't seem to care."

"You don't know anything about my intentions, or my heart. I'd kindly ask you to refrain from assuming you do." Lukas stood stiffly in the doorway, hands full of firewood that he unceremoniously dropped to the floor.

She jumped as the logs clattered at their feet, but her eyes never left his face. For the first time, he felt ... dangerous.

With a tense jaw and flashing eyes, Lukas turned on his heel and left the house. Casper limped after, throwing a quietly amused look at his abashed and uncharacteristically quiet sister as he passed.

"Now *there's* the Hameln hospitality Aunt Aggie requested," he said.

"I guess I'll make my own tea, then," she said to the empty room before slowly, begrudgingly following him out.

Lukas hadn't gotten beyond the smithy courtyard and when Cas walked out, they saw why. Lucie, Clare's best friend and the mayor's daughter, was there with him, looking uncomfortable in a way that only those who had known Lucie her entire life could see—her brows were raised just so, and a slight stiffness to her hands betrayed her.

"Lucie!" Cas grabbed both her and Lukas' attention. "Is everything alright? Clare told me that your father and the Council were caring for the stricken reveler. I hope he's doing better?"

Lucie's pale face brightened and she pushed her golden hair over her shoulder, neat as a pin before moving away from Lukas to greet Cas. "Yes, they have everything under control. But it is dreadful what has happened to the festival. And all these rats ..." She shuddered before collecting herself again. "Mother is very agitated, but Father insisted I come talk to you as soon as possible."

Clare was watching her friend's tight smile carefully. "Did something happen to Margarethe? Or Aunt Aggie?"

"No, no, everything's fine," Lucie assured her.

"Go back inside! Isn't the tea ready?" Casper started fussing over Clare, and the scene quickly became a competition in mothering, as Lucie, too, became alarmed over Clare's apparent illness.

Clare's insistent voice rose above the rest. "I feel much better, actually," Clare said, quelling Casper and Lucie's concern. Lukas was conspicuously quiet on the matter. "Lucie, would you like to come in? Cas just made tea."

"I can't. I'm just here as a messenger," the blonde girl explained, though she ventured farther into the forge-warmed courtyard. Even in the dead of winter, it was a pleasant place to rest a moment, with the weak sunshine peeking around the furnace and more than a few places to sit. As long as you didn't mind sharing the space with a few straw-filled dummies and a veritable armory of weapons.

"Father asked me to give you word—the Obolen may be postponed indefinitely." Lucie was speaking to Cas, but she seemed aware that all three of them were hanging on her every word. "Though he doesn't want you to be concerned. Besides Father Stephen's obvious claim, Countess Katherine has spoken quite highly of your work—what she's seen of it, anyway. With or without the Obolen presentation, you will not miss the choosing ceremony this summer."

"All that work and worry, and I didn't even have to exhibit to be chosen?" Cas demanded indignantly as he collapsed heavily into a nearby stool. "I'd be furious if I weren't so relieved—and confused."

"If you want to speak to Father Stephen, I believe he headed back to St. Boniface," Lucie offered. Much like herself, Clare knew Lucie could never stand a dejected Casper.

"Really?" Cas brightened at the thought. "Yes, Father Stephen. And maybe he'll have more information about the choosing cere-mony." He made his way to leave. "I'll find you later, Lukas. Thanks again for your help today. And Clare?" He turned to his sister. "Be nice."

Clare rolled her eyes and waved him away. She had returned to work almost as soon as the conversation had started, dizzy or not. Nothing soothed her quite like having something to do with her hands. She looked over the state of the forge, picked up a half-finished sheath of nails the Vogt brothers had ordered last week, and grabbed the round stock and nail header to continue the job.

She purposely aimed to look busy, only half paying attention to the conversation around her. She missed her friend, but was worried her eagerness would scare Lucie away. After all, it was the first time she and Lucie had shared a friendly word in what felt like months.

It was generally agreed that Lucie was the most beautiful girl in Hameln. Clare knew that Lucie was actually the smartest.

Lucie's beauty was undeniable: with her glossy blonde hair and large brown eyes, she favored her father, Wilhelm. Though there was something about the shape of her mouth, the quirk of her brow, that was all her mother, Margarethe.

But beyond her honeyed looks, Lucie's mind penetrated in surprising ways, quick to analyze any situation and come to the most favorable solution for all involved.

Clare had always been the more aggressively imaginative of the two, with a biting wit and boisterous laugh. But Lucie's quiet understanding of other's motivations and desires had been superior since they were young girls trying to understand and navigate the insular world of Hameln together.

From the start, trouble found them as naturally as a goshawk took to flight—trouble that Clare was keen to get into, and Lucie was quick to talk them out of.

But lately, Lucie had pulled back from Clare. They no longer spent an idle hour or two together in the courtyard, Clare with her longsword and Lucie lunging lazily toward her with a pole arm, the weapons glinting in the sun like treasure. And Lucie no longer invited Clare to her house, where they had spent many a night holed up in the library, Lucie diligently at work with her distaff and spindle while Clare entertained them both with epic stories, either reading from the pages of Margarethe's books or repeated from the Nixe's dining room.

It hurt, but Clare knew that Lucie was needed by her ill mother's side, soothing and directing as if she were now the mother and Margarethe the child. And Clare was busy herself, taking on more and more the duties of the official Hameln blacksmith, with orders to be filled and deadlines to be met. *Whether I want to or not.*

Clare missed Lucie's sparkling laugh and quiet understanding. *I wonder if she misses me at all*, Clare thought, before turning and speaking to her directly.

"Come on Luce," Clare cajoled her friend. "Spar with me, like we used to. I'll be the evil Erlking, and you can be the courageous Princess Christina striking the murderous villain down!" She picked a longsword at random, feinting just left of her friend, to playfully block her exit.

Lucie's gentle face blanched, as if suddenly sick. "Princess Christina didn't fight a Faerie king. She defied her parents, running away from a loveless engagement."

"Sounds pretty heroic to me ..."

"I don't have time for our old games, Clare." Lucie's voice was sharp, and she didn't wait for a reply before heading for the gate. "I must get back to my mother. She gets unsettled if she's left alone too long, you know that. Especially with the trouble we've had this morning."

Clare flinched, glanced at the two boys watching them, and decided to fight another day.

"Alas, your good sense defeats me yet again, gentle lady." Clare bowed low, her words theatrical, but her tone sincere. "Well met."

Lucie's small smile almost eased Clare's hurt. Whenever she thought she could grab a small piece of her old life, reality came crashing through. The reality of Lucie's life was in some ways even more grim. At least Clare could remember her parents, strong and hale. They all had to watch as Lucie's mother became a weaker shadow of herself with every passing year.

"Should we come see you and your mother later this week?" Clare asked. "I miss your parents, and I know Casper misses the sight of those beautiful clocks ..."

"Of course." Lucie's eyes had already moved beyond the courtyard, to her myriad other responsibilities. "This week, or the next, Clarebear." And then she was gone, leaving a slightly embarrassed Clare to continue her idle work with the blade, testing the balance, oiling the sword, and thoroughly ignoring a certain charming minstrel who had witnessed her exchange with Lucie.

"Wait a moment!" Lukas snapped his lean, dark fingers and his smile widened with delight. "You're Clarebear! *The* Clarebear."

She looked up, confusion clouding her dark eyes. *How does he know that name?* He had jumped up on another stool, both hands pointing toward her, a wide grin lighting up those preternatural eyes.

And what a grin it was. Her chest expanded while her mouth twisted automatically to return the smile.

She shook her head sharply, as if breaking a spell. "You know that name?"

"Wolfhart often spoke of you," he said. "Clarebear, with her plans to roam the world and make a name for herself, far from Hameln—"

"You know Wolfhart? I mean, you actually spend time with him? I was starting to believe you'd forged that letter." She couldn't hide the disbelief. *Who was this boy, casually mentioning the hero of Lower Saxony like an old friend? And why was he really here?*

"Well," his smile faltered in the face of her savage tone. It quickly returned, like the summer sun briefly shadowed by a passing cloud. "I came across him in my travels. A brave hunter like him is renowned throughout the land. The perfect subject for my next masterpiece. Here, let me perform 'Red Riding Hood' for you. It's not finished quite yet, but I'm sure you'll recognize the tale. The brave Wolfhart saving a young girl and her grandmother from the very jaws of death, slicing open a beastly wolf—"

"That's not what happened." Clare rolled her eyes, wondering what kind of fool believed such nonsense. "He couldn't save two people who were *eaten* by a *wolf*. The girl and her grandmother didn't survive. Though, neither did the wolf. Its head currently graces the back wall of the Nixe."

"Sometimes the truth needs a little finessing. Right, *Erlking*?"

She rounded on Lukas and his flinch at her menacing look was particularly satisfying. Then she realized the sword was still in her clenched fist, and turned to place it on the rack instead. "Don't you have errands to run? Room and board to earn?"

"Yes, unfortunately duty calls me from your side, Clarebear. I'm sure they can find something for me to do at the Nixe. Please, don't let my absence hurt your tender heart." His feigned reluctance and mocking smile had her anger rising. Again.

Clare's voice growled out, a bit strangled. "Don't call me that."

"You are a bit touchy about your monikers."

How could she explain it to him? Clarebear was a stupid girl with a head full of lies. And being known as Hameln's blacksmith? That was her father, the steady, wise man who worked so hard to make a life in Hameln. She couldn't bear to be either of those people right now. She didn't have the strength or the purpose.

"Look, those aren't names to me. They're like ... they're like titles. And titles should be earned." Clare turned away to pick up her heavy apron that had been hanging on a nail just inside the smithy door where she'd left it this morning. Had it only been a few hours since that disastrous Obolen?

Lukas looked over the beautiful sword she had just laid aside. The light glinted off it warmly, like a blazing fire instead of a mere reflection of the sun.

"Looks like you should be plenty proud of your work, Clare," he said.

The compliment hung in the air for a moment longer than she was comfortable with.

"I may have need for a striker." Clare stalled, pulling her heavy apron over her head while lifting her dark braid away from her neck. She willed Lukas not to notice the veritable pile of unfinished metal at her worktable. Jakob's help was hard to come by with so many patrons at the Nixe, and Casper could only leverage so much strength with one weakened leg. She was drowning in work, and determined that Lukas would not know how much his help was needed.

"I'm not afraid to get my hands dirty. Though the heat could take some getting used to." Lukas sensibly turned away from exactly the spot she wanted him not to see. "Besides, if I'm helping you at the forge, it won't look quite so suspicious when we're seen talking together."

He paused a moment, as if considering the pile of metals around him. "Just the cover we need if we're going to figure out what happened at the festival today." His tone was just suggestive enough that she could ignore the implication.

She did.

"You might want to change then," she replied with a tiny smirk, casually turning to bolster the flames, not a moment to waste. "Wouldn't want you to ruin your *fine clothes*. I'm not sure you could find a jacket to replace that one … anywhere, really."

8

"I know how it sounds, but you have to believe me," Sophie pleaded with her brother, who had dragged her away from the stage into an empty courtyard. Usually, she'd put up more of a fight, but her head was still spinning with death and treachery and *real magic*. This is the adventure she'd been looking for in Hameln, plus or minus the rodents.

Freddie swung her around to face him, muttering low, though Sophie caught a very distinct "foolish girl" in there.

"This was not a murder, or at least not *just* a murder," she continued. "And I think I could explain the sudden surge of rats, too, if you will just *listen*."

Freddie sighed deeply. She knew he wasn't heartless, and he didn't enjoy disappointing his sister. *I'm betting on it this time*, she thought to herself.

"Spitfire, this isn't a game. This is … this is *chaos* in the middle of one of the biggest political events of the decade, with one person dead, and a mill town full of rats. The grain industry of the entire region depends on Hameln. I don't have the time to babysit you—"

"B-babysit?!" Sophie sputtered, ready to tear his curly dark hair out of his hard head. But he simply held her thin shoulder in one hand.

—while we deal with the crime, the infestation, and whatever actually happens when the Obolen doesn't occur."

Sophie hesitated, reading his exhausted face.

"I am not a silly child," she continued pleadingly, before Freddie could order her back home. "I am a witness, and I can help the people of Hameln. In fact, aren't you always the one telling me it is my duty as an Everstein to do so?"

She could see Freddie fighting for calm, his jaw and fists both tight.

"You are fourteen-years-old." he scolded. "You stole away from home on a lark, and now you want to stay and write about all the excitement in that damned journal of yours!"

"Father knows I am here. And this is not just about my chronicles! It is about saving lives!" Sophie's small hands were clenched at her sides. She would not back down, not when so much was on the line. "By the time Grandmaman was my age, she had already helped negotiate peace with House Lippe and a trade deal with the Southerners. I will not acquit myself with any less honor."

Freddie took a moment to really look at his little sister.

"I want nothing more than to pack you up and drag you back home," he began with a soul-deep sigh. "But mother needs all the help she can get to wrap up this *unpleasantness*. If I can't be here to aid her … you are my next-best choice." He paused. "My only choice, really."

Sophie caught on quickly: Their mother had clearly already ordered him back.

"I can do that," she responded solemnly. "*Of course* I can do that."

"Very well," he relented, speaking slowly. "But you must go to the Council as soon as you have the evidence you need, or it becomes too dangerous. And I will determine when it becomes too dangerous."

"Yes, yes, of course," Sophie gushed before attempting solemnity again. "I trust your judgment implicitly."

Freddie continued, clearly warming to the scheme. "First, keep me abreast of the developments, and keep your head down. Make yourself known only when you are sure of your evidence, and then return to the castle as soon as you are no longer needed."

"I promise," Sophie agreed, nodding fervently. "As soon as I have rock-solid evidence, I will come home."

She then rushed in to hug him, and he stroked her head affectionately. "I am proud of you, Spitfire. But no heroics, do you hear me? And I expect a regular report from you while you remain. If you go silent, I'm coming back with all of Castle Everstein behind me."

"Yes, Freddie." Her response was muffled in his tunic. "Maman and I will come home to you and Papa, all in one piece. I promise."

After that embarrassingly emotional reunion with her brother, Sophie knew it was time to get to business. First order: finding a new, *ratless*, base of operations.

As Sophie left the town center, she hesitated, patting down the hood of her indigo cloak to make sure her head was still fully covered. If her mother saw her now, she knew she'd be sent home immediately. If she wanted to uncover the truth in Hameln, she needed to find a safe haven, and fast. Saint Boniface it was.

As soon as she entered the cathedral, Sophie sat down and got to work. She jotted down her thoughts—a timeline and lists of motives or opportunity, as well as any who had seen the murder, any failed initiates who might profit from an interrupted ceremony, someone who could conceivably lead a town into *treachery*. With her bowed head in quiet intensity, any who came upon her could mistake her investigation for piety. In truth, her mind was still trapped in that tiny bedroom, watching a man die.

Hameln will pay for this treachery.

The man was dying, he clearly knew it, and those were his last words. But how could he blame an entire town for one person's actions? Did that mean it was a member of the Council?

And who gained from the festival's abrupt end?

Her mother had been quietly furious, which wasn't too terribly different from any other day. The ceremony was ruined, and the months of careful negotiations and preparations were for naught. The mayor looked positively ill earlier in the Nixe, and clearly wanted to help the victim. But not enough to call for this Rachel person that Agathe had mentioned. Even Count Ebernberg and Father Stephen moved faster than she had ever seen such important personages move in her young but full life at court.

"Hear it, write it, remember it," she reminded herself, before scratching out a timeline of events as best she could remember. As if she could somehow keep score for the universe with the written word.

Sophie shook her head, readjusted her butterfly mask, and breathed deeply before putting her quill to paper.

Of course, none of this speculation mattered if she didn't go talk to the locals—anyone who might help her understand how Hameln worked and what there was for the Council to fear. She needed an insider to smooth the way like her network back home.

Sophie was looking idly through a stained-glass window in the church, mind churning furiously over her dismal options, when she caught sight of an Obolen initiate's robes in the courtyard.

A witness. Exactly the type of person she should question. Immediately.

"Hello, child!" Sophie called out cheerfully when she stepped into the courtyard, a large rectangle of space covered in concrete pavers and filled with potted plants and benches.

The Obolen initiate didn't even look up.

As she moved closer, she registered that the mass of black robe and brown curls on the ground was actually a boy. And possibly deaf.

She sidled up to him, attempting to remain unthreatening. Instead, she imagined she looked a bit mad, waving her hands down by her knees as she crept up. "Hellooooo there," Sophie called out pleasantly. "I was hoping to talk to you about the ceremony today?"

The boy finally looked up from some complicated device that he was poking at with a screwdriver. And blinked. A long pause grew between them before he finally spoke.

"If you're here to perform, this is definitely the wrong place," he told her, his voice deeper and more amused than she had anticipated. "Father Stephen isn't much for the theater."

She grabbed the ridiculous mask off her face and stood up awkwardly. This boy was possibly older than her, with clear brown eyes that sparkled with laughter in his pale face.

Just as well, she was terrible with children.

"Oh, hello. And no," she answered. "I was just … enjoying the festival. And I had a few questions, if you could help me?"

It didn't take long for Sophie to convince this boy, Casper, that they should continue their interview indoors. She found herself in a long, dry room filled with tidy workbenches. The walls were lined with slate, covered in sketches and equations. She was reminded of her father's laboratory.

"Strictly speaking, girls—I mean, women—aren't supposed to enter this section of the monastery …" Casper glared back at her.

Sophie steeled her spine and pulled herself up to her full height —taller than him, anyway—tilting her head with a sweet smile. "I'm terribly sorry, did I neglect to introduce myself properly? I am Princess Sophia Everstein of Castle Everstein, sent here by my father Count Johann and Prince Frederich to investigate the assuredly criminal activities in Hameln. Those who hinder my investigation ..."

She dropped off with her own meaningful glare. Casper folded almost immediately.

Normally, this little adventure into the heart of the monastery would have warranted its own entry into her chronicles, but she was determined to focus on the mystery at hand.

The boy, Casper, was not just an initiate, but the nephew of a Council member. He had been polite but guarded as she explained who she was—the truth, after her lost, curious little girl story was met with quiet disbelief.

With Casper's access to the Council and knowledge of the ceremony, she knew she had her man on the inside. She just had to convince him of it. He was generally unimpressed with her mission, princess of the Empire or not.

"Look, I have evidence." Sophie continued her pitch, producing a scroll from her traveling sack and spreading it on his worktable, heedless of the tools and bits of metal strewn about. She decided to ignore his dismay. "Here is the list of people that profit from the Obolen. And here," she pointed at a somewhat shorter list beside it, "is the list of people who profit from covering up a murder in Hameln."

"The list is practically identical." Casper pored over the names, wincing as he saw Aunt Aggie and Father Stephen. But he found that she wasn't a hypocrite, seeing how Countess Katherine's name was included. "This isn't helpful at all."

"It shows that there's a conspiracy!" Sophie insisted through gritted teeth. "Who would dare to interrupt the ceremony, unless they knew that the Council would do everything they could to sweep it under the rug? The murderer is being protected, and I think they *knew* that the Council would do so."

"Or it was an act of passion," Casper pointed out. "Or an accident. Or, as the Council has already stated, it was self-inflicted."

"The reveler didn't just die, Casper. God's bones, he turned into a swarm of *rats*," Sophie enunciated, her words clear and cold.

That silenced him for a moment, as he stared into her face, as if he could discern the truth from it. She pressed on. "Right in front of me! That is not normal, even for Hameln, I'm guessing."

"So you say," Casper said, reading her scant evidence closely. "And you think it was a local. Someone we all know?"

"The Council should be livid that the ceremony was interrupted, and out to punish those responsible," Sophie said. "Instead, they're making every excuse to make the murder seem innocent, and move on. It must be someone they all know and want to protect."

"They're just trying to maintain the peace." Casper was uncomfortable and unconvinced. "Telling everyone there's a murderer on the loose isn't exactly good for business." He stabbed his finger at one unexpected name on her list. "And why is Jakob on this list? He's not on the Council, and he gets paid no matter how many tourists show up at the Nixe this week."

"Because," Sophie said, almost reluctant to share her last bit of intelligence, the only thing that she knew kept her relevant if this boy wanted to turn her over to his aunt. "Jakob witnessed the Rat King's death, too."

"He may not be a leader, but he was the only other person trusted enough to look after a dying man with a grudge," she insisted. "Perhaps he administered the dying blow? Or, at least, he could know more about the whys and hows of the assassination?"

Casper snorted, clearly unconvinced. But then he looked back down at the sheath of papers she'd handed him.

Sophie waited patiently, allowing the silence to stretch out between them, determined that he should be the next to speak.

"I don't know about your skills as an investigator," he finally said. "But if this man died angry at someone in our town, and the Council is covering the truth up … What's so important that they're protecting?"

9

L ukas and Clare had spent a few hours working together, the icy tension between them melting in the warm orange glow of the forge. He was a quick study, tying his curling black hair back and moving his body, light and quick, at her every command. *Maybe he's not entirely useless*, she thought begrudgingly.

It wasn't until they'd returned to the kitchen inside and she spied the weapon hanging at his hip that her earlier suspicion roused itself.

"You bought one of my daggers?" Clare asked, recognizing one of Casper's intricate designs on the hilt that now jutted from the minstrel's belt. "Why are you bothering to work here if you have enough money to buy that?"

"Actually, Pieter gave it to me," Lukas answered easily, unsheathing the short blade for a closer inspection. "For services rendered to the Hameln blacksmith."

"He did what?" Lukas clearly expected her to be pleased, or even honored, that her dagger was considered worthy payment for his time. Payment that she never expected to give him, and that she would now not make on her own labor.

"If that son of a—" she sputtered before starting over. "If he thinks that he can skimp out on my payments, he's going to be sorely disappointed," Clare seethed through her teeth. "I've been a full, dues-paying member of the guild for more than two years now. And I expect full payment for my wares."

Lukas' eyes widened as he realized his mistake. "I can pay." He reached for his coin purse. "How much do I owe you?"

Clare waved him away. "No, I won't welch on Pieter's deal. My fight's not with you."

"That's a relief," Lukas answered. Clare's anger simmered down enough that she realized he was actually the one with the weapon in his hand.

Clare stood, deciding at that moment that she had to get out of the close room. "I have to go talk to Aunt Aggie. Although ..." She paused, considering her options. "That means closing the shop."

"I can stay," Lukas said, raising his hand as if she were asking for a volunteer. "Something tells me the paying customers won't be allowed back in the Nixe anytime soon, after all."

"Fine," she answered tightly. "Thanks," she added, imagining Casper's pointed look at her incivility, before heading out the door.

Clare weaved in and out of the crowds that had dwindled noticeably since the crowds of rats had invaded this morning. While the forge had remained mostly unchanged, Clare saw the immediacy of the chaos and fear the rodents brought with them.

"First a murder and now a plague of rats?" One particularly vicious broom-wielder bemoaned, attacking the pests with wide sweeps of her weapon.

It was almost enough to give her pause before adding another trouble to Aunt Aggie's plate.

Almost.

"... Do you think this is punishment?" Clare heard Mayor Wilhelm's voice just as she neared the threshold to Aunt Aggie's office. She knew better than to interrupt Council business, so she stood quietly by the half-opened door and waited. If she happened to hear the rest of the conversation, so much the better.

"No, if he wished to punish us, it wouldn't be with rats." Aggie's derisive snort was almost soothing to Clare's nerves. "We'll have to fix this on our own, I fear. And then we still have Mabon festival to look forward to. Perhaps if we can give him the perpetrator to sacrifice instead, we'll be spared the brunt of his anger."

Who was this "he" they kept referring to? It wasn't like either of them to wax philosophically about God.

"Yes, if the murderer is a child, I'm sure that will do the trick." Wilhelm's mild tone did nothing to disguise his sarcasm.

Clare recoiled at both the mayor's tone and words. *A child?*

"The Obolen ceremony is mostly symbolic anyway. We already knew which children would be accepted, and where most would be apprenticed." Aggie's answer was almost absentminded, and to Clare's frustration, her aunt didn't bother clarifying the subject. "We can fix this during the Mabon festival, announce the placements officially, and still be on track for the Midsummer festival."

"I'm sure you're right."

Clare heard the mayor's slow, heavy steps moving toward the door and raced down the hallway before she was found eavesdropping. "I'll attend to the matter at hand now. Make sure that Father Stephen's men have prepared the body—as it were—for burial."

Whatever that means, Clare thought, body tense with the effort it took to walk forward silently.

"Yes, I'll be along shortly." Aggie's dismissal was clear.

Clare met Wilhelm at the door.

"Ah, Clare! Here to see your Aunt Aggie?" Wilhelm, Lucie's father, didn't quite look her in the eye. "She'll be happy to see you, I'm sure."

"Yes, I just want to make sure everything is well here." Clare spoke distinctly, ensuring her aunt would know she was coming. "You know, the word around town is that there is something almost otherworldly about these rats." She paused a moment, eyes wide in what she hoped was innocent confusion. "Supernatural. Biblical, even."

"Well, a few drinks too many undoubtedly helps to exaggerate the situation." Wilhelm put his hand on her shoulder as he had so many times before when advising her on her studies or listening as she related her latest adventure with Lucie. The familiar gesture didn't put Clare at ease, and she visibly flinched at his touch. Hopefully he took it as worry for the town's plight instead of the strange words she'd just overheard. "As Father Stephen would say, moderation in everything. Even on festival days."

"Wise words, as always, mayor," Clare said, sidestepping his heavy hand. "If you'll excuse me, I need to see if there's anything I can do for Aunt Aggie."

"Of course, Clare. Your diligence, as ever, is a credit to your family." Wilhelm moved on, clearly ready to wash his hands of the Nixe.

For the first time, Clare found herself wondering if the mayor actually cared about the people of Hameln at all.

"And come by the house later, won't you? I know Lucie misses your company. Perhaps you can bring that bard with you? Lukas, was it?"

"Yes, Lukas," Clare replied faintly. At least someone in the mayor's house wanted to see her.

"Perhaps he can even perform for us?" Wilhelm continued his one-sided conversation. "I'm sure Margarethe and Countess Katherine would enjoy a private performance."

"The Countess is still here?" Clare asked sharply, before moderating her voice. "I thought she would have left after the *incident* was handled."

"There is much to prepare if we want the ceremony to go

smoothly this summer after that disastrous Obolen ceremony. Dreadful business," he answered with a vague, cheerful smile.

"What's going—

"Good afternoon, Clare!" he interrupted her before moving swiftly down the hallway.

Frustrated, she knew better than most how well Wilhelm avoided answering even the most innocent of questions. *Looks like I'll have to get answers from Aunt Aggie, instead. Starting with Pieter cheating me.*

As she entered the office, Clare took a moment to study Aunt Aggie's face, her dark eyes bright and skin taut over her bones, tired but still sharp as she shuffled papers around.

"If you're here about the unfortunate event, or the rats, I really can't help you, Clare," Aggie began, not bothering to look up from her papers.

"I need to talk to you about Pieter, actually," Clare said, aware that talking about money never failed to pique Aggie's interest. She couldn't do much about the rats, but she could damned well protect her business. "I'm concerned he's cheating me on my profits."

"That is a serious charge, my dear," Aggie's gaze was now on Clare's face. Nothing focused Aggie more than money. "What is your evidence?"

"He's already given that bard one of my weapons. For nothing!" Clare said, happy to finally find a sympathetic ear. "With some nonsense about bartering for labor. As if the dagger or the labor were his to begin with."

"I will speak to him," Aggie said, before turning back to her books. For a moment, Clare was speechless. Was that it? Pieter would get a stern Aggie speech after disregarding her work and livelihood?

"No." Clare stepped closer, lowering her voice. "I want to file a complaint with the Council. The guild is supposed to protect its members, not use their hard work to hand out prizes."

"I don't think that is the best course of action, Clare." Aggie's

tone was a warning that Clare happily ignored. She had to make her aunt *listen* to her.

"I think Pieter will treat me lower than an *auslander* as long as I allow him to," Clare insisted. "I am not a child, or an apprentice. I am a master blacksmith like my father before me. He is disrespecting my family. *Our* family. You are a burgher now, a crime against you and yours is a crime against the entire community. That has to mean *something*."

"I know it hasn't been easy for you, Clarebear," Aunt Aggie said with a heavy sigh. "It wasn't easy even for me, when Matthias died. Many on the Council wanted me to hand over the Nixe to someone else—anyone with a half a brain and a pin between his legs, to be honest. It didn't matter that the Nixe was my father's inn."

At her words, Clare's rage melted into a bone-deep fatigue. She and her aunt both were just the latest in a long line of Hameln locals: never herself, her hopes, her ambitions.

She turned to Clare now, her expression softening. "I've fought hard for you to take your father's smithy. I knew you would prove yourself, and credit this family. But never forget—they are only waiting for an excuse to push you out or dry your business up."

Clare blinked away angry tears, looking away before Aunt Aggie saw even a moment of weakness. "It isn't right."

"No, it's not," Aggie agreed. "There's a balance that we must maintain. I can't do everything I want, but neither can Pieter. And I will speak to him. Quietly, so he is not embarrassed. But as you said, I am the innkeeper of the Nixe and a member of the Hameln Council. He *will* listen, Clarebear."

"And if it makes no difference?" Clare asked stiffly.

"Afterward, if you are not satisfied with your compensation, we will take the matter before the full Council," Aunt Aggie relented. "You have my word."

Clare hesitated, brow furrowed in disagreement, but knew there was nothing more to discuss. Aunt Aggie did not make oaths lightly.

Clare may not trust the system, but she had to trust her family. What other choice did she have? *Speaking of trust …*

"And the murder—"

"Don't, Clare," Aunt Aggie cut her off, voice high and tone final. "I know your heart; I know you would seek to help. But I beg of you: leave this mess to the Council."

Clare stilled a moment, her freckled nose wrinkling in disgust before nodding stiffly. For all she knew, the culprit was another loathsome tourist, and everything would be set to rights by morning. She headed back home without another word.

10

That evening Sophie moved slowly and steadily behind Casper through the crowds and rats. Though his walk was never impeded, his limp was obvious. In a very un-Sophie-like manner, she hadn't asked him about it yet—finding a place to stay overrode her desire to uncover all of this boy's secrets.

Sophie followed him eagerly, if gingerly, flinching at a squeak that was a bit too close, and tried not to think about the fact that each of the rodents had been a part of a living, breathing person just hours earlier. Were they still?

She shuddered and turned her mind to the more pleasant curiosity that was the home she was headed toward.

Her castle's forge was one of the few places she was routinely chased away from, as the risk of a severely burned princess proved to be too much for the otherwise indulgent servants at Everstein Castle. But today, she would not only see Hameln's forge, she would be sleeping right over it. And hopefully it would keep her warmer than she'd been since she left the castle.

"Christ's teeth, it's cold," Sophie complained as the sun disappeared behind the treetops. The last time she'd worn this dress, it had been in an overly heated ballroom, not the icy December streets.

"You shouldn't curse like that. Father Stephen says—"

"Father Stephen says that my father experiments on our Obolen apprentices like some sort of demented King Midas," Sophie interrupted. "You shouldn't believe everything that Father Stephen says."

"Still. It's disrespectful," Casper insisted, pale hands clenched into fists at his sides.

"Fine! By Thor's hammer! Odin's beard! Frigga's frozen girdle!" Sophie paused to smile ever-so-sweetly at Cas. "Better?"

Casper gave her a grudging smile. "We're here."

Other than a small iron horse shoe hanging over the door, the smithy looked like any other house on the street, two-storied and narrow. There was an open archway beside it that seemed to lead to an open courtyard, but before she could investigate further, Casper opened the door, quickly checked the room beyond, and then pushed her into it, awkwardly kicking aside a rat that thought to join them.

Inside was all polished wooden furniture and metal accents. The entire first floor of the house comprised one large room, with long tables covered in wares. There were weapons of all varieties, along with the everyday necessities: door hinges, nails, and even some surprisingly fine jewelry.

Ringing sounds of metal hitting metal could be heard coming from the back courtyard, periodically interrupted by the *whoosh* of superheated steam. Sophie moved toward the door immediately, before Casper caught her arm.

"Upstairs first," he said, limping toward the third and final door in the room. "We should figure out exactly what we're going to tell my sister, Clare, before you meet her. She can be … protective."

Sophie felt confident she could handle whatever Casper's sister threw at her. She had, after all, just convinced her own brother to allow her investigation. Clare should be no trouble at all in the face of Prince Frederich of Everstein.

"I think we should tell her the truth," Casper said as he led her carefully up the steep, narrow stairway to his home. "None of this curious *auslander* act that you tried with me. Clare doesn't have much patience for subterfuge."

"Whatever you feel is best," Sophie agreed. "As long as you know, I'm not giving up, even if I have to live on the rat-infested streets while I uncover this mystery."

"I believe it," Casper responded dryly. "And your title may convince her more than anything else. Clare does respect authority, as long as it is properly wielded."

"How sensible of her," Sophie said, looking around Casper's small but tidy house in satisfaction. "Your home is quite comfortable, and I thank you for bringing me here."

"Save the compliments for Clare," he answered with a grin. "You've already convinced me, milady."

Perhaps I'd learned something at Maman's endless balls after all.

Sophie casually plucked up an abandoned cup from the kitchen table, examining it briefly before setting it down again—where the half-full drink promptly rolled to the floor, spilling water everywhere.

Then again, maybe not.

"God's bones!" Sophie cursed her clumsy fingers while righting the now-empty cup. Casper wheeled around in search of a cloth, calling out "I've got it!" With a towel in hand, he bent down clumsily to clean the mess she'd created.

"What's going on here?" a new voice called out. From the look on Casper's face, Sophie could tell he was mostly relieved that their awkward moment was interrupted. This must be Casper's sister, then.

Clare squinted suspiciously at Sophie, her muscular shoulders showing through her blouse. "I thought we had an agreement about bringing home Yuletide revelers. You know—not to do it?"

The tips of Casper's ears were burning red-hot as he attempted to make the scramble to his feet look more like a graceful swing around to face his sister.

"Uh, right. Well. Sophie isn't a reveler. She's … investigating the tourist's murder for the Countess. And she's going to be our guest." Sophie admired how his face was suddenly smoothed into a practiced mask.

Clare's dark eyes passed over Sophie, assessing her with a keen glance.

In her brown velvet traveling cloak and soft deerskin boots, Sophie had thought she'd look inconspicuous, a seasoned traveler just passing through for the annual Hameln festival. But now she saw her clothes were too fine and her face was too young to pass more than a cursory inspection.

Clare's scrutiny made her feel like a foolish little girl and a big inconvenience.

"You were sent by Countess Katherine, then?" Clare squared her broad shoulders and planted her feet in front of the door. Her absolute authority in the moment was unmistakable. "It's interesting that Aunt Aggie didn't mention you. And that the Council didn't send word that an investigator from the castle would be staying here, instead of with the mayor? Or at the Nixe?"

Or literally anywhere else, you pretty little liar, she seemed to say to Sophie.

Sophie heard the unspoken words hanging in the air as Casper glanced between the two girls uncertainly.

Sophie called upon every trick she'd learned at court and smoothed her brown curls back, giving Clare a firm look of her own. "Yes, the Countess had become concerned at the news—"

"Hullo! Clare? Casper?" All three turned at Lukas' muffled greeting from the stairs. Casper didn't even try to hide his second sigh of relief, wiping a suddenly damp hand over his woolen pants as he threw the towel aside.

"We're here, Lukas, come on up!" Casper called out to the musician, ignoring an exasperated glare from his sister.

With Lukas' entrance, Clare was forced to move, bringing her hand up to smooth her mussed braid self-consciously. As her hardened posture receded, Sophie realized that Clare wasn't actually that much older than herself. Perhaps only a few years and a few hundred cares separated the two young women.

"Sophie?" Lukas' voice interrupted Sophie's perusal of Clare. She blinked at him, confused and more than a little horrified that her cover had been blown so spectacularly already.

"Do I … know you?" As she said the words, she met his brilliant green eyes and encouraging smile. A flash of recognition hit her. She didn't know this Lukas. She had never met him, or even heard his name before this moment. And yet … she was completely at ease, her body relaxing at the sound of his voice as if they were old friends who just happened to have not met yet. *How … strange,* she thought. "Excuse me, I'm certain we've met. Have you been to the castle?"

"Uh, no …" Lukas' own flustered reaction as he ran his hands through his black, loose curls, sharpened her curiosity. "I mean. I've heard stories about Count Johann's children. In my travels. There aren't many who share my dark complexion, after all, and it's often been assumed I'm one of them. You *are* Princess Sophie, then?"

"You brought home a *princess*?" Clare hissed at Casper before Sophie could respond. "What are you doing?"

"Helping the empire?" Casper answered weakly.

"Try again." Clare's sooty hands were now fisted firmly at her hips.

"I was actually hoping to keep my identity quiet for the near future," Sophie said. "It would be best for my family's investigation, I feel."

"Investigation?" Lukas asked, a slow smile blooming on his face. "We're investigating something now?"

"No, we are not," Clare said tightly. "Would you two please come with me? We have some *preparations* to make for our royal visitor, it seems."

Clare turned on her heel, opened the door to the store room beside her, and waited.

"Looks like we have meetings in the pantry now," Casper said, exasperated. "Sophie, why don't you head to my room? Just through that door." He pointed across the room, opposite the staircase. "Make yourself comfortable, and try not to step on anything mechanical that may be lying around."

With that, the two boys followed behind Clare, Lukas sending one more sheepish look over his shoulder at Sophie as he left the kitchen.

Clare remained silent just until Casper closed the door behind them. "I don't like this one bit. What exactly is she looking for? And why is she hiding who she is?"

"It's probably a good thing she's not throwing her family's name around right now," Casper said. "It would make an investigation a lot harder to hide from the perpetrator. And if people think a bunch of children are interfering—or worse, that the *Everssteins* are interfering—no one would talk. You know how people feel about outsiders right now, even noble ones."

Lukas gave him an amused look. "Yeah, I caught that. Not the most welcoming place once the ceremony ended and the money stopped flowing."

"Yeah, because look what happens when we invite all these auslanders to town," Clare retorted, tossing her brown braid over her shoulder. "We have a murderer, a magical grifter, and now a nosy noble." She turned to Lukas with a viciously sweet smile. "If only we could rid ourselves of any of those problems."

"Look, help her or not, we can't leave her to her own devices. She doesn't know how things work here," Casper said. "If she runs around making crazy accusations before we have all the facts, we'll never figure out what really happened. And no one will hear us out long enough to care."

"Yes, like 'The Boy Who Cried Wolf.' " Lukas's eyes lit up in a

now-familiar gleam. "I've been reworking that one lately. I feel like there's something more there, about the bonds of community broken by our own—"

"Lies?" Clare sneered. "Yeah, that one's actually true. My father knew Klaus as a child. That wolf's pelt is at the Nixe, too."

Lukas flinched at her tone.

"You live in a strange town, you know that?" He kept his voice light, but she refused to look up at him. A quick glance at Casper's carefully impassive face showed that the younger boy wasn't going to help him out, either.

"Well, I had better go prepare a room for our noble guest before someone realizes who she is." Casper moved to the door with determination in the tense silence. "I hope she enjoys her accommodations."

Clare leaned heavily over a barrel, staring hard in the middle distance as Casper left, closing the door behind him. "He's right. If we can't stop her, we have to contain her. Aunt Aggie has made it clear she doesn't want to be bothered with my troubles right now. I overheard her and the mayor talking. They don't know anything, either. I don't think they can help us."

"So, let's help her." Lukas' tone was eminently, maddeningly reasonable. "Cas can keep her occupied while we find the truth. And if they stumble across evidence, even better. Two birds, one stone and all that."

Clare nodded slowly. "We've got to keep them both out of trouble. Steer them away from danger, at least until the Obolen is sorted. That *would* be easier if they were together." She tilted her head, eyes squinting in suspicion. But why are you so keen to be involved, anyway?"

"Sophie is … important to me," Lukas hedged.

"Like, 'She's a princess of the Empire' important, or like 'Sophie the thin, meddlesome girl who is about to upend our lives' is somehow important to you?"

"Yes."

Clare rolled her eyes. "You are impossible, you know that?" she said, now positively fuming at his reticence. "And now I have to worry about all three of you teaming up and finding even more trouble!"

"Clare, did I do something wrong?" Lukas actually seemed shy for a moment. Something in Clare's chest seemed to loosen and grow warm at the uncertainty in his voice. "You appear angry."

"Of course I'm angry!" Clare leaned into the fear and confusion that had plagued her since she'd begun grappling with Casper leaving and Lukas staying, the tangled emotions making her words heavy with conviction. "Cas has worked for this Obolen for *years*. It's the only thing that's brought him joy since our brother left and everyone else died. This is his only chance to leave Hameln, to make something of his life. We need to get to the bottom of this as quickly as possible."

"So it's not something I've done?" His voice was almost plaintive in her ears.

An exasperated puff of air blew tendrils of hair out of her face before she responded. "Of course not. This is about Casper's future. My family's future. It has nothing to do with *you*."

"Yes, absolutely, I get that." Instead of relief, Lukas looked almost disappointed at her words. "We're going to fix this. I say we send Casper and Sophie to talk to any straggling tourists while we talk to witnesses at the Nixe."

"Can you think of any way to distract the Council, too?" Clare moaned into her hands, realizing exactly how quickly her aunt would become suspicious of her continued interest in the interrupted ceremony.

"You mean more than the rats already are?" Lukas asked.

"Good point," Clare said ruefully. "We may not need to do much sneaking around at all, until they're handled."

"How much do you think they want to be rid of these rats?" Lukas asked, drumming his fingers on his folded arms.

"Pretty badly," Clare said, looking up from her cupped hands and belatedly wiping them on her tunic, suddenly realizing how dirty her face must be at the moment. "Obviously."

"Let's see how the conventional measures work first," Lukas said slowly, pulling his fife out from his jacket with a thoughtful smile, a sure sign to Clare that he already had a scheme in mind.

"How utterly mysterious and ultimately unhelpful of you to say," Clare answered, but she found herself smiling back at him despite herself. The boy may be trouble, but he would definitely not be boring.

11

asper knocked awkwardly at his own bedroom door with an elbow while juggling linens, a fresh jug of water, and the fine Castile soap his mother saved for special guests. *A noblewoman was about as special as I can imagine.*

"Come in," Sophie called distractedly from inside, and Casper walked in to find a much different young woman than he had met at Saint Boniface. Sophie had changed into grey woolen leggings and a soft green tunic that brightened her hazel eyes. A fur-lined vest cinched in at the waist with a leather belt completed the outfit.

But it was her hair that had Casper gaping like a hooked fish.

She had loosened it from the long, elaborate braids that had encircled her head, and the dark cloud of soft curls was kept out of her face with only a few simple twists that circled her high, brown forehead. The resulting mane was somehow both regal and practical, setting off her delicate features in the low light.

"Your hair ... " Casper's soft voice trailed off, eyes wide.

He saw her body tense infinitesimally. "Yes?" She pinned her eyes to his, as if daring him to finish.

Casper ducked his head. Not even his customary blank expression could hide the blush that spread across his cheeks, threatening to engulf his entire face. His restless fingers fidgeted with the door handle as he searched for words. "It's so…"

Sophie's face twisted in the growing silence.

"… beautiful."

At that, Casper's eyes darted back to her face, just in time to see Sophie's smile transform into something real and sweet.

"Oh, well…my grandmother was Moorish," she replied shyly before gesturing to his hands. "She said it's normal enough there. Are…are those for me?

"Yes! Yes. Everything you should need. I'll be staying upstairs with Lukas, in Nic's old room, to make sure he understands his duties, and give you privacy, of course. We'll both be in and out at the Nixe or the monastery—and the forge of course. Everyone's used to having me underfoot." His self-deprecating smile bloomed slowly, while his brown eyes became clear and steady.

A girl could get used to such frank admiration, Sophie thought.

Sophie relieved him of his burdens, placing the armful of items on top of the dresser beside her own belongings.

"So how will I find you tomorrow, for our investigation?" she asked. Sophie may not *need* a tour guide, but she knew Casper was the key to many doors that would otherwise be closed to her. Anonymity was tiresome but safe—and Freddie had demanded she be safe while she determined exactly what was going on in this strange city.

"Oh, don't worry. I'll be finished at the Nixe before breakfast. Then we have the rest of the day to snoop around." She turned from the dresser to face him fully. "I was thinking we should start at the Christmas Market."

"I'll go ahead and begin recording what we know so far." Sophie

moved toward his workbench before looking to him for permission. "May I?"

"Of course!" Casper moved past her nimbly, and she found she could hardly perceive his limp now. She suspected he had learned to compensate years before; nearly everything in his room was no more than a step away.

"What do you do here?" She picked up a fine metal chain, the almost weightless links slithering through her fingertips like a tiny snake, were a delight. "This is rather good. Did you make this?"

"Well, I am a silversmith. Clare makes the swords, I provide the smaller, more delicate pieces that we sell." Casper slowed in his tidying, shy but eager to show off his wares. "This is a piece I'm working on for Lucie. It's a locket with a bit of phosphorescent moss so that it will glow in dark places. Lucie's never liked the dark much."

"Remarkable. Is that a Star of David on the back?" Sophie brought the necklace close, caging it in her hands as she peeked in the crevices between her slim fingers to see the soft glow within.

"Yes, she wears one that I made her years ago, but I figured this one would replace it." Casper looked at Sophie, clearly waiting for a judgment.

"So it's beautiful and useful!" She handed the necklace back to him, her smile genuine. "You know, we could use someone like you at the castle. My father is always looking for the practical applications of his theories…"

"That's kind of you," Casper interrupted, though he weighed his words carefully, like the tiny bits of precious metal he worked with so well. "But Father Stephen wants me to continue my studies with him. The world needs enlightenment through good works, and I hope I can help spark that flame."

I'm not just a palace jeweler, he might as well have said. Sophie felt the cut, though kindly meant. But how could she blame him? She herself had been yearning to break free from the confines of Castle Everstein. Casper knew he was meant for bigger things, too.

Like bringing a murderer to justice.

She could imagine Freddie and her father's proud faces, if not her mother's.

After reassuring Casper that she was fine, just tired, a good night's rest would make a world of difference, she firmly closed the door in his adorable, worried face and sat at his tinkering table to get to work on her first report to her brother.

Freddie,

Hameln is already proving to be a hotbed for the weird and wonderful. I have it on good authority that the victim's last words were a curse on the entire town of Hameln, which leads me to believe it was a city resident who attacked.

Even better, I have found local allies in my investigation: an Obolen initiate, Casper and his sister Clare have taken me in for the duration. They have a multitude of connections to the event, beyond being eyewitnesses at the festival themselves.

We have plans to speak with five persons who I believe will prove indispens-able in learning the truth:

Casper and Clare's Aunt Agathe, the operator of the Nixe;

Casper's mentor, Father Stephen of Saint Boniface;

The bartender, Jakob, who I told you witnessed the victim's dying moments;

Lucie and Margarethe, Mayor Wilhelm's daughter and wife, who may have seen the events from above, on the balcony of their home.

As you can see, most of those on my list are intimately connected to the Hameln Council. I believe learning what they know is the fastest way to deter-mine what has happened. I will write again as soon as we have spoken to them.

Please keep me informed of any developments in the case that you glean from your own investigation and communications with Maman. Between the two of us, I am confident the culprit will be found and brought to justice.

Give my best to Papa.

Yours, S.

12

The Rat King's curse had done its job.

Hameln's tourists were the first to flee, taking their gold with them, much to Clare's annoyance. Though she had to admit the holiday atmosphere was a bit ruined when you're surrounded on all sides by beady-eyed rodents gnawing holes in your clothes, terrorizing your horses, and joining you in your bed in the middle of the night.

The Obolen aspirants followed soon after; not even the possibility of fortune and glory could persuade their ambitious parents to tough it out while rats hissed and snapped at their apple-cheeked darlings. And besides, there was no indication that the festival would proceed as scheduled. With the prospect of a full six months spent swimming in rats before the initiates were officially sorted, the younger participants' families decided they could wait another ten years. Clare didn't blame them.

Which left only the Hameln residents to weather the infestation. It soon became apparent that nothing would keep the pests out of their homes and businesses. Mothers covered their sleeping children with cheesecloth after raising their beds on blocks, but still woke to their terrified cries as the rats nibbled at them experimentally. Pantries were soon laid to waste, even with exhausted men and women standing guard over their storerooms to beat back the rats.

And more alarmingly, the grain silos were penetrated, risking all their lives as the winter stores dwindled further day after day.

Rat catchers soon descended, the desperation in the air smelling like golden opportunity. But even they were overwhelmed by the vicious and preternaturally intelligent animals that avoided all traps, instead who worked together to surround the would-be hunters. They jumped and grunted, their shining yellow teeth and tiny paws ripping and clawing the would-be saviors' clothes and bodies. To Clare's disgust, within a few days, the rat catchers escaped the disheartened town, too.

It had been a month since the murder, and Clare had resigned herself to the new miserable routine. Every morning she ate a smaller breakfast—unmolested grain was now a scarcity, a danger that she never would have imagined before—with a smaller crowd, as more and more residents now left the rat-infested city. Jakob would share what little news Aunt Aggie deigned to share, which was always some variation on the same theme:

"We've secured the very best rat catcher in the empire this time," the mayor would assure them yet again. "He'll be here by tomorrow at the latest. Much better than that last good-for-nothing charlatan. The rats are as good as gone."

Clare wasn't the only one unconvinced at his words, then or now.

And sure enough, the rats continued to multiply, until she didn't take a step without first watching for a scaly pink tail in her path or a pair of gleaming eyes in the darkness. Rat catchers came and went, but the rats seemed eternal.

Then she'd head to the forge, sometimes with Lukas, sometimes with Jakob, and rarely with enough orders to fill the day or their pockets.

She was a bit unsettled at how quickly the rats became a way of life, a forgone conclusion to Hameln as if they had been here all along. Wicker food covers were sold next to fishing baskets, and cats became popular—if somewhat ineffectual—pets. And everything from camphor to mint oils were liberally doused around beds to prevent the unwanted guests.

Perhaps she shouldn't have been so surprised. *Look how quickly Hameln had made abandoning my dreams seem normal.*

Strangely enough, however, the rats seemed to have no interest in her home or the smithy.

"It must be my music, scaring them off each night," Lukas explained breezily while lounging in the courtyard, one cold but sunny morning. "Just another service I provide." Clare grinned at his bravado, rolling her eyes.

"Or maybe they sense looming death via burning hot forge," Clare mused agreeably. "Whatever the reason, it is a relief. Walking the streets has become … unpleasant." Lukas wrinkled his nose in agreement before he laid his head back down on the bench he was sprawled across, shielding his eyes with an arm across his face and swinging his leg distractedly. Since there wasn't any real work to do, Clare let him be as she tidied up a bit.

Of course, whenever there was work to be done in the smithy, such as handling the hot metals—moving them, quenching them, hanging them out of harm's way—Lukas was scarcely seen.

"I could use some help with this," Clare snarled at him one of those now-rare busy days, juggling two hot pieces of metal that would be swords in her hands.

"Sorry, I seem to be allergic," Lukas drawled back, not bothering to turn and face her.

"Of what? Hard work?" she grunted, finally moving them to the waiting anvil as she rolled her weary shoulders.

His answering lazy wink over a raised shoulder brought her simmering anger to a boil. She slammed her hammer closer to his hand than either anticipated.

"You do realize we work to keep food on the table, right? It's not just an amusing option to consider when you haven't gotten a better offer."

"Against my religion, you see," he murmured, already inured to her rage and tending to his many instruments.

"Well, feeding nogoodkin lazabouts is against *my* religion," Clare shot back. "I guess I'll just have to go see if Jakob is available after his shift."

She watched the muscles in his back tense up as they always did when the bartender's name was mentioned.

"Ask if they have need of a bard at the Nixe this week," he called out airily, while his soft cloth tackled what must have been a particularly stubborn spot on his fife to burnish. "My coin purse is feeling particularly light lately."

She stomped down the stairs, mumbling angrily, if indistinctly, trying to avoid another disagreement before Cas and Sophie returned.

They convened and shared their knowledge that evening by a cheery fire, a scrap of overheard rumors from Cas or a thoroughly unenlightening interview with another desperate soul who had definitely maybe seen the Rat King.

"Flora told me she saw him at the festival," Sophie reported back diligently.

"Flora who leaves offerings by the Weser every sunrise to keep her beauty?" Clare asked doubtfully.

Sophie paused, making a mark in her notes before continuing. "Hmm. Yes. Her skin *was* almost glowing. Anyway, she told me she saw the Rat King at the festival spitting on the cross and changing wine into vinegar."

Clare nodded. "Sounds like Flora, alright."

The paranoid nonsense was almost as exhausting as the constant misery.

It wasn't until Saturday afternoon that Clare heard actual news about the investigation. When Lukas finally returned after a night out who knows where with his fellow sinners, Clare shared it. He was stretched out like a particularly pleased alley cat in the golden light of afternoon, while she spoke between labored breaths of heated air, wisps of dark hair curling around her reddened, sweating cheeks.

"Word from the Nixe is that Countess Katherine has left town," Clare said, her attention split between the conversation and her work. "She's leading a search for the Rat King's family."

"That's an awfully small job for a noblewoman to take on," Lukas said. "Are you sure your information is right?"

"Who knows the latest gossip better than the bartender?" Clare shot back, the steady rhythm of her hammer faltering.

"I suppose Jakob would never steer you wrong," Lukas conceded. "Just make sure you don't tell him too much about our investigation."

Clare stopped her work altogether, an exasperated frown marring her face. "Jakob doesn't know anything, he doesn't suspect anything. He's just being a good friend."

"Well, let's keep it that way," Lukas replied stoutly. "I'm going to go find Sophie and tell her she can move around town without worrying about her mother. After I get you a cool drink. You're sweating like a pig iron."

"Like he knows anything about iron," Clare mumbled to herself after he left, wiping her face with a damp sleeve self-consciously. How was he so irritating even when he was thoughtful?

She was halfway through the cup of water he'd brought back for her before she realized he'd managed to slip away from aiding her in her work yet again. Despite it all though, she had to admit it was nice to share her evenings with the young noble and the bard.

Tonight was just such a night when she pretended she was far too busy bustling about the room, preparing for the next day's meal to pay attention to Casper and Lukas laughing around the kitchen table. Sophie had begged off to the Nixe, excited to exercise her newfound freedom to obtain any news from Freddie.

Lukas brought out his fife to polish, and Casper, who could never resist any mechanical treasure, was currently coveting it.

"May I …?" Casper asked, face shining. At Lukas' nod, he took the instrument from the bard's hands gingerly, weighing it in his hands and turning it in the light.

The musician looked on indulgently. Nothing pleased Lukas more than frank admiration, after all.

Sophie returned, with no news and a sour look on her face.

"Is that bad mood brought on by a person, a rat, or this never-ending mystery?" Lukas asked as Sophie sat down at the table with them, poring over the scraps of evidence they'd cobbled together.

"I don't expect to be treated like a noble, but it seems being treated like a normal person is too much in Hameln," Sophie grumbled, rearranging papers in a pattern that made sense only to her.

"What happened?" Clare was suddenly alert, moving over to the girl protectively. "Who insulted you? Did they hurt you?"

"No, no, nothing like that," Sophie answered, waving Clare's concern away. "Just the normal derision. God's bones, if some drunken buffoon calls me *auslander* one more time …"

Casper had stiffened at Sophie's first complaint, but seemed to deflate as she explained her dismay. "It's just a word, Soph. They mean nothing by it."

"But you have noticed that, haven't you?" Sophie turned to Lukas, ignoring Casper's words. "How they say '*auslander*,' like they mean something else entirely? And it's not something that's particularly friendly."

"That's just our way," Clare said as she placed a careful hand on Sophie's shoulder. "Just because we depend on them and their money, doesn't mean we have to like it."

"No, Sophie's right with this one," Lukas said, reaching out to squeeze the younger girl's hand sympathetically. "I've traveled through the empire a bit now, and it's weird how this town refers to visitors. Like they're branding you every time they use the word *auslander*."

Clare looked unconvinced. "Look, my mother's family has only been here three generations. But my father's family can trace its roots back more than 300 years in Hameln," Clare said. "You are *auslanders*, here."

They looked at Clare with matching dark looks and she flinched. *I've said the wrong thing.*

"But honestly?" Clare continued. "We could probably use a few more *auslanders* like you around here. If only for the entertainment."

Lukas took that as his cue, plucking up his lute and playing the opening strains of *Unter Der Linden An Der Heide*.

The rats and the murderer seemed far away when she closed her eyes and let his music transport her to one of the many far-flung locales she feared she would never see herself.

13

Papa may not be interested in the day-to-day operations of his county, but this situation in Hameln deserved his attention.

Freddie hurried through the castle, half-familiar faces passed in a blur. While he knew most on sight, and remembered a few names, Freddie didn't know the details about the army of people that kept this castle running. Not like Sophie.

Finally coming to the door of his father's study, Freddie hesitated just a moment. This was new territory for them, speaking together as something approaching peers. Freddie rolled his eyes at his own uncertainty. *Princes do not shirk their duties, no matter their personal preferences.* Squaring his shoulders, Freddie simultaneously knocked on the door while swinging it open.

But the room was empty.

Freddie spun around. "Where is the Count?" He directed his question to the room.

"He left for Aquitaine last night." The reply came from the young guard who had followed close behind him.

"Aquitaine?" Freddie repeated.

"He left a note, my lord. It is with the rest of your correspon-dence, I believe. Something about needing another sample? There was an explosion there last night …"

For a moment, the guard seemed off balance, Freddie's own confusion inspiring uncertainty in his suddenly pale, young face. If he were Sophie, Freddie could tell a joke and convince the young man to tell her some shocking new rumor from the town, and they wouldn't be marinating in this strange, awkward moment that made him want to crawl out of his own skin.

"Quite right," Freddie responded after too long a pause, unin-terested in the troubles of some far-off place when he was stuck in the castle to deal with too many others. He eased his shoulders back and nodded sharply. "The samples, of course." Without another mortifying word, he spun around, heading back for his desk and the pile of letters he had just abandoned. He was beginning to think the world was populated by letters instead of the people who wrote them.

No matter. He would muddle through. And learn that guard's name, no matter his mother's policy of distant respect between nobles and their attendants.

More importantly, he'd stop making everyone around him as edgy as he was.

After his failed attempt to reach his father, Freddie turned to his sister, the only other Everstein he knew would be available.

Dearest Spitfire,

The castle is a truly dull place without you.

The troubles in Hameln begin to affect the entirety of Lower Saxony. Flour is becoming scarce, and I worry that many will not survive the season without importing foreign stores—an expensive but necessary precaution that even Bran-denburg agrees to. Panic throughout the region will only weaken us.

The Countess tells me that she has sent for the Royal Huntsman. Has he reached you yet?

Be careful, but please be quick.
Freddie

The scratching and tapping and squeaking of the rats had become as familiar to Sophie as the rushing waters of the River Weser, the ever-present creaking of the watermills it powered, or the stately bells of Saint Boniface.

But unlike those now well-known sounds, the rats were never comforting. And as the winter months melted into spring, the towns-folk's patience was wearing thin.

Activities mundane and singular were interrupted by the vermin —people lived and died, but not quite in the same way. Families took turns standing watch over food stores so that desperate men and women could sleep. Beloved pets—once ferocious terriers, ferrets, cats—were now terrorized by the unnatural rats and shunned by their disgusted owners. Sophie listened as grieving townsfolk talked of hiring mourners to sit with their loved ones' bodies at night to prevent the infernal rats from desecrating their bodies before burial.

Sitting at the kitchen table, Sophie knew that something had to be done, and soon.

It was time to talk to Jakob, the witness who apparently only she still thought might have something to do with all of this misery. Of course, that meant risking the cover she had so meticulously maintained since arriving in Hameln. As Freddie's letters became more baldly grim, the urgency of the case became almost desperate.

"We are running out of time," Sophie announced to the room glumly as she stared at her copious notes yet again. "Jesus wept. We seemed to have uncovered some sort of strange secret about the Obolen, but we're still no closer to discovering the murderer."

"Do you think Freddie will make you go back?" Lukas asked,

angling his head to try to meet her gaze. The concern in his bright green eyes only made her feel worse.

"Yes," she answered honestly. "Or worse, tell Maman that I'm here, and I'll get dragged out by my ear."

"That's my cue then," Lukas answered, straightening up and reaching for his bag. "Time to dazzle the Council, banish the rats, and hopefully bring a murderer to justice."

"What are you talking about?" Sophie asked, rubbing her temples in exhaustion.

"Just my greatest performance yet!" Lukas answered with a flourish. "Let's see if we can flush out our man by disrupting this plague."

"Sounds great, but that's not really a plan, Lukas," she answered with a tired sigh, leaning back in her chair to stare up at the rafters in the ceiling.

"No plan," he responded, pulling out the leather case that held his pipe. "Just my pipe, and a song."

She watched as Casper reached for the beautiful fife that was nestled in the evergreen velvet interior of the bag. He almost seemed hypnotized by the shimmering instrument.

"If I could just determine the material it's made of, or the method used to craft this instrument, I would really have something to show Father Stephen," he murmured, almost to himself.

Lukas lightly slapped Casper's hand out of the way, and the younger boy seemed to wake from a trance, and Sophie snorted at his owlish blinking.

"Where did you *get* this? I've never seen anything like it." Casper's voice was almost reverant. Sophie noticed Casper's fingers twitch as if he longed to learn all the pipe's secrets.

"It was a gift from my father." Lukas' open, devil-may-care expression may have fooled Casper, but Sophie was surprised to feel a strange mix of anticipation and dread at his words. "The only thing he left me, actually. Not bad as inheritances go, since this fife is what I'm going to use to save your town."

"So it's magical? Did your father make this himself? How old is it, and how do you care for it? Is that shimmer normal, or is it a trick of the lamplight?" A thousand questions seemed to jostle for prominence in Casper's mind, but Sophie could tell that Lukas wouldn't—or couldn't—share the answers Casper sought.

"He didn't stick around to tell me anything about my fife." Lukas' small smile was bitter, an unnatural emotion sitting uncomfortably on his face. But he quickly turned it into a familiar smirk, targeted back at her. "Or even his name. But if good old Johann *is* my father, we'd better use it to keep Sophie around."

She tensed at his ridiculous words. "Papa knows about as much about music as I do about blacksmithing," she said crossly. "Now stop speaking in riddles and tell us your plan."

He sobered quickly enough, just in time for Clare to join them upstairs, hot, tired, and lugging up a full bucket of water.

"Better lower your expectations there, Soph," Clare chimed in, dropping the bucket carefully before leaning her back on the wall. "Riddles are Lukas' first language, after all. Try asking him where he goes on the nights he's not here or at the Nixe, for instance."

"Hilarious as ever, Clare," Lukas said dryly. "And my plan is to drive the rats out of Hameln for good. Maybe into the river …" He stroked the flute thoughtfully, his mind seeming to wander. "It's a little more difficult to convince animals to harm themselves, but these little demons deserve their fate, at this rate."

"You can do that? Just with your music?" Clare's voice was loud, but Sophie didn't blame her. "Make the rats just leave?"

"I can make them fall in love with the water and float all the way down to the North Sea," the bard bragged. "The supernatural rat bastards can go terrorize the Swedes instead."

"Prove it," Casper said eagerly. "Right now."

Lukas looked around the room, before his eye settled on a couple of flies that had been lazily buzzing about the room all day. He brought his pipe to his lips and began playing a low, twisting melody. It brought to Sophie's mind a bonfire, powerful and hot and ever-changing, the yellows and reds and oranges all swirling and dancing, the flames licking up and out, seeking out into the world with superheated, golden fingers.

She watched, spellbound, as the two flies broke their slow, looping circles, flying directly into the candle flames on the kitchen table they all sat around. There were two wet pops, and then a short fizzle, their crispy little bodies falling into the melted wax beneath them. Lukas lowered his instrument, smiling in knowing satisfaction, before looking expectantly at his friends' faces.

Before the moment slipped away, Sophie grabbed for paper and quill, concentrating on every word of their conversation this evening, and the feelings Lukas' music inspired in her. If she could just remember this moment—every word, every detail—then it was real and it happened.

When she opened her eyes again, the entrancing music having slipped slowly into silence, no one seemed to even be breathing. She was still putting her thoughts together, trying to synthesize this new aspect of the bard for her journal, when Lukas spoke, startling them all.

"This particular instrument can be used—in the right circumstances, mind you—to sometimes manipulate an emotion or a desire that I might point the listener toward, if they are so inclined." As shock mixed with her excitement—*magic is really real*—Sophie's eyes darted to Clare, whose expression moved swiftly from curious to closed to downright livid.

"It is much easier to control smaller animals, of course. And it's more like persuasion or influence, than outright control," he hurried to add as Clare began pacing the room. Her silence seemed to put him on edge, as he balanced at the edge of the seat he had taken and watched the young blacksmith. Sophie saw his mouth open and close as if he wanted to fill that silence with explanations or examples or maybe even an apology.

"Wait a minute. Are you saying—are you telling me the whole time we've known you—we invited you into our home, worked with you, ate with you—we, I was *charmed?*" Clare rounded on him so violently that Sophie flinched along with him. Trust Clare to see magic and see the looming danger. "Your music makes people do and feel what you want?"

"You were charmed; I am charming. Same thing, right?" His lopsided grin was a valiant attempt at humor, but Clare's anger was white-hot, making Sophie squirm for Lukas from the other side of the room.

"Not even close," Clare answered, pacing herself right out of the house.

Lukas, clearly bewildered, seemed set on following her. But before he could, Sophie snagged him.

"Could you …" Sophie stopped, catching her breath. "Could you really use your music on people?"

"What?" Lukas was instantly focused back on her, sitting up straight and staring sternly. "No! That was a joke! Why would I ever want to do that?"

"No, no, of course not," Sophie agreed fervently, dropping her quill to clasp his hand in both of hers. "I would never suggest otherwise. I am just trying to determine exactly what this power of yours means."

"It means that he can get rid of the rats," Casper answered, a small smile on his face. "And save Hameln from this dreadful curse."

Lukas tossed a quick grin to the younger boy before taking off, leaving the two of them alone in the blessedly quiet house.

"Think he'll catch up to her?" Sophie asked absently while recording everything they'd just discussed.

"I almost feel sorry for him if he does," Casper responded, equally engrossed in his own tinkering at the table. "I haven't seen her that upset since Lucie told her she didn't have time for their childish adventures and to go bother Jakob."

"Do you think they'll stop annoying each other long enough to realize they like each other?" Sophie asked, tilting her head as she reread her own words on the page.

14

Clare found herself walking swiftly but without a destination as she closed her eyes, shutting out every-thing save the air she pushed through her lungs and the steady pressure of her fingers gripping her own arms. If she tread on a rat, so be it. She felt ridiculous. The *auslander* had promised nothing, beyond a song and an extra set of hands at the forge.

So why did his secrets feel like a betrayal?

Of course it was magic. Just like these rats, a mysterious force that no one could reason with or stop. Nothing she was feeling—thought she was feeling—was real. And she was determined to rip her burgeoning attraction to him out by its roots.

Clare, like every child in Hameln, had seen magic since she was born. There were the small, everyday magics: Faerie rings appearing overnight or the green-gold Northern Lights blazing in the summer's sky.

Or the mysteries of the church, where bread and wine became flesh and blood, or a long-dead Saint's finger could return a blind man's sight.

There were also the little magics that differed from person to person, like Lucie's remarkable ability to remember anything she'd ever read, or how Jakob could change the mood of the room with his wide, genuine smile and a hand clasped in friendship.

But the bigger, showy magics were still rare in Hameln, shared only during those secretive moonlit mysteries or perhaps the more ecstatic festival crowds.

Clare herself had spent many too-short hours examining Wolfhart's enchanted weapons, hoping to unlock their secrets by sight alone. His double-sided axe, sharp enough to split a hair, never in need of a whetstone. And his sword, said to be imbued with the souls of Lower Saxony's noblest fallen warriors, so that it would never break, always striking true to protect the innocent.

Clare was no stranger to magic, but this was the first time she felt she had been its victim.

A strange, beautiful boy came to town and she lost her head. But it wasn't his smile or his eyes or even how Casper looked up to him like he had Nic. *It was a spell.*

Eventually, even her anger could no longer fuel her sojourn through Hameln's deserted streets. For the first time, she noticed how many empty homes had replaced the boisterous streets she knew. "All thanks to those damn rats," she cursed as she snuck back through the evening gloom into the house.

It seemed everyone else had gone to bed, making it easy to avoid the questions she wasn't ready to face. Still feeling stifled once she reached her familiar room, she quietly climbed out her bedroom window, walking with soft, careful, practiced feet along the roof tiles until she was just above the smithy itself. She looked out at the familiar horizon, her well-loved stars and the darkness beyond with not a rat in sight, finally breathing easier.

It wasn't until she was settled, quiet, and still, that she looked up to see that Lukas had already found the same spot for his own late-night musings. *What is he doing here?*

She eyed him critically, taking in the tired lines around his eyes and his downturned mouth limned in the moonlight. Even his gloriously wild curls seemed limp. There didn't seem to be any fight in Lukas tonight.

And I don't want to force one out of him, she realized.

"How does this work, exactly?" Clare asked simply, turning her dark eyes to skim the horizon, the buildings, the tree line—anything but Lukas' face. "Is there a ceremony under a full moon? A sacrifice to your ancestors?"

"No, and no wild parties in the dark heart of the woods, either," Lukas answered sardonically. "Honestly, I could probably take care of the rat infestation before the rest of the town even wakes tomorrow. The magic is in the flute, and it's never failed me before."

She paused to let that sink in. "So, what are you waiting for?" she finally asked.

His immediate silence caused her to turn. The sly smile he gave her showed her that was exactly the reaction he intended, and she rolled her eyes in turn.

His expression turned soft and thoughtful.

"Your brother and Sophie want to solve this murder, but they need time. If parading around town, pretending to "test the ley lines" or "examine rat auras" or whatever other nonsense the Council will believe gives them that chance, I'm going to give it to them."

Clare nodded at his words. His logic was sound, she decided, even if the plan—and his power over her—put her teeth on edge. Casper could lose everything—his placement, his opportunity for the bigger and better life he's earned, his very freedom—if the Council or Countess Katherine learned what they were doing. But Clare knew Casper wouldn't stop until he knew the truth.

Clare weighed her words carefully, fisting her hands to her sides so the tremble wouldn't give her away. "I guess the only thing to be done is to help you, then," she replied in a sensible tone that belied both her fear and excitement.

"That's a rather extreme change of heart." Lukas looked over to her, the smile on his face at war with the resignation in his voice. "What changed your mind?"

"The Council may be hiding something," Clare admitted for the first time. "I heard talk of sacrifices to someone. An appeasement? And that children may be involved? I don't know what it means, but it didn't sound good. So, if I have to choose, it's going to be keeping us all safe."

"That is noble of you," Lukas responded, but looking away from her, as if embarrassed by the compliment he was giving.

"But why are *you* so determined to distrust the Council?" Clare asked. "Aunt Aggie, at least, has been nothing but kind to you."

"In my experience, wherever there is desperation, you will find corruption. And the Council, the initiates, the whole town is clearly desperate," Lukas said. "And Sophie agrees. Why else would she use me as a distraction, meeting with the Council while she searches Aggie's office."

So that was the plan they'd come up with. Simple and direct, at least.

"While *Sophie* is using you as a distraction, I'll be right here not snooping into anything," Clare shot back.

"I have nothing against your aunt or her Council," Lukas said. "But I do trust Sophie. And if she thinks something strange is going on, I'll follow her lead. And my own instincts, of course."

"Of course," she answered, standing slowly, her feet and heart unsteady. He trusted Sophie, she trusted Cas. It was an uneasy alliance, but she could make it work. She just had to focus on *doing* instead of feeling. She *wanted* to trust that they were doing the right thing, anyway. "I think it's past time for me to go to bed. Good night, Lukas."

"Good night, Clare."

She made her way back to her room, closing the window tight before laying heavily on her bed. Clare would finally have her adventure. She just wished the stakes weren't quite so high for everyone she loved: her place in the guild, in her family, in Hameln.

❄

The next day's dawning did little to make her feel better.

"You're meeting the Council wearing that?" Clare asked incredulously. The sun was bright and Lukas' clothing was garish, as usual.

"My mother made this tunic." Lukas admonished her lightly as he picked at a speck of dirt on his sleeve that only he could perceive over the loudly clashing reds, yellows, and greens, herringbone and plaid meeting in an eye-bleeding collision. "I think it makes me look roguish."

"Well, you certainly are wearing clothes." Clare crossed her arms, leaning against her workbench as she looked him over with a critical eye.

"Don't sound so disappointed," he answered lowly, winking at her.

Her cheeks warmed before she opened her mouth to snarl back, sputtering instead of speaking.

"Th-that's not—"

Casper and Sophie clamored down the stairs to the kitchen before she could respond, deep in a discussion about how best to avoid Jakob when sneaking into Aggie's office. She felt the fire in her cheeks and turned to the oven before they noticed her embarrassment.

"Are you all ready?" Lukas asked the room.

"Ready to get to the bottom of this," Sophie answered with a determined tilt to her chin.

"It's 10 a.m. now. The weekly Council meeting is scheduled in the hall in two hours," Lukas said. "We should all be in position by 15 till, and I want the two of you out of her office by 12:30. Find what you need and get out before you can be found out. Understood?"

"And I'll be at the bar in case it all goes wrong," Clare interjected. "I told Jakob I'd be there to help with the lunch crowd at the Nixe today."

"You'll be the perfect distraction!" Sophie said, a smile finally lighting up her nervous face. "Jakob'll never notice us with you around."

Clare glanced at Lukas. He looked particularly unamused by this observation, but stayed silent. *For once.*

"More importantly, I'll be able to pass you the key to Aunt Aggie's office," Clare said, returning her smile.

"Then I guess we're as ready as we're going to be," Lukas declared, pulling out his instrument for a final once over as he waited for the bells of Saint Boniface to announce the morning's march into noon.

At 11:45 precisely, Lukas passed by silently as Casper and Sophie slipped through the Nixe's doors, where Clare had been bussing tables and shooing away rats from the meager leftovers customers left behind. The short walk to the meeting hall seemed shorter still as he felt the familiar rush of nerves before a performance.

He leaned into the feeling, hard, savoring the fast beat of his heart and his sharpened senses. He was through the door and announced to his latest audience before he could think too carefully about finally revealing the true power of his instrument—something he swore to his mother he'd never do, for the safety of them both.

Stepping up to the long table before the fireplace, the Hameln Council was arrayed before him: Aunt Agathe, Mayor Wilhelm, Father Stephen, the Guildmaster Pieter ... and Countess Katherine. Lukas looked at the silent woman evenly before sliding his gaze back to the mayor, hoping the sharp-eyed noble wouldn't notice his surprise at her presence. When had she returned to Hameln? What did that mean for the investigation? And for Sophie's safety? His heart thrummed unevenly, but improvising always made him feel a little more alive.

"To what do we owe the pleasure of your presence, Lukas Pfeiffer?" Aggie asked. Her voice was friendly and light, but he knew better than to waste their time with pleasantries.

"I am here to offer my services in dispelling the rats from Hameln," Lukas replied.

"You're a bard, not a rat catcher." The mayor's dismissal was short and final, bringing Lukas' attention to how impressive a performance this needed to be. "What we *need* is the Wolfhart. Where is he?" His pointed look at Countess Katherine wasn't lost on any in the room.

Katherine returned his look with a raised brow. "I summoned him the night of the murder." Lukas felt her long, measuring glance. "What's the harm in letting him try, as we continue to weigh our options?"

"Should I demonstrate my skill, then?" Lukas quickly brought the flute out from somewhere in the folds of his multicolored tunic and to his lips. He began the song with a high trill before turning it into a melody that swooped rapidly through the air, bringing to mind the magical murmuration of an entire flock of birds moving as one in a lifesaving skybound ballet.

Soon enough, the chamber was filled with calling sparrows and blackbirds circling them overhead before settling in the rafters. Lukas ended the song with a long, high note, and then silence crashed the room, broken only by the tittering birds and wondering Council who all stared, first at Lukas, then the rafters, then back at Lukas. All but Katherine, whose keen gaze stayed pinned on the bard throughout.

He saw the exact moment the calculations began.

"And what are you asking in return for this service?" Aunt Aggie was staring at the animals that had invaded the building before pinning him with a long, measured look.

"In return for ridding Hameln of these rats, I request an audience at the Countess' court." Lukas, staring Katherine down, heard rather than saw the nervous titter run through the Council at this request. "And 1,000 gold pieces."

Everyone knew the rumors of Lukas' paternity, and no one as intimately as the Countess, he was sure. All eyes were on her as she rose from her chair and walked toward the young musician. Despite this triumph, even he feared how everything was about to change beyond his control. "Get rid of these rats, and I'll hand you the money myself, with the entire court in attendance."

Lukas smiled brilliantly before bowing. At least the first step of their plan was a success.

15

While Lukas was dazzling the Council with magic, Sophie padded silently down the hall to Aunt Aggie's office with Casper, the key Clare had purloined for them grasped tightly in his hand.

They had agreed it would be better for all involved if Casper looked like the mastermind of this adventure, a silly boy trying to impress a pretty girl. *He thinks I'm pretty.* Sophie briefly closed her eyes against the flustered thought, watching the exits as Casper slipped the key in the door.

Once inside, Casper closed the door quietly behind them before lighting a candle he had smuggled in his coat and placing it on Aunt Aggie's desk.

"What are we looking for exactly?" he asked Sophie, letting her take the lead.

"Anything about the Rat King, Wolfhart, sacrifices ..." she answered grimly, sifting through the papers at the top of one of the many haphazard piles in front of them.

"Right," Casper said, turning his attention to the shelves on the wall. "Let's get this over with."

The next fifteen minutes were quiet and tense. Working in tandem, they had found, discarded, and replaced nearly every scrap of paper in sight. Gusting a disappointed sigh at yet another useless document, Sophie's shoulders were tense with their pending failure. The only thing they'd discovered thus far was that the Nixe went through a truly stunning amount of food and ale during Yuletide.

Sophie had moved on to searching through the drawers while Casper picked up yet another journal, his eyes swimming through numbers.

"Wait a moment," he said. Sophie looked up from her own seemingly fruitless search. "This is different."

"What did you find?" she asked, moving to his side swiftly. She misjudged the distance in the close, darkened room, and was forced to wrap one hand around his wrist, the other reached backward to the desk, steadying them both before they collided. When Casper caught her eye, she saw only confusion, rather than the trill of nervousness she felt in her own chest.

"It's just a list of names," he said. "But Nic's on here. I think … I think this is a list of every initiate going back … decades. Their ages, assignments. The guilds, or Everstein Castle—and something called the Erlking? And then dates … " Casper's eyes widened in surprise, and she felt the first giddy flush of possible success. "I think they may be death dates. And there are *a lot* of them."

"Let me see." Sophie reached for the book, but before he relinquished it, the door behind them swung open.

"Just what do you two think you're doing in here?"

Casper and Sophie turned as one, wide-eyed and momentarily speechless at Jakob's sudden appearance.

Jakob's face would be almost comical, if Sophie weren't so worried that he would recognize her and immediately send her packing back to her mother. His eyebrows had disappeared somewhere into his hairline, while his eyes were narrowed at them suspiciously.

Sophie recovered first. "Cas was just winning a bet. I had no idea the Nixe went through so much ale in one week, festival or not."

"I-I'm sorry, Jakob." Cas got out, looking appropriately embarrassed. "I was just showing off."

"Well, put everything back as it was and get out," Jakob growled out. "I think it's time that you returned home. And you." He swiveled to face Sophie.

"There's another letter for you that came this morning. From Everstein Castle."

At that, Jakob turned on his heel, no doubt expecting them to follow immediately. He missed the moment that Sophie snatched the journal from Casper's hand and slipped it under her cloak. He opened his mouth, as if to argue, but the complaint died in his throat at her savage look.

Sophie wasn't about to lose the closest thing to a clue they'd found in weeks—even if she had no idea what it would lead them toward. *Dead townspeople? Or were they all initiates?*

As they headed back to the bar, Sophie noticed Jakob catching Clare's eye with a meaningful look before he turned back to his patrons. And suddenly, Jakob was all smiles again, his tense shoulders easing back down and his full, deep laugh filling the room.

Clare looked embarrassed, cleaning up after a particularly obnoxious customer.

"Sorry," she mouthed silently to Sophie.

Sophie knew better than to approach Clare under Jakob's watchful eye. Clare may consider him an older brother, but Freddie never looked at *her* that way.

Catching Casper's sleeve, Sophie led him to the storeroom, eyes down and cheeks red, looking properly chastised. It was a look she practiced for her mother often enough.

"Is something wrong with Casper?" Clare asked, and Sophie heard the real concern coloring her voice.

"He's well, physically." Jakob was quick to calm her, rubbing

Clare's shoulder soothingly. "But I did find him poking about Aggie's office with that strange girl that was snooping around the Nixe earlier. You know, when the … incident occurred."

"You mean the Rat King's … death," Clare supplied.

Sophie crowded her face even closer to the narrow opening of the back door, determined to hear Jakob's side of events. She ignored Casper's warm breath on her cheek, as they silently jostled for space. Only Lukas seemed unbothered, seated at the table.

"Just … be careful with that one, please," Jakob said, lowering his voice as his head inclined closer to Clare's, and disappointing Sophie's hopes for more of the story. After a few murmured phrases, he finally pulled back, signaling his departure. "Nic would have my hide if anything happened to Casper or to you."

"Aunt Aggie trusts him, and so do I," Clare replied stoutly, and Sophie could almost imagine the stubborn set of her chin. "For now, anyway. Besides, you know you're the first one I'll come to if I need backup."

"That's all I ask." Jakob left with a satisfied nod, and Sophie bit back a relieved smile of her own.

"I appreciate you checking on me, Jake," she heard Clare reply. "I'll see you tomorrow morning for breakfast."

Before she and Casper could make themselves known, Lukas let loose a deep groan.

"My gods, is he always so earnest? Talking to him is absolutely *exhausting*," Lukas plopped down on the ground as the door closed behind Jakob, covering his eyes with a dramatically thrown arm. "Can you imagine, living your life with all those feelings just spilling out of you? No self-preservation with that one, just genuine concern."

Sophie giggled, despite herself.

"Everyone else seems to like him," Clare answered mildly as she moved to wipe down the table he'd just vacated. "In fact, he's universally liked, much like someone else in this room."

Sophie's grin turned genuine as Lukas' mouth gaped open, his eyes blazing in something like horror. Sophie decided it was her new favorite face.

"That's because I am delightful. Nothing like that self-righteous tattletale," he finally answered, pointing at the closed door with eyes and mouth wide, dramatically offended.

"I think his honesty is refreshing." Clare defended her old friend as she leaned heavily on the door, glaring at the prone bard. "At least you always know that he means exactly what he says."

"Yes, and how exciting that must be for you," he replied, glittering eyes peeking through. "A real sense of control there."

Sophie shifted, wondering exactly how uncomfortable this conversation was going to get. Maybe announcing her presence wasn't the best move, after all.

"Look, he knows something is up, and now we know that he knows that." Clare seemed to ignore the jab. "He didn't go straight to the Council because he trusts us—well me, anyway. We need to be more careful, unless we want Aunt Aggie knowing that we're poking around in Council business." She moved away from the door, closer to Lukas. "He'll tell her if he sees something suspicious, make no mistake."

"I'm surprised he can see anything, the way his soul is just pouring out of his eyes," Lukas grumbled, but he held his hands up in surrender. "Yes, right, I'll work on my stealth. More questions about rats, not tavern security."

Clare clearly decided that was a victory. She continued moving away from the door, and Sophie chose that moment to enter the room.

"Good! You're both here." Sophie practically bounded through, hauling Casper's slender frame behind her in an excited lope. She shut the back door carefully behind her before slipping out of the traveling cloak that had become her second skin in Hameln. "I think we've got something from Aunt Aggie's office. There were some documents, and they reminded me of a conversation I overheard between two nurses talking about a patient, Margarethe. Something about an old town curse." She gripped her paper and quill in her hands, sitting at the table to begin writing.

"What do you know about the Erlking?" Sophie asked Lukas and Clare.

Lukas finally felt like the wheels they'd been spinning in the mud were coming unstuck. Finding a murderer was one thing—unveiling a vast Obolen conspiracy, spanning centuries and scores of enemies, known and unknown, was quite another.

That's why it was time to play the role he knew best—distraction. If they were going to put on a show, he would make it the best. While he made a lot of noise about banishing the rats—ideal conditions, instruments, acoustics—the others would find out what the Erlking wanted with Hameln. He was determined to shine.

After all, if the entire town is watching me, they're not watching my friends.

He started at the center of town, eyes steady on the ground, periodically stopping as if in great thought. He would bring the pipe to his mouth, blow one clear note, then tilt his head, as if listening for a response.

This exercise continued half the morning, as he stalked to the edge of town, then followed the wall surrounding the village, even letting his fingers graze the stonework as he spoke nonsense syllables to himself. He noted the small groups that would gather to watch him, then move along, either bored or confused with his machinations. *If only they knew how simple the truth of my magic is: one tune and the rats would be gone.* He hid his upturned lips behind his instrument.

He eventually came to the mysterious marker that helped make the myth of Hameln even more irresistible to tourists: a poem written in stone. Its marbleized surface shimmered lightly, and it was slightly warmer to the touch than the surrounded ashlar that made up the curtain wall. Town historians debated its age, the estimates made more impossible by the fact that the pockmarks and fissures in the surrounding stone were absent on the marker.

Etched upon it were two short stanzas that he didn't recognize, despite his many years memorizing folk songs and stories:

> *In Hameln fair,*
> *Choose words with care*
> *Else Fate will stop your tongue.*
>
> *No babe aware;*
> *No crazed mind share;*
> *The past remains far-flung,*
> *The truth is yet unsung.*

Was it a warning or a prophecy? Was it a clue about what had happened to his mother all those years ago? Who had forced them to hide away his whole life?

Lukas knew exactly who to go to for answers. If Casper didn't know something, he would know how to find out.

He found the boy huddled over another delicate creation in his bedroom, slight shoulders hunched as one hand held a small brass bell and the other turned a sharp metal tool inside it.

"What are you working on, Casper?" Lukas made sure to speak softly, as if gently rousing Casper from sleep.

"A miniature version of the bells of Boniface," Casper responded, not looking up from his work. "I want to see if I can emulate the mechanism on a smaller scale for those who wish to recreate the sounds of Hameln when they're far from home."

"I'm sure there are many who are leaving at the Midsummer festival who would cherish such a device," Lukas hummed agreeably. "But I was wondering if I could talk to you about a different Hameln landmark." He knelt beside Casper, bringing him face-to-face with the younger boy. "There's a strange marker in the town wall, and I didn't recognize the stone it was hewn from. Marble quarried elsewhere, maybe? Or a metallic marker your family forged?"

Casper paused in his tinkering.

Lukas waited patiently as the boy carefully placed his small tools on the worktable, combed his fingers through the dark curls on his head, and blinked up at him. Lukas was learning that Casper needed a bit of time to switch between tasks, as if his total attention to detail could only be disengaged and then refocused slowly.

Some might consider Casper absentminded, but Lukas knew the boy's focus was anything but absent.

"You know, it's just always been there," Casper said. "I never really thought to ask where the stone came from, or what it meant. Like a nursery rhyme, you know? Everyone around here just knows it."

"Well, I think learning more about the etching could give us some much-needed insight into this town of yours," Lukas said. "Everyone in this town seems a little too comfortable with unquestioned adherence to ancient ceremonies and traditions. This stone included."

"Well, there are only three libraries in town: the monastery's, Margarethe's and Aunt Aggie's," Casper seemed to weigh their options carefully. "Clare or Sophie could get an invitation to Lucie's house pretty easily, but there's no way Father Stephen or Aunt Aggie would let any of us near their books."

"So, it's a stealth operation, then?" Lukas asked.

Casper stared up at him, his brown eyes squinting in suspicion, as if sensing that Lukas seemed a little too happy with the idea. *Lukas charming—or scheming—his way into people's hearts and houses was his specialty, after all.*

"For Aunt Aggie's office, yes," Casper agreed. He stood easily, but Lukas saw him massage his hip, as if to loosen the joint before settling his weight on it. "But you and I can head to the monastery right now and check the historical records on the town. I'm sure we can figure out when the wall was built, and if that stone was part of the original construction. If we're lucky, they'll have information on who commissioned it, who wrote the rhyme—maybe even who etched it into the stone itself."

Lukas felt the pull of discovery. *Finally, some answers. But ...*

"I'm not so sure Father Stephen will want me in his church." The corners of Lukas' mouth pulled down at the thought of getting Casper—or himself—in trouble with his mentor. "But if I were found in Agathe's office, that should be easy enough to explain away."

Casper looked confused at Lukas' words. "But our monks at Saint Boniface have many different backgrounds! Father Samuel is from as far as Constantinople, and Father Paul came to us from Spain."

"Yes, but how many Jewish monks does Father Stephen house?" Lukas' words and wry grin made Casper blush.

"Oh! I'm sorry," Casper's words rushed out in an embarrassed stream, as if he could wash away the awkward moment with them. "I just thought maybe it was your appearance you were worried about. But we have so many different families that come through Hameln for the Yuletide festival, no one looks twice at any who are different. Even a kid like me whose leg doesn't work. In fact, Lucie and her mother are Jewish, too."

"Have you ever considered a cane?" Lukas asked, changing from one awkward subject straight to another. "You would cut a dashing figure. No one underestimates a man with a cane."

"I find that having both of my hands free to work is much more important than being able to move more quickly," Casper said.

Lukas looked him over, considering. "You kept tripping over it, right?"

"Well, yes," Casper admitted, ducking his head down. "How am I supposed to keep track of where I put a piece of wood when I've got the mysteries of the world to uncover?"

"Hard-headed stubbornness is a family trait, then," Lukas said.

"Can we focus on getting answers, instead of my sister?" Cas replied peevishly. The younger boy was more perceptive than Lukas thought.

The two boys walked through the church and through the dormitory without seeing another soul. More and more of the monks' time was spent caring for the sick and terrorized lately, and while Casper and Lukas weren't forbidden from the scriptorium, even rule-abiding Casper conceded that it would be an easier visit if they were just left to their own devices.

It wasn't until they had entered the scriptorium itself, the afternoon sunlight flooding the small square room with bright light, that they found their first investigative hurdle.

"Casper." Brother Paul met them just inside the door. "What a pleasure to see you. But who is this—" Brother Paul's eyes widened a fraction. "Prince Friedrich, we did not know we were to expect you."

Lukas raised one dark eyebrow in response. Mistaken identity? He could work with that.

Lukas saw Casper turn pale, but that could work in their favor. Intimidation was a natural response to power, anyway.

Lukas shifted his stance. He threw his shoulders back, hoping to gain a few more inches of height, and tilted his head. Then he narrowed his eyes slightly, attempting to look both haughty and amused. *Look noble.*

"Yes, my mother did not want it known by the general public that I had returned for the Council meeting this week," he said. "But I could not resist the opportunity to see your beautiful scriptorium myself. Casper here tells me—" at this point, Lukas clasped the younger boy's shoulder with a bit too much force. Casper shuffled to hide the wince on his face.

"—that yours is the largest of its kind in Lower Saxony. And I am prepared to be impressed. If you would not mind a modicum of discretion?"

"Of course, your highness." Brother Paul looked a bit dazzled, and grateful to be in the prince's confidence. "You know we even have teachings written by Thomas Aquinas' hand from his time in Cologne. They are the jewel of our collection, though he did have some odd ideas on witchcraft. Regardless, I will leave you in Casper's capable hands. And your secret is safe with me."

"Excellent!" Lukas bared his teeth in a beneficent smile. "And I would not be surprised if there were an official commendation from the Count of Everstein in your monastery's future. God's blessings upon you!"

"And with you." Brother Paul responded with a pleased smile before leaving them.

They waited a few seconds after Brother Paul's exit before Casper slipped from under Lukas' iron grip. "Ouch!" he complained, rubbing his now-sore shoulder. "Easy on the props. Especially if they're me."

"Sorry, sorry," Lukas said. "I got a little carried away with my noble routine. I'll be less handsy next time, I promise."

"Whatever," Casper said, focusing on the books in front of them. "The biblical works are on the east wall. Histories should be … here!" He crossed the room to the opposite wall. Most of this investigation had been a lot of sneaking around and listening in dark corners, and lying to most everyone in town, which were not exactly his strong points. But research he could do. "Just sit over there, *quietly*, please. I'll bring the relevant books to the table. Don't touch anything else."

"Casper, I need you to be honest with me right now." Lukas slowly circled the room. "Is this a prisoner situation?"

"What?" Casper's mouth flapped open like a river trout, looking up from the dusty spines he was perusing.

"You come here on purpose?" Lukas asked.

"To learn!" Cas insisted. "But not just here. My more robust studies are usually held in the church's courtyard."

"Good! You do get a bit of sunshine in your life, then." Lukas seemed pleased.

"Now you sound like my sister," Cas responded sullenly. "Here! The town's histories."

Casper and Lukas hunkered down, preparing for a few hours of scouring the place for clues about the marker—or even the original Obolen, if records even went back that far—Cas with obvious delight, Lukas noted with a bemused sigh before opening up the dusty old tome in front of him.

16

ours later, and a few admonishing hisses from Casper for the minstrel to be still, Lukas noticed the younger boy massaging his own hip absently.

"What happened?" Lukas wasn't looking at his leg, but Casper didn't feign confusion at the question. He just snatched his own hand away, clearly uncomfortable at the moment of weakness he had shown.

Casper opened his mouth, about to recite the story by rote, but Lukas saw him hesitate, as if unsure how to tell an old story to a new audience. Lukas had heard whispers while staying in Hameln, a cautionary tale about a family broken by injury, disappearances, and death. But he gambled that after all these months, Casper would be comfortable telling his own story.

"I don't remember it," Casper finally admitted, rubbing over the tight skin at his thigh. "I mean, I remember Nic's face—I've never seen him so scared. And I remember Pa's arms around me, carrying me to my mother. But the fear, the pain? That's long gone."

Lukas stayed silent, patient. He knew what it was to let a long untold story unfurl. It happened slowly, then all at once, a plant stretching hesitantly out to the sun, then growing confidently as the soil proved fertile.

"Nic was holding me, showing me around the forge. Pa had just given him his apron, let him work his own projects instead of fetching water or striking metal or working the bellows. He was so proud, and I remember his excitement. But something happened, I got too close, Nic wasn't paying attention, too caught up in his first real project—I climbed up on the anvil to get a better look, lost my balance and ... I fell back into the hearth."

Casper's eyes were soft, focused inward. *Remembering*, Lukas realized.

"Nic felt terrible. He decided to undergo the Choosing not long after. And then our parents died, Clare was left to look after everything. All because I was a clumsy child."

"None of that is your fault, you know."

"Yes," Casper responded slowly, returning to the present. "And it wasn't Nic's either. It doesn't matter who's at fault, just who's left to pick up the pieces."

Suddenly, Lukas touched Casper's hand, feeling almost timid. "I think I found something."

Casper looked up, blinking away the personal misery he had just immersed himself in. "What is it?"

"Something unusual, written by a Father Marcus." Lukas pointed to the pale, spidery handwriting that looked as if it were about to fade out of existence. " 'On this day 100 years ago, the first of our children were sent to the Erlking.' "

"That is mysterious," Casper agreed. "What's the context?"

"It was written on the day of the choosing ceremony," Lukas answered, before continuing to read. " 'I pray for the souls of those taken to the demon's halls in the hills. And I pray for God's forgiveness at what we have done.' "

Lukas looked up, confused by the words.

"Exactly how long has Hameln been sending its children out into the world?" he asked Casper. "And where are they all going?"

Before Casper could begin to answer the question, he heard the familiar *tap, tap, shuffle* announcing that Father Stephen was fast approaching the door.

Lukas may be able to fool one of the more sheltered monks, but he worried that Father Stephen wouldn't fall for the noble impersonation. He knew Prince Friedrich had spent time with the entire Council.

"Hide behind those stacks," Casper hissed, waving his hands toward the tall bookshelves beside them. "Father Stephen is coming. I'll keep him busy while you slip out. *Quietly*. Try to avoid any more monks, and go tell Sophie what we found about the Obolen. Maybe the Eversteins know more about the role that each member of the Council plays in this ceremony."

Lukas nodded before slipping in the shadows behind the piles of scrolls.

Casper quickly closed the history they had been reading, turning as if to look for another reference.

"Is that you, Casper?" Father Stephen called out, head cocked and listening for his protégé's presence.

"Here, father," Cas called out, moving toward the monk and away from his retreating friend. "Studying, as usual."

"I'm happy to find that you haven't been distracted." Father Stephen moved with confidence in his library, aware of each cabinet and table. He lowered himself down on a nearby chair. "No need to worry about the … unpleasantness."

"But don't you find it odd that no one has come forward to identify this 'Rat King'?" Casper asked, pinning his eyes to Father Stephen's face, in the hopes that the holy man wouldn't notice Lukas' quiet retreat. "How can we provide him a proper burial and mourning?"

"People come from all over the Empire to see our Obolen," Father Stephen reminded him, not unkindly. "Unfortunately, there have been no reports of missing persons. It seems no one is looking for our Rat King. And even if someone did come forward, there would be nothing to identify, God bless him."

"What do you mean?" Casper asked, hoping that this line of questioning would lead to an uncovered clue.

"I am told that the poor soul's body decomposed past recognition within moments of his expiration," Father Stephen explained delicately. "By the time my brothers came to collect his body, there was nothing left but the tattered remains of his clothes and that odd little crown. Some sort of poison on the blade is the culprit, I am sure."

"What kind of poison could disintegrate a man in mere moments?" Casper mused quietly.

"Why this womanly interest in medicine all of a sudden, Casper?" Father Stephen's suspicious look was enough to alarm the boy. "Any illiterate midwife can pass out a poultice for a stomachache. You, my son … you are destined to be the next Archimedes!"

"I am simply curious about the practical applications, Father," Casper was quick to assure him. "If it can melt down a body so quickly, what could such a poison do to rock or metal, I wonder?"

"Hmmmm." Father Stephen took a moment to entertain the thought before shaking his head solemnly. "It is a shame we did not recover the weapon to test such theories. As it is, we may never know what was used to kill the man. Or why, I'm afraid."

When Casper had finally found the right combination of timing and excuses, he hurried home to tell the others that they could safely remove Father Stephen from their suspect list, and even more importantly, the possible cult leader list. But as he limped tiredly up the stairs, he was met by a scene that horrified him even more than the endless parade of rats: his friends huddled over a pilfered Saint Boniface text.

"You stole from the monastery?!" Casper's voice rose up a horrified scale. The book, *the knowledge*, was sacred enough. But stealing it from a church?

Lukas, Sophie, and Clare were all hunched over the book as he entered the kitchen, skittering away from each other with his outburst.

Clare jumped, clapping a hand over her own mouth to suppress a yelp before snarling at her brother. "Don't *do* that!"

Sophie had barely blinked, but allowed herself a deep breath while she tried to steady her spiking heart rate. "Hello, Cas. Lukas was just showing us what you both found."

"Yes, the information I obtained from the monastery, just as we came for," Lukas said, reasonable as ever. Casper gaped at them all for a moment. *Can't they see this is wrong?*

"I obtained information," Casper said, pointing to himself before turning the same finger at Lukas, accusing. "You stole a book! And one of Father Marcus' journals, at that!"

"We were interrupted, and we want to know more about the Obolen, don't we?" Lukas asked.

Casper grabbed the book from his grasp, holding it to his chest protectively while glaring at the bard.

"We could have figured out another way," Casper insisted angrily.

"Next time, I'll let you plan the heist," Lukas responded. "Now that we're all here again, can we please get some answers now?"

"What a wonderful suggestion!" Clare said, clearly annoyed at both Lukas and Casper. "How about this one: Why are you in Hameln, really?"

"Oh, you mean the part where I'm helping you rid your home of rats?" Lukas' sarcasm was sharp and bright. "Or where I'm helping Sophie and your brother uncover a murderer? Or maybe where we're possibly uncovering a centuries-old townwide conspiracy to steal your neighbors away?"

"No, I want to know why you came to Hameln in the first

place!" Clare exploded, refusing to be shamed. "This could ruin Casper's standing with Father Stephen, not to mention any chance he has at finally getting out of here! Don't tell me you did it all for him."

"I think I found something," Sophie said casually. That ended the fight immediately. They turned to find her reading the book, skimming the pages quickly while Casper held it open for her.

It is my belief that there are only three ways to approach our Faerie associates: with faith, with fear, or with fascination. I believe my faith has aided greatly in protecting our town from utter damnation. While we cannot entirely rid our town of Fae influences large and small, we can offer an alternative to their sly promises and half-truths.

But fear can also be a healthy tool. Fear may still feed into the Erlking's power, but gives him no entry into our life. The townspeople do not want his influence here, and he holds no sway on their immortal souls, even while he clouds their thoughts. While many seem content with offering their children's futures—as long as their own are also guaranteed—they seem to understand that this agreement is dangerous. Every tithe year, more Hameln families refuse to participate in the Obolen, even while children come from all over the Empire flood into town to replace their numbers.

It is the third manner, a strange fascination with the preternatural, that I see as the deepest threat in the journey toward salvation. I see already, with Countess Adelaide and her search for immortality; with her new daughter-in-law, the ambitious Katherine aiming for political allies; even with my old friend, Afi, whose yearslong obsession with his lost Esma clouds his senses.

"Countess Adelaide?" Casper whispered, looking at Sophie. "Isn't that your …?"

"My grandmother, yes," Sophie confirmed with a thoughtful frown. "And my mother. But I have never heard either of them mention Faerie tales such as the Erlking."

Meanwhile, Casper felt like the top of his head had been dipped in ice-cold water, seeing his grandparents' names featured so prominently in the monk's journal. *Did our family conspire to hurt people? What's happened to the children? To Nic?* "Clare, what does this mean?"

"It means that whatever the elders in Hameln were involved in, our grandfather was also a party to it," Clare said, taking the book from Sophie's hands for a closer look. "It is true he would have done anything in the hopes of finding our grandmother again, no matter how hopeless it was."

"But who was this Father Marcus exactly?" Lukas asked. "And what happened to him?"

"He was a member of the Hameln Council, the representative from Saint Boniface before Father Stephen took his place," Clare explained. "He was one of the many victims of the plague that struck our town eight years ago. The only plague since … as long as anyone can remember, anyway."

"That's how you lost your parents?" The last of the anger seemed to fade from Lukas' bright eyes as he glanced over at Clare and her defiant chin.

"Our parents, Afi, our Uncle Mattias, the old mayor … There wasn't a family that wasn't touched by the sickness that spring." Casper answered for Clare, a careful hand stretched out to squeeze hers. "The entire Council was wiped out, basically. And most of our elders. Children were spared, mostly, other than Lucie's baby brother, Wilhelm. Even Countess Adelaide stopped attending Council meetings around that time, and so we all assumed she was felled by it, too."

Sophie hummed, thinking over the timeline. "I remember when she became indisposed that spring, but we were never told what happened. She had locked herself away for months in her rooms. Then one day, we were told she had died. But I never actually saw her fall ill."

"That sounds like what I remember from our parents, too," Casper whispered, pained by his grief and now Sophie's.

"So Katherine, Agathe, Mayor Wilhelm … they've all been Councilmembers for eight years now?" Lukas asked. "Working together to uphold the *tithe* this whole time?"

"They stepped in and brought order from the chaos," Clare

confirmed. "Katherine and Aunt Aggie brought a cure from the Grey Cottage—your mother's work, I assume. And the plague hasn't returned since. Well, until these rats."

"Do you think this plague had something to do with the Erlking, then?" Lukas asked. "If Father Marcus was working against him?"

"Father Stephen says that Father Marcus saw demons in every stranger and the evil in every wilderness," Casper answered. "He didn't trust these accounts."

"For once, I find myself agreeing with Father Stephen," Clare said. "Father Marcus had been a kind, gentle man, once. It seemed when the plague hit … he did go a bit mad toward the end."

"Like Lucie's mother?" Sophie asked.

"Something like," Clare said, choosing her words carefully. "Fewer nursery rhymes, more fire and brimstone, though."

"I think it may be time for us to meet Margarethe," Lukas said firmly. "Let's see how deep this Hameln madness really goes."

17

The next day, Clare and Lukas braved the sea of rats searching for food outside Lucie's ornate door, the trees carved into the wood twisting all around the frame.

As she raised her hand to knock, Clare noticed Lukas eyeing the mezuzah affixed to the doorframe of the mayor's home.

"It's a Jewish tradition," she started to explain to him, smiling at the young maid who opened the door for them. "It holds a piece of their holy text—"

"I know what it is," Lukas interrupted her, brushing the wooden case lightly with his fingers as he finally passed through the doorway. "I just wasn't expecting to see it."

"Is there going to be a problem?" Clare felt herself puffing up, already indignant on Lucie's behalf. But the bubble of anger growing in her chest dissipated at his sudden, blinding smile.

"It's like finding a little piece of home, that's all," he said to her, as he held her gaze intently.

"Clare, Lukas, it's so good to see you," Lucie's voice floated down the hallway to them. Clare turned to Lucie's apple-cheeked smile, golden hair piled atop her head in a painfully sensible bun. "Please, Mother is expecting you."

Clare turned her attention to her oldest, dearest friend. The delighted smile on her face almost felt foreign, it had been so long.

There was a time, when they were young, that newcomers assumed they were sisters.

After all, they were of a similar height. Both had heart-shaped faces and bright, dark eyes that never missed a beat. But where Clare's body was like a well-crafted machine, with strong muscles over sturdy bones, Lucie looked more like a delicate work of art. Looking at them now, the superficial likeness had nearly disappeared. It was the difference between a blast furnace and a fine marble fireplace.

No one mistook them for sisters anymore, which suited Clare just fine.

They entered Margarethe's study, and Clare was transported to simpler days, when she and Lucie would hide under tables with food and books and a candle to light the pages. She found her oasis hadn't changed at all in the years since she and Lucie used it as their own personal playroom.

The ceilings were high, carved with intricate octagons and crosses, and a lighted candelabra at the middle that made the dark wood shine. One whole wall was lined with bookshelves, and the opposite with glass-encased cabinets. Each shelf was filled with small statues and an astrolabe that Clare had coveted since she was three years old. There were stuffed animals, both local and exotic next to antique vases and ancient tools whose purpose none still remembered. A collection that took a lifetime or more to acquire, and nothing like the handmade treasures in Clare's house.

At the center of the room, Lucie sat with her mother, Margarethe, who had brought this chamber of wonders to life.

Clare never got used to seeing Margarethe like this. Twenty years ago, she was a celebrated beauty, her raven curls and bright blue eyes capturing the attention of every man in Hameln. But she was no empty-headed girl to be wooed by empty words or strong arms. She collected as many books as admirers before ultimately choosing Albert as her husband, a man whose ambitions for Hameln matched her own.

At one time, she hoped to make Hameln the unrivaled jewel of Lower Saxony, with celebrated artists, scientists, and musicians traveling leagues from all directions for a chance to sit in her study, sharing the culture and knowledge of the realm.

And even after her youth had faded, within Clare's own memory, Margarethe had been a loving mother to Lucie and political advocate for the town. It was only after she lost her youngest, Wilhelm, that her grip on reality was lost.

For weeks after the tragedy, she was found by shocked neighbors, wandering day or night in her dressing robe, calling for her dead child. In broken tones she railed in the streets about a conspiracy to take her son—accusing the Countess Katherine, the child-snatching Erlking, even her own husband.

Lucie had been her mother's keeper ever since.

Today, there was no sign of the broken woman who haunted Hameln so long ago. Margarethe sat tall and calm, her hair pinned back simply and her hands absently caressing a volume in her lap while Lucie read to her. Only her strangely winking fever-bright eyes betrayed a deeper trauma.

As she sensed their entrance into the library, Margarethe looked up and right through Clare, her eyes zeroing in on Lukas instead. The change in her demeanor was immediate.

Winking first the right and then the left, her face grew bright with recognition, then shadowed by grief. "Oh, sweet sister! What have you done? Why have you brought your sorrow back to Hameln, back on our house? What will become of my Lucie? You must go, now!"

"Mother, it is Clare," Lucie's voice was soothing and practiced. She stroked her mother's hand gently, easing the joints loose from the agitated claw they had become. "She's brought a friend, Lukas. He's a musician, and he came to perform for you. Perhaps your favorite Tagelied?" She turned to Lukas, lowering her voice confidentially. "Really, you can sing about anything but the Crusades—we've really had enough of the war ballads."

Margarethe's eerie sing-song voice cut through the air before he could respond. *"In Hameln fair, choose words with care, else Fae will stop your tongue. With claws so cruel, no naive fool can escape, old or young."*

"What was that?" Lukas was instantly alert, and Clare stiffened beside him. Did she know what they were investigating? Did they harbor a spy or a traitor? She forced herself to relax, a friendly smile replacing the strained grimace at Margarethe's words.

"I recognize the tune, but the words aren't quite right. They're from the marker, right?" Clare asked.

Margarethe's laugh was high and light, the mirth sounding almost manic. "Oh, the words. So many words we're supposed to forget, ignore, seal away, never to be seen again. Like the children. Those godforsaken *dybbukim* that steal them away ..."

Lukas went swiftly to one knee in front of Margarethe, taking her hands from Lucie, speaking low and kind. "Is it a ditty well-loved in Hameln? I can add it to my collection and share it in my travels."

"But you are obviously his child. You have his eyes, his skin, his gift." Margarethe's tone was fond, but her words made Clare's head spin. "But there! These are dear Rachel's deft fingers. I always knew she could have made beautiful music, instead of those tonics and poultices. She could have saved my Wilhelm, you know." At her child's name, her voice went low, and she drew Lukas forward, caressing his cheek.

"How do you know my mother?" his eyes searched Margarethe's frantically. Clare felt she was quickly losing the thread of this conversation. "And whose eyes? My father? Do you know him, too?"

Margarethe recoiled at his fierce tone, turning from him to find

Lucie's sweet, concerned face. "No longer a child, yet so ignorant of the present's past. Hameln is a dangerous place for such a babe. Too much knowledge learned too quickly will bring his eyes on us all. I think it's time for bed, don't you agree, my dear?"

Lucie helped her mother up, whispering soothing nonsense in her ear, while nodding apologetically to Clare and Lukas. "You must excuse us. I'll return shortly. Please, make yourself comfortable. I know Mother would love to know you were enjoying her study. Like the good old days."

"Of course," Clare said.

"*Of course, off course, wrong horse,*" Margarethe sang brokenly. "Do you know where your brother is?"

Margarethe's words floated behind her before the door closed. Clare pounced on Lukas. "Who is Rachel? Aunt Aggie mentioned her after the Rat King was attacked, said she could have helped."

Lukas sat heavily in the elegant chair Margarethe had just vacated.

"Rachel is my mother, and she is a skilled healer. But I don't know how either of them would know her. We've lived in our cottage, far from any town, ever since I can remember." Lukas sighed heavily, clearly frustrated with the day's riddles. "She's never spoken of Hameln, other than to persuade me to avoid the Yuletide festival."

At this, he looked up at Clare with a knowing grin. "She tends to avoid silly adventures, too."

Clare felt the hot rush of annoyance at his words, but before she could snap at him, Lucie was back.

"I'm sorry, Clare." Lucie ducked her blonde head, looking embarrassed. "She has her good days, but sometimes meeting new people makes her remember those she's lost."

"Like Rachel?" Lukas was smooth and polite, quelling Clare's interruption with a glance. "And Wilhelm?"

"Yes," Lucie's desire to protect her mother seemed to be battling her normally open manners. "Wilhelm was my little brother. He lived barely a month, and mother always claimed her sister could have saved him. But Rachel left more than fifteen years ago for Castle Hanover, and we haven't heard from her since."

Somehow, Lukas seemed to collapse even further into himself at her words, and Clare's heart jumped to her throat at his miserable appearance. She'd never seen him look defeated, and it didn't suit him.

"If she were at the castle, Sophie would have said something," Clare interrupted. "She heard Aunt Aggie mention her at the Nixe that day as clearly as we did, and didn't seem to recognize the name. This Rachel could be halfway around the world by now."

"Or at the Grey Cottage." Lukas sounded grim and certain. "Raising her son with no friends or family to speak of."

"The Grey Cottage?" Clare's annoyance was forgotten in her wonder. "But that's where the witch lives. She peddles poisons and love potions … "

"… And takes wicked children who trouble their parents," Lucie finished, alarmed.

"Now who's peddling Faerie tales, Clare?" Lukas said with a grim smile that didn't reach his stormy eyes. "My mother helps all who seek her, but there's no magic in her work. And it looks like the only child she ever took away was me."

"Your … mother?" Clare repeated, dazed. Lukas came from the Grey Cottage?

My dear brother;

Our investigation has been particularly maddening these past few weeks. Every stone we turn over has a slippery Faerie tale beneath it, instead of the solid facts we seek. What is clear to me is that many on the Hameln Council, past and present, believe that there is some shadowy presence—an Erlking—who is manipulating the town in some nefarious manner. And somehow our family is mixed up in it.

Did you ever hear anyone in our family (other than Papa, of course) talk of immortality? I have found evidence at St. Boniface that Grandmaman was actively seeking a way to extend her life unnaturally, and anything you could find to corroborate this allegation would help me determine how reliable this new evidence really is.

Be careful, as always. Send my love to Papa.

Faithfully yours,

Spitfire

P.S. Would it be possible to have Papa write a formal commendation to the monks of Saint Boniface? The honor may already have been promised on your behalf. —S.

Sealing her letter for Freddie, Sophie was quiet and careful, watching Clare go through her nightly routine in a daze. Lukas was nowhere to be found, but that wasn't exactly unusual. Clare's silence was. Even in her worst moods, she was quick to let you know what was wrong and how it was (or wasn't) your fault.

Running around after witnesses was getting them nowhere. And all of the books they'd found had just sent them into a supernatural spiral.

Maybe it was time to focus on motives instead of suspects. She turned to a clean sheet and wrote "MOTIVES FOR MURDER" at the top.

"Why would someone want to kill the Rat King?" Sophie asked aloud.

"He was a complete ass," Clare responded, to her surprise. "Sorry, I didn't mean to startle you."

"No, it's fine," Sophie answered, scowling more at the fact that she had flinched at Clare's words than at the intrusion. So much for her careful watch. "You met him?"

"I had the very brief and distinctly unpleasurable honor of his acquaintance, before the guards dragged him away, yes," Clare answered. "He was a little too intoxicated, even by festival standards."

"So he had been bothering the tourists? That's bad for business," Sophie said thoughtfully. "But not exactly a capital offense. I'm sure the jail would have fixed the problem just fine."

A new thought hit her. "Do you think the murderer knew about the rats?" Sophie asked, looking up from the book she was writing in.

"Do I think that someone killed him specifically to bring the plague?" Clare looked puzzled. "No, because that is completely mad."

"But maybe it was a frustrated initiate?" Sophie persisted. "There are things my father's been working on that seem completely unbelievable. And with the number of learned men in the city ..."

Clare paused, considering her words. "I guess we can't rule it out. But then we're right back at our original problem: The people who are most hurt by the plague are exactly the people we've found are involved in some sort of ... conspiracy. So, are the murder and the missing initiates related, or aren't they?"

"Was the Rat King's murder just a way to punish the Council? Or did the Council kill him, and then this plague was his retribution?" And now Sophie found herself questioning all of her previous assumptions. "Perhaps instead of one mystery, it's two?"

"And will we find the answers to both if we get to the bottom of one?" Clare asked, flicking her brown braid over her shoulder.

"Answers would be nice," Sophie agreed.

"Especially from someone we can actually trust," Clare sniffed.

"Was that dig aimed at someone in particular?" Sophie asked lightly. "Or the increasingly corrupted world in general?"

"Lukas," Clare admitted.

"What has he done now?" Sophie asked.

"He's from Hameln," Clare told her simply.

"What do you mean?" Sophie asked. "And how is that a bad thing?"

"His mother was an initiate, trained by the former Countess to do who knows what. More than that, she was my mother's best friend." Clare shook her head slowly, eyes unfocused and mouth pursed thoughtfully. "All this time, he acted like just another wandering minstrel. I never imagined he was so … intimately related to our town."

Sophie paused, taking a moment to digest her news. For some reason, it felt … incomplete. "You didn't trust him from the beginning," Sophie said. "Now you're disappointed that your suspicions were confirmed?"

"I didn't want to trust him," Clare responded. "But I was beginning to. And now … he's Lucie's cousin. Their family has lived here for centuries. His mother left to study … with *your* grandmother. And when she came back, it was … it was a scandal, honestly. Specifically, his birth was the scandal."

Sophie scowled. She didn't know who Lukas's father was, but she would never believe it was her Papa.

"That's not his fault," Sophie reminded her gently. "And maybe now it is a little easier to understand why he came here at all. He's looking for answers, just like the rest of us."

"True," Clare conceded, tilting her head as if to literally see another angle to Lukas' actions. "None of this is his fault."

"But?" Sophie sensed Clare was still discomfited.

"But if he would lie about his family, what else would he lie about? His powers? His loyalties?"

"His motives?" Sophie finished for her.

Clare finally met her eye, with a grim set to her mouth. "Exactly."

Sophie sighed, looking down at her papers. "This is going to be a whole new list, isn't it?"

"Probably," Clare agreed.

"So that's two—bordering on three—mysteries to solve, one increasingly impatient brother to answer to, and a few hundred rats to dispel from the town." Sophie ticked off the items on one hand. "Do you know what I think we should do tonight?"

"What's that?" Clare rolled her head lazily to meet Sophie's steady, determined gaze.

"Relax. Let Lukas serenade us for a bit, and then tackle our problems with fresh enthusiasm in the morning."

Clare smiled at the princess fondly before leading her from her bedroom to the kitchen where the others had gathered. "Deal."

And true to her word, Clare greeted the musician with a smile that she almost certainly did not feel.

"It's been a hard day," Sophie announced broadly to the room. "I think we all deserve some entertainment."

"Is that so?" Lukas asked dubiously.

"Come on, bard," Clare said teasingly. "Spin us a yarn."

"All right, all right," he conceded easily enough, pulling up a chair to sit front and center before the glowing hearth. "Tonight, I'll tell you all about the fairest of them all: Snow White."

Casper and Sophie settled in to enjoy the tale, while Clare pretended to be too busy cleaning up the evening meal to pay him too much attention. But soon, her busy hands had stilled, and she cupped her chin as she watched him tell his story. It felt so like the old days—her and Nic at Afi's knees, listening intently to his latest tale—and she let herself slip into the happy, long-lost scene.

" ... *The huntsman disobeyed his queen, for he knew his first duty was to the people, not her evil machinations. And so, he led the young woman, weak and pale from the blood loss of childbirth, and her newborn babe deep into the wilderness to escape the queen's vengeance. This is how they met the seven dwarves.*

The Fae had traveled from the distant mountains, laden down with heavy rocks quarried for the home they were instructed to build for Snow White. And so she stayed safe with them, and the evil queen was instead served a stag's heart on a silver platter."

"Gone for ten years, but some things never change, I see." Clare and the others had been so thoroughly engrossed in Lukas' story, that none of them had heard the opening door, or footsteps coming up the stairs, as a wide-shouldered man filled the kitchen doorway almost entirely. Lukas jumped up and forward, moving as if to cover his friends as he reached for his dagger.

But Clare was frozen where she stood, a heart-sized lump in her throat that she tried to swallow down, not daring to believe her eyes. "Nic?" she whispered.

18

"Nic?! Are you actually here? It's really you?!" Clare knew she sounded hysterical, but she *didn't care*. Nicolaus had come back to her. Instead of rushing into his arms, she simply held her fingers out to his chest, almost expecting them to pass right through.

But Casper didn't hesitate. His normally graceful, controlled movements devolved into crashing limbs and sobs, pulling Clare into their embrace. Nic scooped them up and into his broad chest, as if it was the most natural place for his normally stoic siblings to be. Maybe he needed the reassurance just as much.

"I'm here, not-so-little ones." Nic's words were said into Casper's neck, but directed to them both. "Word is that you've found a little bit of trouble."

Clare was barely conscious of her body falling heavily into a kitchen table chair. Her nerveless fingers smoothed over her leather-clad thighs rhythmically. Her tears only registered as she pressed her face into the dampened tabletop, breathing in slowly.

Everything was going to be fine. Nic was back. She wasn't alone to deal with everything.

Clare vaguely registered that Nic wasn't alone, either. Lucie had been right behind him.

"I saw him coming home, from my window," she explained, a bit weepy. "I was reading by my window, and there he was, just walking down the street. I could hardly believe it!"

A dark-skinned girl stood at the door, stepping lightly into the room. Impatience tightened her beautiful face. The dying firelight that fought the deepening gloom only seemed to emphasize every dip and slope of muscle that wasn't covered in her hard leather armor. Armor that, if the multitudes of scars and dark stains were any indication, had protected this woman's small but powerful body in a battle or two. Clare glanced between the newcomer and her long-lost brother, suddenly nervous.

"This is heartwarming, Nic, really," she drawled, voice warm as a midwinter gale. "We have a murder to solve, if you want to head off that war my father's planning."

At this, the lithe young woman Nic brought with him sat at the table, her back to the fire. "Now, tell us everything you know about the incident."

Clare narrowed her eyes at the tone of easy command in the woman's voice.

"You are?"

"Helena," Nic supplied. "A friend. Ignore her manners, she never bothered to learn any."

"Faerie deals in boons and blood, not meaningless rituals and chitchat," Helena countered airily, though her green eyes narrowed.

It didn't take long for the group to tell Helena and Nic what they wanted to know, even with the lot of them frequently interrupting and stumbling over each other's narratives. And when it was all laid out, Clare realized with a sinking heart that Hameln actually wasn't the safe, reliable home that she had always believed it to be.

"First of all, Father Stephen seems to be completely unaware of the pact," Casper said.

"And this isn't just your affection for the old monk talking?" Clare asked.

"No, he spoke of faeries like angels—they exist, but he's never seen one," Casper replied. "I don't think he knows what a Faerie actually is, much less that the entire town is in league with them. No offense, Helena."

The Faerie girl nodded in acknowledgment. "What else did you learn?"

The group had been discussing the tangled web of clues they'd unearthed for twenty minutes now, Lukas' Faerie tale long forgotten. Every once in a while, Clare shot Lucie a long, nervous glance, but after years listening to her mother's broken conspiracy theories, it seemed she was impossible to shock. Besides, Nic and Helena didn't look concerned about her presence.

Instead, they seemed to hold a full conversation in the space of one shared look over Clare's head. She noticed that they did that a lot. And it really pissed her off. *He was her brother. Wasn't he supposed to confide in her? Who was this auslander, anyway?*

"I do not see how the innkeeper's books are pertinent for our mission," Helena said stiffly, finally addressing Nic aloud. "Especially since the Rat King's death was not ordered by the Council. Berchtold would have been aware of such a directive."

Sophie narrowed her eyes in sudden understanding. "Are you two spies?"

"I prefer to think of us as scouts," Nic said. "But sometimes we have to get a bit creative before the calvary arrives."

"Nicolaus." Helena's tone was like a warning.

"So … she's your commander?" Sophie looked over at the strange girl with new interest.

Nic's barked laughter sounded like home. "Oh, yes. She definitely outranks me."

"Well, full disclosure: I am also acting as a spy. Sort of for my brother, Freddie, but mostly for me," Sophie said.

"Who's Freddie?" Lucie asked timidly. "And why does he care about the murder?"

"And there goes our cover," Cas said before turning to the room. "Anyone else want to declare their intent toward espionage?"

Clare noticed that Sophie was eyeing Lucie strangely but remained uncharacteristically quiet.

"I'm just here for the fascinating company. And to see what will set Clare off next," Lukas confided conspiratorially.

"Why are you all in my house again?" Clare asked, glaring at each of them in turn.

"See? It's a good game." Lukas elbowed Cas while gesturing toward Clare with his chin.

Helena had remained quiet for most of this episode, but Clare saw something changing in her face. Helena's eyes had a shimmering, changeable aspect: at one glance they were the color of the clear morning sky, at another they looked more like the gray clouds that would move rapidly on a cold winter's day to hide it from view. *There's a storm coming,* she thought nervously.

"We do not have time for this. I have no idea who Freddie is, or of his interest in these proceedings. We are here, Clare…" At this point, Helena stood, striding to the window overlooking the quiet, if not peaceful, town. "…because Nic tells me this is the safest place in Hameln."

Clare noticed Lucie looking anywhere but the corner of the room where Nic and Helena were now whispering at each other fiercely, close and intimate. And she remembered how Lucie had loved Nic just as fiercely as Clare herself did.

Despite the world-weary man in front of her, she still saw him as the eleven-year-old boy who held his age and height over her, an annoying, necessary part of her young life. She tried to see him with Lucie's eyes: golden and lean, with a few more worries than she remembered. His broad shoulders and an almost effortless competency snared your attention—and maybe even fear. Yes, she could understand how his steady presence could draw the eye of Lucie, and even Helena.

Understanding attraction was a part of growing up that she hadn't mastered—she had barely even experienced—yet. And the only experience she had with love was a Faerie spell she'd gotten caught up in when she'd first laid eyes on Lukas.

She found herself at a loss, wanting to comfort Lucie, but certain that her friend would be horrified that her feelings were so easy to read.

"Lucie, do you think your mother still has that tea that used to soothe us to sleep as children?" Clare appealed to Lucie's instinct to care for those she loved, instead. "I feel so jittery, and her tea always calmed me down. We could use a little magic like that right now."

Lucie glanced at her, standing almost automatically at the request. "Yes, that's exactly what we need, Clare. I'll be back short-ly." With one guilty glance at the two hunters, their heads still close in quiet conference, she was gone.

Being needed isn't the same as being happy, but it was the best Clare could do. If only there was a tea for the heartsick, she figured it might do her and Lucie some good.

Not long after Lucie had left the room, Nic turned from Helena to Sophie and Lukas.

"Now that you've caught us up on your investigation," Nic said, turning his attention to Sophie, "do you mind telling us why you're here?"

"I am Princess Sophia Everstein of Castle Everstein, and I am here to understand what magic has taken hold of Hameln," Sophie said. "And to … stop it, I guess."

"Aren't you a bit young for such a mission?" Nic asked, tilting his golden head and squinting at her.

"Aren't you a bit presumptuous?" Sophie responded, her eyes and voice suddenly hard. "I do not answer to Berchtold's men."

Nic remained silent, but his watchful eyes showed his attention had not wandered. Clare realized he probably made a very good spy, putting strangers at ease with his easy camaraderie and loud laugh.

"And you?" Nic turned to Lukas. "Why are you here, in my family's home?"

Lukas had settled into an empty corner, watching them all while his restless fingers moved in a silent cadence he had set. "Me? I was just here for the ceremony, and I'll be moving along as soon as this unpleasantness is dealt with, I'm sure." Clare rolled her eyes at everything Lukas didn't say. But Nic just accepted his words with easy grace.

Nic grinned at the minstrel. "That's something we have in common, then. Welcome to Hameln."

That evening, Clare watched the storm clouds roll into town, taking the bitter-cold sting from the air and replacing it with a soft, cheerless rain. It was a gentle, persistent downpour that seemed to make the whole world melt and blur around the edges. The type of dreary weather that was great for the crops and terrible for just about everything else—including Clare's mood.

It felt much later in the day than it was, an inauspicious end to what she had hoped would be a day of revelations. She needed answers. More importantly, the town needed answers: about the rats, about the murder, about the Obolen.

Hameln was one bad turn from chaos. She felt it in the air, noisy with curses and squeals from townsfolk and rats. When Clare came across a strange young girl outside the Nixe at dusk, she knew she couldn't put her head down and just keep walking, not when you could almost taste the bloodlust in the air.

"Excuse me, miss," Clare spoke out brightly, as if to an old friend. As if she could put the whole town at ease if she just pretended this was a normal Hameln evening.

The girl turned to face her, and Clare stumbled to a stop. Her dark skin was glowing like moon-soaked pearls in the weak light. Were strange, beautiful women just dropping from the sky this winter?

The girl in front of her was ethereal, her dark skin seeming to shine from within. Her dazzling crystalline blue eyes focused serenely on Clare's astonished face, and for a moment Clare sensed an almost feral intelligence. While slight, Clare realized this strange woman wasn't as young as she looked from across the street—perhaps in her early 20s—and not nearly as frightened as Clare thought she should be.

"Hello, young one," the woman responded, arching her elegant dark eyebrows over crystal-clear blue eyes. "I hope this evening finds you well. Can I help you?"

"I…I was actually wondering if I could help you." Clare had expected to find a frightened young girl who needed assistance. But the calm this stranger radiated told her she was simply interrupting her early evening stroll through town.

"Perhaps. I am looking for my daughter." She was not such a young woman, then.

"Look, I don't know where you're headed, but I think you should follow me." Clare looked over her shoulder, watching the now nightly procession of watchmen was heading toward them, and Clare knew they would feel more than entitled to stop and question the beautiful woman, just for something to do. Curfew was approaching.

"Unless you have seen my daughter …"

"Yes! Your daughter!" Clare snatched at the name, at the chance to head off an ugly scene in the making. Helena and even Sophie were far too old to be this woman's daughter, but she would beg off at the mix-up and help her find her actual daughter once they were both *off the streets*. "It is possible that she came to town with my brother, Nic. I can take you to them."

"Please, lead the way." The woman nodded, seemingly unaffected by Clare's agitated manner. "It has been so long since I have been in Hameln, I do not know how long I would have wandered before finding her on my own." She bowed her head slightly, smiling. "My name is Ursel, and I am in your debt."

Clare led Ursel through twisting footpaths that she prayed the patrol would avoid. She barely understood why she was helping, and didn't need an angry interrogation from a pack of men who were determined to solve all potential problems with casual violence. They passed several figures passed out with drink, held up only by the walls of the buildings around them. Ursel simply walked through, silent but watchful.

"My smithy is this way," Clare whispered urgently. "And my home above it. We can figure out exactly where your girl is, once you're safe."

Ursel followed without complaint, and Clare noticed that the soft, persistent rain didn't seem to touch her. Not even the hem of her cloak seemed dirtied by their surroundings. She'd have to learn that trick someday.

She idly wondered if it were the lady or, like Lukas' pipe, her cloak that was imbued with magic, before hurrying ahead.

When they finally reached the courtyard, Clare ushered Ursel through the gate and door silently. Once inside, she could finally breathe easy.

"Just up those stairs—"

"Are these your creations, my dear?" The confounding woman seemed to forget her urgent mission that had her roaming foreign streets in the middle of a townwide crackdown—to look at her weapons, of all things.

"Yes, and if you're interested in buying any, I'd love to haggle prices." Clare couldn't keep the edge out of her voice. "But maybe we should find your daughter first? Like I said, people are a bit … unsettled … about strangers right now."

"Oh, my dear, I wouldn't know what to do with a sword." Ursel's light laughter did nothing to calm Clare's nerves. She reached out and stroked the hunting dagger Clare had made years ago with Nic in mind. Of course, he had never before returned to use it. And now he could make his own.

"Yes, well. That's not for sale," Clare told her grimly, approaching to take the weapon from Ursel's small, elegant hands. "Now, what was your daughter's name? And where did you last see her?"

"That is a fine *hirschfanger* you've made." Helena's eyes never left its blade. "Please, I just want to take a closer look at the detailing of the handle."

Clare held the blade out, but didn't surrender it to her guest. She may be stupid enough to show a strange woman kindness, but she wouldn't hand her a weapon.

Clare noticed a brief flash of pain on Ursel's face as her fingers caressed the metal. "Please be careful, the blade is sharp," she cautioned.

"I am well, my dear." Ursel brushed away her concern. "Just worried for my daughter."

Stupid. And reckless. Clare thought to herself. She'd led a strange woman to her home, one who was now entirely too concerned with the weapons that filled the house.

Eyeing the stairs, she considered whether backup or disarming the threat was more important.

Ursel again stroked the handle, murmuring words too low for Clare to catch. "Yes, it is exquisite. You have quite an eye for detail, as well as a talent for forging swords."

"My brother Casper handles the finer work," Clare replied as Ursel handed the weapon over, sheathing the dagger and then looping it around her own waist. It never hurt to stay alert, and her own uncharacteristically slow instincts reminded her Ursel was not as she appeared to be.

"Upstairs, you said?" Ursel asked with a bland, beautiful smile that reminded Clare of nothing more than Sophie's mother, Countess Katherine. Clare motioned her toward the staircase, following her up with one hand still on the dagger. She could afford to be more welcoming after they caught the murderer.

Upstairs, they found a cheerful fire and two somber soldiers. They glanced up to greet Clare, but were both on their feet and alert instantly at the sight of Ursel.

"What are you doing here, milady?" Helena's cold manners could not hide her agitation.

"I came with a message for my daughter." Ursel met Helena's gaze unflinchingly. Somehow, Clare sensed a reproach. "Her father grows restless and I fear what he will do if left to his own machinations much longer."

"Hameln is not a safe place for unknown faces, milady." Helena continued to give a strange kind of deference to this strange woman, bowing her head slightly when addressing her. Clare realized this woman must outrank Helena and Nic both, then. "It would be best if you could leave this town as you came, before anyone else is hurt."

"Nevertheless, I must speak with my daughter, even if I cannot pry her from this town." Ursel's tone was light, but her intent was clear. She would not leave.

"Maybe you can describe her?" Clare found her mind clearing, and suspicions rising. "Her name, for instance?"

"I will accompany you," Helena cut in, while gesturing Ursel to the exit. "I can get her out of Hameln safely this night."

"But what about her daughter?" Clare was ready to end their unspoken game, but that didn't mean she wanted to see bloodshed. Even with Helena's two wickedly curved swords strapped to her back, it didn't feel right to allow either of them out in the streets after curfew. She knew from experience how easy it was for neighbor to turn on neighbor, much less easy prey like Ursel.

"No one will harm either of them." Helena eyed her partner warily. "Nic, I think it is time to attend to family matters, yes?"

Nic had been curiously silent through the exchange, but he now drew himself up, as if preparing for a particularly grueling battle. "Yes, I'll explain—what I can—to Clare."

Without another word, Helena went out into the clear, cold night with her charge.

Hours later, Helena returned with good news. Ursel had been reunited with her daughter and sent back to her own home, far from the madness that gripped the city.

And Helena brought back a gift from the grateful woman: a delicate porcelain ring that she insisted be given to Clare before she would leave.

Clare pocketed it without looking too closely; she had never cared for such trinkets. She had far too many mysteries on her hands as it was—not to mention a couple of blockhead brothers to look after.

19

"Clarebear, I can't stay," Nic's voice pleaded. "I'm here because Berchtold commanded it. And I will have to leave when he commands, as well."

"But we need you here." Clare's head drooped down to her chest and Sophie could see she was fighting for control. "*I* need you here."

"I cannot be the man you want me to be—the big brother with all the answers." Nic's hands covered Clare's.

Sophie became uncomfortably aware that this intimate moment was not for her eyes.

"My job is to hunt down a murderer in Hameln. That is the best way I know to keep you and Casper safe."

She rose, brushing his hands away, and reached for the door. "Then I hope you find him soon. And never come back again."

Casper reached for her, but stayed beside Nic. "Clare, you don't mean that. He's our brother!"

"I do!" She whirled around, teeth bared, and both brothers flinched.

Sophie didn't blame them. Clare was fierce on her best days, and right now she seemed rubbed raw.

"I wish you'd both just leave. Then I could live my life without worrying how either of you are going to ruin it again."

"You know what I think?" Casper's voice was uncharacteristically loud. "I think you're both ridiculous. Service to your friends and family is not a prison sentence, it is an act of love."

"Stop being martyrs. I'm not your responsibility." Cas pointed at Clare. "And my…injury is not your cross to bear." This time he pointed to Nic. "Find the courage to be who you really want to be. Otherwise everything we already lost is for nothing."

He stomped heavily to his bedroom before slamming his door shut.

Nic was speechless for only a moment. "Well, he definitely doesn't get that from me," he started.

Clare stared at him, mouth hanging open in disbelief. "That's the lesson you're taking from this moment? That Cas is too angry? That somehow this is my fault? You were his hero, Nic. Even after all these years. And what have you done to actually help us?"

"Heroes are just people who haven't disappointed you yet," Nic replied tonelessly, but his hands were trembling. When he saw Sophie looking, he grabbed his cup with both hands and drank deeply. "I told Aunt Aggie I'd check in with Jakob. I'll be back before morning. Try not to start any wars without me."

And then he turned to Sophie.

"Look, I appreciate all the information you've shared with us," Nic told her, softening his tone. "But we're here on official business, and I can't have my little brother and his little friend following us around."

"Little friend?" Sophie said, indignant. "This was my investigation first, Nicolaus. You can't push me out now that Berchtold has seen fit to care about this town's plight."

Nic narrowed his eyes and opened his mouth.

"You have good instincts. And they have served you well,"

Helena interrupted calmly, as she placed a quelling hand on Nic's shoulder. "But we work better in the shadows, and we do not wish to lead you into danger."

"Danger came here," Sophie argued. "We didn't seek it out."

"Nevertheless—" Helena started.

"I am here on the explicit instructions of Count Johann of Everstein and Prince Friedrich of Everstein," Sophie interrupted, drawing herself up to her full height. "Obstruct my investigation if you dare, but know that they will both be highly displeased by the interference."

The two shared a few whispered words, their tone transitioning from disbelief, amusement, and finally begrudging acceptance. To Sophie, it read like a whirlwind of condescension.

"I propose a truce," she said, ignoring their wordless conversation. "We will continue our investigation—which has already produced good evidence of a conspiracy that you and Ebernberg seemed completely ignorant of, might I add—and you will continue yours. Of course, where our efforts meet, we will be happy to cooperate."

And then she bared her teeth in what could barely be considered a smile.

"But otherwise, you don't get in our way, and we won't get in yours," Sophie said.

"Very well," Helena agreed, looking at her steadily. "Then the first order of business is to discover the spy in your midst who has informed the Erlking that Princess Sophia is in Hameln investigating the Rat King's murder."

"The Erlking?" Sophie felt her body go hot, then cold at Helena's words. "How does he even know I exist?"

"And how do we even know that *he* exists?" Clare interjected.

Helena ignored them both. "And then we can determine why it is that the Council seems to be so interested in making a deal with Lukas," she said, before leading Nic back downstairs.

Sophie turned to Clare, preparing to comfort her. But Clare's calm mask of indifference greeted her. "I'm *fine*," she said savagely before turning to leave.

"Good night, Clare," Sophie spoke to her retreating back. Were other people's families all so … complicated? She suddenly missed Freddie.

Sophie took a breath, glancing out the window where the rain had finally diminished into a gloomy mist. She spied a figure, crouched down in the mud, both arms covering his head like a two-year-old hiding from the dark. A very large two-year-old. She moved past Lukas, heading downstairs to get a closer look.

Once she stood at the doorway leading outside, she realized it was Nic sitting there, alone in the courtyard, very quietly losing his mind.

Sophie walked outside, approaching slowly and steadily. She made just enough noise so that he would know she was coming, but not enough to make him think she expected him to greet her.

His breathing was jagged and shallow, but ever so quiet. He shifted to sit on his own hands in the straw, just inside the over-hanging lip of the roof. His unfocused eyes looked out into nothing. Not wet or muddy, then. Just cold and desperate. *Trapped,* she thought.

Sophie settled into the silence, letting the minutes stretch out, filling the uncomfortable space between them with an easy cama-raderie. In fact, Sophie welcomed the quiet interlude to think about the evening's revelations. She had so many strong impressions of the two spies, and the Erlking's interest. If only she'd brought something to write with, to organize her thoughts.

Casper's now-familiar uneven gait drew her out of her thoughts, and she looked up to see him and Lukas standing uncertainly behind her.

"Did you two follow me out here?" Sophie asked, smiling.

Casper looked at Lukas askance. "I did," he confirmed. "I wanted to make sure you were both all right. Lukas just came along for … inspiration, or something?"

"Misty evenings are so delightfully atmospheric, aren't they?" Lukas answered with a slight grin.

Casper shrugged at her apologetically.

Lukas rolled his eyes. "I would think a creative soul such as yourself would understand."

"Thank you," Nic said, too softly to be brusque. "For staying in this space with me."

"So it was the right thing to do, then?" Sophie asked, relieved. "Good, good. Maybe we can do this again sometime. Except for the panicking part, of course."

"You have a lot of experience with episodes like this, then?" Nic asked, finally looking at her directly. He seemed unconcerned with Cas and Lukas' presence, so she followed his lead, zeroing in on his unfocused golden gaze.

"Not exactly," she admitted, stretching out her now-stiff limbs. "But I do have a particularly focused father. When he gets too far into his own head, I've found it's best to just be with him. Helps him remember there's a world outside of his own thoughts."

Nic snorted at that. It was almost charming.

"Casper." Nic finally spoke to his brother. The two shared a stoic look that Sophie couldn't decipher. After a pause, Nic continued. "You were right, of course. I suppose I jumped into the Obolen to escape my shame." Nic spoke softly. "That won't surprise you to hear. I do tend to leap without looking, I suppose. And I am sorry."

Sophie saw Casper, backlit and solid compared to the foggy world around her, relax in his rigid stance.

Lukas laughed. "Well, we're just a walking band of cautionary tales, aren't we?" He turned and presented himself to Casper with an exaggerated, courtly bow. "Pleasure to meet you, sir. I am known as 'the consequence of unbridled lust.' "

Casper shook his hand heartily, while patting his leg. "How do you do? They call me the 'danger of a curious child.' Alternatively, 'the peril of a white-hot forge.' "

Helena had by then returned, arms laden with saddlebags. They turned to her expectantly, but she seemed unamused and slightly bewildered.

"We'll just call her dangerous," Nic supplied helpfully, standing up to retrieve his supplies. "And it's time for us to go."

"You don't honestly think I am staying behind while you confront the spy," Sophie asked incredulously. "He put all of us—and worse, the investigation—in jeopardy!"

Casper eyed her carefully, but said nothing. *He really is a smart boy.*

"We don't know who we're looking for. But I need to speak to Jakob. He may know nothing at all …" Nic explained, clearly tired. "We're not going to walk in the Nixe and accuse him of anything. That's not how you get information."

"To clarify, it is not how you start an interrogation," Helena said. "Depending on how this conversation proceeds, an accusation may be just what we need to knock him off balance."

"I can appreciate that approach," Sophie said, nodding thoughtfully. *Maybe I can learn something from them.* "Fine then. I'll follow your lead. But if it looks like you don't have him …"

"Do not fear, youngling," Helena said. "We will have him. Stay quiet and pay attention."

Within the hour, the four of them were seated at the Nixe, waiting for Jakob's break from the bar. Sophie had to admit, it was a good location for a clandestine meeting. The hall was just noisy enough that they would not be overheard. But even here, the rats hung over the revelries. Rat pie on the menu, and live rats scurried by, heedless of drunken dancing feet or their own possible fate as dinner.

She watched as Jakob filled a few more tankards, slapped a few more backs, and then sat down with them, clearly pleased to see his old friends Nic and Casper.

But his pleasant smile melted as soon as his gaze hit Sophie's face.

"I know you," Jakob said, narrowed eyes looking her up and down. Sophie straightened her back and tilted her chin, a low-level panic beginning to swirl in her gut. "You were here for the Obolen, and never claimed your bed."

"She is one of the nurses from the war encampment," Nic interceded, putting a calming hand on Sophie's shoulder before she could reply. "Berchtold was concerned this might be another outbreak, and wishes to stop it before it can decimate his troops."

"A bit young for a war nurse," Jakob replied, his eyes never leaving Sophie's face. "Wait, that's it! You were in the Rat King's sick chamber when he …I saw the rats …" Jakob was now sputtering, unable to put the strange accusation into words. *Does he really think I summoned the rats somehow?*

Nic's grip on her shoulder tightened, ever so slightly. She may have forgotten to relay that particular detail to him. *I only hope his other hand will grab Jakob, if the occasion calls for it.* She'd never seen such a menacing look on Jakob's face.

"She was there on Berchtold's orders, naturally," Nic continued. "The Rat King's death was a strange affair, make no mistake. Whether the attack was natural or unnatural, he wanted an expert at his bedside."

Jakob settled back down in his chair, seemingly willing to accept Nic's version of events. For now.

"To be honest, I've been looking for you," he said, still talking to Sophie. "I must have hit my head. The entire attack, or … whatever it was … it's all a blur. I remember he was moaning, and there was so much blood. I left for just a moment, and when I came back, he was gone. Instead *you* were there. You and the rats."

"You remember nothing else?" Helena probed delicately.

Jakob eyed her with a humorless smile. "If you are Berchtold's servant, then you know my memory alone isn't enough to unlock my tongue."

"If you could just try," Helena said, taking his hand. Sophie tried to hide her surprise at the suddenly intimate moment.

Jakob furrowed his brow as he chose his words carefully. "His entire body seemed to recoil at the monk's touch. And then he called down a curse on Hameln, saying that … that Hameln's peace would end with his death. The Erlking would abandon us for 'the lady's wicked betrayal.' " As he ended his speech, Jakob seemed struck dumb by his own words. "How?" he asked Helena, wide-eyed.

Sophie shared his alarm. *What lady? Only Agathe and my mother hold Council positions.* But Nic said this couldn't be a Council action. Another lady, then?

"I think that's enough for now," Nic responded instead. "Jakob, what you have seen is dangerous. Promise me you'll keep your head down?"

Jakob gave his old friend a wan smile. "This isn't how we thought we'd end up, eh Nic?"

Nic smiled back, the look somehow more genuine and sad at the same time. "How many half-drunken nights at the Nixe do we owe each other, you think?"

"Too many to count," Jakob answered. Sophie took a moment to admire Nic's ability. He'd be the perfect courtier, easing tense moments with his charming smile.

"Let's see if we can catch up a bit tonight." Nic stood, clasping his friend in a warm embrace.

"I look forward to it," Jakob answered, nodding at Helena and Sophie before returning to the bar.

"So that's it? We're not going to push any further?" Sophie asked quietly as the three others rose from the table. "He seems to know more."

"We won't get any more from him tonight, anyway," Nic said with a short, dimpled smile. "Jake always did hate rats."

Sophie shivered as they walked through the door, remembering the swarm of rodents that had crawled over her body that day. "Is there anyone left in Hameln that doesn't feel the same?"

Turning to share a smile with Casper, she watched, horrified, as a particularly burly drunk crashed right into Cas before careening on his merry way. Casper crumpled soundlessly to the ground. The squeak of a displeased rat echoed in the now-silent street.

"Cas!" she cried, running to him. Cas shook his head dazedly, before grabbing her offered hand and hauling himself up. "I'm fine, I'm fine. Hazards of walking in Hameln, I suppose," he said with a forced laugh.

She could tell he wished for the moment to be over, and so she changed her grip, twisting her hand so that it instead rested lightly on his arm as he stood.

Nic was no longer walking beside them. He had stopped short in the street, still as a statue. Sophie saw that his golden eyes were glazed over and wide with fear, as if trapped in a nightmare.

It wasn't until Jakob rushed by, knocking his friend's shoulder roughly as he moved to Casper's side, that Nic finally seemed to breathe again. With two slow blinks, he focused first on Sophie's face, then Jakob's.

"Sorry about that, Cas," Jakob said, quiet and firm. "Sometimes cutting a customer off his drink leaves him a bit fearsome. You all right, there?"

"Yes," Nic said, moving swiftly to take Cas from Sophie's grasp. "But let's get him home, all the same."

At that, Nic practically carried Cas toward home.

Sophie shared a look with Helena, who shook her head briefly at Nic's obvious nerves before changing the subject.

"We have two more pieces of information," Helena said, and they quickly followed the two boys. "One: The killer was a woman. And two: Jakob is not the spy."

"How did you come to that conclusion? He admitted he was looking for me!" Sophie argued, still unsettled by the bartender's overtly suspicious attitude toward her. Why did he seem to trust Helena immediately?

"Yes, and that he did not know who you are," Helena said with a quelling look. "The spy my mother warned me of knew specifically that Princess Sophie was in town investigating the murder. Not a nurse from one of Berchtold's war camps."

"Fine," Sophie grumbled gracelessly. "And there goes our entire list of suspects. I guess that leaves us with Jakob's lady, though I don't know how we'll find her."

"It is time to simplify this situation," Helena continued. "Lukas needs to get rid of these rats."

20

After a few angry hours pacing around her room, an exhausted Clare crawled out of her window onto the roof —her oldest sanctuary, one she used to share with Nic. She welcomed the clear, cold air that stung her nose and cheeks after the oppressive mist and rain they had endured most of the day.

This was her favorite part of the day, when it slipped slowly into night. Clare watched as inky darkness seeped through the sky, creating a dark rainbow arching down to the horizon—black to blue to gold to the mere slice of red sun that she could just see over the western line of hills beyond the river.

The dying light transformed the town, making shadows of every familiar building and tree. But the most magical part was watching as the stars slowly blinked into view, piercing through the night sky like a thousand needles through rich velvet.

"I thought I'd find you hiding up here." Clare heard Nic's voice, warm with affection. "Nice to know some things never change."

"I'm not hiding." The defensive tone was clear, and she struggled to sound reasonable. Adult. "I just come here to think. Or not think, as the case may be."

She felt him scramble up beside her, keeping her eyes to the sky. She didn't trust herself to look into her brother's face yet, unable to hide every emotion she was feeling. Anger, obviously, but also despair that she would be so easy to leave behind. *Again.*

The silence stretched between them, absorbed into the thin night air. It was childish, but if he had something to discuss, he could start talking.

"I thought you were better off without me." Nic grinned over at her, looking almost proud. "Now I'm back, with everything I've learned and seen and done ... I still think you are."

"What's that like? Being so sure that you know what's best?" Clare questioned him mockingly.

She waited so long, she was certain he wasn't going to answer her.

"It's hard," he admitted. "And lonely."

Clare didn't answer, and they let the silence lay between them, heavy and almost comforting.

"Who do you really think the spy is?" Clare finally asked.

"It could be anyone," he admitted. "It could be someone who'd been to Everstein Castle recognizing her in passing, or an educated guess by any who saw a young girl with dark skin."

"But the Erlking knows she's investigating," Clare argued. "That goes beyond a royal spotting."

Nic rubbed his eyes. "Yes, that's true. We have to assume it was someone from the Council. Or someone who works for them, at least. That means anyone from the Patrol, or the monastery."

"What about from your side? The count, Berchtold?" Clare asked slowly, eyeing her now-strange brother.

"No." Nic was firm in his response, surprising Clare enough to stop being gentle with him.

"What makes you so sure? How well do you know him?"

"I know that he spends his life teaching children to defend themselves. Not putting them in danger. Not like ..."

"But at least we know Jakob is still on our side." Clare finally responded when it was clear that Nic wouldn't finish that particular thought. She'd have to trust that Nic would steer her true, even if he couldn't open up.

"I just hope that's enough," Nic said grimly.

Clare's recurring nightmare never failed to surprise her.

This time, she'd pushed a shrieking young Casper into the spring-thawed river as Nic laughed, her mother scrambling up to help Cas out of the frigid water. The sun shone, the yellow and pink spring flowers were in bloom. *Everyone is happy and—most importantly—everyone is alive.*

"Clare!" Cas sputtered as he failed at his first attempt to grab their mother's hand. "It's *cold*!"

Clare laughed, delighted. "Of course it's cold, silly!"

That's when nightmare creatures slunk along the riverbanks. They seemed like a trick of the light at first: translucent creatures, no bigger than forest foxes, creeping toward her family and friends, silent and wicked. If she turned her head too quickly, they nearly disappeared in the tall grasses.

Only she saw them, and she yearned to cry out, but the warning stuck painfully in her throat. She tried waving her hands, but no one noticed her terror, not even Pa, who lifted her in his strong arms and prepared to swing her into the Weser.

"Into the river with you, Clarebear!" he chuckled, watching her face.

"Wait!" she cried. "Look o—" But he ignored her warning, and she flew into the water.

Breaking the surface and sputtering, Clare cried in horror as one of the creatures slowly climbed up Casper, still shivering in the water. It latched its round, needle-lined maw to Casper's forehead. The confusion and pain registered in his eyes before he fell silently back into the river before she could reach him.

Clare was paralyzed as Nic was attacked next, from behind. The creature clamped onto the top of his head as he slowly collapsed. *No!!! I have to do something!* Her mother fell next, splashing into the river and floating away as the monster rode her lifeless body like a raft.

Pa faltered, dropping her to the ground before he slumped down beside her, more amazed than scared at his own death. His empty eyes were wide, his mouth open, but no sound came.

"No!" Clare finally screamed, too late. "Please!"

It's my fault. They're dead and I couldn't stop it! I'm all alone!

Clare jerked awake, wiping tears from her face.

She didn't need a monk or a healer to translate her dreams for her. She knew what fueled the nightmares: her family already half gone. After all, in all the ways that matter, she'd already outlived them. *How long will it be before I'm truly alone?*

She sighed once before throwing her blankets off and hauling herself out of bed. It was finally morning, but early enough that the sun didn't seem to know it yet.

Once outside, Clare felt that the star-pocked sky suited her just fine, matching her dark mood. She walked through the courtyard quietly, moving things about with no particular purpose. She felt like bringing some order to the smithy, but Clare knew her mother would have called it something else. "I'm fussing," she murmured to herself.

"Excited about my performance today?"

She jumped at Lukas' voice, a scream aborted in her throat.

"And here I thought you *weren't* my biggest fan." His smile was wide and his teeth white.

Clare glared, but remained silent, not yet willing to relinquish her moment of solitude. She'd earned this loneliness through the years, actions and words pushing everyone to a safe distance. Why didn't he leave her alone, too?

"If you don't mind." Her voice was low and tight. "I've already disappointed the entirety of my family. I'd prefer to limit the number of people who hate me today."

Lukas sat down beside her, as if he hadn't heard her speak at all. He crowded close, his back straight and knees bent up as he rested his elbows on them, then his chin on his crossed arms. It would only take one deep breath, and her knees would touch his own. She could pretend it was an accident, and not a silent plea for borrowed comfort and warmth.

"You know what the best part of having a family is?" Lukas said, staring steadily into still new flames of the forge across the courtyard.

"There's always someone there to remind you of every mistake you've ever made?" Her voice was watery and shoulders unsteady with tears she refused to let fall. Why couldn't she pull herself together?

"No, it's—" He cleared his throat roughly and shook his head before starting again. "It's proof that you weren't a mistake. Your parents fell in love, sure, but any couple of reckless teenagers can do that. What makes family special is the choices that were made: to stay, to work, to build something together, even if they can't remain with you to share it forever."

Clare allowed herself one deep breath, letting the icy air expand her lungs until it seemed that she could feel every muscle and sinew in her chest burn. She felt her leg press lightly into his, and his answering pressure. Maybe they both needed comfort from past regrets and future fears.

"People aren't mistakes." She felt the truth in the words as they left her mouth on a deep sigh.

"And you are not your mistakes." Lukas moved to rise, nimble and quick, his hand giving a slight squeeze to her knee that had her stomach pleasantly clenching and her toes flexing. Even after he left, his words floated behind him, and she closed her eyes to imagine them hanging there in the air above her, a reminder and a promise.

Maybe she wasn't so alone.

Eventually, the sun banished last night's gloom, and the day dawned in full force. It seemed Clare and Lukas weren't the only ones who had awoken early. Half the town was eager to witness Lukas' performance. The festival-like atmosphere was nearly vibrating all around, uncertain energy making her feel off-balanced and jittery.

Clare and Casper joined Lucie on her bedroom balcony overlooking the heart of the town. Clare kept a close eye on the Council below them. She didn't doubt that they wanted the rats gone. But did they want to continue the initiation, or do something else entirely to the children? To her brother?

Lukas' desired audience had congregated. While the pessimists remained in town, secure in their continued miseries, the optimists were gathered on the other side of the Weser, faces curious but cautious. Their eyes stayed on Lukas, watching impatiently for a miracle in the form of the piper whose power they hoped would be irresistible to the rapidly burgeoning rodent population.

Lucie seemed particularly nervous as they waited for Lukas to begin his performance, and Clare grasped her friend's white-knuckled fingers, squeezing in an attempt to comfort them both. If Lukas failed to get rid of the rats today, there was no telling how the Council would respond—banishment, jail, even turning a blind eye to an enraged mob after another broken promise.

He came into her view, and she smiled in spite of herself. He was in that hideous multicolored costume again. He claimed it was all part of the show, but she knew he just enjoyed *being* the show.

The hum of quiet whispers eventually died down, as it became clear Lukas would only start once he had the audience's full attention. In the hush around them, he raised his flute to his lips and played.

It was a rollicking melody, more like a sea shanty than anything, but in a haunting minor key. She felt herself and Lucie swaying slowly with the music, and a sudden, almost painful urge to run into the open waters swept over her, like a wave of want.

Just a quick swim, that's all I need, she thought giddily.

But looking down, the effect on the rats was more than a little horrifying, stilling her instincts to run. Hundreds upon hundreds of them had emerged from every nook and hidey hole in Hameln, squeaking and growling in helpless panic. As the shocked townsfolk watched, mouths agape, the rodents moved, jerky and relentless, to the river. Clare could see their beady eyes bulging in terror as their heads thrashed back and forth, unable to stop their own bodies as they followed the bard's call. She shivered, and felt Lucie's own tremors through their interlocked hands.

They ran headlong into the water, not even attempting to swim. Instead, they walked along the bottom of the river bed, racing as if the Weser were simply a road to take them to another town to terrorize.

"That was …" Lucie began.

"… terrifying," Clare finished for her.

And these were just rats. Clare tried to imagine the power Lukas could have over other people. Over her. Loosening her grip on Lucie, she wrapped her arms around her stomach and willed the thought away. Lukas would never consciously lead them all to danger. She was almost certain she could trust him with her life.

It was her heart she was worried about.

Three months after the failed Obolen ceremonies, Hameln was finally able to celebrate. The roar of the crowd was deafening, and those who remained in town ran to see what had happened. The two crowds collided, hugging and dancing to Lukas' rousing drinking song.

Any ale and victuals they'd managed to save from the vermin were brought out and shared with all. Even the usually sanguine

Council joined in the fun, Aunt Aggie dancing for the first time in Clare's memory.

As the star of their long-delayed festivities, Lukas was more than happy to accept the city's appreciation.

Clare, still reeling from Lukas's power, was sitting on the Nixe's storeroom steps, chin in her hands, in an attempt to escape the townwide party. The Rat King's betrayer remained, after all. "All we're missing is the parade," Clare grumbled to Jakob as he rolled yet another keg to the bar.

"A parade of those damned rats into the river was more than enough for most people, I'm sure," he responded, pausing in his labor to scratch thoughtfully at his chin. A sparse beard had begun to sprout on his face, and she imagined the scruff was just as itchy to grow as it would be to feel. "Cheer up, Clare. This is good news!"

As he continued out the door, careful to avoid her on the wide, shallow steps, she could admit, to herself, that many in Hameln had cause to enjoy a rat-free existence.

But there are so many other problems we have to solve.

Who was the murderer? And if they had killed the Rat King in order to unleash the plague of rodents in the first place? As for the apparent Obolen agreement, it seemed Father Stephen was being kept in the dark—literally—about the town's relationship with Faerie. But how responsible was Aunt Aggie in all this? Or her parents, and Lucie's parents, and Sophie's parents?

And even her beloved grandfather?

No, she'd celebrate once she'd cleared their names, at least in her own mind. There was too much work still to do for drinking and dancing.

But it seemed the investigation would have to wait until tomorrow. Searching the crowded dining room of familiar faces, she finally found Nic as Lukas had ended his latest song to thunderous cheers. And her brother was singing Jakob's praises to an obviously skeptical Lukas.

"He's loyal and kind. But most of all he's brave," Nic said, spinning his tankard in lazy circles and watching Lukas beneath lowered lashes.

"Sounds like exactly the type of guy I make it a point not to like," Lukas responded cheekily. But in spite of his irreverent tone, the look he shared with Nic was long and steady.

"As you will," Nic said. "Just know that you can trust him. I've trusted him with Casper and Clare for the past ten years, after all."

"I think you underestimate them," Lukas said, leaning forward despite himself. "*Especially* Clare."

"I won't make that mistake with you, the great hero of Hameln," Nic smiled, finally stilling his drink. "I don't know yet if you're a good man, but you've proven to be a powerful ally."

His power is what unnerves me, Clare thought, narrowing her eyes.

Nic clasped Lukas by both shoulders, grinning down at him. "Berchtold will be pleased at your progress. The Rat King's ability to morph into those foul creatures was always a damned nuisance. Now that we've mitigated that Fae creature's plague, we can focus on what the rest of the Council is trying to hide."

"The Faerie?" Sophie jumped on the loose fact like a ball. "So the Rat King was a Faerie, not just some drunken imbecile unlucky enough to be cursed?"

"I shouldn't have said that," Nic said, eyes growing wide.

"Yes, well, what's a little secret-telling among friends?" Lukas asked. "And we can use this information. So the plague is more like a "dying breath" curse from an enraged creature, not a side effect of the broken Obolen pact."

Clare watched Lukas lean forward, as if ready to pounce. She felt something spinning out of control, their words becoming loose and fast.

"No, I should not have been *able* to say any of that," Nic insisted. "What kind of magic is happening here?"

"The magic of you going easy on me, maybe?" Lukas winced under Nic's tightening grasp. "Your hand is doing that squeezing thing, there, Nic."

"The curse has never affected you, has it?" Nic said. "And you are over sixteen. So why can you talk freely when it stops our mouths? And why can I now talk freely of it in your presence?"

"Maybe you just needed an outsider's perspective?" Lukas volunteered. "I never agreed to an evil, centuries-old pact. Why should it affect me?"

"What pact?" Clare rose to break Lukas free from Nic's hold. "What's going on Nic?"

Lukas answered instead. "I'd wondered how much the initiates knew. Or the townsfolk, for that matter. What have you gotten in return for the children you give away? Gold? Protection? Or was this payment for a wrong committed by people long dead?"

Nic and Clare just stared at him.

"This isn't the place, Lukas," Helena warned.

Nic was shaking his head. "That's not how it works. Or, that's not how it's supposed to work, anyway."

"I demand to see Lukas the piper," a loud voice cut through the merriment. "I am here on Council business."

"Must be reward time." Lukas winked at Sophie, switching back to the devil-may-care bard in a heartbeat. "I'll get you your answers soon enough, Sophie."

Josef pushed his towering frame through the crowds until he was standing in front of Lukas, flanked by Nic, Sophie, Casper, and Helena. "You are the piper who rid our town of the plague of rats?"

"Yes, that's me. Lead the way, good sir," Lukas said jovially.

Josef's face hardened. "You are under arrest for murder and extortion. Resist and die, by order of the Hameln Council."

21

The party quickly dispersed around Sophie, her head spinning after the arrest of the guest of honor. She stayed right where she was, unsure what to do after the astonishing turn of events. But the end of the party didn't stop people's tongues. The townsfolk were at turns curious and then furious at the news that their hero was a charlatan. Certainly no one spoke up for Lukas.

"I invited him into our home, shared meals with him," Sophie heard one woman behind Casper grumble.

"I kept him in drink most nights here at the Nixe," an old man returned. "I knew there was something wrong with him, what with all his odd questions he had about the town. Looking for answers that no *auslander* is entitled to know, no matter how many tricks he has."

As another *auslander* with a lot of questions, Sophie felt her blood run cold. When would the angry mob turn on her? She decided to keep her head down until she made it back to the house with Casper and Clare.

"I don't believe it," Casper said stoutly, once they were safely in the kitchen of their own home.

"Of course you don't, Cas," Sophie answered. "None of us do." She shot a sidelong glance at Clare, who had been uncharacteristically quiet even before Lukas had been dragged away.

Clare still said nothing.

"Nic and Helena will sort this out," Sophie continued. "Your Aunt Aggie will listen to them."

She had hardly gotten the words out before she heard Nic's tell-tale heavy tread on the stairs.

"Not this time, Princess," Nic answered, his face and tone dark with anger. "It seems the Council doesn't have time for Berchtold's associates." Helena was behind him, though her footfalls were silent.

"So what do we do?" Sophie nearly wailed in her disbelief. *How could they turn on Lukas so quickly?* "Who do we talk to?"

"I've sent word to the Count," Helena said shortly. "We wait for his orders."

This time it was Cas and Sophie who seemed to exchange a question, answer, and agreement all in one short glance.

"So, we wait," Sophie said to the room. *Until nightfall, anyway*, she vowed to herself.

The house was quiet, if not peaceful, when Sophie and Cas crept out of doors, determined to get Lukas out.

"He'll be at the mayor's house," Cas whispered as they walked quickly from shadow to shadow. "Unless they're still interrogating him."

More quickly than she had anticipated, they were at the back door of the mayor's large house. She was about to ask what the next step was, when Cas pulled a small leather pouch out of his pocket. He chose a slim metal rod with a long hook at the end.

"Are those lockpicks?" Sophie's amazement turned to annoy-

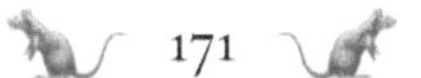

ance. "Why haven't you done it before? We could have used that kind of skillset in this investigation!"

"I created them as an exercise, to help me better understand the locking mechanisms," Cas explained, though his focus was now on pushing the pins to the shear line. "I've never actually done it for—oh, that was quick!"

Casper stepped back, holding the door open for them.

"God's bones, what would Father Stephen say if he could see you now?" Sophie didn't even try to hide her delight as she teased him. "Using your powers for ill-gotten gain."

"Father Stephen thinks that my sister is an aberration and that Helena is a demon," Casper replied darkly. "He can go to hell."

They paused in the hallway after closing the heavy door quietly behind them. Letting her eyes adjust to the weak light of the oil lanterns on the walls, she was struck by the easy opulence around her—dark wooden walls shone beneath portraits.

Uneasy, Sophie glanced at Casper. "Where are we—"

"Cas, is that you?" Lucie's voice floated down the ornate staircase, alarmed. "And … Sophie? What are you doing here?"

So much for their clandestine rescue.

"I-I was worried," Cas stammered, fumbling for a likely response. "I heard the Council was meeting; I knew you were here alone with Lukas."

Lucie was staring down at the leather pouch still open in his hand. "Did you break into my house?

"I-yes? And no." Casper looked lost. "Look, don't be upset, it's just …" He took a deep breath before staring Lucie straight in the eye. "Lukas didn't kill anyone. And I came here—with Sophie—to let him go. Before the Council comes back and does something terrible."

Lucie's astonished expression turned thoughtful at his words. Sophie noticed her mouth tremble as she looked toward a door at the end of the hall. With a quick nod, she was moving. That's when she saw Lucie already had a set of keys in her own hands.

"Let's go. Before Josef returns from the kitchen," Lucie said, leading them up the stairs. "Though you're going to explain to me how you came across those. Who taught you to use them?"

"You're helping us?" Casper was astonished, but that didn't stop him from hobbling quickly after her. "I thought you said we had to trust in the system?"

"Yes, well, the system's rotten," she snapped back at him.

"What?" Cas asked. Sophie noticed he seemed as perplexed as her.

"Put those away!" Lucie hissed at him, pointing toward the lock picks. "This will be hard enough to answer for."

Sophie swallowed her own questions down. Following Lucie's instruction quickly, they crowded into her back as she put the key in the lock, all the while watching for a lurking patrolman.

"Heaven help us all," Lucie whispered, opening Lukas' cell door.

They found Lukas laying back in a rather comfortable bed, feet kicked up on the wall. Sophie rushed to his side. "Did they hurt you?"

Lukas pulled Sophie into a short, tight hug. "No," he answered grimly. "They just left me here. I've just composed the first stanza in my newest epic while I waited. It details the tragic sorrow and awesome revenge of a wrongly jailed musician. I was still deciding the ration of bloodshed to romance—surely this hero deserves a lady's favor in reward for saving an entire plagued town."

"Can you be serious?" Sophie stomped her foot.

"Me? What about you?" he whispered back. "What are you all doing here?"

"What does it look like?" Casper asked, looking reticent after Lucie's earlier questioning.

Sophie was annoyed on his behalf. *Do they think we're useless?*

"Gather what you need," Lucie said. "The patrolmen think you're to be questioned by the Council."

"The patrolmen think the Council sent you and Casper to fetch me?" Lukas asked Sophie incredulously.

"No, they think the Council sent me," Lucie said. "Now move."

"I half expected to find you trying to unlock that door yourself." Casper spoke quietly as Lukas gathered his hat and the traveling sack with his pipes. "You haven't figured out how to charm a lock open yet?"

"Give me time," Lukas said with a grin and a wink.

Lucie's impatient whisper was low and piercing. "Come on!"

After a particularly terrifying trip back to Casper's house, Lukas was met with a different interrogation altogether.

"What did you expect to happen, after a display of power like that?" Clare growled at the newly freed bard. "Of course you became the prime suspect. You can control rats!"

"This is all nonsense." Helena interrupted her. "He clearly didn't stab anyone. As if that mortal blade could kill a Faerie."

"Someone has framed Lukas, and they have done a fine job of it," Nic agreed. "Even if it means ignoring good sense."

"Yes, the Council is mistaken about many things," Clare admitted. "But you must have done something to make Aunt Aggie distrust you. And it's not like you've been totally forthcoming with all of us."

"I have *never* lied to you," Lukas insisted, stung at her distrust.

Clare narrowed her brown eyes.

"About anything important," he amended.

She raised a single dark eyebrow.

"Important to you, anyway," he amended again, this time with both hands tangled in his black hair.

"What are they arguing about now?" he heard Sophie whisper to Cas.

"I doubt either of them really knows," he responded with a

weary shrug. "And we need to get him out of here before anyone notices he's gone."

"Would you both sit down and listen to me." Lucie was irritated enough to raise her voice, and that got everyone's attention. "I know Lukas didn't kill that horrible little man. I did."

"What?!" Clare shrieked. Lucie just looked at her miserably.

Sophie moved from Lukas's side, eyes narrowed on the blonde girl. "I knew I remembered you from somewhere. I saw you with a blade the day I came into town!"

Lukas watched Lucie shudder and fold in on herself.

"You don't understand. Katherine promised she'd help my mother." Lucie tucked her chin, blue eyes glittering with tears. "Mend her mind. All I had to do was stab that *auslander*."

"My mother?" Sophie shrieked this time, rising to her feet. "What could she possibly do?"

"I don't know, exactly. But she *promised* she had a way." Lucie's tears were coming down fast now. Clare and Casper huddled around her in concern, while Nic remained apart, cold and impassive. "For years, ever since my brother died, she's been crazed, insisting that it wasn't her Wilhelm, someone had taken her son, and this child was an abomination."

"At first, she just thought he was ill. And it's true, he stopped thriving, his pallor was pale, and he seemed lethargic." Lucie's gaze was far from the room they were in. "And then she began looking at him sideways, with one eye and then the other. And she said she saw horrible things. With her right eye saw a chubby, happy newborn. But with the left ... she claimed he was dead, the flesh peeling from his face and black, dead eyes. He would eat or laugh, and she saw only a swollen purple tongue in his little head. She was crazed with fear and disgust."

Lukas saw Clare flinch at Lucie's words, then put a careful hand on Lucie's stooped shoulder, bringing her out of the memory and back into the firelit kitchen with them.

"And that's when everything went terribly wrong. Wilhelm didn't just die, Clare." Tears fell from Lucie's eyes, and she wiped them away impatiently. "Mother killed him. And Rachel helped her."

"She did *what?*" Lukas bolted upright at her words, anger making his voice shake. "My mother is not a killer. You're wrong."

Lucie looked up, clear-eyed and steady. "They did not set out to kill anyone, I know. But my mother went to her sister for help. And now my brother is gone."

Lukas felt the blood drain from his face at her words. *Sister. Lucie's my cousin. And the murderer.*

"I am not so sure that whatever your mother was caring for was her son at all," Helena interrupted from a chair at the other side of the room, thoughtful. "I have long heard tales of children carried off, sickly creatures left in their stead. It may be that your brother had been gone for much longer than anyone realized. And both Margarethe and Rachel would have known the signs."

"Margarethe's mind must have been shattered with the guilt and the grief of losing her son. There's only so much my mother's skills can do," Lukas said, running a shaky hand down his face.

Maybe taking her son away from the madness of Hameln isn't the worst that a mother could do, he realized.

"After a while, her perception shattered, too," Helena continued. "One eye sees life as the Council commands us. The other sees the rotten core of the Fae pact."

"The Council!" Lucie suddenly stood up, horrified. "They're meeting the Erlking in the woods. We must go if we're to know what they're planning. Immediately."

22

They headed to the wild woods, where the beasts and the outlaws and the truly desperate of Lower Saxony converged. It was the only place that belonged to everyone, and therefore no one at all. Under a furry coat of ice, Sophie imagined the trees were living beasts standing guard with hidden, patient eyes. She shivered from the cold and their heavy gaze.

The winter chill was strong, with weeks to go before spring broke through the icy grip that had claimed the region. After months of bitter cold, the trees and rocks around the town had been covered in a deep layer of hoar frost, making everything look bigger and more menacing in its icy armor.

Sophie looked around anxiously, still unused to the sounds of the wild and the unseen creatures that moved in the dark all around them.

"You're nervous."

At the back of the line led by Lucie, Sophie found that Nic had sidled up beside her as they moved quickly, quietly through the trees. Startled, she pulled her chin up to meet his gaze. "This is hardly the first time I've been in the woods."

"No...it's good. That the forests can still make you ... nervous, I mean." Nic stumbled with his words a bit, looking down at his hand wrapped around the pommel of his sheathed sword. It was another nervous tic he shared with Casper, she noticed. And somehow it helped calm her own nerves.

At her silence, he continued, looking up and through the shadowy gloom around them that was punctuated only by naked, white trees. "It means that when all this is over, you still believe that you have a safe place to go home to," he said. "It's a good thing."

Sophie thought back to Everstein Castle, filled with family and comfort, all of her books and belongings, and the servants she'd known her whole life. Home. It wasn't exciting, in fact it was downright stifling, but it was hers.

And much more than any of the rest of them could expect to have when they returned to Hameln, she realized glumly.

"Yes." She met his eyes with a growing determination to protect this new group of friends she had found for herself. She would not abandon any of her people, least of all those who had stood by her during this nightmare. "Let's make sure we all have safe homes to go back to."

Lucie stopped them all, a hand in the air to stop both their steps and their mouths. It seems they had arrived.

Sophie recognized it. The Calvary. The clearing outside of town where Hameln's most despicable criminals met their ignoble ends. She had heard many a story about the horrific deaths here, all overseen by the Council and witnessed by the silent woods.

The Council that was here already, just as Lucie had said they would be, a half circle gathered around a particularly sinister tree.

The nightmare tree had grasping, bare gray branches that reached out in all directions, heedless of the sun shining above it. No leaves grew upon it, but still it expanded, as flesh-colored mushrooms sprouted, stair stepping up its trunk. The children said it grew on bad dreams and curses they whispered into its gnarled bark, gaining strength from the fears they poured into it. The oversized bramble crouched at the edge of the clearing, somehow reaching both low to the ground and high through the canopy at once.

She was surprised, of course, to see those skeletal branches twist around. No tree should move like this, but if any would …

As the branches settled around the dark low trunk, Sophie realized with creeping horror they'd formed a dour wooden throne, fit for a demented king. And that's when another nightmare emerged out of the encroaching mist.

Is that the Erlking?

Sophie stifled a gasp, reaching out instinctively for Nic's tense arm for comfort. She tore her eyes from the boogeyman in front of her to focus on his face, hoping for reassurance. Instead, his forehead was beaded with sweat and his eyes burned with hatred.

"Clare. Clare, look at me." Sophie saw Lucie take both of her friend's hands, her tight grip forcing Clare to focus on Lucie's unnaturally pale face, her dark eyes glittering with fear. "Do you trust me?"

"Of course, Luce. But what are we doing here? You hate the Calvary," Clare said.

"Just …" Lucie's eyes seemed to spy something that hardened her resolve. "Be still. All of you. Don't come any closer, no matter what you see."

"Lukas?" Helena's voice was low and firm, with nothing of the panic Sophie felt coming off Nic in waves. "Play something to soothe and distract. We must not be seen if we're to learn anything."

Lukas hesitated before giving Lucie a short, reassuring smile and played a few soft notes that sounded a soft evening breeze, carrying lonely birdsong and rustling pine needles to Sophie's ears.

Sophie watched, aghast, as Lucie squared her shoulders before leaving the thick evergreen underbrush where they were hidden and walked into the clearing. *What is she doing?*

She was soon joined by a half dozen others.

Sophie recognized most of those present: Lucie's father,

Wilhelm; Aunt Agathe; her own mother. And none of them looked surprised at the presence of the Erlking. Cloaked in gloom and silence, with a bone crown atop his head, Sophie felt an unnatural weakness in her limbs, and she was grateful she hadn't let go of Nic.

She was even more grateful that he hadn't let go of his sword.

When the Erlking pulled back his hood, his two hands sparkling with countless rings made of bone and jewels, this time there was no double vision to shield the truth from anyone's eyes.

The man's face was half rotted off his skull.

What kind of creature was this? All the hair on her body stood on end, as if prepared to panic. Lukas' song stalled only a moment, and Sophie saw his shoulders rise in a fortifying breath before the music continued, quiet and peaceful.

The Erlking was pale in the gloom, but it was the sickly glow of bleached bone and writhing maggots on a corpse, not glittering starlight or even cold reflected moonlight. His face was covered in deep fissures that crisscrossed his skin, looking more like scars than wrinkles of age. Cloudy white eyes practically glowed in the darkness, surrounded by hair as dark as pitch, and when he opened his mouth to speak, it was filled with razor-sharp teeth.

Sophie's eyes grew wider, as if seeing more of his horrible visage would somehow make it look normal again—instead it was the opposite. Every new feature—his terrible eyes, with no eyelids to hide them; the bony ridge where his nose should be, terminating in two dark openings above a grim, lipless mouth—made her realize that there was nothing human about this dark figure.

"Everything is prepared?" the Erlking asked. His voice was smooth and hard, like glass.

Lucie's father stepped up. "Yes, yes. All of the children will be claimed at the Midsummer festival. The ones who were already spoken for go to their expected patrons. All others will go to you." He waved his hand rapidly, as if clearing away smoke and not the lives of more than 100 children.

"But what about my Margarethe? She stays with us? You get

your tithe, and we keep my wife." Wilhelm's voice wavered, and even Sophie could taste his eager desperation. *He must look like a fool to this monster of a man,* she thought.

"Of course," the Erlking responded. "Lucie did her part admirably, and Lukas is taking the blame. It is unfortunate that Katherine did not tell me of her plans sooner, but with such a generous tribute this year ..." The Erlking kept his eerie eyes on Lucie's father as his hand whipped out and grasped Katherine's arm. The Countess didn't even flinch.

But Sophie did. The Rat King's last words echoed in her mind: *the lady betrayer.* Her eyes ached with unshed tears.

My own Maman. Thank God Freddie isn't here to see this.

"Faerie is satisfied. Hameln remains true, and safe."

Sophie's thoughts swirled chaotically. *What had the Council—with Lucie's help—gained from sacrificing their own children? And what had* Maman *done?*

"We need to move. I don't know how much longer Lukas' music can disguise us." Helena's low, insistent words barely registered in her muddled brain. Sophie glanced over, and noticed the sweat beading on Lukas's dark, furrowed brow.

Sophie heard something else hammering quick and loud, so loud that everyone must hear it, before realizing it was her own heart. She scrambled into the relative comfort of the woods, head tilted up to catch her bearings and her breath.

She closed her eyes, for once, in this moment, not wanting to see, to understand, to remember.

23

Clare was lost, her ears thrumming with the shock and horror of the true Obolen. She followed Helena blindly, going over the Council's meeting again, and it always ended the same way: her aunt betraying her, the town sacrificing its children, her safe world completely destroyed. This morning they had saved the town—tonight they were fleeing it.

She tipped her face up, seeking air clear of loss and horror. Instead, she saw the skeletal branches of the now sinister woods, making her skin crawl as they reached up, as if attempting to hide the glittering stars from her view.

But there, through the branches: Polaris! Clare's guide light home. Just as Afi promised.

And that quickly, her thoughts snapped into place. *I know where we have to go. The one place even the stalwart Josef dared not go.*

"Come here," she whispered. Grabbing Lukas' belt and Casper's hand, she dragged them back toward the Weser River. "It's this way to the Grey Cottage, at least according to all of Wolfhart's stories."

It was a testament to their exhaustion that they went willingly enough toward whatever new destination she had planned. Lukas cut his eyes at her and Casper merely grunted. Even Helena and Nic followed wordlessly after only a brief hesitation.

Surprisingly, Clare found that Lukas was soon leading the way, eagerly even.

They'd been walking for what felt like hours, though the stars had barely moved in the sky. And before too long, a dilapidated cottage came into view.

Oh, no.

The mud walls were caving in, and it looked like animals had poached the straw, small sticks and pebbles helping to hold up the walls for their own nests.

"This is the Grey Cottage?" she asked in dismay.

There was a great hole where a chimney used to be, with mere ashes to mark where she could only assume the warm hearth once was. The thatched roof gave way to a wizened pine tree growing up through it, the only life that cottage had housed for generations.

We need to get as far away from this place as possible.

They came all this way for safety, to regroup, make a plan. And clearly Lukas was insane.

"Lukas, look at me." Clare tried to get his attention gently, seeing the warm smile on his face as she stepped beside him. He was overjoyed to see this broken-down wreck. "There has to be some- where else we can go."

He turned to face her, confusion furrowing his high brow. Then his green eyes lit with mirth. "Oh, no, Clare. All is well. Take my hand." He grabbed her, then reached out for Casper, as well. Just like that, the decrepit wooden shack was gone. Before her was an impressive square stone keep, thirty feet high and seemingly much older than the trees that surrounded it.

Clare squeezed Lukas' hand sharply as her head turned up to take in the full stature of the Grey Cottage. A steep staircase led to an arched wooden doorway, which itself was flanked by two narrow towers. Gleaming windows were all that interrupted the smooth, shining grey stonework. And now the only thing glowering at her were the small gargoyles perched on the parapets. It was dazzling.

"How … ?" Clare started to speak and then stopped, dizzy with relief.

Clare glanced back at Sophie, and the younger girl's shocked smile sweet after the day's horrors. It seemed that Helena had opened the young noblewoman's eyes to the true Cottage, as well.

"It's just a glamour," Lukas explained, as if it were the most natural thing in the world. "My father may be absent, but he cared enough—or had money enough—to make sure we were safe in the woods."

Before Sophie could get, what Clare assumed would be, dozens of questions past her lips, the large keep door opened, and all but Lukas and Helena were forced to shield their eyes from the unexpectedly bright light within.

"Lukas! You're home!" a woman's voice rang out, all joy and relief. Clearly, this was his mother, Rachel. The witch of the Grey Cottage. Lit from behind, Clare could just make out a halo of dark curls around her head.

"And who is that with you? More strays who need my help, I suppose?" The cheer in her voice eased the sting of her words.

Yes, Clare realized. *A stray band of children running from a cursed town.*

Rachel gasped. "Esma? You've returned? After all these years?"

"No …" Clare answered softly. "I'm … her granddaughter."

Rachel quickly hustled the exhausted group through the doors of the suddenly magnificent Grey Cottage. Once inside, Clare practically wept at the feeling of warmth and safety.

She turned an anxious eye on Lukas' mother, and easily discerned the woman's resemblance to her beautiful sister, Margarethe.

Rachel's clear grey eyes took in the scene before her calmly. She pulled her dark, curly hair back from her face with one hand while the other brushed over the chatelaine around her waist, an almost practiced gesture.

There were many familiar objects hanging at her hip from the well-made silver chain over her simple brown dress: a pair of shears, tongs, a small pouch, a ring of keys—along with a few others Clare could not identify with a quick glance. Hurried footsteps and a fluttering dress drew Clare's eye.

Beside Rachel, the oldest woman Clare had ever seen began to fret over Lukas.

"Do you know how long it's been since we had word from you?" the ancient woman exclaimed over him, rubbing the smudges on his face. "And now you come back, dirty and your tunic in tatters. What mess did you get into now?"

"I'm fine, Madge," Lukas responded with a soft smile.

"Kane, heat water on the hearth and gather bandages," the crone called out to the kitchen. "And check the storeroom for provisions for dinner. We've been saving that venison haunch for a reason."

She finally deigned to glance at the rest of the children. "You all look like you haven't had a good meal in your lives."

"Hush, Madge," Lukas chided her, grabbing her gnarled hands and kissing the palms to stop their further assault on his person. "We needed a safe place to land, not a giant pot of stew."

Her displeasure filled the room until she was suddenly much taller than her small frame had first suggested. It seemed that the only thing that outnumbered the wrinkles on her face were the freckles dotting her pale skin, which did nothing to soften her piercing glare. At Lukas' blanch, Clare warmed to Madge immediately.

"Not that I'm going to turn down a warm meal," he continued, releasing her hands with an apologetic grin. "Carry on, Kane!" he called out to the unseen person behind her.

Rachel chuckled fondly, stepping around Madge in order to

wrap Lukas up in a warm embrace. "It's good to have you home, Luke. No matter the trouble you've dragged in with you."

"The Grey Cottage is a sanctuary for the downtrodden," Madge said, turning her careful, probing eye on the rest of them. She took in their stunned expressions before nodding stiffly to herself. "Food, bath, and bed for all of you. Then I'll listen to the nonsense you've gotten up to."

Clare caught Lukas by the shoulder in a strong, desperate grip as Madge herded them all up the wide, winding stairs from the foyer. "Lukas, are you sure we're safe here? You swore you'd protect Sophie and my brother."

"No one can harm us within these walls, you have my word," Lukas assured her.

"Especially not Elisabeth's children," Rachel added. "Not under my roof."

The witch of the Grey Cottage knows my mother, my grand-mother, and exactly who I am.

A slight boy who could only be Kane appeared in the doorway at the end of the foyer that they had yet to move beyond. "Everything is ready, Madge," he said, his voice low and weak. As they were ushered by, Clare noticed his fever-bright eyes over flushed cheeks. With a closer look, she realized the young boy could be no more than 10, though his gaunt cheeks aged him another five years. "Are you …"

"Kane is fine," Madge interrupted. "Back to your room, boy. We have an early day ahead of us. Let's get you all fed and to bed." Clare watched him obey without another word, and felt a slight ache in her chest at his resignation. But a quick glance at Lukas showed her he was unconcerned, at least.

Clare herded the others to follow the old woman into the kitchen, attempting to give Lukas a moment alone with his mother. She practically melted in front of the cheerful fire, quickly grabbing the chair closest to its warmth.

They all sat around the oversized kitchen table while Madge

bustled around preparing the meal. As Madge lifted the full cauldron, her body was seized by a quaking cough. But before Clare could move to intervene, the pot was over the fire and Madge was upright again, either by magic or force of will.

"Maybe you should sit down," Clare offered. "Perhaps I could help you with a few of the more strenuous tasks tonight, since Rachel is engaged."

"That is a kind offer, Clare, and I am happy to accept your company and your aid," Madge answered, easing into a kitchen chair.

"Have you been ill long?" Clare asked, as she picked up the knife and sliced the potatoes on the table. Sophie joined her, organizing the herbs in a manner that showed exactly how little experience she had in a kitchen.

"This old thing?" Madge asked, thumping her chest. "Oh, I've had it forever. Old age brings other unpleasantness, believe you me. I'm much stronger than I look, youngling."

Clare looked at her incredulously, but remained quiet, letting the familiar sounds of cooking fill the air instead. The Erlking's pale visage suddenly intruded in her mind's eye, and she shook her head in a daze.

Clare looked closely at the old woman, busy in her work. Madge reminded her of the river driftwood she collected when she was young: Soft and smooth to the touch, bleached in the sun, and tough as rocks.

Clare found that she liked Madge.

As much as Lukas had insisted they weren't hungry, an hour later Clare descended on the venison stew as soon as the bowl was placed in her hands. It was perfect: the fragrant meat was cooked until tender, and the peppery sweet taste of parsnips and carrots melted on her tongue.

"It's nice to see a familiar face, even if it belongs to a stranger." Rachel smiled warmly at Clare. "I was just so shocked to see any resemblance to someone I loved so dearly And you never even met your grandmother, Esma, did you?"

Clare shook her head silently, making quick work of clearing her place at the table, eyeing the others for a reaction to this small speech, but they were all busy filling their own stomachs.

Her family's joys and sorrows were hers, and she guarded them jealously. Clare lost her parents when she was only five years old, and too often listening to others speak about them felt like they were stealing them away from her, or as if they weren't hers to begin with. She clung to her memories, worried that talking about them would somehow dilute or stain them.

Too often, speaking about her lost family still felt like prodding an open wound. She couldn't bear to speak of them with a stranger.

No matter how curious I am.

The next day, Clare woke from her borrowed wooden bed easy and warm to comfortably familiar sounds: Casper's uneven gait and absentminded humming, snatches of a half-formed melody from Lukas' flute, and Sophie's uninterrupted stream of questions.

"How does anyone find you out here? And the glamour—do they see it? What if they return, does it still work if you know the house is glamoured?"

She stayed tucked between the feather mattress and woolen blanket, her eyes closed, stretching her muscles lazily, letting herself pretend for a moment that everything was normal, that her entire life hadn't been upended.

Then she let go of the fantasy, opening her eyes to the completely unfamiliar place.

The woods. The Erlking. And her aunt—the entire Council— aiding him.

And yet, beyond the horror, she felt the undeniable thrill of adventure, a challenge, a purpose to her life that had been missing until this hidden spectre was finally revealed. Followed closely by the now-familiar guilt of wanting more than being the unwanted blacksmith in a stifling town.

Clare swallowed hard, attempting to push away those dark thoughts, and dressed and prepared for the world beyond the bedroom door. A world full of the unknown, and all the good and bad that came with it.

When she finally did join the others in the kitchen, it was bustling and bright. Rachel was the energetic center that seemed to hold them all, steady and clear-eyed.

At the moment, she was organizing the herbs that took up most of the tabletop, while Sophie and Casper peppered her with questions about her preparations.

"Is there a specific order in which you add the ingredients to make it effective?" Casper asked, leaning over a satchel Rachel was preparing and sniffing cautiously.

"Or an incantation?" Sophie asked eagerly.

Rachel laughed. "No spells. I'm just timing the blanching process. If it is boiled too long, the medicines leach out."

Cas and Sophie nodded in unison, eyes shining. Lukas just smiled indulgently at the scene from the corner, plucking absently at a well-worn lyre.

"Oh, good morning, Clare!" Rachel called out, voice like a bell. "It's astonishing, really. You really are a nearly perfect double of Esma."

Clare startled at her words, then smiled in disbelief.

"My grandmother? The gorgeous woman my Afi spent his life waiting for?" she finally asked.

"Yes, she was a beautiful woman. And how Afi doted on her." Rachel sighed, her head tilted as she recalled the memories. "She always threatened that she'd leave him some day, find a country that the sun had not forsaken."

Clare smiled with her, remembering how her Afi had always bundled her up tight as the days got shorter and the cold nights longer.

"He blamed himself, I know," Rachel continued. "One last voyage before settling down for good, somewhere warm for Esma. Hameln held so much promise for your family, then."

"He always said it was mermaids that carried her off. In the Weser River," Casper volunteered softly, and Clare remembered that, the very first tall tale her Afi ever told her. It was also the one he told most often, as if repeating it would help explain his wife's inexplicable disappearance.

Rachel hummed agreeably. "We all handle the loss of our loved ones in different ways. He needed that hope that he would see her again someday. It's not a bad way to live, though it isn't real."

"I'm not so sure," Clare said, now sitting at the empty table. "Hope is wonderful, if it gives your life purpose. But Afi ... some days he would wake up raving about how beautiful my grandmother was in the river's reflected moonlight, how they talked for hours the night before at the banks of the Weser, and she promised they would be together forever, if only he would join her there."

Clare looked up to see Rachel's concerned face before continuing. "That wasn't hope. That was delusion, and it made him half-mad with grief and guilt. During those episodes, he always felt he was choosing between his family and his love. And that either choice was wrong. After he got sick, he went to die at the river. I think he just wanted the guilt to stop."

Rachel stopped in her work to sit beside her carefully and gathered Clare's hands in her own. "Your Afi loved you fiercely. And nothing short of death would have torn him from you. That devotion is the most precious gift he gave his family. And Clare, no matter who you look like, something tells me you will *always* take after your Afi."

Clare felt the warmth of that statement fill her chest, proud and sad at once.

"Now," Rachel continued, standing up again briskly. "Let's get you breakfast."

At that moment, Madge's bickering voice was heard from the foyer.

"Come in, come in, and don't bring the cold with you," Madge fussed. "No, no, I've got the door, just tend to your mother."

"Thank you, mistress," Lucie's low voice answered.

24

Clare hurried to the foyer, where she saw Lucie gripping her mother with one arm and holding her own head in the other.

"Luce?" Clare called out. "Are you well?"

"Clare! Thank goodness, you're safe," Lucie answered, relief flooding her pale, stricken face. "I needed to get mother out. You were all gone, and I didn't know where else to go."

Rachel moved forward, taking Margarethe by both shoulders, sorrow in her eyes.

"My dearest Maggie," Rachel whispered up into Margarethe's wane face. The hard years showed there: wisps of grey at her temples and wrinkles at her eyes seemed to smudge her appearance, like a kerchief washed too many times. "Sister, what have they done to you?"

"Come in, if you're coming," Madge interjected grumpily. "You can talk and eat just as well sitting down by the fire, I'd imagine."

"Thank you for your hospitality," Lucie said, anxious and stiff, as Madge herded them all into an airy drawing room with seats enough for all of them. "I … I wasn't sure we would be welcome."

"You are family," Rachel answered firmly. "It is no trouble at all, and I am so happy you came here for comfort."

After all, Rachel and Margarethe were sisters. The similarities were there, if you looked beyond Margarethe's manic, gleaming eyes and Rachel's careworn face.

"Father agreed that the house was far too stressful an environment anymore, what with the Council investigating Lukas' disappearance," Lucie went on, her breath thready and voice strained, as she led her mother to an empty chair. Margarethe was blissfully compliant. "I could not leave her there. Who knows what the Erlking will do next to punish Hameln."

"So he has made his move against Hameln," Rachel breathed, dropping to her knees beside her sister. "It is what we've feared for years now. He's no longer content with fresh blood every ten years. The war must've turned badly for him. And if so…this is exactly where you and Margarethe need to be, if we are to stop him from consolidating his power."

"I'm not sure what good a crazy woman can provide in this war," Lukas interrupted, almost apologetically. "Though I am pleased that she is safe."

"Margarethe did not go mad. She adapted," Rachel corrected him sharply. "If your world turns upside down, what can you do but stand on your head?"

Lukas looked almost ashamed, but Rachel waved away whatever his next words would be. "Madge, let's take my sister to a room. She has had a long journey."

Clare watched Lukas throw himself into a chair, the better to watch Lucie by the softly crackling fire.

Lucie had perched herself on the edge of the chair opposite, wringing her red fingers, either from the cold or nerves.

"I would like to start by apologizing to you. All of you," Lucie began.

"So it was you all along," Clare blazed back at her, all the doubts and pain from their fractured friendship boiling over. "You were the

Council's spy, the betrayer we were warned about. You helped keep the entire town in the dark while all of those children were sacrificed!"

"Oh, my darling friend." Lucie moved to embrace her, but the expression on Clare's face must have warned her away. Instead, Lucie held her arms up, palms out, approaching Clare as if she were a skittish horse. "Everyone already knows."

Clare paused. This was not the big confrontation she was expecting. "What?"

"The entire Council, the guilds, Aunt Aggie, Nicolaus, even your old hero Wolfhart … The Obolen, the choosing ceremony that takes away our best and brightest, this is the system that keeps Hameln the safe, prosperous town that we've all worked so hard to create." Lucie continued to speak in soft, soothing tones. "For you, for me, for everyone."

"Everyone … knows?" Clare repeated dully.

"Well, except for Father Stephen, the woman-hating old fool," Lucie said with a grim grin. "He thinks we're all speaking in Christian allegory every second of the blessed day. Just as well, he didn't grow up here. He doesn't understand our ways."

A bitter laugh stuck in Clare's throat. Her old nemesis, Father Stephen … the only innocent in Hameln?

"I don't believe you," Clare said slowly, distinctly. "And I am going to make sure that you and the Council never hurt another family again."

"I'm not in the business of hurting families," Lucie responded hotly. "Everything I did—for my father, for the Countess, for the Council—was meant to make life in Hameln better."

"You mean easier, for you," Clare rejoined.

"Easier for everyone," Lucie corrected her.

"Easier is not the same thing as better," Clare shot back.

"Do the people of Hameln go hungry? Do they worry about pirates or marauders, or even land disputes among distant nobles? No." Lucie's eyes blazed. "Because the system keeps us safe."

Clare sucked in a painful breath. "But not everyone, right Lucie? Not *my* family."

Lucie's gaze faltered, the righteous anger in her eyes fading into something softer, something sadder.

The others watched this volleying exchange in silence, until finally Rachel intervened. "Clare, Lucie is not the one you're actually angry with," she said firmly. "Remember your real enemy."

Clare stopped, closing her eyes and breathing in deeply. "Of course. The Erlking."

Helena cleared her throat, instantly commanding the attention of the room. "While we're admitting our secrets," she said evenly. "You should all know: the Erlking is my father."

Everyone, save Nic, stared. Clare suddenly felt too tired to react, and was quite glad to be sitting.

"That could be good news, right?" Sophie spoke up, finally. "Perhaps he can be reasoned with, if Helena can make him see our side? Mama always says that if you keep your opponent talking, they'll be too busy to attack you."

Helena looked unconvinced.

"I don't think that we can depend on him to treat Helena with the typical love of a father," Nic answered for her. "It's just as likely he'll force her to return home for a … reeducation, of sorts."

"Surely he has some human feelings?" Casper asked. "After all, he has been working with the town for hundreds of years."

"Do not confuse the Erlking's subtlety for mercy," Helena warned him. "He will not lie. But that does not mean he will not bend others to his purpose to have such promises shattered."

"As soon as he feels he is strong enough to crush his enemies, he will. You spoke of love earlier." At this, Helena looked over at Lucie, who suddenly looked shy at her attention. "Dominion is his only passion. For hundreds of years, as long as I've been alive, he's led a war to bend all of Faerie to his will. And he will allow nothing to threaten his plans."

Clare straightened her spine, anger overcoming the despair

she'd allowed herself to wallow in. She looked Helena straight in the eye. "What are you saying?"

"My father," Helena seemed to hesitate, as if thinking of him as such was new for her as well, or perhaps just too painful. "He won't stop. Ever. Which means someone needs to stop him."

"So that's what we'll do," Lucie answered, lifting her hand as if to place it on the elfin girl's hand, before instead bringing it up to pat down her own curls.

"What can we do?" Clare demanded.

"Anything we can," Lucie said, the sensible tone of her voice familiar and welcome to Clare's ears. "We cannot stop all the evil in the world, but we have to at least try to leave the world better than it was before."

"I never took you to be an optimist," Helena teased tonelessly.

"I'm not," Lucie shot back, smiling softly at Helena. She took a deep breath. "I've been selfish, thinking only about myself and my family. But not anymore. We're the only ones we can trust, so we have to fight back, for our families, our friends, ourselves."

"Oh, now your mother is threatened, you want to do something about it?" Clare snapped back at her oldest friend.

Lucie flinched, looking completely cowed. "Yes. Her and you. And Nic. And Casper. All the people I've let down, looking for a way to heal my mother at the expense of their lives. I owe you all so much, and the Countess didn't even keep her promise. It's time to fix some of the damage I've done."

"You're right," Clare said, standing. Hameln was her town, and she wouldn't let anyone hurt it, especially not her own family. "As usual. We can't fight each other, we have to fight *them*."

Lucie smiled up at her, and Clare felt the easy camaraderie slipping back into place between them.

"But we definitely need backup, too," Clare continued. "So let's put our heads together and figure this out. Quickly."

"So the question is," Sophie began eagerly. "Who is powerful enough to stop the Erlking? Or at least to convince the Council that he can be stopped?"

"The Wolfhart?" Casper ventured.

"No." Lukas was firm. "He has the will, but not the strength. He's beholden to the nobles, and breaking his vows to them … he'd lose much of the power he has."

"I can only think of one man who could help, though I don't know if he will," Nic said, turning his attention to Helena. "Count Ebernberg."

Helena's face was grim. "That particular option comes with its own dangers," she said. "But he might just be the only one we have, for Faerie *and* Hameln."

"I say we pay both men a visit," Sophie decided with a firm nod. "We don't have time to waste traveling all around Lower Saxony. And I think we need to start by finding Wolfhart."

25

Late into the night, Sophie had found another corner, this time in the study, to continue her missive to her brother while the others fought over where would be best to begin their search for Wolfhart. She had so much to process, so much to share with Freddie.

If seeing the monster her mother and the rest of the Council was in league with hadn't already left Sophie shocked speechless, the sudden appearance of a castle in the middle of the woods did. While the Grey Cottage wasn't impressive compared to her own home, its sudden appearance in the middle of the woods certainly was.

She had plenty of questions: Whose spell hid the castle? For what reason? How was it revealed to them? And how did anyone in need ever find it in the first place?

And so, before long, Sophie was in the corner of the kitchen, dinner hastily inhaled, with quill and paper in hand, attempting to record every terrifying moment, until Lukas and Casper finally coaxed her into a spare, comfortable bed to sleep.

. . .

As soon as she woke, she was back to her journal. She looked up from her list of questions and through the room. A beam of sunlight cut through it, creating a spotlight of dancing dust motes. There was some quality to the light—the angle, perhaps, or its placement—that suddenly brought up a swirl of images, scents, and sounds that overwhelmed her senses.

She closed her eyes, and she was no longer in the study, but instead inside a kitchen filled with dried, hanging herbs, various multicolored bottles, and afternoon sunlight. Quiet laughter caught her ear, and the steady grind of a practiced hand creating a poultice with mortar and pestle. She heard someone speaking, but she couldn't quite comprehend the words, as if the conversation was spoken in a lilting, unknown language.

Sophie struggled to focus, straining her ears, willing her mind to understand …

Seven-year-old Sophie and her friend Lukas were seated cross-legged on the stable floor together when Wolfhart found them, Lukas humming a tune only he knew before blowing experimentally into his silver pipes to test the new melody, as his favorite audience of one, Sophie, looked on.

He clearly took no pleasure in interrupting the boy's process, which Sophie always saw as a kind of inexplicable magic inspiring joy or sorrow, even fear, as the song dictated.

But they all knew he took even less pleasure in disappointing the boy's mother.

"Your mother's looking for you, young man." Wolfhart's voice was fond, if gruff. Lukas took to daydreaming like a duck to water. While Sophie started at his familiar voice, as if caught, Lukas' dark face simply smiled up at him, clearly unrepentant at shirking his duties.

Wolfhart held his arms out, steadying both Sophie and Lukas as they scrambled up from the dusty floor. "Up you get," Wolfhart groused, trying and failing to hide the smile on his face. "She was asking about the eggs you promised to fetch a few hours ago?"

Lukas' answering grin was just sorry enough to make most people forget he never actually apologized. "Right! The eggs. I think I left those—"

"Right where the hens laid them?" Wolfhart filled in.

Lukas' ducked head and jaunty wave were all the answer he would get before the boy ran to the coop, his latest magical tune hanging in the air like the sweet scent of honeysuckle on a warm summer day.

Sophie closed her eyes and breathed it in.

"I distracted him," she began, eager to defend her friend. "He really was on his way to fetch the eggs."

Wolfhart smiled down at her before grabbing her up and hoisting her on his back as she shrieked delightedly. At times like this, it was hard to believe this bear of a man was normally tasked with protecting all of Lower Saxony from super-natural threats of all kinds. "Likely story, sprite," he said. "Let's go find that cake Rachel is hiding in the house, eh?"

Sophie shrieked happily as Wolfhart swung her up and over his shoulders, carrying her back toward the house.

The next thing Sophie knew, she was in a soft bed, with soothing music and more low voices. But these, at least, she immediately recognized. Lukas and his mother were positioned like sentries over her.

" … certain you said nothing of her time here?"

"Not when it was so clear she had no idea who I was," Lukas said, from somewhere to her left. The music continued soft and sweet, though she could hear the tension in his voice.

"And she didn't ask about your family? Or how it may be connected to hers?" Rachel continued, hovering on her right side.

"Of course, I know about the rumors." Lukas seemed too tired to be angry. "I'm sure others did, as well. But I never mentioned the Countess, or how she had been coming to visit the Grey Cottage for as long as I could remember."

Sophie sat up in bed, Lukas' words cutting through her lethargy and filling her with uneasy confusion. Somehow, at some time, Sophie had been in the Grey Cottage before.

"Yes! I came here as a child. Mother said we were visiting a wise woman, who would help with Papa's work. How … how did I forget all that?"

The music stopped. She found Lukas seated on the floor beside her, while Rachel sat on the bed with a tray full of instruments and herbal concoctions.

Lukas, eyes wide, nodded. His relief at her recovery, and of one less secret to keep, was palpable. "It was so many years ago. Katherine would bring you when you were younger, and Mother told me to entertain you. But nothing made you happier than Wolfhart's stories. We had that in common, before Katherine stopped bringing you along. I guess she didn't want you to ask too many questions."

"She must have … stolen my memories somehow. Maybe through one of her experiments. Or a curse, like Hameln's?" Her brain was fitting memories and emotions into slots long kept empty: enjoying Madge's apple pastries under the table with Lukas while their mothers pored over documents above them; piggyback rides and tall tales from Wolfhart; falling asleep to a melody Lukas was composing in the library.

"I wonder what else I've learned that she's taken from me?"

"She's not the only one who has kept secrets from all of you." Rachel's voice sounded behind them. "I think it's time we all cleared the air." She beckoned Lukas to follow her into the kitchen. "But hard news usually goes down easier with a good meal."

Lukas stood, coming to Sophie's side. "Can you get up? Or would you rather eat here?"

Sophie closed her eyes for just a moment. But she had spent enough time in the dark. Opening them again, she pushed the covers off, ready to move. "I can stand. And I think the truth will make me feel better than any medicine your mother could give me."

And, of course, Sophie had many questions.

"You mean you could *see* the magic in Hameln? This curse that

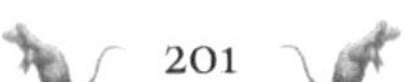

binds everyone to secrecy?" Sophie asked, anger making her more peevish. "What does that mean? What did you see exactly?"

"It was like a spidery gauze wrapped around your eyes." Lukas narrowed his gaze on her, and she lifted her hand as if to physically wipe the binding from her face. "On yours and Clare's and Casper's. But it's gone now."

"It's all part of the pact," Rachel explained. "It's not exactly a curse on the children themselves, just a way to protect them from the Fae, bind their sight until they're old enough to understand how the town works. Most people never see the supernatural, or if they do it's just another opportunity to trick the mortal. But in Hameln … mortals and Faerie creatures mix together every day, for better or worse."

She looked at Lukas now, love and concern furrowing his brow. "Hameln's folk have mingled with Faerie for centuries, long before the town became another battleground for the Erlking. He cultivated the families, claimed to protect their interests, and then began harvesting the children for his own ends. And if the children knew, if they could see the horrors before they were old enough to take part in that oath … well, the Erlking made sure that wouldn't happen."

"You said you saw the curse on me and Casper. But not Lucie?" Clare's voice was strained.

"No," Lukas confirmed, looking uncomfortable. "Instead, her mouth was bound, like nearly every adult in town."

"She must have taken the oath already," Rachel explained. "Or my poor niece had just seen so much so soon, they felt she needed the binding before she came of age."

"So she's known, this whole time. And she didn't tell me." Sophie's heart fell again at Clare's heartbreak.

"She *couldn't* tell you, Clare. That's what we're trying to explain." Rachel's voice was soothing, and suddenly Sophie understood why so many had come to this woman for help over the years. "She had no choice, if she wanted to protect everyone she loves. Once you know how the town works, the binding prevents you from speaking of it. The consequences are … well, you've seen my sister. It's a terrible responsibility to place on such a young girl."

"But that doesn't explain my memories," Sophie said, desperate to understand. "Why couldn't I remember you and Lukas until I came here?"

"I don't know what Katherine did, Sophie." Rachel sank to the empty chair beside her at the kitchen table. "She stopped bringing you to us years ago, and I assume she had the Erlking ensure you wouldn't remember us. But I don't know what happened to make her take such an extreme step."

"And I missed you." Lukas' smile was shy now. "You were the closest I ever had to a real friend all those years. I worried about you when you stopped visiting, wondered what we did wrong …"

"The Erlking's magic has no power here," Rachel interrupted. "Katherine must have known that and kept you away so that you would remain enchanted. It's why Margarethe and Lucie never came to us, as well. The Grey Cottage is not literally a secret; too many have come for aid over the years. It's simply hidden from those who would do harm to any beneath its roof. And disguised to those who do not need to know."

Sophie felt something loosen and expand in her chest. "That means my mother wouldn't harm you. She must be a victim, just like Luce."

Maman isn't evil. She clung to the fact like the last patch of solid earth in a bog of mysteries and secrets. Her mother meant no harm. Casper met her gaze with a friendly smile.

"So now we all know what we're up against, what this curse really is: a way to control all of us until we're bound by the pact and powerless to help ourselves," Casper said. "What do we do now?"

"I've been thinking about that. Since we've got a royal Fae here." Lukas spoke almost casually. "From Faerie's perspective, what exactly does the Obolen do? Are the initiates some sort of sin offering?"

"Sin?" Helena huffed delicately. "What use do we have of sin? Human nature is just that—natural. What we have is more of a mutually beneficial agreement. The Erlking offers protection: bountiful harvests, freedom from illness, mild weather. And Hameln offers Faerie the best of her people. As long as the oath is kept."

"A payment, you mean?" Lukas asked.

Helena bowed her head in silent assent.

"That does not make me feel better," Lukas said grimly, as he began to pace the room. "And that means we have to figure out how to end it altogether. Or at least come up with a better option for that payment."

"Wait, if you're a princess…" Lukas pointed one slender finger at Sophie. "And you're a princess…" he swung himself and his finger around to Helena. "That means we've got two princesses? I feel like there's got to be some kind of advantage here."

"If you are considering a hostage situation …" Helena said.

Lukas puffed up, affronted. "I would never!"

"… I have already determined the odds of success are low," Helena continued. "My father will not give up power for me, and I doubt he will allow the Countess to derail his plans, even if she wished to."

Lukas blinked twice before responding. "I was thinking more along the lines of sabotaging their plans, or turning a particularly stupid ally?"

"Those ideas do have merit," Helena conceded. "Perhaps that weaselly businessman Pieter would reveal the Council's latest plot with the right persuasion."

"You are one scary princess," Lukas said.

"Thank you." Helena really did seem pleased. "But what we really need is your mortal champion, the Wolfhart. Wherever he may be."

❋

Hours later, they had talked themselves into a quiet funk.

While the others prepared the evening meal, Sophie was left to recuperate. Alone again in the study she digested not only the alarming news of the conspiracy, but the myriad memories that were settling messily into her brain. And there were quite a few that were frightening, disorienting, or just plain confusing.

Like the jumbled memories of a dark, chilly, cavernous space filled with the cries of others, low, terrible moans, and pitiful tears.

A girl dressed as an Everstein maid reaching out to her, her hand with too many joints on each spindly finger that ended in bloody nails raking the air before her face. Tears streamed down her own face, silent and unending. "I'm so sorry," she gasped into the dark. "God's teeth, I didn't know. I didn't know …"

Sophie came back to herself, huddled into a protective ball in the library, rocking her head back and forth as if she could sort out the new and nightmarish thoughts with a good shake. Were these true memories? Or were these nightmares she'd been spared through magic?

Caught in her own hideous thoughts, Sophie hadn't noticed Nic enter the library, or even when he settled close by, at her feet. It was only his low, rumbling voice that finally penetrated her agonies.

"… despite what it feels like, you're not losing your mind, princess. Just breathe," he said, not unkindly. "This is all knowledge you've always had. Now you actually remember it."

"I wish I didn't," she answered hotly. "I wish … I wish I knew what to do with these thoughts, these *experiences*. If I can believe them."

"I know a little something about not being able to trust your own memories." Nic's normally inviting smile was replaced by the grim set of his mouth. "Questioning your eyes, your thoughts …"

Sophie held her knees tight to her chest, as if she could keep her body from flying apart.

"With all those experiences and feelings just stripped from me until now, how can I trust my feelings on anything?" Sophie whispered. "These memories are filling in blanks of time I didn't realize I was missing in the first place. But what if it never makes sense?"

The fire crackled in the silence that followed.

"I wish Freddie were here," she mumbled to the ground.

"You're not alone, now or ever," he said, answering a question she hadn't actually asked. Then again, maybe she had.

"But … I have to go back. To Hameln. Alone, preferably," he explained quietly. "We can't just wait around for the Wolfhart, and I don't need Casper or Clare seeing my and Helena's work. It can be … brutal."

She looked up sharply, but he was staring deeply into the fire again.

"To protect everyone?" she asked, recognizing how quickly the situation could deteriorate in the little town. They weren't the only ones from Hameln who knew the truth, but they seemed to be the only ones who wanted to do something to stop the Council. *Someone has to help the children.*

"It's my duty as a member of Berchtold's Wild Hunt to stop Faerie from interfering in the mortal world, to protect the people I can. Something tells me you can understand a little of that," he answered. "Just … don't tell Clare and Casper yet. They need a moment to breathe before I leave them again."

"Of course," Sophie answered, suddenly exhausted again. "We can protect them, too."

26

After speaking with Nic, Sophie realized it was time to get some answers about all of these memories rushing back into her head. What had Maman done? And how many more family secrets were there?

Was Lukas her brother? Could Papa betray her mother so basely and then abandon his own child completely? She couldn't even conceive of it.

Sophie finally found him in what she now remembered was a favorite hiding place from their childhood, high in the rafters of the lofted barn. Staring up at him quietly, she finally spoke.

"Are you my brother?"

Luke looked down at her sharply, as if he was surprised. He cocked his head to the side, considering before sliding down to sit beside her on a rough-hewn bench, though careful not to touch her. Perhaps he feared her rejection even now.

"I don't know," he finally said. "I have always hoped to be. I wanted to think Katherine had been kind enough to allow us to grow up together all those years. The one concession she could give me, since I could never really be an Everstein." Sophie stared at him. *I never thought about being the family he could want.*

"And there has never been a clue from your mother?" Now that she had forced herself to entertain the possibility, she fought to keep her voice calm, though her heart was racing. "She never speaks of your father, or their time together?"

Now his clear green eyes darkened, more like low-lying moss than the spring green she knew. "I know that they met at Castle Everstein. I know that your grandmother forced her to leave. And I know that—whoever he is—my father protects us even now with the powerful magic of the Grey Cottage."

"But my father doesn't believe in magic," Sophie said, grasping eagerly at this flaw in his reasoning. "He is a man of science, not a sorcerer."

"He dabbles in alchemy, does he not?"

"Yes, but—your flute," Sophie continued. "You said it was a gift from your father. My father cares for music as much as he does tales of chivalry. Which is to say, I've seen him asleep face down in his own dinnerplate whenever another noble knight attempted to impress him with his deeds of heroism."

"I told you, Sophie, I don't know," Lukas said. "A rich and powerful man could have many such instruments at his disposal, even if he chooses not to believe in them."

Now he caught her hands in his own, pressing them to his chest. "But brother or not, I swear to you, I am your friend. And I've done nothing but try to help and protect you since I saw you in Clare's smithy."

Sophie set her head carefully on his shoulder, as much to hide her confusion and disappointment as to seek out comfort. *Brother or not, he's always been my friend.* In that moment, she decided to trust Lukas, even if he was a mystery she hadn't yet solved.

Besides, there were so many other mysteries she still had to solve.

. . .

Which is why she found herself alone in the kitchen with Rachel mere hours later.

At that moment, Rachel was preparing some kind of treatment at the dining room table, consulting a book covered in spider-like writing and gorgeous lifelike illustrations of various plants. The type of book that looked exactly like a grimoire to Sophie's eyes.

"What are you working on?" Sophie asked by way of announcing herself.

Rachel looked up and smiled. "Something to help Kane. He's stronger than he looks, but he was born very weak. Over the years I've been able to treat him, and it's made a world of difference since he first came to us. I think if I can tweak his medicine a smidge, I can help ease his fatigue."

She looked down at her pestle thoughtfully, before flipping a few pages in the book next to her, as if searching for a different answer.

Sophie nodded absently, still wrung out over her conversation with Lukas. She looked over the various tools, herbs, and books covering every available surface in the large working kitchen. It seemed something was always cooking in here, but at a nice gentle simmer, instead of the oftentimes hectic, overheated kitchens of her own home. *It's nice,* she thought. *Homey.*

"It's wonderful that you're able to help him," Sophie said, easing into what she feared could be an uncomfortable conversation. Her mother would be surprised at her diplomacy, she thought with a smile. And then grimaced, remembering the swirling doubts she now had about her mother's share in the evils plaguing Hameln and her friends, new and old.

"I know it's been years since we've seen each other, but with the way my memories are rushing back …" Sophie faltered. "Sometimes it feels like I just saw you a few days ago, and other times, it's as if you're a complete stranger."

Rachel finally stilled her hands from her work and gave Sophie her complete attention.

"I'm sorry," she responded. "I'm sorry for what's happened to you, and for not being able to stop it. I didn't realize … Katherine never really told me her plans, so I really don't know what she did or why. I always hoped for the best, that she would continue your grandmother's work, finding healers to help the people. So when she stopped coming, I had so much else on my plate, it was months before I even realized there was something wrong."

She stopped, seeming to catch herself from spiraling the conversation into territory that neither of them could traverse easily.

"I'm sorry," she said again.

Sophie nodded again. "There are still some blank spots for me. Would you mind … would you mind telling me more about this place, about you? And Lukas?"

"What do you want to know?" Rachel asked, smiling before turning back to her concoction.

"Well … how did you come to be here?" Sophie pushed past her own discomfort, finding solace in the one thing that always gave her a feeling of control—an interview.

"I got on the wrong side of some very powerful people," Rachel answered, simply. Though Sophie was quick to recognize a vague non-answer when she heard one. Sophie stepped in closer to look more closely at the older woman's calm face. But if a lifetime at court had taught her anything, it was how to project a sense of ease —at least until you were in a position to push someone right to the truth.

"Just you and Madge, with Lukas and Kane? That sounds lonely." Sophie frowned, considering. Katherine hadn't abandoned her, even with the rumors. And her mother wasn't the forgiving type.

"Oh, no, we've had many allies over the years." Rachel reached out to pat Sophie's hand absently. "My friends in Hameln did not forget us entirely. And there are always the desperate souls willing to trade foodstuff or services for my tinctures and herbal concoctions."

"Don't forget Wolfhart, Mother," Lukas said.

Sophie silently blessed the bard who had chosen that moment to join them, with his teasing grin and twinkling eye. She could see the tension in Rachel's shoulders ease, and hoped his presence would loosen her tongue, as well.

"We would not have survived without the Wolfhart all these years, that is certain," Rachel said. "The Wolfhart has a sacred duty to protect the people of Lower Saxony, and we are lucky to have such a loyal friend."

"Why do you keep calling him that?" Sophie interrupted, causing them both to turn to her in confusion." "I mean, you make 'The Wolfhart' sound like a title, not who he is."

"You answered your own question, Sophie," Lukas answered. "There is story after story about the brave hunter who saves victims throughout the empire. Did you think it was all just one man's deeds? The Wolfhart is a calling, and the title is handed down generation by generation."

"So Wolfhart is actually the however-many-times-great-grandson of the Wolfhart we hear about in your stories?" Her curiosity left no room to be embarrassed by her own ignorance.

"No, it's not an inheritance. It's an honorific." Rachel continued to speak to Sophie as if she were a member of the family, indulged instead of brushed off. Sophie found she had missed this cama-raderie that she hadn't known existed days before. "The last Wolfhart discovered our own and decided he was most worthy to carry on the mantle." Sophie stayed silent, willing Rachel to continue.

Rachel looked almost preoccupied with her own reminiscences. "It was actually the former Wolfhart who helped us to the Grey Cottage. And at great personal risk. I've no doubt he's the one who charged our Wolfhart to continue looking after this house when he took up the mantle. It's the only secret I believe he ever kept from your grandmother, the old Countess."

"*Grandmaman?* What did she have to do with any of this?" Sophie asked.

But suddenly Rachel was a flurry of activity, chopping an herb, and sweeping it into a mixture that was bubbling over the fire.

"Sorry, dearest, but the timing of this recipe is particularly persnickety, as Madge would say. I need to concentrate."

"Of course," Sophie answered faintly, watching the healing woman at her work, completely absorbed in her task. She had another pressure point: bringing up Papa directly. If she pressed forward now, would Rachel shut her down completely?

"But I really am curious—"

"You always have been," Rachel interrupted ruefully.

Sophie grinned back. "You clearly worked closely with my mother, and apparently you knew my *Grandmaman?*"

Rachel looked a bit confused at Sophie's question. "Of course, your grandmother was in charge of choosing Everstein's initiates in those days. We worked together developing medicines and treatments. Just as Katherine does now."

"But she doesn't," Sophie said, sidetracked by confusion. "I've never seen a single initiate in *Grandmaman*'s study, or her greenhouses. We've had plenty of soldiers, a few craftsmen, but no doctors or naturalists."

Sophie herself knew that Everstein took in Hameln children. But even with her new memories rushing in, the Hameln children claimed by her family just ... weren't there. *But you did just remember something, bloody hands in a cage. Was that vision real?*

Was her own mother disappearing them? Or did she simply hand them over to that monstrous Erlking? And, knowing that her mother never acted against her own interests, what was Katherine getting out of such a strange deal?

"The Erlking ... did he ever come to you?" Sophie whispered.

"The Erlking? Here?" Rachel closed her book with a thud, eyes glinting in displeasure. "Of course not. Now leave me to my work."

Freddie;

    I'm not sure when I will have the chance to write again. We were forced to leave Hameln after an alarming discovery. First, let me reassure you: I and Maman are unharmed. But it seems that Maman has gotten caught up in something fairly sinister, and she is participating because of someone called the Erlking.

I need you to look through her study for any evidence of blackmail or coercion—any connection with this villain at all. In particular, any mention of Lucie or Margarethe could be helpful, or even a list of past Obolen initiates and their fates.

In the meantime, I and my friends in Hameln will seek out allies. If you see the Wolfhart yourself, make sure he knows of our need.

So much has been revealed and reordered in my own mind, much of it too shocking to even allude to here. There have been many past misdeeds that have only recently been uncovered for me. I hope we will see each other again soon for there is much to discuss. And I think right now, I need my brother.

Be careful. I do not know if the Erlking's eyes extend into our own castle walls, with or without Maman's presence.

Yours,

Spitfire

She sighed heavily before pushing herself up and taking her letter, intending to send it to the post.

"To the pigeon post at Wolfhart's Lodge," she murmured to herself, and then paused to revel in her newfound knowledge of how Lukas' world worked. What else did she used to know? And how long would it take her to recover it all? Would she even know when she had?

Filled with purpose, Sophie reemerged from her room, and walked directly into a fairly domestic scene between Rachel and Clare. It seems Sophie wasn't the only one looking for answers. And the amused glint in Clare's eye told Sophie that Clare was having much more success in her quest.

"And he asked for this, this pattern and these colors, specifically?" Clare asked.

"Yes, I made him this tunic to his *exact* specifications. Not that I like bragging about it, but what are you going to do?" Rachel asked them with a helpless shrug. Clare's low, rolling laughter filled the room, and Sophie found herself joining in immediately.

As if sensing trouble, Lukas skidded into the kitchen at that very moment. His narrowed gaze flitted from his coat to his mother's distasteful look to Sophie's uncontrollable laughter and finally to Clare's wide-eyed, delighted expression at his entrance. The last seemed to cause him physical pain.

"What is going on in here?" he asked, voice too careful and tight to be strictly casual. Sophie sat back, still giggling and intent on enjoying his embarrassment.

"My dear," Rachel began, a far-too innocent smile playing on her own face. "I was just telling the girls about your ridiculous little tunic …"

"Stop, stop. Everyone just … stop talking," he said, voice suddenly high and rushed. He spied the letter in Sophie's hand and moved toward it like a lifeline, pushing and pulling Clare and Sophie out of the room. "It's time to go. Let's see if Wolfhart has returned to the lodge. Or maybe he's written to us. The pigeon post, let's go there. Hurry, hurry. No time to lose. The light is almost gone." Lukas was nearly jumping out of his skin in his apparent panic.

"Whatever is the matter, Lukas?" Rachel asked, with a touch of bewilderment. "Clare was just telling me how fascinating she finds your pied tunic. For some reason, she thought it was my design, though?" With Clare's answering howl of laughter from the other side of the doorway, Sophie saw that he actually *flinched*.

The look he cut at Rachel showed exactly what he thought of this particular betrayal.

"Yes, that's quite enough, thank you, *Mother*," he said as he hustled the girls out the door. "Maybe you can all share a laugh about me when the world isn't ending? How about that?"

"Thank you, Clare, so much," Sophie huffed to her friend between her own peals of laughter, finally feeling that heavy knot in her chest ease, just a little. "I really, really needed that."

27

Unfortunately, the laughter didn't last long.

"It's time for me to go back to Hameln," Nic announced to the room, walking in side-by-side with Helena.

"What?" Clare yelped. "No you're not! It's too dangerous! What if they arrest you next?"

"I am a spy, Clarebear, remember?" Nic said. "And I can't do my job hiding here where all the action isn't. If I'm going to help stop this madness, I have to be there."

"What good is all this Faerie magic if we can't keep the people we love safe?" Clare practically stomped her foot in frustration.

"We have three objectives here: find the Wolfhart, report to Berchtold, and warn Hameln about the Council's new deal with the Erlking to rip every child in Hameln away. And since I am Berchtold's eyes and ears, I can at least take care of the last two." Nic caught Clare up in his arms and spoke soothingly into her hair. "I'm not doing much good hiding here in the woods when war is on the horizon."

Clare's mouth pulled down as she glared up at him. "I don't like it."

"Your brother will be fine," Helena interjected. "It's hardly enemy territory. The Council cannot attack him without raising even more questions about their true motivations. At most, they will interrogate him."

"That's what I'm counting on," Nic said with a sardonic grin. "No better way to get information than an interrogation, you know."

"Even when you're the one being questioned?" Sophie asked quietly.

"Especially then," Nic said. "They don't even think about everything they're revealing when they think they're in control." Then he turned to Clare and Casper.

"This is what he was trained to do, and has done many times before," Casper said kindly, hugging them each in turn. "Don't worry about me."

"I'm going with him," Lucie announced stoutly to the room. "Mother's safe. And I can concoct some story of following you into the mountains to explain my disappearance and keep them away from the Grey Cottage as long as possible."

Helena and Nic seemed to nod in approval, while Clare could only make a strangled sort of noise in her throat, her face down and fists clenched.

"You can't go back," Clare said, glaring at Lucie. They were all finally—relatively—safe, but they all seemed intent on rushing back into danger.

Lucie went to her. "I need to do this. For you and for my family. I have to pay my debts and stop my father from hurting any more people, if I can."

Clare nodded wordlessly. She understood the need to protect family, but she hated it.

"I'll keep her safe, Clarebear," Nic said, more cheerfully than any of them felt.

"So will this," Helena interrupted, squeezing something small into Lucie's right hand. Lucie squeezed Helena's hand back with a smile before bringing the small white ring up for inspection.

"That isn't—" Nic began.

"It is horn." Helena quelled him. "One of Berchtold's, like yours. With a minor ... adjustment, for my own purpose."

"But Lucie hasn't sworn fealty. And no sacrifice or favor has been exchanged." Nic spoke fiercely, every inch the protective brother Clare remembered, though she didn't understand why.

Helena ignored him, reaching for Lucie's other hand. "This token is freely given, with no expectation or reward. Show it to any who would harm you. You will return it to me when the danger has passed."

Lucie nodded slightly, looking both confused and a bit breathless. The odd, stilted words felt ceremonial, and the danger they were all in seemed much more permanent and real. Clare touched her own ring and wondered what magic it might possess, before realization hit at their words.

Clare looked between the two, confused. "You're not going with them?" she asked Helena accusingly.

"Someone has to report back to Berchtold," Helena explained, eyes lingering on Lucie. "That doesn't mean I can't lend a hand."

Helena turned to Nic, clasping his neck to bring his forehead down to her own. "Safe travels and fair winds, my brother-in-arms. May your purpose fly true."

"And yours," Nic sobered, closing his eyes as their heads met, his own hand wrapped over Helena's shoulder. Then he stepped back, jovial as ever. "Don't hurry back from Berchtold on my account. Lots to see and do back home before you drag me back to the barracks."

Helena's small smile was bright as the sun on her normally placid face. But her golden eyes burned with concern. "Do not court danger, my friend."

"But what if it asks for a dance?" Nic rejoined, before herding a suddenly quiet Lucie toward the door. "It isn't nice to keep a lady waiting."

They trouped out of the Grey Cottage, Nic and Lucie toward the town, while Sophie, Clare, Cas, and Lukas turned in a new direction, toward what Sophie now dimly remembered was Wolfhart's lodge. She looked back for a moment, wondering if the Cottage would become a ramshackle ruin again before her eyes. But it seemed the glamour, once pierced, was changed for good.

It was strange, this newfound affinity for the bard—for everyone at the Grey Cottage, really. Sophie's head carried all these memories of deep bonds, and her heart was still catching up. An uneasy sense of misunderstood loyalty to Lukas all these months finally made sense, though.

And possibly smitten with Clare. She turned her eyes from his tense shoulders to Clare's distracted attention. Just another changing dynamic to attend.

It was a complete tangle in her head, all these feelings and memories and long-held fears of a world that made no sense. Lukas was right. They needed to act to prevent the children's abduction, to end the curse, to ensure her mother wasn't hurting anyone.

And then maybe she would have time to figure out what she was feeling and thinking and who she really was.

New-old memories were constantly welling up thanks to now-familiar trees, birdsong, and the scents of the forest all around her.

Sooner than she anticipated, she saw the massive treehouse supported between two ancient trees and the large porch that surrounded the circular structure entirely, giving perfect sightlines for miles around. There was a complicated pulley system with a platform to ride or hoist up larger loads, and a simple rope ladder next to that.

"Casper would love this," she thought wistfully.

The windows were dark, but a thin tendril of smoke still curled from the chimney, promising a welcome respite to the brisk morning air. She opened her mouth to ask what they were supposed to do next, when to the left, she saw an alarmingly large shadow moving toward them out of the gloom.

It was a mountain of a creature, shoulders broad, footfalls steady and heavy, and what looked to be a monstrous amount of arms—or was it legs—coming from what Sophie could only assume was the thing's torso. She felt her throat tighten, panic making a scream impossible. *God's bones, would anyone even hear them out here?*

"If you're here for mischief, I suggest you move along," the being rumbled. "The hound won't hurt you, but my bird can get a mite prickly when provoked."

That voice wiped the panic away. And Sophie noticed Lukas and Clare relax, as well.

A few more steps, and the mist fell away, revealing an ordinary man. Well, ordinary as the Wolfhart could be.

Sophie's heart soared at the sight of her old friend, and his dirty, weary, dear face. His light brown hair was greyer, and his beard to match, but those sparkling blue eyes were the same. And with only two legs and two feet, she saw it was only the deer slung over his shoulders that gave him such a terrifying appearance in the low light.

Sophie saw a falcon perch on the railing overhead. The hound simply watched it all, with a flick of his ear and a slowly wagging tail.

"Lukas, Clarebear, and Sophie, is it? All together?" the huntsman sounded surprised. "Something is either very good or very bad in Lower Saxony, I take it."

"Very bad," Clare answered grimly. "Where have you been?"

"Hannover for a bit," the huntsman answered. "Then I came back south to hunt. There are many in these woods who depend on the extra meat as it gets colder."

"But we needed you!" Clare answered. "You're supposed to protect us!"

Now the older man looked confused, dropping his quarry to the ground. "What are you talking about?"

"The Council! And the Erlking! And my mother!" Sophie began listing, in lieu of an answer. "And did you know how she bewitched me?"

The Wolfhart paused, staring hard at each of them in turn. "Easy, sprite. I need you to explain to me—slowly—what is going on in Hameln."

Her eyes pricked at the easy nickname. She took a deep breath and started over again.

While they spoke, he silently dressed the deer, expertly separating skin and bone, muscles and sinew, until there were two distinct piles: meat and carcass. He then collected the doe's bones, covering them with the animal's own skin in a process that felt more like funerary ceremony than simply discarding a body.

"I'm going to bury her now." Wolfhart gestured to the door of the Lodge. "When I get back, we'll figure this out. You're welcome to join me, or go warm yourself by the fire. You've already gotten through the perimeter, and no doubt Lukas knows where all my traps are by now."

"I did have an expert instructor," Lukas grumbled. But Sophie could see the relief in his face. The Wolfhart was here, the hero of every tale they'd been told at the knees of their elders. The Erlking was just another villain he would soundly defeat before they all lived happily again.

28

As the small band made it back to the Grey Cottage, Sophie was buoyed by hope for the first time since they'd fled Hameln's woods. The Wolfhart, protector of the mortal world, was on their side. She watched his broad back as he carried the venison and Sophie spied his hound—"Cavall," she remembered—trotting beside him.

"It's to be an empty house yet again, I see," Rachel said, as she opened her door, looking at their uncomfortable but determined faces. She sighed. "I knew I couldn't keep any of you here long, with all those war councils about the chaos just outside these walls."

"Long enough for a visit, at least," the Wolfhart answered, striding in to easily transfer the meat from his shoulders to her kitchen table. "This is for the desperate who find your door. Present company excluded, of course." He playfully cuffed his slavering hound about the snout, before turning the fake blow into a gentle caress.

"I'll put it in storage," Rachel answered, her capable hands taking the cargo and moving to put it away.

"A rather cold greeting, don't you think?" Wolfhart stopped her, catching her around the waist from behind to place a smacking kiss at the crown of her head. Lukas rolled his eyes good-naturedly, clearly used to their affection, while Clare's eyes kept darting between the two.

"You old fool," Rachel laughed affectionately.

"Now, now," the Wolfhart said. "I thought I was your prince!"

"I stopped waiting for my prince the day you smuggled me and Lukas out of Hameln," Rachel answered, her voice sweet and dry. "But I suppose I'm stuck with you now."

He was gazing after her with a soft smile, and Sophie smiled at the easy affection she was witnessing and remembering all at the same time. Memories that she only now realized were so precious to her. And she refused to believe her Maman would take them from her without a very good reason.

Maybe her mother was the Erlking's accomplice. But she could not—would not—believe her mother was a *willing* partner. If poor Lucie could murder a man for love and duty to her mother, what could the Erlking be holding over the Countess? Her family or even Everstein's safety? She had to learn more about how Faerie and even her own world worked, and fast. *I have to save Maman from this evil.*

Luckily, asking questions was her specialty. "What's our next move?" Sophie asked. "I'm ready for answers and action."

Wolfhart chuckled before putting the pipe away, apparently ready to get down to business.

"We will need every advantage we can get. That means convincing Berchtold that now is the time to act," Wolfhart said, one hand deep in Cavall's fur. "And while you are children, I feel you will be more important to a victory than we can now tell."

"Does your magic tell you that?" Sophie asked.

The hound looked up at her master's words before rising to lightly bump Clare's hand with her massive head. Clare stroked the hound, and Sophie noticed she was deep in thought.

Wolfhart hummed discordantly at his words as his pipe smoke drifted toward the ceiling.

"I have no real magic of my own, or no more than most of you grew up with," he answered slowly. "And Fae magic—real Fae magic— is innate to their kind. It's about intent and purpose and a strong will. If you trust them, their hold over you is even stronger. Which is why, generally speaking, humans should not trust Fae. And we cannot fight them on our own with any guarantee to win without magical assistance."

"So we go to Faerie," Clare said with a tone of finality. "We meet with Berchtold and we make him understand. It's time to end Hameln's pact."

"It is risky," Helena said, but the look she gave Clare had an air of respect. "There is no guarantee he will not immediately hand us over to the Erlking. Hierarchy in Faerie is … inflexible."

"You don't really think that, do you?" Lukas asked her. "That he would give us to the Erlking?"

Helena paused in thought, her brow wrinkled and her golden eyes far away. She snapped back into the present. "No, I do not. Berchtold will help where he can. He hates this war as much as anyone. It interrupts his hunt."

"Hunting? At this time of year?" Sophie asked.

Helena allowed herself a grin. "Oh yes. For wicked Fae who prey on naïve mortals. Faerie's version of Wolfhart, you might say."

After their venison meal, Casper sprung what felt like his latest trap on his sister.

"Someone needs to go back to warn the townspeople that the Council has been lying, and I'll only slow you down in Faerie." Casper's body was stiff, and Clare couldn't tell if it was pain, exhaustion, or something more. She wouldn't mother him in front of the others, not when he'd made it clear how he felt about his siblings' concern back in Hameln. She had to trust that Casper knew what he was doing.

She pushed past the immediate panic and thought carefully about their options, none of them safe.

"It'll be dangerous, going back," Clare spoke slowly, placing her hand lightly on his shoulder. "But I'll feel better knowing that you and Nic are back there together. Besides, if you're gone too long, Father Stephen will grow suspicious. And Aunt Aggie has never been able to tell when you're lying, at least."

"A lame man's advantage," Casper grinned grimly. "No one looks at you too closely, as if an injury were contagious. I'll make sure Nic does not rush into danger, and we'll both make sure Lucie is safe."

"And I will accompany you, at least as I make my way to Castle Everstein to see the Countess. She's expecting me," Wolfhart said, rising from his seat by the fire. "And it's long past time I got some answers."

"What if my mother isn't there?" Sophie asked him.

"Then I'll be where the trouble is, as usual," he answered. "And this time, it looks like that means Hameln."

As it turned out, after the decisions were made, it didn't take long for them all to spring into action: Casper, Nic, and Lucie journeying to Hameln, with Wolfhart reporting to Castle Everstein before joining them; while Helena led Lukas, Clare, and Sophie to Berchtold's fortress. Relief thrummed through Clare's chest. *Finally, we're going to fix this. And with true allies.*

After Rachel ensured that they each had all the supplies they could possibly need (*"Mother, it's not even a full days' journey!"*) they were off.

At least Casper and Wolfhart knew exactly where they were off to.

"Where are we headed?" Clare was willing to follow the elven girl,

but not unthinkingly. " 'Toward the road' is not actually a destination."

"For us, it is," was Helena's reply.

"I don't understand," Clare countered. "And until you make me understand, I'm not walking another step. We have family and friends in danger."

At her tone, Helena finally stopped. But the exasperated amusement on Helena's face did absolutely nothing to tamp down Clare's anger or despair.

"I need to go to Faerie… to report what we have found… and get aid for Hameln." Helena spoke slowly, but whether it was for their benefit or her own, Clare wasn't sure. "Faerie is not difficult to locate, precisely, but it also is not everywhere all the time. There are certain places—*kinds* of places—where we may enter. And thoroughfares, crossroads specifically, are one of those kinds of places."

Helena pointed ahead. "The intersection is just there," she said. "Just hold my hand, and keep your mind as empty as possible. I don't want your stubborn will bending our purpose," she instructed. "I will get us there."

Clare grumbled, but grabbed Sophie's hand, while the younger girl reached out for Helena's shoulder.

The world blurred for a moment, and Clare blinked violently. By the time her vision had cleared again, they were nowhere near the road they had been on just a moment ago and time had shifted.

Looking around, Clare saw that even Lukas looked a bit pale in the moonlight. Because suddenly the clear afternoon sky was dark and sparkling with stars.

Clare spun in a quick circle, seeing a dark, empty, *unfamiliar* countryside all around. Faerie was dazzling, even in the low light with her clumsy, mortal eyes. The landscape was a kaleidoscope of colors, bright, glittering, and knife-sharp. The Fae world assaulted her senses with deep saturation, and she barely recognized the foreign hues as the reds and yellows and blues swirled and melted around her. Softpetaled wildflowers dotted the rolling hills, their colors melting lavender and pale pink and deep blue; rushing spring waters shifted light to dark from within, flashing silver then aquamarine then inky black; and above it all the swirling winds caressed pearlescent clouds high above them as stars danced in a blue-black velvet sky.

She felt woozy with delight.

"Helena, I'm going to need you to explain what just happened."

Helena spared them all a moment to gain their bearings before gesturing to move along with her in a direction that she seemed quite sure of.

"Suppose you're walking in the woods, and you come across a river. You climb into the boat and the current carries you along." Helena's voice was flat as she stalked ahead, which was probably as close to patient as she could sound. "Are you still in the woods, or are you on the river?"

"So, we just … found a dock and paddled away?" Lukas' green eyes glittered in the low light.

"You misunderstand, youngling."

Clare heard Helena's gentle amusement.

"Faerie is vast and eternal. *Your* world is the fast-moving stream."

Still casting about to find the moon, Clare abruptly realized that these were not her stars, either. "This sky is different. What happened to the constellations? And the North Star?"

"Well, the analogy isn't perfect," Helena shrugged. "There are many things in Faerie that you would not find in your mortal world —and the opposite is true. But we've got to keep moving. Berchtold doesn't know what my father and Katherine are plotting. He needs to be prepared."

"What about Nic and Casper?!" Clare stopped in her tracks, forcing the others to a standstill. "We left them there, to deal with Agathe, Jakob, and the Countess—we don't even know what they'll do to Lucie, and the Wolfhart is only one man!"

"What's that supposed to mean?" Lukas looked offended, but whether for his cousin or his hero, Clare wasn't sure. When she turned her eyes to Sophie, the younger girl was looking down, unable to defend or attack her own mother. At the moment, Clare didn't really care about either of their feelings.

Regardless, Helena was already striding away again toward a point that only she seemed to recognize. It was all fields and stars as far as Clare could see. "Casper will explain everything. And Nicolaus is a warrior, who's as prepared as he can be until we can get back to them. Berchtold will know what to do."

"Who is this Berchtold you and Nic work for? And how can he stop the Erlking and my mother?" True fear laced Sophie's words for the first time, and Clare heard the unspoken message: *If I can't trust my mother, how can I trust this stranger you're taking us to?*

"Well, you know him as Count Ebernberg. But he's not simply a powerful count in your kingdom. He's also the leader of the Wild Hunt, the commander of ten legions of Faerie, and the only other being that the court may listen to."

"Sure, but why would he listen to *us?*" Lukas finally broke his silence.

"Why do you think Nic and I were in Hameln to begin with? Berchtold sent us specifically to assess the situation after the Rat King's murder. He's expecting my report, and won't be shocked to hear that the Erlking is involved." Helena threw the words over her shoulder, never breaking stride. "And he is my uncle."

"Your uncle?" Sophie sounded as astonished as Clare felt. "Why didn't we go to him earlier, then?"

"Blood does not bind us the way it does you mortals," Helena explained. "We put more faith in oaths than relations. Oaths cannot be broken."

"Still ..." Sophie responded grumpily. "Does diplomacy mean nothing in Faerie?"

Looking over to Lukas, Clare discovered that it wasn't just the spring-green blades of grass that were suddenly fascinating. She had an almost irrepressible urge to skim her fingers over the soft, luminous skin just inside his wrist. She found herself wondering how his bottom lip would taste on her tongue and was moving toward him with intent to wrap herself around him like a strong vine to a tree before Sophie's sharp voice brought her back to reality.

"What manner of tree is *that*?" She pointed to her left, and her eyes followed the path of the swift river cutting through the meadows to its head, where golden-billed kingfishers flew quick and low to capture their fish feasts. And there she saw an entire world in a massive, blooming tree.

Clare craned her head back, but found it impossible to see the entirety of the gigantic—ash? It pierced through the clouds above them and into the starry night. She caught sight of a bird of prey—or maybe just its shadow?—soaring easily overhead. The dome of this green oasis was 100 times wider than it was tall. It was the tallest tree she had ever seen.

If they all linked arms and encircled its trunk, they would not even span a quarter of its girth. "This tree must be ancient," she breathed.

"Christ's toes, is this the actual tree of knowledge?" Sophie asked, reaching out but not moving toward the tree.

"It is called that by some," Helena responded, moving closer to it with little regard to the flora and fauna around them. "Or the Tree of Immortality, or Yggdrasil, or *Etz ha-da'at, tov va-ra.*"

That's when Clare noticed a strange type of bundle swinging in the branches, before realizing it was an old man hanging by his feet. His arms ended in bloody stumps, just brushing the ground below.

"Is that a man?" Clare asked, horrified at the macabre sight in an otherwise idyllic landscape. "Left there to rot?"

"That is what happens when you rebel against the Erlking," Helena replied darkly. "He won't die. We Fae are made of tougher stuff than you mortals."

"That's not actually better," Clare said. "What could he have possibly done to deserve this?"

"He was a general under my father, just like Berchtold, and he started speaking of a truce with the other side. Secretly. This is his punishment, and a warning to others who may try to do the same."

After one last glance at the unfortunate man, Helena moved on. Clare shuddered at the Erlking's fearsome display of power and quickly followed.

They walked for what could have been moments or hours, each seemingly lost in their own thoughts.

In Clare's case, *she* just felt lost, and was alarmed to find that she enjoyed it. Fiddling with her pendant, she quickly ascertained that due north was precisely—nowhere. Inexplicably, she was almost giddy with delight instead of dread. This was an entirely new world, open and waiting for her to explore.

Meanwhile Clare watched a dazzled Sophie, silent and taking in the sights around her with a slightly open mouth, her hands twitching like she wanted to write it all down. "Maybe I can map this all out later."

"Doubtful," Helena answered.

Clare sidled up to Lukas in the instant he hurried to join a reticent Helena, peppering her with questions.

"So, considering you're a Faerie princess, I must admit I was expecting shimmering wings and silken robes, not armor and battle axes," he said archly. Clare barely smothered the grin forming on her face. Too-serious Helena and rarely earnest Lukas were an entertaining combination.

"I am what my kingdom needs me to be. And we've been at war for as long as I can remember. Which is something like 500 of your human years."

"Five hundred years of destruction?" Clare was appalled. "How is anyone—anything—still standing?"

Helena shrugged. "Hameln is still standing, as well. People adapt. And here, the land adapts, as well."

They crested a hill and Clare gasped, dropping her charm as if it burned her. Had she conjured the sight before them?

Laid before them was Berchtold's fortress, startling white and overwhelming in scale. Fort Sternenfeuer was ablaze in torch and Faerie light. Five massive stars, sometimes concentric, at other points interlocking, comprised the stone bastion fortress as big as a city, far larger than Hameln—moats and battlements and hillocks whose sharp points jutted into the landscape at ever higher elevations. The entire overpowering bastion stronghold culminated in a shining white citadel, towering over the surrounding hills and forests.

"How ..." Even worldly Sophie was speechless. The structure before them was imposing, beautiful, and impossible—there was nothing like it in their world. But there it was.

Helena finally grinned at them. "We've arrived."

29

Freddie walked into his mother's grand study, the air grown cold and stale with disuse the past few months, the red-, blue- and gold-tinted light from the wall of stained glass giving it a melancholy feel.

"Might as well make it a little brighter—and warmer—in here if I'm going to be snooping," Freddie thought. He grabbed one of the lit torches off the wall beside him, intending to try his luck at starting a fire in the room's grand fireplace.

No sooner was the torch in his hand, he heard the telltale twang that every noble child is taught from an early age to listen for. A crossbow? The hair on his arms stood on end as he reached for the omnipresent dagger at his waist to fend off a would-be assassin.

Instead, the movement his eyes caught proved to be his own spooked reflection—eyes wide, mouth stretched absurdly—in the large silver-backed mirror that stood facing his mother's workspace.

The brave future Count of Everstein, scared by his own reflection.

Shaking his head ruefully and thankful that he was alone in this shameful moment, Freddie refocused on the strange noises coming from deep within the fireplace itself: a brief grinding rumble of stone on stone that ended in a soft, mechanical click. He turned round just in time to see the entire left side of the firebox swing open.

Freddie paused a moment, his pounding heart still trying to escape his chest. He looked between the torch in his hand and the newly opened doorway leading to a secret passage *in the fireplace* as a bemused smile bloomed over his face.

"Sophie is going to be furious that I found this without her."

He nearly dropped the torch from nerveless fingers at the sight before him. There, sitting in the corner like a forgotten doll, was the missing chambermaid. *What happened to her?* Her face seemed trapped in a terrifying facsimile of a smile, rigid and far too wide to be natural. Her teeth jutted every which way, like tiny ivory spears, cutting into her face. Blood and tears dripped down, filling her cupped hands. He rushed over, realizing before he was at her side that it was too late. *She's gone. She's gone, and she was murdered.*

The entire room was filled with his mother's ... experiments. He collapsed against the cold, damp wall behind him, suddenly breathless. Alongside Katherine's human victims were mutilated faeries. *Did Maman do all this? How? When?*

He stumbled back through the dark passageway to his mother's study and then came upon the one person he was not yet prepared to see: Maman. Surrounded by her guards, she sat calmly behind her desk. As if she were waiting for him.

"When did you return?" he asked, voice high and thin.

"The Wolfhart wished to talk to me," Katherine said, looking at him intently. "He said he had news of Sophie. It seems she had a few...interesting ideas about what was happening in Hameln."

"Yes, and so do I!" Freddie's voice became louder as he returned the torch to its place on the mantel.

"Not here, darling," Katherine said soothingly, looking over her shoulder at her grand mirror. Freddie thought he saw fear in her eyes. "Let's talk this over in your chambers."

"I demand an answer *now*, Maman." Freddie refused to be moved.

"Of all the times to choose to be a leader, you pick this one," she said, covering the mirror with her traveling cloak.

Ignoring the sweat trickling between his shoulder blades, Freddie cleared his throat as the nausea crawled up it. "This isn't a jest!" he croaked out.

"And I am not laughing!" she screamed back, hands raised into fists.

"Johann isn't the only one who can use trial and error to perfect results. And this particular plague was going to help make us powerful enough that no one could stand in our way, not even the Erlking. Of course, there were unintended consequences."

Freddie scoffed at her calm, understated words that reflected nothing of the horrors he had just seen.

"No matter. Ten years ago before the last Obolen, I meant for my little disaster to only strike down those with Fae blood, but I underestimated the power of a dying Fae," Katherine continued. "It's all part of the scientific process your father loves to talk about. I've simply abandoned those plans for other, more productive lines of inquiry." Her voice was colored by regret, but Freddie couldn't be certain if it was for the dead, the tortured town, or her abandoned science.

"You're talking about the plague that killed nearly half of Hameln when I was just a child? That was orchestrated by you?" His voice was dull now, despair coloring his words.

"With the Erlking's aid, of course," Katherine admitted. "He has to try out new weapons somewhere his enemies won't see them, after all."

Freddie recoiled again, throwing his body as far from his mother as he could, while still somehow staying on his feet. He wiped the sweat from his face, breathing hard. "How long have you and the Council been torturing these people?"

"The Council?" she laughed mirthlessly. "Those shortsighted

fools. They only go so far as the original pact dictates. And even in that, they are cowards."

"So you took it upon yourself to become the Erlking's servant. While all along you prepare for war with Faerie?"

"And thanks to my work, House Everstein will be celebrated for generations. Any who dare stand in my way won't live to regret it. Man or Faerie, as the Wolfhart just learned."

Freddie shook his head, trying to clear it, but all he could hear was screaming: his mother, her victims, his own. He pieced together her words, slowly. *The Wolfhart? Didn't Sophie want me to warn him?* "What did you do to Wolfhart, Maman? Where is he?"

"He's gone," she answered. "The arsenic in his stew didn't agree with him, and neither did my personal guard." A battered soldier standing over her left shoulder winced, and Freddie noticed his tunic was covered in blood. *Too much blood.*

"He's … dead?" Freddie stared at his mother, as if he was seeing her for the first time. Her eyes seemed colder now, her self control inhuman. This woman was a complete stranger. "You killed him? Y-you sacrificed all of these lives … the lives of our own people, children … "

"Their lives were ours to sacrifice!" Katherine interrupted savagely, her blue eyes blazing and teeth bared. It seemed she was done trying to bring him to her way of thinking. "We provide them the land that they farm, the protection of our armies. And if we need their aid, that is our due."

Freddie's mind was racing, along with his pulse. "Where is my father?"

"Where do you think?" Katherine turned from her son, dismissive. "None of this is new. If your father cared to venture beyond his laboratory, he may even have joined me years ago."

She raised her pale hand into the air, as if addressing an unseen crowd. "A woman who searches for ways to save life is an unnatural servant of the devil, hellbent on perverting God's will. A man who aims for immortality is a venerated alchemist."

At his silence, she changed tack, transforming herself into the doting mother he loved and admired. Somehow, it hurt even more.

"You must understand." Katherine's tone was soothing, confident—the voice he heard in his own head every day of his life. "You've seen what the Rat King could do, even in death, and he was a low Fae, so far below the Erlking's notice. You see why I had to protect our interests, our heritage—our very lives. And why you *must* help me find your sister. To bring her back!"

He brought his head up, looked deeply into those clear eyes that had mirrored his own hopes and fears for so long.

He needed to go to Hameln if he was to help. It was the only way to protect everyone, everything he'd been born to serve. That meant pretending to work with his mother, to give Sophie the time she needed to reach aid. Perhaps Berchtold could be persuaded.

He straightened his weak knees and swallowed heavily. Freddie only hoped he would be enough to end his mother's madness, to protect his people, his sister. Like a true Everstein.

"Yes, *Maman*. I understand."

30

I t was lucky that Lukas had recently grown used to an armed guard watching his every move, as it made their phalanx of escorts to Berchtold a little less unnerving. Not that the Hameln patrol could really compare to the professional soldiers at Fort Sternenfeuer, with their shining armor and crimson capes.

Helena led them confidently through the cold hallways filled with light and little else, until they came to a massive oak door inlaid with an equally massive amber tree. Lukas barely had time to enjoy the artistry of its twisting branches before Helena had barged them right through.

No time for manners during a war, he supposed. Even if he was still a bit spotty on the details of said war.

"General," Helena began, addressing the tall man at the other end of the long, narrow room. The space was alight with torches dotting the wall and a massive, roaring fire behind him. "Why do you look—"

"I need your report immediately, Helena," he interrupted her.

She cleared the confused look from her face. "Yes. The Erlking is on the move."

"Yes, I determined that without my best spies, actually," the Berchtold replied. As they drew closer, his features were revealed: burnished brown skin and hair cropped close.

"You are not Berchtold," Clare declared, moving to cover Sophie. "Who …"

"He *is*, Clare." Helena shushed her, eyes darting between the agitated blacksmith and her boss. "He's simply let go of his—"

"Glamour," Lukas finished for her. Berchtold's deep-set sea-green eyes were instantly, uncomfortably familiar. *Like mine*, he thought grimly.

"Apologies if you were alarmed." Berchtold nodded slightly. "We're running out of time, and I am not skilled in human pleasantries. The Erlking disappeared from my sight, and I heard that the boy was to be executed …"

So Berchtold *did* notice him.

"Did you decide not to attend your own execution, or are you simply waiting to make an entrance?" Berchtold asked him.

"Was … was that a joke?" Lukas asked, unable to mask his surprise. "You guys know how to do that?"

Sophie made a particularly unprincess-like snort.

"You are an Everstein heir?" Berchtold asked Sophie after a short pause.

"Yes, Count."

"As you wish," he answered. If she meant to surprise him with her knowledge, Lukas saw that it didn't work.

"Then … I am here to speak on the County's behalf," she continued.

"Hmm," Berchtold responded, before turning back to Helena.

Helena, already proficient in ignoring him, moved on quickly. "Milord, why are you … ?"

"I just returned from Hameln." Berchtold patted down his black cloak, simply cut but with a fine, silvery pattern embroidered throughout. "I was expected when the Council called an emergency meeting, especially since I was ostensibly spearheading the investigation that led to …" Now he turned to Lukas. "…your capture."

"It didn't take," Lukas explained helpfully.

"We know the true culprit," Helena began.

"I wouldn't call her a culprit," Clare interrupted. Lucie didn't deserve the wrath of a Faerie general, no matter how fair Helena claimed he was.

"And it was Countess Katherine Everstein," Helena continued, quelling her with a sharp look, clearly displeased with a partner far less disciplined than Nic.

" …More like a wicked, wicked criminal attempting to circumvent the tithe to Faerie through murder and rat plagues," Lukas amended, sending Clare a reassuring wink.

"We don't know that," Sophie hissed. "I still think she's being manipulated, just like Lucie!"

"That…complicates things." Berchtold looked down at the table he was standing at, and Lukas knew that if there were a chair there, the general probably would have fallen into it. A large hound snoozed by the fireplace. Berchtold whistled a three-note tune, and the brindled mastiff was instantly awake and moving toward its master, who scratched behind the dog's ear, almost indifferently. It reminded Lukas so much of Cavall and the Wolfhart that he felt a sudden, painful twinge in his chest at the sight. He would never take his home for granted again.

"Does this mean their alliance is dissolved, or was this merely the Erlking's plan to hasten full-scale war with the rebels?"

"Alliance?" Sophie asked, and she did openly lean against the table. "God's bones. My mother and the Erlking really have an … agreement?"

"I do not know the full extent of their partnership, youngling," Berchtold looked down at her, almost kindly. "I know she was messing about with magics she did not understand. That she had orchestrated the plague that had nearly stopped last decade's tithe—"

"What?" Sophie cried out.

At the same time, Clare surged forward. "What do you mean *orchestrated?*" she snarled. "You're telling me the Countess killed my family?"

"Yes. Or her and the Erlking." Berchtold's tone never shifted. "As far as my spies can determine, she meant to develop a weapon to use against the Fae. I'm not sure if it's meant to be used in our side's civil war, or if she's planning to oust the Erlking from her lands. But she forgot how long the people of Hameln have been walking between the two worlds, mingling mortal blood with magic."

"That's…that's impossible." Clare's face paled, and Lukas watched as she stumbled to the table, reaching for support. He moved swiftly to catch her, easing her onto a chair, and rubbing her shoulders.

"I know, I know," Lukas soothed directly into her ear, unsure if she could even hear him in the moment. "Stay strong just a little longer."

"The tithe went on, of course." He continued, heedless of Clare's obvious pain, infuriating Lukas further. "The Council moved swiftly to contain the panic and hold a truncated ceremony. The Council, or at least factions within it, will continue to work with the Erlking. That will not change, even with Wolfhart's intervention."

"And now they will be looking for Lukas, without a doubt," Helena said. She had moved closer to Sophie, who looked horrified at the latest revelations about her mother. It confirmed all their worst suspicions, and his heart ached for both his friends.

"And your father's already looking for you," Berchtold's voice became stern. "Your mother is frantic, Helena. You were supposed to report back to both of us, you know."

"The situation was escalating more rapidly than I anticipated," Helena replied stiffly. "I felt that saving lives was more important than reports. But I apologize for disobeying both of your orders."

"I need you to go to your mother," Berchtold ordered, even and firm like a man used to being obeyed unconditionally. "And I must find a way to ready our troops and avoid the Council until I have a clear picture of Katherine's—" here Sophie made a small sound of dissent "—*and* the Erlking's motives. I cannot be caught flat-footed while your father starts another needless war, this time with the entire Holy Roman Empire."

"That cannot be his aim," Helena said.

"I do not trust his aim anymore," Berchtold answered. "He has become greedy and shortsighted, determined to bend or break every Fae to his will. This partnership with the mortals clouds his judgment, and he forgets that his first duty is to protect Faerie, not expand his own reach."

"Can't you just go to Hameln and lie?" Lukas chimed in, looking away from Clare for a moment to join in their family squabble. "I'm sure you've got some men here who can do the organizing and the arming and the … whatever it is you military types do to prepare for killing people."

"No, I cannot just lie," Berchtold said, staring at Lukas like he was a particularly thick-headed child. "And telling the Erlking the truth at this juncture would start a larger war that I have been desperately trying to head off for centuries. Beyond that, I am bound to the tithe as surely as the Erlking is. A contract is a contract in Faerie."

"Right, deception, not the Fae's strong suit," Lukas said. "Except for how the Erlking has been manipulating an entire town to lie for at least 100 years now."

"And why should *my* people keep dying for *your* war?" Clare added. Anger colored her words, and Lukas was grateful that she could even speak.

"Deception is just another form of free will," Berchtold spoke slowly, as only the very old or very stupid do.

Lukas had not yet decided which this general was.

"You humans can create your own reality through stories—and yes, through lies. And in this pact with Hameln, he decided to use your mortal power to his advantage. I think the Erlking resents that power that you can wield so carelessly."

"But that doesn't explain why you won't come to Hameln and help us defeat him." Lukas was exasperated, and struggled to continue reining in his anger. Anger could lead to mistakes, and he couldn't afford to make any in front of a potential ally as powerful as the Count. "We need the power that *you* wield if we have any chance at stopping him from taking every child in Hameln."

"You need a plan," Berchtold corrected mildly. "And I can be no part of it—knowingly, at any rate—until the Erlking breaks the bargain himself. I am still one of his vassals, no matter how much I wish I could stop his ambitions. Whatever you are planning, I wish you success. But I cannot know your intentions. When the time comes, he cannot be able to force your plans from my lips."

"You sound like Wolfhart," Lukas scoffed. "You're the leader of the Wild Hunt. That's the force that finds lost Fae in the mortal world and punishes those who use magic to harm us. As long as they're not the Erlking, right? All this talk from powerful men about honor and the rules they have to follow, but you don't *do anything*."

Lukas saw Berchtold's eyes flash with what could have been regret.

"Without these rules, powerful people become like the Erlking."

"So we came all this way for nothing." Lukas couldn't hide the despair from his voice. "If you wait until he breaks the tithe, it will be too late."

"I am as much a liability as an asset at this juncture," Berchtold continued, before speaking to Helena. "After you relieve your mother of her worries, you must ready Fort Sternenfeuer for any and all contingencies." He paused, a furrow worrying his brow. "And stay away from your father's court."

At this point, Berchtold turned to face Lukas fully, his bright green eyes boring into Lukas' own. "And you and the rest of your friends are going back to the Grey Cottage."

"But I can help you here!" Lukas objected.

"You do not understand the forces that are allayed against you," Berchtold said. "You are not prepared, and you cannot help me."

"So make me understand! Prepare me," Lukas insisted. "I have abilities. I'm not a child!"

"You *are* my son, of course you are powerful." But the Fae lord paused there, giving Lukas what felt like the most thorough inspection the bard ever had. Behind him, he heard Clare gasp, but father and son ignored both.

Lukas felt Berchtold's eyes practically peeling away the brash bravado Lukas had carefully cultivated to mask the desperation he had felt ever since he'd noticed Berchtold's eyes. *My eyes.*

"Son or no, my ability to protect you begins and ends at the Grey Cottage," Berchtold continued. "I swore to protect the Erlking's throne hundreds of years ago, when he married my sister. Your mother understood that, and I need you to, as well."

"You can't fight him?" Lukas whispered. He felt crushed by the weight of his disappointed dreams of a kind, if not loving, father. "But you have so much power." Someone—Clare, he realized—held his shoulder, rubbing soothing circles into his back.

"We used to have the power of gods," Berchtold said, finally. "And dominion over two worlds. But as our influence diminished, so did our power. Some—*most* are content to recede, to watch over Faerie and leave the mortals to their own devices."

"And others?" Lukas asked. "And to be clear, I'm talking about the Erlking here."

"Others," Berchtold continued, "are furious that we lose ground every day to both science and the Christian god. The Erlking fights a war on two fronts—one to hold dominion over all factions in Faerie who deny his supremacy. The second to stave off irrelevance in the mortal realm. Our own have seen their immortal lives cut short by centuries of bloodshed, and the Erlking see mortal lives as the only acceptable alternative. And that is how we find ourselves today, dependent on humans to continue a war of attrition in which I see no end."

"And you use children to feed the war. Why?" Lukas asked.

"Mortals have always been more … pliable than us," Berchtold explained. "We are eternal, unchanging. But humans are creative and curious enough to adapt to the most unusual conditions, especially the younglings. It is not until a mortal ages that they will become rigid, fixed in their ways. And so we decided to take children, to mold their mortal lives into the components we need. Soldiers, yes. But also inventors and healers, philosophers and diplomats."

"But what if we took away those mortal lives?" Lukas spoke almost absentmindedly, a terrifying scheme beginning to come together in his mind. *What if the Erlking couldn't use Hameln's children?*

"I despise death for death's sake." Berchtold's voice rumbled, clearly appalled at the minstrel's apparently flippant attitude toward murder.

"No, no," Lukas said. "I mean, what if we took away the option of using mortals? What if the Erlking had to depend on his own people's lives? I don't think they'd stand long for their own mass slaughter."

"There are already many who question the never-ending war," Berchtold admitted. "Though none with any real power."

"A resistance," Sophie nodded, and Lukas could see determination in her eyes. "Those who want to break the tithe."

"Those who want to end the war," Berchtold corrected her. "Immortal beings are not used to fearing for their lives. Hundreds of years of killings have made some desperate to end the Erlking's despotism. But there are not enough willing to act to change the course of the war."

"Could it be done?" Sophie pressed. Lukas wondered if she was thinking of ending her mother's alliance with the Erlking, as much as saving the children of Hameln.

"It would be … complicated," Berchtold said reluctantly. "There are treaties that bind your people to service, and even without them, the Erlking might begin to simply take what is not freely given to him."

Lukas took a deep breath, considering all the angles, the players, the goals. It was a relief to focus on other's problems, not the disappointing end to the search for his father.

"You said 'complicated.' Not impossible," Lukas pointed out, a grin beginning to grow on his face. "I can definitely work with 'not impossible.' "

I spin stories for a living, surely I can unravel a few words. Use my magic for good.

"The Fae deal in illusions to mold the world as we see fit. And illusions are easy enough and highly effective. If you make something appear to be, it will become what it seems, eventually," Berchtold paced the room as he spoke. "But to truly change something, its fabric and purpose, not just how others perceive it to be … that takes blood magic. A sacrifice so strong that the world pauses in its rotation to take note. That's the power the Erlking thrives on."

"That's what the pact is about," Lukas nodded. "But in order to break it?"

"Even more sacrifice," Berchtold said. "Equal to what is demanded."

Lukas nodded slowly before bringing his attention back to the shimmering map of Faerie on the wall, a plan unfolding in his mind. "Tell me more about this Faerie resistance."

31

After their shocking meeting with Berchtold, Clare and Sophie were led to an antechamber as Helena and Lukas prepared for their departure to the Grey Cottage.

Clare knew she had only processed a fraction of what had been discussed.

She felt as helpless as when she was five years old, trying to understand how she would never see her parents again. And then Nic. All lost to a curse, one way or another. Just pain and suffering, and for what? More war.

Clare looked around dazed, glimpsing a half-opened door to their left. She moved toward it dully, discovering a darkened room, filled with strange weapons, paintings, and tapestries.

Almost wooden, she walked inside, not caring if the others followed. Her eyes pored over glass display cases that shone weakly in the light from the other room.

She saw bejeweled helms and softly burnished weapons with intricate designs etched into the blades and handles, much more delicate work than even Casper could manage. Above each, there was a battle scene depicted on canvas or tapestry, with every gorgeous piece of metal portrayed in battle, worn proudly, or held aloft triumphantly by the obvious heroes of the piece.

She stifled a shriek of alarm when she noticed what looked like one such figure in a painting to her left move in her peripheral. But then she recognized her own dark eyes in her noticeably paler face.

"It's just a mirror," she murmured, clutching her chest before laughing weakly at herself. "Some brave adventurer you are, Clare." She moved closer to it, moving to touch it to reassure herself.

"You are supposed to be the general's guest, actually," a woman's voice said dryly from behind her. She whirled around, reaching for her hunting dagger instinctually.

"I would not draw that blade," the guard said, tense but gentle.

Clare dropped her hand.

"It is time to go," the guard said.

Clare followed the guard docilely enough, keeping her head down and her hand away from her dagger. As they walked, her nose began picking up the unmistakable smell of hay, manure, leather, and horseflesh.

She looked up to find Lukas and Sophie waiting for her. Sophie looked thoughtful, Lukas determined. And they both looked at her with pity that she wasn't ready to receive.

"You have all ridden before, I presume?" Helena called out to them, riding her own dark bay. "The horses of the Wild Hunt move as ordered, and if any of you fall, it could be a while before we can backtrack to find you again."

"Yes," Clare answered.

Sophie nodded as well, while Lukas just gave the horse a nervous, sidelong look. "I suppose …" he said.

"You can ride behind me, Lukas," Sophie offered awkwardly.

He gave a short bark of laughter before haltingly swinging onto the back of the brown-and-white pinto he was presented with. "I think I can manage," he said.

Ignoring the others, Clare settled onto her own grey, patting its neck and digging her fingers into its withers comfortingly.

Helena must have given a silent signal, because the herd leapt forward and up as one, into the dusky sky.

Clare clung more tightly to her wild mount's mane, tangling suddenly cold-numb fingers into its wiry hair so tightly that she feared she would hurt the animal.

"Whoa, easy!" she whisper-shrieked, discomfited at the realization that she had no power over her mount. No power over anything, perhaps.

But her horse ran on through the air undeterred, as if Clare wasn't even there. She sank down into its warmth, felt its neck, withers, ribs all moving together, straining parts of a glorious whole, working toward one goal.

Fly fast and free.

Clare had screwed her eyes tight against the wind, but she now forced herself to peel them open. Immediately, she felt tears streaming from her face back into the hair at her temples. When she moved to brush them away, she noticed the tears gleamed like captured starlight on her fingertips.

This was the adventure she had always dreamed of.

She heard a howl rise through the air before realizing it was coming from her own throat; it quickly became delighted laughter. *I didn't know I could still feel this ... happy.*

The cold night air was purifying, and her thoughts were suddenly clear and bright as the world blurred beneath her.

This could be her life now. Nic had returned to the smithy, as her father had always intended. Casper would become a master of the world, engineering a brilliant new future where anything was possible.

Clare was free to live the grand adventure she had always dreamed, discovering everything in this great wide world—two worlds, now that Facric had made itself known and enchanted her so. Clare felt the sorrows and responsibilities of the past few hours, the past ten years, like a large, immovable block, cracking and crumbling away to dust. But she longed to open her arms and embrace all the magic and possibilities this world had to offer.

Through her euphoria, she finally caught a familiar sight—the brilliant white light of her own moon, nearly full, illuminating a cloudless night sky. And there, Polaris, bright and steady as ever. She felt the reassuring weight of Casper's necklace pressing into her skin, and there was sweet relief in knowing it would point her in the right direction again, regardless of strange lands or skies.

The Wild Hunt responded as one to an unseen command from Helena. Before long, she felt the impact of hooves on solid earth, softer than she expected, and realized they were back on mortal land. It seemed they had slipped through Faerie unperceived, back into the forest she had grown up in once again.

Clare slid off her horse slowly, adrenaline thrumming through her body as she leaned into its trembling side. She turned, still unsteady, to find Lukas braced as if to catch her, clearly anticipating her clumsy dismount. With a grin, she threw herself into his arms. His answering smile told her he felt the same rush of excitement, as he allowed her momentum to whirl them both round once.

Looking up in his face, she now allowed herself to acknowledge his had become the first she looked to in a moment of panic or sorrow or …

Joy.

The moonlight brought his dear, dark face in stark relief—the high cheekbones, long, straight nose, and wide grin. Even when she didn't know what direction to turn, she knew she could depend on him. Magic or not, if she only had this moment before the Erlking's nightmares came to devour Hameln whole, she wanted to make the most of it.

Without a word, she pulled him down, pressing his lips to hers. In a flash, his arms tightened like a band around her ribcage, holding her close. It was a hard, desperate kiss, full of longing and passion. It was an unspoken promise that they both knew might never be kept; surviving the next hour was uncertain, much less tomorrow.

I will live, she thought, *if only to keep this moment.*

32

It took an embarrassingly long time for Clare to realize that something was wrong. A horsey snort and a clip of blunt teeth to her shoulder were all the notice she got that the herd was still moving. She pulled away from Lukas and had just noticed the dazed, pleased look on his face before a coldly amused voice sounded from somewhere in the clearing.

"The Wild Hunt, so much more predictable than the name suggests," the stranger said. "Give them a few dozen newly lost souls, and they will come to claim them."

"Or maybe," Helena's voice rang out into the night. "We are here to run down a villain. You shall do nicely, Elegast."

The Fae, presumably Elegast, stepped forward, gesturing broadly behind him with his still-wet sword. Clare's stomach lurched, and she now felt fully grounded again, with horror and disgust. The blood-drenched dell was covered in gore and … pieces of people. Mortal or Faerie, she could not tell.

"At last, princess, you have proven your worth, delivering my quarry." Elegast tilted his dark head mockingly, black eyes blazing. "And thank you, Clare, for showing yourself so nicely to the Erlking.

I always expected that spy mirror would prove to be a useful tool at Sternenfeuer, though it took longer than I expected."

Clare stood as still as possible, though her mind was whirling. This despicable man knew her name? And something about a mirror …

The movement in the display hall. The one she wasn't supposed to be in.

It hadn't been her imagination, or her own face. Her curiosity had alerted the Erlking to their presence in Faerie, and for what? A spiteful quest for adventure when she felt she was ignored. Her joy from just moments earlier twisted into cold shame in her stomach. She felt Lukas snag her hand, but kept her own limp in his grip.

Seeing that his words had hit their mark, Elegast turned to Helena. "Berchtold does not revisit his deeds of valor as often as the king expected. This is the first time the mirror has shown us anything useful," he said. "I suppose his vanity lies in other places."

Her silence did not seem to bother him. "You will join us to your father's court, I expect?" Then his face transformed into a gruesome smile, with far too many teeth in his mouth. "Or would you like to challenge me?"

Helena slowly forced his blade down with her own, though her flashing eyes never left his face. "I do not seek your position, *champion*," she sneered at the title. "Perhaps you should seek out my mother's sword, instead. Or are you sick of losing to her, as well?"

He growled low in his throat, but made no move against Helena or the rest of them. He wasn't a complete idiot, then.

"Enough," Helena scolded him like a wayward pup. "No more unnecessary blood should be shed tonight. Take me to my father. And leave the Wild Hunt to their purpose."

"Not so fast, princess. Our king wants the children, too. After all, they've already been promised to our side." Elegast used his sword to point to each of them in turn.

"But we're—" Clare started to argue, but Helena held her back.

"I don't have the authority or power to stop this." Helena's words were soft, belying her steely gaze. "But I will get us out of this, Clare. On Nic's life. Trust me."

"Don't swear on my brother's life, Helena," Clare shot back. "I understand what a promise means in Faerie. Just … just help me keep them all safe."

Clare glanced around at the mounted hunters who had made quick work of gathering the disparate bodies together, carrying the poor lost souls, one and all, in black bags.

They were now the Erlking's prisoners. *Is this my fault? When I was snooping around in that hall, the Erlking's spies really saw me there?*

"Where are they taking us?" Clare hissed at Helena.

"To my father," Helena answered simply.

Elegast made a complicated series of gestures with both hands, and they were suddenly surrounded by men who were herding the four of them into the dark woods. She saw Sophie and Lukas briefly before the men surrounded her, heard the profane tirade Sophie unleashed on their new captors as Lukas tried in vain to calm her—and shield her small body from retribution. But the soldiers just laughed.

"And then? Will he try to kill us? Send us to the frontlines of his war?" Clare asked.

"No," Helena said. "Not right away, at least. I am sure he has grander plans than that."

"And that doesn't scare you?" Clare asked, her voice rising with panic. "Don't you feel anything?"

"Would that be helpful to you?" Helena asked coolly, scanning their surroundings, as if cataloguing and calculating everything in her sight.

"*Helpful?*" Clare fumed. "It would be helpful if you gave some indication that any of this actually mattered. That in two weeks' time we won't just be a distant memory as you continue playing the pawn between two immortal men who see the entire world as their chessboard."

Helena finally focused on her, but said nothing.

"You're just a … a statue, aren't you? A beautiful marble statue." Clare paused, searching for the right words. "It's not your glowing skin, or shining eyes. Everything is effortless for you. We're fighting and scrapping to survive, and with you…nothing touches you."

Clare brought fists to both of her eyes, squeezing the tears out and away.

"You're beautiful. God, you're luminous," Clare said. "But you're so remote. It's like trying to reach the horizon. I know I never could, not in a million years. How do you *do* that?"

"You make me sound like a heartless creature," Helena said, now staring steadily ahead as they were marched toward a green hillock that grew impossibly large as they drew closer. "If I knew how to, don't you think I would try to stop whatever it is that makes me so … alien to you?"

"I just want to know that this *matters* to you," Clare admitted on a sigh. She looked Helena dead in the eye. "None of us are expendable. Don't toy with any of us. Or you'll learn what us mere mortals are really made of." She raised her hand to the dagger at her waist that their captors hadn't even registered as a threat.

It was a bluff, and not a particularly convincing one. But Helena nodded in understanding before a giant cave, threaded with ancient, crumbling tree roots, opened in the hill and swallowed their party whole.

The Erlking didn't bother sending for his unwilling guests, squirreling Clare, Lukas, and Sophie away unseen—no gloating monologue, not even a snide comment. They were just shoved through a door and left in an enormous, gorgeously appointed ballroom to imagine the worst.

Just as well, since Clare had no desire to see him ever again.

Clare inched toward the wall, casually inspecting their surroundings. There was a painting on the wall in an elaborate golden frame, showing a party in full swing. She realized the scene was very much like the one they were currently in, though the hall was full instead of empty.

She realized the picture—or was it a mirror?—was enchanted in some way. Sophie stalked about the crowd, angry and watchful; Lukas' knowing grin over her shoulder. Mesmerized, she watched them move through the crowds of Fae.

In the scene each of her friends slowly transformed before her eyes—Lukas' face elongating, his green eyes blazing out of his head like a demented jack-o'-lantern alight for Samhain. Sophie marched about, her form becoming ever more fuzzy and indistinct, until she was just a dark, human-sized smear in the background, like a dirty mark on a stained-glass window. Horrified, Clare reached for her fading friend, but touched only cold glass.

A miserable, hunched figure on the floor appeared as Lucie melting into the marbled floor like ice into water, until there was nothing left but a shimmering puddle.

Clare finally gathered her nerve to shift her gaze to meet her own face. Again, her image was faithful at first. But before long her haunted expression turned into a devious smirk, and her mirror-self produced her hunting dagger from its sheath, licking the wicked blade that glinted in the harsh light of the chandelier. Clare pounded on the glass now, shivering in terror, as her reflection smiled back with a mouth full of teeth and blood that now trickled down her chin to the cold, white floor.

She turned from the terrible images, and saw that her friends were all still around her, whole and unharmed. Only a tinkling of devious laughter from the mirror creatures behind her told Clare that her personal nightmare had not played out completely unnoticed by some supernatural force.

I really hate Fae magic.

Lukas, attuned to her distress in a way that she wasn't yet comfortable owning, was at her side in an instant.

"I thought I'd find my father in Hameln," Lukas admitted, a

bemused look on his face, as if he could scarcely believe his own naivete. "I knew that's where Mother was from. I thought I'd find him carousing at the festival. Or if Johann was my father, that I could charm Katherine into an invitation to her court. Instead, I found you."

At his confusing words, she finally turned to look at him, searching his face for meaning. Which was probably his intent all along, she realized ruefully.

Clare snorted indelicately, cutting her eyes away. "I'm sorry about that."

"Why?" Lukas brought his hand up, gently tracing her cheek with his fingertips. "I'm not."

"Don't," she said, cutting off both his words and his touch. "You don't know yet."

"Know…?" he trailed off, eyebrows raised.

"I - It's my fault," she answered, ducking her head so that she wouldn't see her own horror reflected in his face. "The Erlking, or one of his minions, they saw me at Fort Sternenfeuer."

"What do you mean?" his voice was gentle, but he didn't try to hide his confusion.

"I was mad," she said, finally lifting her head. "We were sent away like useless children, and I … retaliated. I went exploring and, and … and I was *seen* somehow."

"That Elegast fellow," Lukas said with sudden understanding. "That's what he was talking about."

Clare nodded, glum and ashamed.

"Well, I can't really scold you for sneaking into an interesting room, seeing how my jail break was what put us on this path in the first place," he said, bending down to catch her eye again. "And who's to say there weren't spies there to report our movements anyway? The Erlking doesn't seem like the trusting sort. Going to Berchtold was always a calculated risk."

Clare narrowed her eyes. "But it was my behavior that got us caught," she insisted. "My decision, my shortsighted, stubborn—"

"So it was your turn to make a mistake," Lukas interrupted her. "Now maybe you'll be a little more kind to the rest of us mortals in the future."

"Hameln is depending on us," Clare hissed. "That means we can't make mistakes."

"Did you forget your elder brother? And she's playing it coy, but I'm pretty sure that Helena can hold her own, being older than Christ and all," Lukas responded, twisting a curl of Clare's dark hair around his fingers.

"Nic and Helena aren't always *here*," Clare said, gently slapping his hand away again.

"So it's up to us to fix the whole broken world, then?" he asked.

Clare shook her head, slowly but firmly. "Not the whole world. But I have to take care of my family first. They—the whole town—need us to fight for them."

"I came to Hameln to find my father, not defeat a pack of monsters and break an ancient curse." Lukas looked so lonely in that moment that something in her heart seemed to snap. Clare grabbed his hands, and his full attention. She pushed past the shiver that the intimacy brought, focusing on tackling the danger that twisted her stomach in knots even now.

She held her breath as Lukas paused, tilting his head back, to give her a long, appraising look. "But we can't let them down."

"Whatever happens, whatever we come up against, I know we can handle it. As long as we're smart and we work together," she insisted.

Lukas took a deep, fortifying breath before pulling his hands away, holding them in his own lap. "I understand. Vanquishing evil before finding love. But maybe … maybe after?"

"After," Clare agreed with a determined nod and a faint smile, tendrils of heat slowly twisting in her chest as her heart chugged almost painfully.

33

The door before Sophie and the others opened to a resplendent receiving hall, airy and glittering like frost in dim morning sun. Braziers blazed silently throughout the cavernous space with Faerie fire to cast a cold blue hue throughout the room. The Faeries dressed in silk and satin, immortal nightmares in material that looked like sculpted gloom to disguise their more horrifying disfigurements. Sophie attempted to hide her fear behind the courtier's mask she'd cultivated for years, but her hands were cold with dread. Each child she passed was dressed as they must have been the day they left home, she realized, some of their outfits looking more like costumes from yesteryear.

When she paused to watch them more closely, she wished she hadn't. *God's teeth, look at them! They've been ... mutilated.* Many of the children had permanent smiles etched on their faces, or ears where their eyes should be. Some were missing parts of their fingers, cut down by one and two knuckles; still others had only a thumb at the end of a wide palm. *How had they endured it?*

One unfortunate boy's vacant blue eyes reminded Sophie so much of Lucie's that it took her breath away. *Will I end up like them?*

"Why—how did this happen to them?" Sophie asked the room.

Helena glanced at the unfortunate children before looking away again, shame on her face.

"The ones who don't fight are used as servants or … entertainment. The Fae in my father's court are not kind, especially to those they don't consider equal."

The flickering blue-green half-light made every face a bit sinister, with amusement, sorrow, and joy cycling through the expressions of the dazed humans, but she saw nothing like compassion in this hall of horrors. No such emotion lived long in the deadly Faerie court ruled by the Erlking.

In fact, most in the crowded hall continued to feast unabated as she and the others were brought through the crowd, whispering while cracking morsels like nuts between their shining teeth. They looked suspiciously like tiny human fingers displayed on platters of bone and inlaid silver. Amber chalices were filled to the brim, the blood red liquid dripping down the grinning faces of those who imbibed more carelessly.

Sophie turned away, physically revulsed by the toll of this pact. *This isn't just wrong, it's horrifying. And Maman had built this?*

She decided it was better not to look too closely, though she found her fingers itching and her mind racing, mentally composing this entry in her journal.

The dark and sparkling kaleidoscope crowd parted seamlessly as they were brought before the Erlking's throne, this one made of bone instead of wood. Helena was there, dressed in lavish silks instead of her usual armor. No matter the costume, she always looked fierce and proudly beautiful. Her dark face was impassive as always, though Sophie noticed she avoided her eye.

How will we survive this?

Without preamble, the Erlking pulled a familiar silver object from the folds of his cape. Lukas gasped. Now it was Clare and Sophie holding him back as he attempted to reach for his flute.

"An amusing trinket." The Erlking interrupted the delicate whispers of the court, holding Lukas' flute in one ring-encrusted hand, as if it were a child's toy. And perhaps it was, to the king of the Fae. "Faerie-made millennia ago. But how could a boy such as you, hidden away in the woods your whole life, have come to own one of our artifacts, hmm?"

"It was a gift from my Faerie godmother," Lukas sneered, defiant. "I used it to call for my carriage before it turned back into a pumpkin."

This time, the Erlking did laugh. The answering titters from the court made for a sinister sound, and Sophie's hair stood up.

"You are just delightful!" the Erlking's smile widened, slow and sweet as honey. "I can't imagine why the dwarves were hiding you away."

Sophie furrowed her brow. *In all her visits to the Grey Cottage, she never saw any dwarves.*

"Perhaps because your face is very ugly, and you terrify small children," Lukas said. "Though it could also be the genocide."

"Rachel, of course, with her generous heart, can be excused for harboring a changeling child for so many years. She always did love the … *misunderstood*," the Erlking's grotesque features became more terrifying when the smile dropped from his face.

"What do you mean, 'changeling child'? Are you speaking of Kane?" Lukas' voice rose, suddenly gruff with emotion. "What do you know about me and my mother?" Sophie felt her frame shiver with tension, willing Lukas to stay calm.

The Erlking turned his attention to the girls at his side, and Sophie stiffened her spine, refusing to look weak in front of the villain.

"And you, Clarebear." The Erlking leaned forward on his throne. "Your magic is threadbare for Hameln, it is true. I had hoped that *auslander* blood would keep you from becoming a thorn in my side, and it nearly did the trick. You're just strong enough in my lands to vex me yet. If only I'd kept you away from the

Wolfhart's influence and Esma's blessing. I'd hoped you'd prove to be more … malleable. Like our dear Lucie."

Sophie felt her friend trembling, but whether it was fear or anger, she couldn't tell. And she refused to turn her head and look, in case the Erlking sniffed out her concern like a hellish bloodhound. *He's playing with us. He* wants *us confused and terrified.*

But of course, he sought her out. It was her turn to be mocked.

"Sophie. Almost as beautiful as your bewitching mother," the Erlking mused as his eyes glanced over her features.

Sophie snorted in derision.

"Now there is a lady who uses her gifts well. A little too well, sometimes. But your family served my purposes well enough. I thank you for your service to my crown. It may be the only thing that saves your mortal life tonight." Sophie blanched. As if she was supposed to be grateful for dooming her people.

With rising dread, Sophie glanced over at Clare, who was clutching her charm once again, tangled up with Casper's iron sword and a shell ring. The clearly terrified girl somehow cleared Sophie's own resolve. She had to do something. Without Lukas' flute they had no magic, but there still must be some way to escape. Maybe Helena would cut her father down and take—

"Halt, my lord husband." A clear sweet voice cut through the foreboding silence before the Erlking's interrogation could continue.

The interloper came to stand in front of the exhausted children. She was beautiful, with glowing dark skin and silvery white hair cascading down her back. Her gown shimmered in the Faerie light, matching perfectly the fiery opals in her crown.

"I owe a favor to one of these mortals. And she calls upon it now."

The Erlking leaned back, the only indication he had even processed an interruption in his evil monologue.

"A favor?" His voice was even and low, tightly controlled, which terrified Sophie even more.

Confused and relieved, Sophie's breath left her body in an

audible gasp. A Faerie queen coming to rescue them? God's bones, she'd take it.

The queen held her hand out to Clare expectantly. Clare hesitated before slipping her necklace off, giving the ring back to the queen. The pearly ring shone in her hand, and where she saw beauty, the Erlking seemed to see a foiled plan.

"A favor," the queen affirmed. She turned to Clare. "You wish me to take you and your friends to safety?"

Clare nodded fearfully.

The queen turned back to the Erlking. "Do you challenge my charged further, lord husband?" she asked mildly.

He stared at her a moment, speechless. Looking at the ring like a maggot wriggling in her hand, he gave a disgusted motion of his hand.

"Fine!" the Erlking's tone belied the word, ripped from his lipless mouth in a snarl. "Take them. But they go without this instrument the boy loves so." And he crushed the pipes in his monstrous fingers, until they were nothing more than a small ball of shimmering metal.

Lukas was too proud to make a sound, but his body collapsed into itself, as if he had lost the ability to hold himself up. Sophie scrambled beneath his weight to keep him from falling.

So that was it. Their one advantage, crushed by the Erlking like it was nothing at all. Helena had clearly chosen her father's side, and perhaps Lucie had, as well. *We have no magic, no allies here, and barely a hope to protect Hameln now.*

Utterly deflated, Sophie followed the beautiful queen out of the hall.

As they gathered in the queen's chambers, Clare was shocked to see one familiar face—Lucie, her smile tight, her eyes despairing. She rushed to her oldest friend.

"What are you *doing* here?"

"Father thought I needed to learn a lesson about ... oh, who knows. Terror, I guess?" Lucie's chin wobbled before she steeled herself. "So he sent me here. Luckily, Queen Ursel had need of a chambermaid."

Suddenly flooded with relief, Clare looked over at the queen, flanked by her silver-armored guard. So different from the woman she had "rescued" in Hameln only months before Clare had endangered them in the first place.

Lucie squeezed her hands. "I don't know what that guilty look is about, but I know you did the best you could. That's all we can ever do."

Lucie really could understand. "We were captured because of me. My thoughtless actions let the Erlking know we were in Faerie."

"No," Lucie said, turning fierce. "You were captured because the Erlking is a monster. And we're all getting away from him because Helena and her mother are not monsters like him." Clare watched as her friend walked to Helena's side, hooking her pinky finger to the Fae princess', smiling fondly at her.

A flicker of warmth filled her chest at Lucie's defense. Clare gave a small nod before focusing on the hasty update from Helena about their current precarious position.

"...your instincts are good," Queen Ursel was telling Lukas with a grave smile. "And I admire the grandeur of your first kill. But the nixies are all in an uproar. They have been pulling drowned rats from their waters for months, now."

"That was ... not my intention," Lukas answered. "Please give them my sincere apologies."

"Nevertheless, I would steer clear of the rivers for a bit," the queen told him. "Just until they forget the stench of rats clogging up the tributaries."

"Right, I'll avoid water," he answered.

"Be careful and brave, my nephew." Queen Ursel caressed Lukas' cheek affectionately. "And remember that you have everything you need, even if you never find the answers you seek." Without another word, she seemed to melt into the shadows, leaving only the sound of rustling silken skirts and water falling far away.

"Nephew, eh?" Lukas scoffed into the dark, empty corridor before turning his heel to hiss at the rest of them.

"Welcome to the family, coz. Such as it is," Helena mused quietly as her mother vanished into the gloom.

"Wait, does this mean you're royalty now, too?" Clare asked, finally having a moment to let the news wash over her.

Lukas rolled his eyes in frustration.

"No, technically he's just related to royalty," Helena answered for him.

"I am related to my mother, and that's it," Lukas answered through gritted teeth.

At that, Lucie looked up at him sharply. "Hey!"

"And Lucie," Lukas amended begrudgingly.

"Wait a moment, then," Lucie spoke thoughtfully, twisting the Star of David around her neck. "If you're Lukas' cousin. And I'm Lukas' cousin. That would make us …"

"Nothing," Helena replied, all business. "Our connection is less than tenuous, and it would be completely lost along with Lukas' life. Which, by the way, is my father's fondest wish. So maybe we should focus on canceling the family reunion? Our shared blood will be painting the walls if we do not leave. *Now*."

"Where are we going?" Clare found herself gasping for breath minutes later as they raced through the damp underground tunnels of the hillock, more from pure terror than exhaustion.

"I am taking you to Berchtold," Helena said, pausing only to push the others ahead. "The choosing ceremony takes place tomorrow, and we must gather our forces to Hameln before the ceremony begins."

"Tomorrow?" Clare skidded to a stop before Helena pushed her again with an almost feral growl. "*How?*"

"Christ's teeth, I thought we've only been gone for two days!" Sophie said, incredulous at the news. "What do you mean two months have passed?"

"Why is it so difficult for you mortals to understand that everything works differently in Faerie? Of course that includes time," Helena replied. She didn't even break her stride, rushing them through a maze of dark hallways. Sophie just hoped Helena knew where she was taking them.

"You know, this actually does explain a lot," Lukas piped up from the back. Somehow, he wasn't even breathing hard. "Like, how you can be older than the pope and yet still be so easily duped by a bunch of us mortals?"

"Enough! We have to get out of here." Helena's eyes bounced around, searching desperately for an escape. "We may not survive whatever my father has planned in the mortal realm, but we have no chance at all in his world."

"But the Faerie queen saved us," Sophie argued. "He said he had to honor her oath. And he can't *lie*."

"Yes, and the Erlking knows exactly how far that oath extends. He chose his words carefully, as always, and I don't doubt he has his minions hunting us down already. Follow me."

Quite suddenly, they came upon a blue-green lagoon fed by a beautiful waterfall, ten-feet-tall and only twice as wide as Clare's body.

"Through here, hurry." An impatient Helena pushed first Lucie, then Lukas, Sophie and finally Clare through the rushing water. Clare winced, anticipating the icy fall on her skin, but discovered instead that she was merely sloshing through the pool where the water was falling at her feet.

She turned around, delighted, just avoiding a collision as Helena came through the misty veil of rushing water.

As everyone in the group paused to get their bearings, Clare peered down into the still waters outside the waterfall's reach. The pool acted as a brief respite for the twisting Weser River. She had spent many a lazy afternoon dipping her feet in its shallows.

"Berchtold will be here." Clare heard Helena's insistent voice betraying more emotion than was strictly normal. "Time can be difficult for us, but he will come."

"Where are we, exactly?" Sophie asked.

Helena closed her eyes and raised her face to the sky, as if tasting the wind. "Back in your world. A few miles north of Hameln."

Clare had wandered back to the water's edge, looking down at her watery face smiling sadly back at her. But as she stared into her own dark eyes, she realized that they were looking frantically beyond her shoulder. She watched her lips move in warning, a hand reaching out of the lake to point behind her urgently.

"*You must go!*" her reflection commanded, in a voice Clare did not recognize.

Eyes widening, she twisted up and around while reaching for her hunting dagger. And there she was faced with her greatest fears come to life: The invisible bloodsucking creatures who had haunted her sleep since before she even knew what a nightmare was.

The terrifyingly familiar translucent monsters approached, and she couldn't suppress her fear facing their feral, toothy mouths. This was real. Her nightmares had broken through to her waking hours, and now everyone she loved would be lost.

Only Helena's triumphant hunting horn broke through her paralyzing terror. And somehow, it had brought Nic to them, as well.

"Haven't fought these ugly creatures in an age, eh, Helena?" Nic was actually *laughing* in the face of these monsters.

"They are not my favorite of the Erlking's pets," Helena replied, with a businesslike thrust of her sword into the nightmare's face. "How does he keep dreaming up such hideous beasts?"

"I think it was me, actually," Clare admitted. "I've had terrible dreams about these monsters for as long as I can remember."

"Well, he does like to intimidate any he sees as a threat." Helena smiled at her grimly. "Like a stubborn blacksmith determined to protect her town."

"I am not a threat," Clare said, taking out her dagger. "I just keep finding myself in all the wrong places."

Helena's reply was lost as the creatures attacked.

34

Helena and Nic moved as one, spinning and advancing back-to-back, slashing at any nightmare that stood against them. Clare felt Lukas and Sophie hovering at her sides, as she drew her hunting dagger—a pitiful defense against the creatures, but surely even magical beasts preferred to avoid the sharp end of a knife.

"It actually feels good to fight back," she murmured to herself, a fierce sense of accomplishment rushing through her bloodstream.

Lukas grinned in approval. "I'll be the gentleman and let you take the lead in the killing, then."

It was Lucie who was soon surrounded by the nightmares, the first to get through the waterfall, and therefore the furthest from the others. Her face was pale, but she stood her ground, swinging a large branch around to stave off their teeth-lined snouts. Lucie's breath was already coming in short gasps, struggling to hold the blunt weapon aloft.

"Lucie!" Helena called out.

She broke her formation with Nic, launching herself toward Lucie and moving like quicksilver among the monstrosities. Helena cut them down as if they were no more dangerous than scarecrows, made of straw instead of razorlike teeth and claws. Lucie moved back to get out of her way, tripping over her own feet to land hard on her backside, reduced to staring at the creatures.

Clare sensed movement behind her, but Lukas was already there, thwarting a creature's attack with a low grunt.

The bloody business was over quickly, the creatures dead at their feet.

"Mindless lackeys," Helena sneered. "Too stupid to know they can't win. You are fine?"

Helena looked no more perturbed than if she had just ended her favorite dance with a particularly undesirable partner.

"You saved my life," Lucie breathed up at Helena, with a wide, pleased smile. Helena stooped low to bring Lucie to her feet, using one arm to balance them both while Helena still gripped her sword.

"You are a strong ally," Helena replied, her eyes scanning for more enemies, never landing on Lucie. "We need—"

Lucie stopped Helena's lips with her own, gently directing Helena's face up for a sweet, shy kiss. Seconds later, she released the princess, slowly pulling away before opening her soft blue eyes.

"Thank you," she whispered.

Clare had never seen the Faerie girl shocked to silence, and she found it was quite enjoyable, even in their current desperate situation.

Helena brought her fingertips to her own lips, pressing gently as if to memorize the feel of Lucie against them. "We should go. My father will soon know his attack failed. We can wait for Berchtold no longer."

They turned as one to gather themselves and flee. But Lukas' sharp cry had Sophie running back toward him and the water without a thought. Nicolaus was faster, wrenching one of the nightmare creatures from the minstrel's back with his bare hands. It was a mistake. The monster twisted in Nic's grip, latched itself around his neck, and bit down viciously.

"Nicolaus!" The scream tore from Clare's throat as Nic fell. Running with a speed that she didn't know she possessed, Clare stabbed at the monster, even as she knew the ordinary mortal blade would do nothing more than annoy it.

To her astonishment, her dagger hit true. It cleaved the creature's snout from its head, and both fell to the ground with a sickening squelch before dissipating into a reddish mist.

Clare sheathed her blade quickly and with no time to question her good fortune dropped to Nic's side. He groaned weakly as his eyes had rolled back into his head. Sophie watched over them anxiously as Clare supported his neck, twisting it around gently to see the wound. Sophie swallowed hard at the sight of a nasty, circular wound at the base of Nic's skull. His leather armor was already soaked through with his own blood. *No! Not Nic!*

Clare held him up in her lap, while Sophie ripped off her cloak to bunch it under his head, both for added support and to stanch the alarming flow of blood.

Helena dispatched the others quickly, moving Sophie aside to join Clare and Lukas by Nic's side. Lucie moved beside her, squeezing Sophie's hand tight.

They all looked on as Helena moved the cloak aside before replacing it quickly with a grimace. "We need to get him to Rachel. Now."

Clare looked around her in a panic. Could they even move him and keep him from bleeding out at the same time? Her vision tunneled and she felt the panic climbing up her throat until Lucie's voice cut through her haze.

"Clare, he will be fine, once we get him to Rachel. I've seen her cure those on the edge of death, and Nic is far too stubborn to give up now." Lucie rubbed soothing circles on Clare's back, practically sitting in the water in order to comfort her. "We will carry him, we can—"

Suddenly, Lucie fell into the water, so quickly and silently, it seemed to Clare as if she had just winked out of existence. There was barely even a ripple on the water's surface by the time Clare had reached the shoreline.

"Lucie!" Helena ran up from behind Clare, but Lucie was gone. Clare watched her slam her twin swords in their sheaths before grabbing fistfuls of her own silvery hair in frustration. "Damnable nixies! They must have hauled her back to their lair in Faerie."

Clare felt the hysteria overwhelm her again, her lungs squeezed in her chest. The capricious water sprites were rumored to eat the still-beating hearts straight from doomed sailor's chests. Or else just keep them in their underwater caves to keep humans like coddled pets. What could they want with Lucie? "Did the Erlking send them?"

"There is no way of knowing," Helena said. She was looking down, now knee-deep in the river. "And it does not matter, she is in danger in either case. We do not have time …"

Helena was grimly silent a moment, and Clare could see she was wracking her brain for the best solution to this latest catastrophe.

Clare stepped toward her. "You go after Lucie. After you've got her, we will go directly to Berchtold," she ordered. "I'll take Nic to the Grey Cottage now, it is one of the only safe places left for any of us."

With that, Helena dove into the water after Lucie. It would have been romantic if not for the horror they now faced without Helena.

"How are we going to do this?" Sophie asked, teary-eyed.

Clare was torn. Could she leave Cas to fend for himself in Hameln, so quickly after Nic was attacked? But of course, this catastrophe was larger than just their family. "I will take Nic back to the Grey Cottage," she declared firmly, the tremble barely noticeable even to her own ears. The rest of you, go back to Hameln. Buy us time."

"By yourself?" Lukas yelled. "You can't!"

Clare had already begun tearing strips of her dress to secure Sophie's cloak to Nic's head. Perhaps she could use her belt to attach him securely over her back?

"I'm stronger than you think. I'm Hameln's blacksmith, after all."

"And Lucie?" Sophie asked, her eyes casting back to the water.

"We just have to trust that Helena will find her," Clare answered. "And that Berchtold will send aid."

Sophie moved forward jerkily, nearly falling into Clare's arms.

"Everything's falling apart, Sophie," Clare whispered into her ear as they embraced. "I'm sorry I can't protect us from this madness."

She felt Sophie squeeze her tight in response. As she released Sophie, Clare saw a new determination in the younger girl's eyes. "We won't let the Erlking take anyone else."

The return to Hameln was quiet and tense, with Sophie intent on finding out the truth about her mother and Lukas lost in his own seemingly dark thoughts.

"Lukas?" she called to him.

"Do you trust me?" he asked.

"Of course!" Sophie answered without hesitation. "You're like a …brother."

Lukas didn't seem to notice. "I just need time. Time and an instrument …"

"What are you thinking about doing, Lukas?"

He glanced at her briefly, before looking down at his own feet again. "I need your trust for a little longer, too, Soph."

The clouds hid the sun in the sky, making the early afternoon feel more like early evening. But the long shadows suited their purposes just fine, so she took it as a good omen.

What they thought would be the hardest part of the journey—getting past Hameln's twenty-two guard towers without being seen—proved to be the easiest. The towers had been unmanned, and the Everstein soldiers were instead roaming the streets.

These men were nothing like the roving bands of town deputies at the Obolen festival. They were professional soldiers who were clearly on some sort of mission.

Sophie's troubled countenance cleared immediately at the sight of her mother's men. A lifetime of pranks and camaraderie had her eager to make her presence known. But she was stopped from popping out behind the barrels where they crouched, Lukas' strong hand to her shoulder. He shook his head sharply.

"We don't know if they're searching for us, or rounding up any children they can find," he told her gently.

She felt the blood freeze in her veins. Stupid. She was still thinking like a silly, pampered princess.

She nodded her head, acquiescing before settling back on her heels, waiting them out. Lukas breathed a quiet sigh of relief. The longer it took for anyone to figure out where they were, the longer they had to find Casper and the allies. Then they could stop the ceremony.

After studying the troop movements for a turn, Lukas gently nudged Sophie along, heading for the forge. Using the key she still had, they moved quickly and quietly through the showroom and upstairs. They soon found Casper at his workbench, muttering darkly and hands moving quickly over his latest creations.

"It's nice to see some things never change around here," Lukas called out cheerfully as he entered the room.

Startled, Casper twirled around awkwardly with a wordless yell, flinging his newest device forward in alarm. The scowl on his pale face transformed into a delighted grin only when he realized who had entered.

"I almost killed you!" Casper cried, hastily returning a strange stick in his hand back to the table.

When he caught Sophie's eye, she didn't hesitate, crushing him in a hug. Lukas moved to grasp both of them together, and they held each other as if it had been years.

"I'd almost given up on you," Cas mumbled through the press

of limbs. "Nic said he was going to bring you back, but it had been so long."

Casper stopped, craning his head around. "Where are Nic and Clare?"

Lukas stepped back, though Sophie refused to loosen her hold.

"They're at the Grey Cottage," she told him. "Nic was injured, but Rachel will fix him up. Clare should be here soon, as well as Wolfhart, I imagine."

"No Wolfhart," Casper said, red eyes darting to Lukas over Sophie's shoulder.

He's been crying, she realized.

"I've been writing with Freddie. He…your mother had him killed, Sophie," Casper said.

"What?!" Sophie shrieked, pulling back to search Casper's face. "No, but he was coming here, right after…he said he'd stop this!"

Lukas didn't even speak, falling into an empty chair and staring into the middle distance.

Casper looked between the two of them before gently disentangling himself from Sophie's arms.

"The Everstein soldiers arrived in town soon after. Now there's a curfew, and all families have been confined to their homes. Three days ago, the children they could find were taken to the Nixe. We didn't even have time to try to get anyone out…"

Sophie gripped his hand. "This isn't your fault, Cas. None of it."

He gave her a weak smile. "But what about Berchtold? *He's* coming, right?"

Lukas' face hardened at the question before he leaned down, pressing the heels of both hands in his face.

Sophie breathed deeply, trying to catch her breath before she finally stumbled through the tale of their imprisonment and narrow escape. "We cannot depend on Faerie," she finished. "We must fix this ourselves."

Lukas roused himself, jaw locked and lips pursed. "So we're doing this alone." He looked resolute, if pale, as he glanced over the weapon Casper had drawn on them moments before. "What's this?" he asked, pointing to the device that looked to be made of wood rather than metal.

"I've been thinking about a walking stick," Cas answered casually. "The world seems a bit more dangerous lately, and I thought it would give me an edge if I need it."

"Moving swiftly has become a regular occurrence lately, yes." Lukas looked over the drawings more carefully. "But what is this metal hook on it?"

"Oh, that's where you pull back the crossbow and nock the arrow, right along the track in the middle there. So far, I can only fit one projectile, but I'm still working on it," Cas explained with a glint in his eye. "I thought it best to be swift and dangerous."

Lukas nodded in approval. "Nice to see you're making something for yourself for a change."

"And I made this for you," Casper said, grabbing something from underneath still more papers. The boy had no time for pleasantries, and Sophie supposed he was right. The Erlking could strike Hameln at any moment. Sophie looked down at the pendant swinging from a leather cord in Casper's grip. It was another Star of David, though much bigger than the one he'd created for Lucie—as big across as his own palm.

"Casper, thank you, but I can't accept this." Lukas looked at the necklace almost fearfully. "It's made of tin, not iron," Casper replied, clearing Lukas' refusal away with a swipe of his other hand. "Clare told me about the gloves you wore while you worked at the smithy. How you avoided touching the iron there."

"She was talking about me?" Lukas' slow, easy smile spread on his face.

Sophie stared at him in amusement. "We don't have time for your crush, Lukas."

"We were talking about how you always seem to know how to avoid real work," Casper explained, carefully looking only at the pendant. *A loyal younger brother to the end*, Sophie thought.

"I'm sure." Lukas tentatively reached out for the star, clearly pleased.

"You see that latch there?" Casper pointed to the back of one of the straight, parallel pieces of the star. "There's a mechanism. If you pull it up, the pieces should make …"

Sophie watched as the interlocking pieces slipped down perpendicularly to form a line of a tiny metal bar growing shorter, left to right. It looked remarkably like…

"A pan flute!" Lukas looked astounded yet again by Casper's ingenuity. "Can I play it?"

"See for yourself!" Casper's self-satisfied grin gave him his answer.

Lukas carefully blew over the tiny pipes. A sweet, clear chord rang through the room.

"This is marvelous, Casper." Lukas grasped the younger boy's hand while looping his new pendant over his own head. "I don't know how you managed it. Thank you!"

Sophie smiled, working hard to ignore the jealous realization that Casper hadn't made anything for her. "It's wonderful," she agreed.

"I know it's not the same," Casper said. "They can't replace what the Erlking took, but I didn't want you to forget you're the greatest musician I've ever heard, with or without your magic flute."

Lukas' smile turned grim.

"They're going to tell tales of our deeds today," Lukas said. "Let's go save the town's children."

The next order of business for Cas and Sophie was sneaking into the Nixe and figuring out the Council's plan for the more than 100 children who were now imprisoned at the inn.

"Do the people even know why they've been rounded up?" Sophie asked, incensed on their behalf.

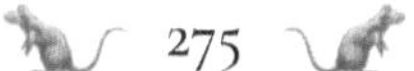

"The Council told us that heathen invaders from the East are seeking to take children to slave markets," Cas explained. "It was determined—by them—that the children would be safest there, since the church would be targeted first."

Sophie snorted. "That's a strange way to describe Faerie, but not entirely false."

Going in through the cellar, Cas and Sophie crept quietly down the hallway to his aunt's office toward the sounds of the two women fighting.

"You didn't have to kill him. You could have sent him away," Aggie argued, so close to the Countess that their heads nearly touched. "He was an ally, and when the next chosen Wolfhart finds out how their predecessor was treated, they won't be eager to work with us."

"I don't need to defend my actions to the Wolfhart—or you," Katherine snarled back. "Regardless, the tithe is safe and ready to be delivered."

"I have gathered them at the Nixe to be protected, not rounded up for slaughter." Aggie's voice was hard as steel, though she kept her volume low. Sophie had never seen anyone speak to her mother in such a manner. "You cannot think we would just hand them over?"

"What choice do we have?" Katherine responded. "Do you think he won't come here and take them himself, if needs be? Do not underestimate the Erlking."

"Their parents have entrusted them to my care. Not yours," Aggie said. "The ceremony will not proceed. We can live through plague and pestilence as well as every other town in the empire. The Erlking asks for too much this time."

"You will bring ruin on us all," the Countess sneered. "You believe he will settle for simply rescinding his protection? He will actively go after everything we hold dear. And we are not yet ready for a full assault."

"Not yet ready?" Aggie's tone became suspicious to Sophie's ears. "What have you been plotting, Katherine?"

"Just an insurance policy for a future in which we no longer live and die at the whim of Faerie," Katherine said. "But I cannot bring that future about without more time. A year, at least. Until then, this is the sacrifice we need to make."

"It seems to me you're not making much of a sacrifice." Casper stepped out awkwardly, ignoring Sophie's whispered curses to *stay put* as he limped into the office, walking stick in hand. She followed behind reluctantly. How was *she* the cautious one now?

"Sophie?!" Her mother gasped, staring but not making a move.

"Casper, where have you been?" Aunt Aggie demanded, standing up from behind her desk and rushing to him.

"Hiding from you and whatever horrible future you seem to have planned," he answered. "I want to know the truth about the tithe. And I want to hear it from you." Sophie shivered at the steel in his voice, grateful that she had never had that tone directed at her.

"We owe you *nothing*—" Katherine was cut off by Aggie.

"If I'm going to sell you to the highest bidder, you should at least know why," Aggie spoke over her. She took a deep breath. "Over the centuries, the tithe has attracted many Fae to our town. There has been an … intermingling," she spoke slowly, tasting her words carefully before they left her mouth. "The oldest families have the most Faerie blood, of course. But no one knows for sure where our humanity ends and the Fae blood begins."

"It has brought us great fortune, you know." Katherine spoke now. "Greater intellect, beauty, grace, luck … there is a reason Hameln prospers where so many have fallen."

"But at what price?" Casper whispered.

"That is the correct question," Aggie said approvingly. "Just our obedience these many years. A small price to pay for such freedom and fortune."

"Says you," he answered.

"We have protected Hameln's future," Aggie insisted, eyes bright and steady.

"No. You've forfeit Hameln's future for a comfortable life of your own," Casper shot back quick and hot, his anger making Sophie almost dizzy. He closed his eyes a moment, regrouping. "All of these children—including *me*—are at risk because of the deal the Council made. The deal you continue to make with every Obolen that passes."

"*You* will be fine. You're going to Everstein. As for the others … It is the price we pay for *protection*," Aggie responded weakly. "And I believe it will eventually provide a way to break the tithe. The more Fae Hameln becomes, the less a human agreement binds it."

"*Eventually*? What about right now? Were you protecting all these kids from the truth?" Casper asked. "Or were you protecting yourself from our questions?"

Aggie closed her eyes, letting the words sink in. "Both, probably," she said wearily, before sitting down again. "You foolish children," she whispered. "You think you invented rebellion? Do you think any one of us haven't been horrified by the truth we learn when we come of age?" She banged her fist into the table, as if reinforcing her words. "But we continue for the common good, rather than destroying everything. You think you have nothing to lose, and you are so eager to burn it all down."

"And whose fault is that?" Casper asked, angry tears forming in his eyes, making Sophie step closer to him. "It is the Council that has left us with nothing! Those who leave become slaves or traitors who left the other children to the Fae. And those who stay become failures to everyone else in the world."

"Hameln only works if we are able to trust each other," Katherine said, smiling prettily, her voice smooth and soothing. "Maintaining our relationships, cooperating with each other, is the only way we're going to make it through the dangerous times."

"You've created those dangerous times," Casper said, banging his cane in frustration. "You were protecting a way of life, when you should have been protecting our lives."

"It's more complicated than that!" Aggie insisted. "There's a delicate balance we maintain, with many interlocking and competing interests. This is the system we've developed that works best for everyone, with the least amount of bloodshed."

"Aunt Aggie…" Casper said. "I cannot follow you in this."

"You will do as you're told," Katherine said, reaching for Casper's arm. When Sophie blocked her hand, she rounded on her daughter. "And Sophia, you are to go home with your brother. Now."

"Freddie? He's here?" Sophie whispered, delighted even as Casper attempted to wrench himself from Katherine's grip. Tears filled her eyes and a she felt a faint glimmer of hope. *Finally, an ally in this town.*

"Fine," Sophie sniped back, flicking the moisture away, and pretending to ignore the rest of the room, every inch the snotty princess her mother expected. "Take me to my brother."

35

Freddie felt paralyzed by his mother's fast-moving schemes. Paralyzed and useless. *I could make a run for it, try to find help. If I ride west, how long before I make it to Papa in Aquitaine?* He stood there, considering all his bad options, when the door crashed open, his sister's full attention consumed by cursing the soldier escorting her and another limping youth.

"Let me go this instant, you *Schweinehund*! I told you, I want to see my brother!" she snarled, snatching her arm from her forced escort.

"Sophie!" he rushed to pick up her slight form, burrowing his head in her shoulder. Freddie felt delighted laughter bubble up from deep inside. "You're safe!"

"Freddie?" she squeezed him back. "God's bloody left foot! You've got to help us stop this!"

He chuckled humorlessly. "I was about to say the same to you, Spitfire."

She related all that had happened to her over the past several months, starting with the last letter she had sent. She spoke breathlessly, out of order, with only a few nudging remarks from Casper to keep her narrative straight. When she was finally done, shaking with anger, she fairly collapsed in his arms.

Freddie held tight, but gave no false words to soothe her. He couldn't lie to her, not now.

"Do you know the most absurd part in all of this?" Sophie asked, turning in Freddie's arms to look him fully in the face. "I was staring down my own death, and the only thing I felt was regret that I would die before I had been able to share all of these discoveries and warn our people about the dangers they would face."

"My brave, foolish Spitfire," Freddie said, stroking her hair and holding her close. "Have a care for yourself, especially when I am not there to care for you."

"Oh, Freddie. Now we face Maman," Sophie said. "That is vastly more terrifying, believe me."

Freddie blanched at her words, turning away from her, wondering how much of their mother's schemes he should share with his darling little sister. "You have no idea, Sophie. You—you didn't see, what she did, what she's done for years, and to so many …"

Sophie came up behind him, reaching over to smooth her thumb over his brow, then flicking it lightly before clasping both his hands into hers and bringing them up to her lips.

"Freddie, what has happened?" He saw her school her features, as if to try to project strength and peace. Freddie had done so himself so often for her. "Tell me, and we will figure this out together."

Freddie nodded, and after a couple of false starts, told them both what he found in the bowels of the castle. "She's even killed the Wolfhart, once he finally answered her summons, and warned her that we'd sought his help," he said. "Now she's prepared, and it's just the four of us against the entire town, Maman, and some ancient Fae boogeyman."

At Sophie's ferocious glare, he shrugged apologetically.

"We don't know what he told her," Sophie argued. But her words were weak.

Freddie sighed. They were Eversteins, and these were their people. He had to come up with a plan that kept everyone safe, even if working against his mother turned his insides ice cold.

"You two go, I will stay and tell Maman I sent you both home," Freddie finally relented. "When they move the children, I will meet you at the river, where the rats were drowned. The Council will be waiting for them at the clearing, which gives us an opportunity. And then …" he faltered.

"Then we intercept the children and take them to the Grey Cottage before the Council knows they're gone," Casper declared. "There is protective magic there. It will have to do. We don't know how bad it has to get before Berchtold determines that the pact is well and truly broken—that he is no longer bound by his oaths to the Erlking."

"But she'll be furious with Freddie for letting us leave," Sophie argued, gripping his hand tightly, and reaching for Lukas standing on the sidelines.

"I'm the heir, aren't I?" Freddie gave the least-convincing smile of his life. "She won't hurt me, she can't risk it."

Casper chuckled ruefully. "This'll be the second time we've escaped this house. I don't think there will be a third."

The decision made, Freddie was quick to move. He opened the door to find two soldiers dressed in the blue and yellow Everstein colors.

"You are to take my sister and her companions to the smithy, where they will be safe." He nodded toward Lukas and Casper.

The soldier tipped his head, but his hand did not move from his sword hilt. "I'm afraid that is impossible, Prince Friedrich."

Freddie scoffed. "Don't be ridiculous. Take them yourself, and the rest of you can take me to Countess Katherine. Now."

"Your mother—"

"My mother is very busy with the business of the land." Friedrich let an edge of impatience color his bored air. "And you are my mother's man. You know what's to come. These children have no business here."

"Then they can join the congregation at Saint Boniface," the guard answered stubbornly. "I'm told that Father Stephen is holding a continuous mass until the demons leave our midst."

"With the doors locked and guarded, no doubt." Casper's face was twisted in disgust.

"They'll be safe," the man answered stoutly, though his eyes never left Freddie's face.

"You are talking about holding Princess Sophia Everstein prisoner, then?" Freddie's voice now cold and steely. The man froze, suddenly unsure of himself.

"What do you think my father would think of that plan? And make no mistake, I will be telling him. Everything."

The man wavered at his words, torn between the orders of two Eversteins. "Very well, milord. I will escort these two to the blacksmith's shop."

Freddie gave his sister a quick glance, and her lack of outrage was all the answer he needed. They would work with what they could get.

"And I will be sure to tell the Countess your orders." The clear threat was delivered with the utmost politeness. He really was Countess Katherine's man.

Freddie felt a cold sweat at his words, and only hoped that by the time this man got his mother's ear, Sophie, Cas, and Lukas were long gone.

They had scarcely a moment to say their goodbyes, and no privacy at all. "I will see you back at the castle soon, Spitfire," he reassured her. "We—and father—will make everything right again."

He clasped hands with Casper. "Don't let my sister get you into too much trouble."

"Trouble is the basis of our entire friendship, milord," Casper shot back.

Freddie grinned in spite of himself. "At least you know what you're in for," he conceded.

One last look, and Sophie, Cas, and Lukas were gone.

Sophie waited with Casper and Lukas by the river as long as she could stand it before they finally convinced her they had to move. She continually looked for her brother as they made their way down the deserted *Bungelosenstrasse* for the clearing outside of the city walls, in the shadow of the mountain. Freddie hadn't come and it was too late for another plan. They would have to stop the Erlking, alone.

The town's children had already been herded into the glade, seemingly too exhausted and confused to even be scared. The Faerie were already there. Creatures of all colors, sizes, and shapes—with no glamour to hide their inhuman visages—arrayed before them, with the Erlking seated at the center of this terrifying tableau.

"Lukas, what are we going to do?" Sophie whispered.

He breathed in deep. "I think … I can get the children away from the Council, away from Hameln. Just remember that you trust me, right?"

"You're going to use your flute, aren't you?" Casper responded hesitantly.

Lukas answered with his showiest grin. "Buy me some time, yes?"

Sophie opened her mouth to question him further, but low, discordant words filled the space, reaching their ears first.

"Good people of Hameln," the Erlking intoned. "I hereby accept this decade's Obolen, as is my right, on behalf of Faerie. With this sacrifice, the ancient pact between our peoples has been honored, and I absolve you of all debts to my kingdom this decade." He raised his arms "Rejoice in ten more years of prosperity."

At his words, Sophie trembled with anger. And even though they had planned it, Casper's clear, defiant voice in the air shocked her.

"I reject your claim, Erlking," Casper shouted, full of conviction and ire. "You will take no one this day, or any other."

As he was recognized, a murmur went through the crowd, and Aunt Aggie moved toward him. But the Erlking's raised hand was all it took for her to become quiet and still. He turned his attention back to Cas.

"Ah, our broken little Casper," the Erlking said, motioning lazily at the boy. Sophie glared at his apparent amusement. "You know, we have been watching your development with great interest for years. Ever since that horrible accident in the smithy. So nice to see that you have overcome dashed dreams, instead of succumbing to it as your sister has."

"You don't get to talk about my sister," Casper gritted through clenched teeth. "Ever."

"Should I talk about you, instead?" the Erlking asked. "I must say, I am quite surprised you are now standing up to be heard. After all, your whole life has been spent staying as quiet and compliant as possible. You don't want to be a burden to your sister or your aunt. Don't want to wander outside your comfort zone, in case you literally fall on your face. After all, what is worse in life than being laughed at?"

"Being a murderous monster, for one," Lukas spoke up nonchalantly from the edge of the crowd. Sophie had never loved him more than in that moment. "And an absolute bore of a public speaker, for another."

The Erlking continued on, heedless of the interruption. "And after that little adventure of yours the past few months, what did you hope to achieve? Did you honestly think you could keep up with a girl like Sophie? You are slow to speak, slow to act. Can you do *anything* quickly?"

"Geometry, I suppose," Casper said, bringing up his cane and releasing the mechanism for the crossbow. Sophie grinned despite the tension in the air. "I know the exact angle I would need to aim this arrow straight down your throat, for instance."

At his words, Sophie saw Lukas move to cover him. The Erlking did not seem the forgiving type.

"And you, my impetuous nephew." The Erlking turned to Lukas. "Have you yet spoken to the woman who raised you? Do you know who your people are, who you are?"

"I know who I am," Lukas growled. "More importantly, I know who *you* are. And we will not let you take these children today."

"Avoiding the truth will not make it less real." The Erlking waved him away. "And lies only weaken you further. Family or not, I will destroy any who stand in my way."

Now Sophie moved from the shadows to join her friends.

"Sophie, what is the meaning of this?" Katherine marched forward, hissing at her.

"I won't let you take my friends," Sophie responded, though her eyes never left Casper's face. "I couldn't abandon the town. Don't do this, Maman. It is wrong."

"You are a child, and you will listen to your elders," Katherine responded savagely, swooping down to grab her arm. Sophie wrenched free, diving back behind Lukas. The Countess wavered when faced by the bard, as if the power of Lukas' strange green eyes and savage grin were enough to ward her away.

"You know, there is one more thing the elders of Hameln can teach us," Lukas responded calmly. "How exactly can we get to Faerie without raising the Erlking's alarm?"

"Sophie, come here this instant," her mother commanded, ignoring the bard. "You will not interrupt these proceedings again."

Sophie shrank back. She realized what an idiot she'd been, constantly begging the world to show her something noteworthy and new. Now she wanted nothing more than to be back in the kitchens, curled up with cook's terrier, sneaking treats and listening to idle gossip.

Not like this. Not like this. I didn't mean this.

"Maman," Sophie was pleading now. "You know this is wrong. We're supposed to protect the Lower Saxony—"

"*I am Lower Saxony!*" Katherine screamed, and for the first time Sophie could see the madness she had hidden from them all so well. *Maman's a monster.*

"You are a parasite, sacrificing children instead of saving them." Lukas advanced on her, eyes glinting in the low light.

Sophie's mother had finally grabbed her, clutching her shoulders tightly, and Sophie could no longer tell if Katherine was protecting her or using *her* as the shield. She struggled against her mother's desperate grip, intent on joining her friends.

"This has become tiresome." The Erlking, who had not moved from his gruesome throne, gestured lazily. Silent and quick, two nightmare branches shot toward Katherine, and her hands fell away from Sophie as the branches punched through Maman's chest, dragging her to the Erlking's feet.

Chaos descended around Sophie instantly, with the children screaming, the Council arguing, and the hound baying in canine despair. Casper threw himself at Sophie, struggling to lift her and pull her back toward the safety of the crowd. As if anyone were safe now.

Only Lukas was completely still in the aftermath.

The Erlking brushed splatter from his cloak, as undisturbed as if the bloodshed were merely a light summer rain.

"The ceremony will commence," he intoned.

"I don't think so." Lukas' voice was soft but certain. He had moved toward the crowd of children, inching closer to the mountain that loomed above them all, and once again Sophie wondered what he was doing.

"And what do I care what you *think*?" the Erlking sneered.

"You forget who I am." Lukas grinned, looking up, his eyes blurred with tears.

"A half-grown, half-blood vagabond?" The Erlking had gone from bored to amused. Somehow, it seemed more deadly.

"No, I'm a bard." Lukas brought his necklace to his mouth, blazingly defiant and gleeful, with the confidence of a madman. "And a very special bard, at that!" Lukas continued, stepping away from the mass of children, while pushing Sophie gently toward them.

Hoping that she was reading his signals properly, she gestured to Casper that they should all move as far from the Erlking's throne as possible.

"I am no longer a child, and lately a resident of Hameln," Lukas said. "The mayor's nephew and a celebrated musician at the Nixe. I can even claim the title of blacksmith's apprentice, though Clare insists I'm terrible at it."

The Erlking raised one supremely unimpressed eyebrow.

"I know, I know," Lukas said. "It's unseemly to brag. But here's the best part: I am also Fae. Now that came as a shock, let me tell you. And not just any Fae, but a son of the Wild Hunt, recognized by the royal family! Do you prefer 'Uncle Erlking' or can I call you 'Uncle Evil'?"

"These titles mean nothing—" the Erlking's voice raised beyond a whisper for the first time that night.

But Lukas, dear, insane Lukas, just kept talking.

"And if I read the pact correctly, that means that I can claim all the children I want, for both Faerie and Hameln. And so…" He raised the Star of David that his nimble fingers had been blindly rearranging into pipes throughout his lunatic speech. "I think *I'll* just take all of them."

He began his song: sweet and melancholic, and a dazed Sophie found herself moved irresistibly forward, forward, always forward and away. The same strange compulsion seemed to hit the assembled children like a sudden rainstorm in a clear blue sky, instantly damping down all other sensations or cares.

Sophie and the 130 children, unable to resist, rushed toward the sheer side of the mountain faster than the astonished princess would have ever thought it possible for her feet to move.

Meanwhile, the assembled adults of Hameln—friends, family, and otherwise—were suddenly collapsing behind them. Sophie looked over her shoulder, watching as they were overwhelmed by slumber, falling slowly to their knees before resting their heads on whatever happened to be beneath them—the ground, their own arms, the bodies of their neighbors.

The Erlking and his retinue found that their own bodies were frozen in space, with joints refusing to move, their mouths open, but no words passing through their lips. Only the Erlking's hatred seemed to blaze from his milky, opaque eyes. It was the last terrifying sight Sophie glimpsed before the mountain cracked open soundlessly, a giant, misty maw, and swallowed them up. And in that moment, she was relieved.

Hours later, Clare found Casper collapsed on the ground at the clearing, sobbing alone and wretched. She was too late.

"Where are they, Casper?" Clare lifted his shoulders from the ground, wiping the dirt from his face. "Where did the Erlking take them?"

"It … it wasn't the Erlking. God's bones, it was Lukas," Casper got out between great gulps of air. "I couldn't keep up. I tried to stop them, but I couldn't keep up and they *wouldn't listen*. They're gone."

"Lukas?" The world blurred around her as she lost the breath in her lungs. "But he told me we were all going to be safe. Sophie, Lucie … you. We were all safe."

Casper's mouth became a grim, trembling line. "Safe from who, exactly?"

She swallowed the rest of her panicked questions—*Where are all*

the children? What had Lukas done?—wrapping her arms around him instead.

The late afternoon light angled through the trees, dappling the hushed valley all around them in silver-golden light. It was peaceful, enchanting—if you overlooked the Countess' motionless body hanging from the nightmare tree. Clare shivered, chilled to the bone in the warm summer sun.

EPILOGUE

The children were gone. The curse was lifted. And that's when Hameln's troubles really began. *And still no Wolfhart to aid us*, Clare noted sourly. It had been months since the children disappeared, and she was left in a very different Hameln.

It was not as if the Valkyries of death swooped in at once. Nor did the Four Horsemen leap through a fissure in the earth to claim dominion. At first, the town was just far too quiet, subdued with shock, until people began telling their stories. And it seemed *everyone* had a story: fantastical Faerie tales they had all lived for years and never been able to speak of before.

There was the veiled woman in white, whose weeping face transformed into a screaming hollow, bleeding through the lace when Anders had approached her.

Or the imp that Anna found at her wheel beside the hearth, spinning straw into gold, disappearing when she asked his name, leaving behind only a few strands of precious gold.

And the glittering slippers that old man Sven had put on as a child, entranced by the shining jewels inlaid in the buckles. But then he began to dance, and could not stop, even as those beautiful shoes filled with his own blood. It was his mother and sister who finally stripped them from his feet, and he had walked with a limp ever since.

Clare couldn't help but imagine how delighted Lukas and Sophie would be to find the entire town now full of such Faerie tales. Charming Lukas would urge everyone to tell their stories again and again, paying them for their time with a song. Sophie with her pointed questions, narrowed eyes, thoughtful clarifications.

Even Lucie …

But she couldn't bring herself to think of Lucie right now, or whether Helena would find her. One townful of problems at a time.

They were all gone. They have been for more than three months now…

Instead of driving herself mad with useless worry, Clare continued on, eating breakfast at the Nixe, working the forge, and, like today, visiting a recuperating Nic at the Grey Cottage. She readjusted the cape of her red traveling cloak, preparing for the damp of the autumn forest on her way to Rachel's home.

"Good morning, Red." Clare saw a tall, lean man with shaggy dark hair and dark eyes smile and walk out of the shadows of the wood.

"Good morning," she returned evenly, bringing her hand to the dagger hanging at her waist.

"Who could you be visiting all alone in the woods, sweet one?" he asked with a wolfish grin on his sallow face as he approached, fast and sure. "Your sick grandmother, perhaps?"

In an instant, Clare held her hunting dagger to the scoundrel's throat, its blade gleaming in the dappled light.

"Oh dear," she said, clicking her tongue in annoyance. "It seems you've mistaken me for a helpless victim. Not a common mistake in these parts anymore."

His eyes grew wide, first in anger and then fear as she carefully sliced through his shabby gray tunic, just scratching the skin of his throat. Whether his shocked silence was a result of the pain or the young girl inflicting it, Clare didn't much care.

"You're crazy," he growled, backing away from her blade carefully.

"That's more like it." Clare nodded approvingly. "Now off with you. I have important business to attend to. But if I hear about a man of your description—hairy, big eyes, too many teeth—harassing any other girls, you'll be seeing me and my dagger again."

He prowled off with a snarl, but he was gone. That was the important bit. She breathed out a shaky breath. *And that's why we need the new Wolfhart. To ward off scum like that.*

Clare carefully wiped her dagger clean before returning it to its sheath and continuing her journey.

And that's how she found Helena sitting at Rachel's kitchen table with Nic and Casper. Her family was back together again, she mused, just as she had dreamed of only months ago.

Before everything had changed.

"They will not talk to me," Helena explained over the hot mug of tea Cas handed her. "Even my mother's pull means nothing at this point. The nixies have ordered me to bring them back the heart of the Piper, instead."

"His heart?" Clare was aghast. "They want him dead? Over a few rats in their waters?"

"Not his literal heart, his figurative ..." Helena sighed impatiently. "The nixies want you, Clare," she said. "Something about his eyes being too big for his stomach, and teaching him a lesson in manners?"

"Helena, I want to find Lucie as much as anyone, but I won't sacrifice my sister for some miffed nixies," Nic protested.

"As if I would let them harm her," Helena scoffed. "You offend me. I am sure we will just be sent on a few quests to amuse them, until they lose interest and go back to drowning sailors."

"Thank you for reminding me that I will never actually understand Faerie," Clare said absentmindedly, her jumbled thoughts already turning to any business she would have to finish up before leaving on this new quest: turning the forge over to Pieter, sending word to Freddie at Castle Everstein, convincing her brothers and Rachel to let her go ...

It was daunting. But despite it all, she found her veins thrumming with excitement.

"We've got a lot to do, then," Clare finally responded, standing from the table. "Let's go find our friends."

DID YOU ENJOY HAMELN?

A few sentences on Amazon or Goodreads helps a lot!
E-mail us at murasakipress at gmail dot com with your published review and join our VIP list as thanks for your time!

PLEASE WRITE A BOOK REVIEW!

THANKS FOR SUPPORTING THE WORK OF NJ KNIGHT!

ACKNOWLEDGMENTS

Sure, a lot of words go into writing a book, but no one becomes an author on page count alone. *This* author needed a lot of time. Time to imagine, stress bake, talk a particularly tricky scene out with my editor, blast some K-pop, and fall dramatically on a friend's sofa while whining about my story.

First and foremost, thanks to my husband and son for giving me that time. Pat and Rhys, your unconditional support made me feel like I could run this marathon long before the finish line was in sight. Nothing without you.

My first and most loyal readers kept me well-fed in compliments and demands for more pages. Abby Horton, Angelica Giuffre, Kiana Shelton, and Jenn Sigwart, whenever my motivation was flagging, I knew you'd pick me right back up. I'm the luckiest.

The extraordinary editor Britta Jensen gave me the confidence and knowledge to keep moving forward when it would have been so much easier to stop. I hope everyone has a Britta in their life—and a Jenni Choi to introduce you to her!—for when doing the thing feels too big and scary to attempt alone.

Special thanks to publicist Fran Carpentier for her invaluable expertise and proofreader Heidi Kasa, who always knows exactly the right words. You both made this book better, and I am incredibly grateful.

Sarah J. Coleman and Douglas Draper Jr., your designs brought Hameln (my magical, twisty version) to life. Thank you for your artistic alchemy that helped turn my manuscript into a real book.

Years ago, my family and I received a warm welcome from Hameln's Marketing and Tourism Department on a very cold December day. Exploring those winding streets was the true high-light of my book research that I'll never forget. *Danke Schön!*

I recently learned that I'm a fairly strange creature in the novel-writing world: an extrovert. I'm thankful that my *Mixed Bag* crew welcomed me into their world, trading my endless questions and silly jokes for invaluable insights and grace. Roanna Flowers, GESS, Ilene Haddad, Hollie Hardy, Kara Lenore, and E.A. Williams, you are the writing community I'd always hoped for. I love y'all.

To all my amazing Knights, Puseys, and Streets, thanks for cheering me on along the way. Ray Flandez, Kim Galvan, Ethan Lascity, Susie Lee, Natalie McManus, and Jim Shea, I hope the book lives up to your years of hope and hype.

I've undoubtably forgotten someone. I'll make it up to you in the next book. <3

ABOUT THE AUTHOR

NJ Knight grew up on the Eastern Shore of Maryland, where her family has owned a haunted wood for more than 300 years. She earned degrees in journalism and anthropology from the University of Maryland, College Park, before working as a journalist for more than a decade. Knight has been published in *The Baltimore Sun*, *Chicago Tribune*, and *L.A. Times*, among others. She currently lives in Austin, TX, with her husband, son, two dogs, and many, many books.

Knight's short story, "The Rules of Sabertooth Sanctuary," was published in the *Mixed Bag of Tricks* anthology in 2023. This is her first novel. She's currently writing the sequel to *Hameln* and a new fantasy novel. Keep up with the latest news and join her newsletter at njknight.com.

 instagram.com/njknightbooks